Also in the Laura Caxton Vampire series:

13 Bullets
99 Coffins
Vampire Zero
23 Hours

Other titles by David Wellington:

Cursed
Ravaged

32 Fangs

A Final Vampire Tale

DAVID WELLINGTON

piatkus

PIATKUS

First published in the US in 2012 by Broadway Paperbacks,
An imprint of the Crown Publishing Group,
a division of Random House, Inc., New York
First published in Great Britain as a paperback original in 2012 by Piatkus

A CIP catalogue record for this book
is available from the British Library.

ISBN 978-0-7499-5726-1

Printed and bound in Great Britain by
Clays Ltd, St Ives plc

Papers used by Piatkus are from well-managed forests
and other responsible sources.

MIX
Paper from
responsible sources
FSC
www.fsc.org   **FSC® C104740**

Piatkus
An imprint of
Little, Brown Book Group
100 Victoria Embankment
London EC4Y 0DY

An Hachette UK Company
www.hachette.co.uk

www.piatkus.co.uk

For everyone who read the previous books.

You made this happen. You guys rock,

and I can't thank you enough.

32 Fangs

Justinia

... The miserable mortal who has been
once caught firmly by the end of the
finest fibre of his nerve, is drawn in
and in, by the enormous machinery of
hell.... my prayer is for the impossible,
and my pleading with the inexorable.

—Joseph Sheridan Le Fanu, Green Tea

[1702]

"What kind of monster are ye?" Father demanded, as he slammed his fists again and again into Uncle Reginald's stomach. "The girl's but seven years old!"

"James, I beg of ye, stop! I am wholly innocent!" Uncle screamed. Just as he'd been screaming since the beating began. "She demanded I give her a piece of candy, and I simply refused, but—"

"'Tis not the way she tells it," Father insisted. He turned away for a moment, seething with rage, and took up the first thing to hand—a pair of iron sheep shears, honed to a razor edge. He drove the blades of the shears deep up under Uncle's rib cage and twisted them. Uncle Reginald stopped screaming then, but his whole body convulsed as the blade dug through flesh and sinew. Foam flecked his lips, and his eyes, which had been swollen shut with bruises, bulged outward from their sockets. "She says ye offered her some candy if she would take down her small clothes. Seven years old!"

Uncle made no reply. It did not occur to the girl that he might already be dead. Clearly it did not occur to Father, either, as he drove the blade of the shears home again and again. The girl stepped backward as blood spread across the straw-covered floor of the barn. Behind her the sheep stared placidly at the scene, wholly disinterested spectators.

Eventually Father threw down the shears, and wiped one gore-coated hand across his mouth. He was breathing heavily and sweat poured down his bald head and pooled in his ears. He turned to look at the girl and the expression on his face was one she would never forget. He was not angry anymore. His face had gone as pale as paper and his mouth hung open, his slack lips wide to suck in breath. In his eyes was a look of desperate *pleading. He wanted something from the girl. But what? Thanks, for what he'd done? The validation of knowing he'd done the right thing, been a good father? Or simple forgiveness?*

She would never know. She would never, in fact, see her father after this day. He would be taken to the assizes, given a quick trial, and hanged in the town square as a fratricide.

But all that was in the future.

This special moment, this very first of her murders, was frozen in time as she stood before the sheep and away from the spreading pool of blood that threatened to touch her shoes. She was too young to comprehend what had just happened. She was only peripherally aware that something very important, something consequential, had changed in the barn. There had been three people there. Now there were two.

Father dropped the shears and ran out through the wide doors, into the sunlight. He did not speak to her before he left. The girl was left alone with the corpse. Uncle's eyes had receded back behind their lids and he wasn't moving, not at all.

The blood parted as it rolled around her shoes. She felt it soak through the thin cloth and touch her flesh, and though she had expected to be revolted by the feeling, disgusted by the wetness of it, instead one simple fact impressed itself upon her. The blood was so very warm.

She splashed through it toward Uncle's body, as if she were playing in a puddle in the rain. Red as rubies it was. When she reached Uncle she leaned over close to peer down into his battered face. How different he seemed now from the man she'd known all her life. How funny a person could change so quickly. He looked a million years old already. She leaned down further, and kissed him on the forehead.

He had been wholly innocent, just as he claimed. She had made up the funny story. How easy it was to make things up. How easy it was to make things happen.

"Ye should have given me the candy," she whispered to him.

From outside the barn she heard her mother calling, her voice cracked with alarm. "Are ye in there, child? Are ye in there? Justinia—where are ye?"

The girl turned toward the door and made a mask of her face. A mask of fear she did not feel. She forced tears to her eyes. "In here, Mama," she shouted. "In here!"

1.

Television and the Internet had given the public the false impression that it was impossible to get away with a crime in the twenty-first century. That advances in forensic science and law-enforcement techniques meant a criminal could be tracked by the subtlest of evidence. That if he left behind a single fiber from his clothing, or so much as a fraction of a fingerprint, a burglar or a rapist was as good as caught.

If it was that easy, Clara Hsu's back wouldn't hurt so much.

At the ripe old age of thirty-one, she was already starting to feel like an old lady. Squatting on the floor of a convenience store in Altoona, a jeweler's loupe screwed into one eye, she groaned with every duckwalking step as she studied the bottom shelf of a display of snack cakes. She was looking for anything, and nothing in particular. Fibers were next to impossible to spot at the best of times. Dusting the entire store for fingerprints would take days, since every surface had to be studied individually under special lights and from multiple angles. If she found anything, even so innocuous a clue as a scuff mark on the floor tiles from the perp's sneakers, she would be happy. She'd been working this scene all day and into the twilight hours and so far she remained unhappy.

Outside, beyond the wide glass windows that looked out on gas pumps and colorful signage, a single flashing light and hundreds of feet of yellow tape cordoned off the crime scene from the summer night that thrummed with the noise of crickets. Inside the store every available light was burning so she could get a better view, while the store's audio system droned out some pop music hit she'd never heard before. That had been the first sign that she was getting old, that she had stopped keeping up with the Top Forty. The way her knees popped when she stood up helped reinforce the feeling.

There was no blood anywhere in the store. The teenaged kid who had been working behind the register had been found dead at his post, but without a speck of blood on him. That had been enough to get Clara's attention. For two years now she had been looking for just that kind of murder. The State Police and the local authorities of twelve counties all knew to call her whenever a bloodless murder occurred, and she always went when they called. Ninety-nine times out of a hundred, it only meant that the victim had been killed with a blunt instrument that failed to break the skin. But still she went out whenever they called, and still she gave every case her full attention.

Most forensic specialists wanted blood on the scene. Blood was easy to work with—between DNA, blood types and factors, spray patterns, trails of blood leading away from scenes, bloody footprints retaining the tread pattern of the perp's shoes, and a dozen other kinds of clues, blood always talked.

But there was one kind of killer who didn't have DNA. Or fingerprints. Who almost never wore shoes. And who, unless they were rushed, would never leave so much as a droplet of blood behind. Vampires tended to be very thorough.

Luckily for everyone, they were just about extinct.

There was only one vampire left in the world. Justinia Malvern, the one who got away—or so Clara believed. She'd been looking for Malvern for two years now, with no official support. Her bosses believed that Malvern was dead, burned to a crisp during a riot in a women's prison two years prior. Clara knew they were wrong, but so far couldn't prove it—for two years, Malvern might as well have disappeared off the face of the earth.

And in her business, proof was everything.

She sighed as she pushed aside a stack of frosted mini-donuts and squinted for fibers behind them. Nothing. She checked behind the frosted chocolate cupcakes. Nothing. The cinnamon twists mocked her. She grabbed one pack and tore it open, then shoved a spiral pastry in her mouth and bit down. She'd worked straight through her dinner break and her energy level was low enough to excuse breaking her diet. As she chewed the dry dough, she let the loupe fall out of her eye socket and caught it with her free hand, then shoved it in her pocket. She dropped the empty snack wrapper on the floor in front of her, and then massaged both eyes with the balls of her thumbs. She pressed hard enough to make flashes of light burst behind her eyeballs. She blinked the afterimages away, then reached for a fruit pie.

A shadow fell across her arm. Just for a moment, then it was gone.

"Hello? This is a sealed crime scene," she called out, thinking one of the local cops must have come in to see how she was doing. "I need to maintain the integrity of the space, so—"

The door to the convenience store's bathroom stood open, revealing nothing but shadows. It had definitely been closed before.

Clara put a hand on either thigh and started levering herself up to a standing position. Every joint in her legs complained. Whoever was in the store with her would, she was certain, hear her knees popping over the beat of the sound system.

"Hello?" she called again. There was no answer.

Most forensic specialists didn't wear sidearms. They typically weren't cleared for them, and anyway they never approached a crime scene until the uniform cops had already cleared the place and taped it off. They didn't need weapons. Clara, on the other hand, had been taught by a very paranoid teacher to always stay safe. She reached for her holster, intending only to unfasten the safety strap.

Before she could do that, however, a shoe came out of

nowhere and cracked her across the jaw. Clara's head flew to the side and back and her feet went out from under her, spilling her to the floor.

2.

Clara toppled into a rack of magazines, spilling glossy pages all over the floor. The attacker punched her in the kidney and she fell down in a heap.

She hadn't even gotten a good look at him yet.

If she were someone else, someone stronger, faster—if she were *Laura,* she thought, she would already have this guy down on the ground and cuffed. But Clara was no action movie cop. She'd never wanted to be. She'd wanted to be an art photographer. She'd wanted to be famous for her tasteful nudes or maybe just poignantly expressive still lifes.

Signing on with the police had just been a way to pay the rent.

A fist caught her in the side of her head and she nearly passed out. Spots danced in her vision and her hands felt numb. Her hands—her hands had been reaching for—for—

Right. She had a gun. She managed to get the catch undone as the assailant stomped on her shoulder. She whipped the gun out of its holster and fired blindly into where she thought he might be.

And—she hit him. She felt shreds of flesh fall on her face, like pulled pieces of chicken. The flesh was strangely cold. She expected to be soaked in blood but wasn't. She did not have time to wonder why, or to be disgusted, though she knew she was eventually going to have to throw up.

The attacker screamed, a high-pitched wail that didn't sound anything like what she'd expected. For all the pain she was feeling she'd expected the attacker to be some hulking guy, seven feet tall and just as wide through the shoulders. He sounded more like a demonic puppet.

Wait—no—it couldn't be—

He didn't stick around to let her get a good look. He bolted through the store, bouncing off a rack of paperbacks by the register, and out the doors into the night.

Clara blinked, trying to clear her vision. It felt as if he'd detached one of her retinas.

Overhead the sound system launched into another pop song.

She had to go after him. She had to catch him. That was what Laura would have done. That was what a cop was supposed to do. Well. Technically she wasn't a cop, she was a forensic specialist. But then technically the cops were supposed to have already combed the scene and made sure there weren't any drug-crazed madmen hiding out in the convenience store's bathroom. Clara struggled up to her feet. Everything hurt. She slipped on the glossy magazines and nearly cracked her head open on the floor tiles. But she got up. She stood up and looked out through the windows at the front of the store, hoping to see a blood trail. Something she could follow.

Instead she found her attacker standing out there, looking back in at her. He was over by the gas pumps, lit up bright as day by the store's floodlights. He wore a pale yellow hooded sweatshirt that concealed his face, and he was clutching at a wound on his arm—almost certainly where she'd hit him with her shot.

There was no blood on his sleeve. *Damn it*, if she could just see his face, she would know for sure. His face—or maybe his lack of same.

When he saw her he gave another little shriek and ran.

"Coward!" she shouted at him. She doubted he heard her through the glass.

She pushed through the door of the store and gave chase.

"*Gentlemen,*" *Justinia said, smiling as she made eye contact with each of the three players, "the game is whist. Strict silence shall be observed." She held the cards up close to her décolletage to keep attention away from her hands as she dealt. Thirteen cards to each player, and the last to determine trumps. This time, hearts were trumps. The single red pip like a blot of blood landed in the center of the table and play began.*

Over their heads, in the room upstairs that Justinia shared with her mother, a bed began to creak. The man across from Justinia, her partner, chuckled at the sound, but she waggled one finger for silence. In a world so filthy and full of sin as this, the quiet rhythm of the game was sacred to Justinia. One clean thing she could call her own.

Which was not to say she didn't cheat with the cards.

It had not been easy for the Malvern widow and daughter to stay out of the workhouse. Without a man to support them they had fallen on untraditional occupations to pay the rent and keep food on the table. They had both learned quite early that the world was not fair, and that there was no reason that they must be fair to it in turn.

Justinia's partner dropped the knave of hearts, a strong lead. The man to his right, a tinker who smelled of grease and road dust, threw the nine. Justinia played the queen, preserving her king because she knew that the tinker's partner couldn't beat her play. She had used a little sleight of hand to appear to shuffle the cards, while in fact merely arranging them so that she knew everyone's hand. The deck, in other words, was stacked—though in such a careful, apparently haphazard way it would take a true master of the game to see through her ruse.

At the ripe old age of seventeen, she'd already learned how much better it was to be clever than lucky.

She took the trick, and the next two, but let the tinker and his partner have enough that when she won it did not look like more than skillful play. The tinker scowled, but just then her mother came down the stairs wearing little more than a nightdress. Mama looked tired, but she waved for the tinker to follow her back up.

Another game began with new players. Another guffaw when the ceiling began to creak. The sound was carefully timed to draw attention away from Justinia's shuffling. She and Mama were getting very good at this gimmick.

By the end of the night she'd garnered seven shillings from the game, while Mama had earned as much upstairs. As she packed the cards away and rose to blow out the candles, she found the tinker waiting for her by the door. "I've tupped the dam, now I'd sample the filly," he said, with a leer that showed missing teeth.

She pretended to be shocked and nearly slammed the door in his face, but he held up a pair of shillings and she let her eyes go wide.

"Ye'd bid so little?" she demanded. "There is one thing every girl possesses which she may only sell once. She should ask a proper price, at least."

The tinker's smile did not change, but one of his eyes screwed up in doubt. Still, he doubled his offer. After a little more protestation, Justinia threw the door open and welcomed him back inside.

Though she hadn't actually kept count, it was probably the hundredth time she'd sold her maidenhead. She lay back on the bed and pretended to be in pain while in her head the cards spun and fell across the table, the pips so black and red.

3.

It hurt to run—Clara's jaw felt like it was floating loose inside her head, and every time it bumped into the rest of her skull it sent a new jolt of agony down her neck. Yet she poured on the speed as her attacker raced across the road and into an empty field on the far side. Dry, dusty weeds slithered across Clara's pant legs as she followed, all the vegetation stained gray by the light of the crescent moon. It was dark in the field and she might have lost her quarry if not for the buzzing orange sodium lamps of the nearby highway. The yellow sweatshirt he wore was a patch of slightly paler light in the gloom, and she focused on hurrying after it, her legs pumping as she hurtled over the uneven ground.

Ahead lay a picket fence stained with mold. He vaulted it with his good arm, barely pausing to look back and see that she was still after him. When she reached the fence herself she climbed over it and dropped to a crouch in the shadows of the far side. He could have been waiting for her there in ambush, and she very much wanted to avoid another beating.

She saw no sign of him. Nor did she hear his footsteps running away. He had to be close, she thought.

Beyond the fence lay the back lot of an auto parts store. The chassis of a rusted-out car hunched low in the weeds that sprang up through the broken concrete. A pair of hulking Dumpsters stood against the back of the store, a pool of shadows between them that could hide anything. Clara trained her weapon on the space between the two Dumpsters and tried to calm her breathing. She couldn't hear anything over the beating of her own heart.

The only smart thing to do in a case like this was to go back to the convenience store and call it in. Give the local cops the best description she could and let them chase the bastard. But Clara knew the chances of them ever finding the guy were slim. She hadn't seen his face and she couldn't even say if he was white, black, or Asian. He might have left fingerprints all over the convenience store, but fingerprints were only useful in identifying people who had been in jail or the armed forces, and even then it could take weeks to get a match.

If she was right about the assailant's identity, she would have less than a week to catch him and question him. And there were a lot of questions she wanted to make him answer.

She had a small flashlight on her belt. Fumbling it out of its holster with her left hand—right hand still gripping her pistol—she flicked it on but held it low down at her side. She didn't want to give her position away if she didn't have to. Duckwalking to the side to get a better angle, she flicked the light up so that its beam speared the shadow between the two Dumpsters. Two eyes reflected the light like tiny lasers and she gasped in surprise. She hadn't expected that to work—

—and it hadn't. The eyes belonged to a feral cat, which stared back at her as if wondering why she had interrupted its dinner.

"Sorry," she breathed. Then jumped again, as the door of the rusted-out car behind her flew open and the yellow sweatshirt bolted out of it, into the alley on the far side of the store.

Clara cursed and jumped up to run again. She bolted around the corner, her weapon held out away from her body, barrel pointed at the ground just like she'd been taught. She shoved the flashlight into her pocket as she came around the front of the store and saw her attacker standing at the curb, looking one way, then the other as if he intended to cross the street.

Except the street was a four-lane highway, and every few seconds a car went rocketing past at sixty miles an hour.

"Stop there," Clara called out, in her best cop voice.

Yellow Sweatshirt looked back at her, his face still hidden by shadows. Then he ran right out into traffic.

Clara threw herself forward, but a lifetime of conditioning kept her from entering the street. She got as far as the curb and found herself wobbling back and forth as if she were standing on the roof of a building looking down at a twenty-story drop. She could see her attacker darting side to side as he crossed one lane, then the next, while car horns blared and headlights made bright trails across her vision.

Laura would have run into traffic to pursue the bastard. Laura was fearless, Clara told herself. *Laura would have—*

She heard the squeal of air brakes and the deep, chest-shaking blare of a truck horn and looked up. She saw Yellow Sweatshirt staring into the lights of an oncoming semi. For just a split second she thought she saw the look of horror on his face as he edged back and forth, trying to decide which way to jump.

He didn't have time, regardless of what he decided. The truck plowed into him at seventy-five miles an hour. Or rather, the truck plowed right *through* him. His body didn't crumple. It wasn't dragged for half a mile on the truck's bumper. When it hit him, he simply disintegrated, turning into a cloud of flesh and bone fragments like a water balloon when it's pricked with a pin.

The truck slowed to a stop, far too late.

The horror of it barely registered on Clara's mind. She couldn't think about that, not when she finally *knew,* for certain. In that split second when the attacker had been lit up by the truck's lights, she had seen exactly what she'd suspected. He didn't have a face. The skin on the front of his head had all been clawed away, scratched off by his own broken fingernails.

He had been a Faceless. A half-dead.

The un-living servant of a vampire.

4.

"I'm okay," Clara said, as Glauer poked at the fresh bruises on her jaw. "It's not broken. Ow! I said I was okay!"

"I've already sent for an EMT crew. They'll look you over, make sure you're alright," Fetlock told her. "Then you're looking at a mandatory seventy-two hours of recuperative leave."

Clara stared up at her boss, trying very hard to mask the pure hatred she felt for him. U.S. Marshal Fetlock was a by-the-book kind of guy. The kind of guy who believed that if something wasn't in the book, it didn't exist. This wasn't the first time he'd tried to screw up a case by insisting on protocol.

"Sir," she said, "with all due respect. This is a lead we have to follow up on. It's the first clear sign we've found in two years that Malvern is still active."

"It's nothing of the kind. Justinia Malvern died at SCI-Marcy. She's not the one we're looking for." Fetlock folded his arms and stood up, breaking eye contact. He was done with the conversation.

Clara was still sitting on the curb, exactly where she'd been when her team came for her. The state police—who still owed her a few favors—had blocked off the highway and set up road flares so she could see. In the two hours it took Fetlock and Glauer to arrive, she'd already collected several dozen bone fragments and scraps of the yellow sweatshirt and begun to piece them together like a jigsaw puzzle.

A puzzle missing most of the pieces. She'd found no part of the dead thing's head, much less its face, and unless she could prove that it displayed the classic pattern of faceless self-mutilation, she had no real evidence of her theory.

And she was going to need real, tangible proof. Fetlock's own theory, that Malvern had died in the prison riot two years ago, was flimsy at best. The body they'd recovered, which he claimed belonged to Malvern, had been burned beyond recognition. It had been missing one eye and it was dressed in the charred remains of Malvern's clothing, true. But Laura Caxton, the disgraced vampire hunter and Clara's former lover, had left them a message saying that Malvern had faked her own death, and was still out there. She had then escaped from the prison and gone on the lam, with the stated intention of finding Malvern and ending things.

Fetlock had secured the prison—by the book. Which meant hundreds of women had died or been seriously wounded, but none of his own team had been hurt. For handling the situation and for finding Malvern's "body," he'd been promoted and given charge of his own special unit tasked with hunting down and capturing Caxton, now a fugitive from the penal system. Clara and Glauer were not members of that unit—nobody really trusted them to arrest Caxton if they found her. Instead they'd been left to their own devices, in a kind of paid retirement. They were permitted to follow their own leads and do all the detective work they wanted, though Fetlock never followed up on the clues they found. Clara suspected he only kept them around because he expected Caxton to get back in touch with them, and he wanted to listen in on that phone call. So far he'd been disappointed in that hope.

Clara and Glauer both hated Fetlock, for very good, if personal, reasons. They both kept working for him because he was their only chance to close the case. To find Malvern—and Caxton—and put this gruesome chapter of history to bed.

"Sir, the man I chased showed the classic signs of being a vampire's servant. His face was gone. Scratched right off his head. He did not bleed when I shot him. When I find a piece of his arm with evidence that I did, in fact, hit him, that will clinch it. But the fact that he was turned into pulp by the truck collision, and that there isn't a single drop of blood on the road at the collision site—"

"Special Deputy Hsu," Fetlock said, in that slow, smoldering tone that meant he wasn't listening to a word she said. "The man you chased couldn't be a half-dead. Half-deads can only be animated after a vampire drains their blood. They rot away very quickly—on average, they last less than a week following their animation."

Clara fought the urge to roll her eyes. She didn't need a lesson in the facts of undeath. But she knew better than to stop him midrant.

"Since the last extant vampire was killed two years ago, it's quite impossible that this subject," he went on, gesturing at her mosaic of bone fragments, "was a half-dead. He would have rotted away long, long ago. I don't have an explanation for why there's no blood on the scene. But I don't need one. Clearly you were mistaken. You only saw the subject's face for a moment and in unusual lighting conditions. I don't have to point out how easy it is to make a misidentification in those circumstances. What you're claiming is impossible. And once we rule out the impossible, the improbable, however unlikely, must be the truth. J. Edgar Hoover used to say that."

Clara's eyebrows drew closer together. She couldn't resist saying what she said next, as much as it might hurt her. "Sherlock Holmes, you mean."

Fetlock shook his head and laughed. "No, no, no. Holmes's famous line is 'Elementary, my dear Watson.'"

Clara squeezed her eyes shut. She might have laughed out loud if Glauer hadn't touched her jaw again. "Ow! Stop doing that. Sir. U.S. Marshal Fetlock, sir. I need to follow up on this. Just let me run some tests. That's what you hired me to do."

"Seventy-two hours of mandatory recuperative leave," Fetlock repeated. "Those are the rules. I'll have the local sheriff's department come down and collect evidence here. They'll check it out for you. If you like, I can have them send you the results of their inquiry—but only after you've finished your recuperative leave."

"Yes, sir," Clara said, unable to suppress a sigh.

Fetlock wandered off to talk to the state police on the scene. Probably to compliment them on what a fine job they'd done setting out the road flares in exactly the approved pattern. Clara buried her head in her hands and tried not to cry.

Glauer poked her in the side.

"Jesus!" she shrieked, sitting up again. "Did you not hear what I said? He kicked me right there. And yes, it hurts!"

Glauer didn't apologize, but his eyes were so full of concern she couldn't help but relent. He was a big man, very broad through the shoulders, with a bristly mustache and a mouth that was always frowning. He looked exactly like what he had once been—the best cop on a local force in a town that never saw much crime. He came from Gettysburg originally—a place that owed a lot to Laura Caxton. Like most people who met her he'd been sucked into the vortex of her intensity, her driving need to destroy the vampires. Now, like Clara, he was still working Caxton's last case for her, because she had taught them you couldn't just give up when it came to vampires. That you couldn't stop until you were sure they were dead.

Glauer was a good man. He loved Caxton, in a very complicated way. A sort of messed-up mix of hero worship and religious awe—the way some people thought about their favorite sports heroes. He liked Clara like she was his own daughter, even though he was only about five years older than her.

"Laura used to tell me, if it hurts, it's still working," he said. "And if you're not bleeding, you can still work."

"She also used to tell *me* that she and I would be together forever and that I meant more to her than killing Malvern," Clara pointed out.

Glauer's face didn't change. The Laura Caxton he idolized was allowed to lie, if it could help her track down more vampires.

Clara sighed again. "It was a half-dead. You believe me, right?"

Glauer shrugged. "Enough that I want a copy of the sheriff's report. You want a ride home?"

"No, my Mazda's still parked over there at the convenience store. I don't want to leave it here overnight." She struggled up to her feet. For a second she looked down at the bone fragments she'd been playing with, but she knew there was no longer any point in trying to make sense of them. "He's going to screw up this lead," she said. "Fetlock's good at that."

"He keeps his people safe. Most of the time. That's not the worst thing you can say about a boss in law enforcement."

Clara nodded. She knew that was true. "Caxton always tried to protect people. But she understood that sometimes you have to take a risk."

Glauer had no reply to that. "Listen, I talked to the locals. They felt pretty bad about you getting attacked. They should have found that guy when they originally taped off the convenience store. Apparently when they went back in, after you chased him off, they found some ceiling panels had been moved in the bathroom. The guy must have been hiding in the ceiling the whole time they locked down the scene, then while you were working. Maybe he thought the cops had finally left, or maybe he just got bored with waiting."

"It would be a lot easier to hide up there if he was a half-dead," Clara pointed out. "They don't get stiff from sitting in a cramped position all day. They don't even breathe, so if he just kept still they wouldn't have heard him."

Glauer nodded, accepting this. "They finally got done checking out the store's security tapes. Your guy was definitely the one who killed the clerk. They've got footage of him walking in there and beating the guy to death—and then tearing the security camera off the wall. What happened after that is anybody's guess. But you shouldn't feel guilty about chasing him into traffic. We have proof he was a killer."

Clara's eyes went wide. It had never occurred to her to feel guilty. That was weird. Of course, Laura had taught her you didn't need to feel guilty about killing half-deads, since they were evil, soulless abominations.

If it turned out that her attacker had been, as Fetlock seemed to think, just a regular human being—

"Wait a minute," she said.

He raised an eyebrow.

Clara had that prickling feeling she got whenever things didn't add up. She shook her head as if she could knock the mystery loose. "There's . . . something weird here. Half-deads don't drink blood. The guy I chased was the killer, but there was no blood on the scene."

Glauer frowned. "Malvern must have come with him. She

probably can't move on her own now. It's been a long time since she drank enough blood to be able to walk."

Clara waved one hand in the air. She'd assumed as much already. "Right, right. So he brought her there. He killed the victim. She drank the blood. All that makes sense. But then she left. And he didn't."

Glauer never reacted the way Clara wanted him to when she was feeling clever. He didn't jump up and down or laugh or tell her how smart she was. He just watched her face, waiting for her to draw the conclusion.

"Malvern left the store, and probably not under her own power. So that means there were other half-deads present. They all left with her, because she needed them to carry her. But not this one, not the one in the yellow sweatshirt. He stayed behind. He wasn't waiting for the cops to leave."

"No?"

"No! Damn it, he was waiting for *us*. For *me*. Malvern left him there—ordered him to stay, and only come out and attack when I showed up."

"Interesting," he said.

She wanted to lean right up into his face and scream for him to react more. For him to recognize that this was important. This was the first time Malvern had shown her hand in years. It was the first time she'd tried to kill them since she left the prison. Why now? Why at all?

That was the problem with Malvern. You never understood why she did the things she did until it was way too late.

"So what do you plan to do about that?" Glauer asked.

She sighed and ran her fingers through her hair. What could she do about it? "I guess I'm going to keep looking for clues," she said, defeated. Malvern had tried to kill her, and the best thing she could do in reaction was keep looking for fibers.

Just like she had been for two years.

She looked down at the bone fragments she'd been studying.

There would be nothing there, she was sure, nothing she could follow. She suddenly felt very, very tired.

"You sure you don't want a ride home?" Glauer asked.

She turned and stared at him. His face was impassive as usual, but his body language was strangely expressive—he kept jerking his chin, as if he wanted to look over his shoulder but didn't want anyone to see him looking over his shoulder.

He was trying to tell her something.

"You have a lead of your own," she said. "On a . . . a different case."

"It's probably nothing," he said. His eyes went wide, which meant he was lying. She had known him long enough to have all his tells.

"The case we don't talk about," she said, very quietly.

"I'll give you a ride," he said.

Which could only mean one thing.

Glauer thought he knew where Laura was.

[1715]

The same year that Mama died, Death began to attend upon Justinia's gaming nights.

He never played, but sat in the back of the room, an untouched glass of liquor before him. He had skin as pale as consumption and the devil's eyes, red and glowing with a light of their own. Rude as it might be, he kept his hat on indoors, a low-brimmed slouch hat that shadowed his face. He did not smile. He would wait until the games had all played themselves out, until the queue formed of men who would be staying after hours to pay court at Justinia's bedside.

But Death was not waiting on her favors.

Always at the end of the night there would be one man, one broken fellow, down on his luck and down at the heels, who would stare about him in wild confusion as if wondering where all his money had gone. With many a backward glance and a pleading look (though he must have known there was little credit to be had at the gambling table, and less sympathy) he would take his leave, drunkenly running one hand across the stained wallpaper. And when the night's loser took his leave, Death followed.

Justinia grew to look forward to his visits. She would pass him smiles he never returned as she laid out the cards on the red baize. Give him knowing looks though he never met her eye. Because she knew what was coming.

She had a rash of pinkish blemishes on the soles of her feet and her left palm. She had seen the French pox before. It had taken Mama, and now it was back for her.

The night that Death finally met her eye, she was ready. She nodded slowly to him, then rose from her chair and announced that she was tired and was calling an early ending to the night. The men around the table groaned and protested, but they left all the same when she put the cards away in their velvet sack and started blowing out the candles. One by one they trooped out, with money still in their pockets and lust still in their eyes, until Justinia and Death were quite alone.

"Will ye be so kind as to let me have one last drink?" she asked, taking up a decanter of brandy from the side table.

He waved the fingers of one hand in acquiescence. He was a patient man, Death, and seemed to have all the time in the world.

Justinia drank deep. The liquid fire coated her throat and made her cough, but it warmed her chilly bones. "There," she said. "I'm ready if—"

He did not seem to move, but suddenly he had her by the throat. He forced her down to her knees on the hearth rug and now, for the first time, he truly met her gaze. "My name is Vincombe," he told her. "And I need what you possess."

"As ye like," she said. His hand around her neck was as strong as iron. He held her down so she could not get away. She resolved to herself that she would not struggle. Her time had simply come. It was right that things should end this way.

"I'm no evil man," he went on, and she wondered that Death should say such a thing, but she withheld her counsel. "I only take those as should welcome it. Though they never do."

"I see," she told him.

Then something strange happened. His eyes went wide. He released his hold on her. It was as if he'd seen something inside her. Something he didn't understand.

Death—Vincombe—took a step back. He looked down at her again and opened his mouth wide. She saw the rows of teeth in his mouth, triangular and long and sharp as knives. The teeth of a vampire.

She reached up and untied her neckerchief, then drew it away from her throat and dropped it on the floor. Then, slowly, she tilted her head to one side, presenting her jugular vein.

"At your leisure, sir," she said.

5.

Laura Caxton was learning the value of boredom.

From where she sat on the porch she could see all the way down the side of the ridge. She could see the brown ribbon of dirt road that led nowhere in particular except down to the Hollow below. She could see the gulfs of wasteland that flanked the road on either side, slopes of green where weeds grew ten feet tall and the summer's new crop of saplings burst up through the soil, fighting for a chance to reach the sun. This whole ridge had been clear-cut and then strip-mined once, leaving it terraced and raw to the elements, but that had been decades ago. Nature only needed to be left alone for one good summer before it took over again, and in the intervening years it had reclaimed the whole ridge for its own. Tangled in amid those plants were the rusted-out wrecks of old mining machines, scrapers and diggers and loaders. When the afternoon light hit a piece of broken glass from a shattered windshield it shone like gems scattered across the top of a green baize pool table. Small animals ran desperate and hunted through that expanse of verdure, shaking the stalks and making tiny noises that got lost in the rustling of the plants. The heat of the day made columns of warm air that rose as invisible pillars of wind, strong enough that the hen harriers who patrolled the ridge could ride them all day, hovering as dark specks up high, waiting for their chance to swoop down and make a kill.

The birds were teaching Laura all about boredom.

If you wanted to be a predator, you had to learn how to wait, and how to watch. You had to be patient. You had to sit and be still and let your prey come to you. It was boring as hell. It wasn't like when she'd gone on hunting trips with her father, back when she was so young that even an hour spent out in the cold woods had seemed like an eternity. That had been all about tracking, and spotting a deer from a hundred yards away, and then the sudden noise and movement of the shot. No. This wasn't like that at all. The birds were teaching her about conserving her energy. They were teaching her about keeping her eyes open all the time, not just when she expected to see something.

And they were teaching her that even boredom had its value. Because the more bored you got, the more annoyed you were at having to wait so long, the more grateful you would be when you finally got your chance to act. When the moment of the kill came, you would be so ready for it, so desperate for it, that you would not hold back. The harriers didn't need conscience, or philosophy, or high technology. They just wanted to kill something so badly they made it happen.

The screen door behind Caxton banged, but she didn't jump. Anyone coming *out* of the house was safe. By the sound of his boots on the doorstep she knew it was Urie Polder, who owned this particular shack, and who was sheltering her from the police.

Urie Polder had one good arm. The other one had been replaced by a tree branch, with long thin twigs for fingers. Because he was a Pow-Wow, a conjure doctor, he could make the wooden arm move almost as well as the one of flesh and bone. He wore a white T-shirt and a trucker cap (sans irony) and he was holding a Mason jar full of yellow liquid. Something dark stirred at the bottom of the jar.

"A little early to start drinking," Caxton said, without bothering to smile. He would know she was teasing.

Urie shot her a shit-eating grin and held the jar up so she could see it. The dark shape at the bottom of the jar turned out to be three rusty nails tied together in a knot. "Fox urine an' a charm," he explained. "For keepin' vermin out of my garden, ahum. Coneys and moles, and the like."

He opened the jar and sprinkled the contents over the tomato and cucumber plants that sprawled over the side yard of the house. When he was done he fished the nails out of the bottom of the jar and buried them in the center of the vegetable patch.

He was not the weirdest person Caxton had ever met. But he was up there.

When he was done he headed back inside without another word. He knew better than to disturb Caxton in her vigil. Idle conversation could be pleasant, but it distracted you. It kept you from paying proper attention.

The harriers had taught her that, too. They were solitary creatures. Predators usually were. They didn't need company while they waited out their prey. They kept to themselves, not chattering at one another, barely aware of each other's existence. Mating season was over. Now it was time to hunt.

Caxton liked to think of herself as akin to the harriers now. She had gotten rid of all the human parts of herself that made her different from those hunters. She had perfected her method. She'd had no choice, really. If Caxton was a hen harrier, then it wasn't field mice she was waiting on. It was a grizzly bear. The only chance she had was to pay attention.

Of course, she did what she could to even the odds. Sitting next to her on the porch swing, hidden under a blanket, were a twelve-gauge shotgun, two Glock handguns carrying thirteen rounds apiece, and a scoped hunting rifle that could put a round right through a steel pipe at three hundred yards. The harriers just had their talons and their hooked beaks.

6.

There were still two hours of daylight left when word came down from the house that a car was coming up the road. A few minutes later Caxton saw it for herself. With a pair of binoculars she checked its license plate, then confirmed that the driver was alone in the vehicle. A teenaged girl in a calico dress—one of Patience's acolytes, probably—stood by until Caxton nodded that it was okay. The girl headed back inside, and Caxton rose from her chair but didn't leave the shade of the porch.

The monster she lay in wait for was known to set traps and snares, and use people she knew against her as bait. She stayed very close to the guns.

The car, a late-model sedan, had trouble on the steep grade, but eventually it chugged to a stop just before the house. It brought a plume of dust with it that cut down visibility from Caxton's aerie, but there was nothing to be done for that. The driver sat at the wheel for a while, staring at her as if she was a ghost. He was about twenty years old, dressed casually in a black T-shirt and sunglasses, which he slowly removed while they looked at each other. Caxton did not wave to him or give him any kind of signal. If this was a trap, or if he was coming here for the wrong reason, it was up to him to signal her.

Instead he popped open his door and stepped out into the yard, a bundle of small packages balanced precariously in the crook of one arm. He looked up at Caxton and smiled, and didn't seem to take it the wrong way when she failed to smile back.

"I got your message," he said. "Obviously."

His name was Simon Arkeley. He was the son of the man who had taught Caxton most of what she knew about killing vampires. The boy was far less formidable than his father, but he had his uses. For one thing, he had a credit card.

"Urie will be pleased," she said, nodding at the bundles in his arm. She stopped looking at him and went back to staring down the ridge. "He's needed those roots for a while now. They don't grow this far north."

"They don't grow anywhere except Mexico. At least not legally." Simon came up the three steps to the porch and looked like he expected a hug or a kiss or at least a handshake. Caxton just kept watching the ridge. "Should I—go in? I guess?" he asked. His smile melted from his face. "Mom always taught me never to just walk into another practitioner's house uninvited."

"You'll be welcome here. You're from one of the old families." Caxton let her guard down for a split second, just long enough to look him in the eye. Then she sighed and accepted that she could not, physically, monitor the ridge twenty-four seven. "Let's get you inside."

She held the screen door for him and followed him into the darkness of the front parlor. An old grandfather clock ticked away the hours in there, its pendulum swinging as it had for nearly two hundred years. When the coal company had come through this ridge, looking to tear open the earth, three villages had been completely displaced and their houses torn down. Only the Polders had managed to keep their land. They had refused to sell at any price, because there was no way to safely move that clock from where it stood. No one now remembered what would happen if the clock stopped ticking, but Urie Polder made sure to wind it every night without fail. Caxton thought it was probably just an old superstition, but she never said a word to Urie about his little ritual.

"Through here, to the kitchen," Caxton told Simon. She took him into the main sitting room, where Patience Polder and her disciples were kneeling on the floor. The three girls facing Patience looked like something from another era. They all wore dresses that were old-fashioned fifty years before Caxton was born. What she'd grown up thinking of as Holly Hobby dresses. Their hair was braided or piled up in buns on the backs of their heads and they kept their eyes down when Simon entered the room.

Patience herself was dressed similarly, but all in white. Fifteen years old now, she was growing into a beautiful young woman, though no boy down in the Hollow would think of making time with her. Patience was destined for something special. Everyone knew that. Her mother, Vesta, had told them. Vesta hadn't lived long enough to say exactly what that destiny entailed, but no one ever doubted her.

The girls had their hands together as if in prayer. They had pushed back the faded Persian carpet from the floor and had drawn a pentacle on the boards with a piece of sticky black bitumen. What they were calling on, or calling up, Caxton didn't know, but she didn't much care, either.

Simon stopped moving when he saw Patience. His eyes locked with the girl's and for a moment the room grew very cold. One of the disciples shivered convulsively. Caxton had seen this sort of thing before and she knew to just wait it out. Eventually Patience looked away, and Simon headed toward the kitchen again as if nothing had happened.

Yet when he dumped his armful of packages on the kitchen table, Caxton saw that he'd gone white as a sheet.

"You okay?" she asked, to be polite.

"She—that girl—" Simon shook his head. "I don't know if I should bow every time I see her, or call in an exorcist." He tried to laugh it off, as if he'd been joking. "She's got some real magic in her. I mean, I can feel it."

Urie Polder came in from the backyard and closed the screen door with his wooden arm. "She's somewhat else, my Patience," he said, nodding appreciatively at Simon. "Ye can tell magic by the way it makes your hair stand on end. I should think ye have that talent. Ye're Astarte's boy, ahum."

"Mr. Polder," Simon said, and shook the man's human hand. "We met once at my father's . . . funeral, but we never got a chance to talk. You knew my mother well, from what I've been told. I'm afraid she never talked about you to me directly."

"There's a reason for that, ahum," Urie replied. "Seein' as your daddy and my wife, Vesta, was lovers, contrary to their marriages. Bad blood there." The placid expression on his face didn't change. "No reason for us to perpetuate it, though, is there? Seein' as all three of 'em is dead now."

"No—no, of course not," Simon said.

"That's good, ahum. Well, ye're welcome in my home. Now let's see what you brung us, and what good can be made of it, shall we?"

7.

Urie Polder used his twig fingers to gently peel open each of Simon's little packages, revealing tight little bundles of plant material that looked almost identical. Yet with each new discovery, the conjure doctor's face lit up with a new gleam. Caxton had no real idea what they were good for. She only knew the names she'd given to Simon when she wrote to him. John the Conqueror root, monkshood, fetchbane, witch grass. Many of them were prohibited by drug laws, though none were simple narcotics or hallucinogens. Urie Polder had suggested he could do great things with them but that he had no access to them, geographically limited as he was.

"You're probably wondering what's going on," she said to Simon, leading him out onto the back porch. She cast one quick eye over the back of the ridge, but she was comfortably certain the attack wouldn't come from that direction, so she turned back to make eye contact.

Simon shrugged. "When I got your letter, it took me a couple of days to even realize who sent it. You didn't sign it, there was no return address—well, I guess I understand that."

Caxton nodded. She was a fugitive from the law. An escapee from a maximum-security prison. The U.S. Marshals were after her, and they had a history of catching even the smartest criminals eventually. She had remained free this long only because she used to be one of them—a special deputy in the Marshals Service—and knew their methods.

"When I left the prison, I knew there was only one place I could go. It was a risk, but there weren't any safe options. So I went to see Urie, in his place in Lancaster County. That's what he calls his 'city house,' even though the closest town is an Amish village ten miles away. He took me in with no questions. We were old friends, and that counted for something. I was also the woman who killed Jameson Arkeley. Your father."

Simon nodded, but he didn't meet her eye.

Caxton had no time anymore for sympathy. "Jameson had killed Vesta Polder, Urie's wife, and turned her into a half-dead. He appreciated what I'd done, he said, but he couldn't keep me at the city house. So we moved back here—to his country place." Pennsylvania was an old state and heavily populated, but it still had its wild places. Old strip mines had a reputation for being toxic and inaccessible, so the real estate developers stayed clear. The ridge was about as far as you could get from human civilization and still be inside the Commonwealth.

"He just packed up and moved for you?" Simon asked.

Caxton sighed. "The city place had been mostly for Vesta's benefit. She had a profitable line in card reading and removing curses from farmers' fields. Urie's work is mostly by mail order, so it doesn't matter where he lives. He can still get to the post office from this place, if he doesn't mind driving an hour and a half. Anyway, he wanted to come here. This is a good place for him, where nobody stares at his wooden arm. Everyone who lives down in the Hollow is kin. They're your family, too, though pretty far removed."

"Witchbillies," Simon said.

"I beg your pardon?"

Simon stared down at his feet. "That's what my mom used to call them. Witchbillies. Like hillbillies, you know, but—well. She didn't have a lot of respect for them. Said they were all bumpkins, and most of them couldn't tell the difference between a real hex sign and something you would get at an Amish tourist trap."

"They're not so bad," Caxton said. "They worshipped Vesta Polder, too. So they're sympathetic to my cause. I'm safe here. Nobody enters the Hollow or comes up the ridge without being seen, and they let me know so I can go hide if I have to."

Simon put a hand on her shoulder. "I'm so sorry you have to live like this. I know it can't be easy. Listen, Ms. Caxton. You saved my life. When Dad—when he—he—"

"The word is *killed*," she said. "Or *murdered*. Your pick."

Simon went pale, but he didn't object. "When my dad murdered our entire family, you saved my life. So I did what you asked. When I got your letter, I had no idea how to do what you wanted. I'd never been to a botanica before. Those places are weird. Little old ladies with eyes that look right through you. Jesus and Mary candles all over the place, and the stores all smell like vinegar and brimstone."

"That's how you know you're in a genuine botanica," Caxton said. "That's the smell of bitumen."

Simon shrugged. "Okay. Whatever. I went into a bunch

of those places looking for the roots you needed and they had them, oh, sure. But they wouldn't sell them to me until I proved I was Astarte Arkeley's son. Even then they kept making signs against the evil eye and spitting on my shadow. I mean—I know magic is real. My mom used to do some pretty witchy stuff, and she even taught me a thing or two. But that was all about tarot cards and spirit rapping and . . . and . . ." He shook his head. "I've been trying so hard, trying to . . . to put this stuff behind me. This life, magic, all of it . . . I just . . . just . . ."

"You did fine," Caxton told him. "And I appreciate it."

"Like I said, you saved my life. I owed you."

"Good."

Simon turned to stare at her. "Good? You could say thank you, or—"

"I already said I appreciated it. I meant, good, because there's more I need you to do. I have another list—don't worry, this time it's all stuff you can get at any hardware store. Small electronics, some building supplies we don't have access to here. That sort of thing. I do need you to go back to the botanicas, but only because I need some information. Now that you've bought from them, those creepy old ladies will trust you, and maybe they'll even tell you what I need to know. After that, I'm going to need you to spy on my old friends in the USMS for me, and find out what leads they're working on."

"Hold on, I—"

He stopped because the screen door creaked open and Patience Polder came outside onto the back porch. She wiped sweat off her forehead with her bonnet before putting it back over her golden hair. "It's going to be a warm evening," she said.

Caxton favored her with a tight little smile that left her mouth before it really had time to form. "Good afternoon, Patience. How are your girls?"

"Coming along nicely. Mr. Arkeley, we weren't properly introduced before," she said. She held out a hand, fingers down.

Simon reached for it, but he looked like he didn't know if he was supposed to shake the hand or kiss it. He ended up bowing a little as he squeezed her fingers. Caxton and Patience both stared at him then, as if he'd instead chosen to tickle Patience under the chin.

Patience relented first, dropping her hand and beaming at the boy. She was five years younger than Simon, but she had done a lot of growing in the last few years and she was just about his height, Caxton realized.

"You'll stay for dinner," Patience said. "It's a full moon to-night—the entire community will be dining together, down in the Hollow."

It wasn't a question. Simon sputtered out something about wanting to get back on the road before dark, but Patience had already turned and gone back into the house.

"You actually don't have a choice here," Caxton told him, and slapped him on the back. "Not when she has that tone in her voice."

"Is she like in charge here or something?" Simon asked, look-ing pained. "I mean, is this like a—a cult, and she's the holy child, or what?"

"You misunderstood," Caxton told him. "She didn't com-mand your presence at dinner. She foretold it."

"There's no fear within ye. None?" Vincombe asked.

Justinia said nothing.

"What's wrong with ye, that ye won't fight for life?" the vampire asked. He grabbed her up again, hauling her into the air by her throat. He pulled her close to those slavering jaws, to the enormous teeth and the burning eyes. She saw now that he possessed neither eyebrows nor lashes. That he was not so human as he'd looked before when he sat alone at her gaming nights. And she understood why he had never smiled. Too difficult to hide those gnashing teeth.

Those beautiful white teeth. They looked like the blades of Father's shears. They smelled of blood.

The thought came unbidden to her mind. Red as diamonds, red as hearts. Red as rubies. She remembered the way the blood had been so warm. How nice it would be to bathe in her own blood. To let it wash everything away.

Vincombe threw her down in a heap. He stalked about the room, grabbing things up and smashing them—her plates, the bottles of cheap liquor on the sideboard. He took up the velvet bag and tore it to shreds and threw her cards at her so they clattered and fell across her where her face touched the rug.

"Always they beg. Always! One more day, they pray me. One more hour."

On the rug Justinia slowly sat up. She began to wonder if the vampire intended to talk her to death.

But his fury had left him as soon as it came on. He sank down in a chair behind her, where she couldn't see him. She understood, and did not turn around.

"Death comes for us all, in its proper time," she said. "Easier to turn the tide and make the sea swallow Ireland than stave it off one second. I'm not afraid."

He groaned, and she wondered that she could give him such pains.

She could only speak the truth, though. "I am twenty years old, with pestilence inside me. I have the French pox. Is it not better to die now, young and beautiful, than to suffer on many years more as my nose rots away and the lesions cover my back?"

"Wouldst thou suicide, then?" he asked, his voice very soft.

She had to laugh. "Given a choice? No. I'd live on. But who has a choice?"

"I do," he told her. "Ye talk of life as of a game of cards."

"Is it not? We are each dealt a hand, and one rarely to our choosing. We play our tricks as we may, with shrewdness or with wild luck." She shrugged. "And in the end, the final card turns, and we see what we have won or lost."

"Some players cheat," he told her.

Justinia smiled warmly. "Oh, yes."

He was in front of her then. He moved so quickly it was as if he did not need to cover the intervening space, as if he could will himself to be somewhere and on the instant he arrived. He grabbed her by either side of her head and she felt the strength in his hands again. Knew that if he liked he could squeeze and crack her skull like an empty eggshell. Instead he just looked into her eyes. His own red eyes burned. She began to say something, but he laid a finger across her lips to silence her. She would not learn until later the vast importance of that silence.

He stared into her soul and she looked back with nothing inside her. No love or fear or hate, no sympathy or pleading, no warmth and no coldness. His eyes burned through her like coals.

And then he was gone. She felt only a little breeze as he moved, a stirring of the air. The door slammed shut behind him and he was gone. And she thought how strange it all was, and she thought it was over.

But nothing, at all, was over.

8.

There was still some human part of Laura Caxton that could appreciate fate joking around with human lives, and which enjoyed Simon's frustration and surprise. The boy tried to flee before his appointed dinner with the witchbillies. He gave it his all—after saying a quick good-bye to Urie Polder, he hurried around the side of the house (the better to avoid Patience) and jumped back in his car, moving like devils were after him. The only problem was that the car wouldn't start. He tried the ignition again and again, but the car just groaned and begged him to stop.

Urie Polder eventually came out and popped the hood. The conjure doctor knew cars pretty well, but after fiddling with the engine for half an hour he had to admit he was stumped. "One of these new computerized vehicles, ahum. No decent man can tell what's the matter, less'n he's half robot. And I'm half tree." That made him laugh, a wheezing, burbling noise that made Simon grimace in distaste.

"She sabotaged my car somehow," Simon said when Caxton came over. "Or you did."

Caxton shrugged. "I'll point out, for the sake of logic and rationality, that you're an unemployed recent college graduate."

Simon flushed. "Yes, and?"

"The kind of man who can't afford a new car. So you bought this thing used, am I right?"

Simon stared down at the steering wheel. "I used some of the money from Dad's life insurance. I couldn't afford much."

"So you bought a clunker. The kind of car that just breaks down sometimes. Also, you're at a much higher elevation here than where you normally drive the car. That can cause vapor lock, or just mess with the carburetor." Caxton shrugged. "I didn't touch your car, and I doubt that Patience would even get within ten feet of it. She disdains modern technology. Face it, you're staying for dinner."

It was enough. Simon gave in.

The two of them headed back into the house. The Polder family always contributed to the full-moon dinners, which meant hauling a lot of food down to the Hollow. Urie Polder had gathered a bushel basket full of his tomatoes and cucumbers from his side garden, and ears of wild corn from a patch down the back of the ridge. Caxton helped him bring platters of chicken parts out of what he insisted was called an icebox (an antique but fully functional electric refrigerator) while Simon threw cold water on his face. As Caxton came out of the kitchen she was nearly stampeded by Patience and her acolytes, who came racing down the stairs with their bonnets in their hands, giggling and whispering among themselves. Caxton wasn't completely sure, but she thought Patience was blushing.

Urie Polder scratched his head with one twig finger when he saw that. "Ye'd think she were a reg'lar gal for her age, wouldn't ya? Somethin's up, ahum."

Caxton frowned. "I don't think Simon's going to like it, whatever it is."

The Hollow, where they'd be having dinner, wasn't far at all—even if it felt that way when you were carrying fifty pounds of produce. Still, it would mean giving up her vigil, if only for a few hours. When they reached the porch Caxton stopped and looked out over the valley at the ridge on the other side. Her eyes narrowed. "Your wards are all set?" she asked. She never felt right about these communal dinners. It meant far too long away from her aerie. She glanced at the blanket that hid her pile of guns. She had a pistol in a holster at the small of her back, but it would be little help if Malvern attacked during the dessert course. "The teleplasm cordon is intact? When was the last time you checked it?"

"All's accounted for and correct, yessir," Urie Polder said.

"She hain't comin' tonight, Laura. There's the full moon. Anyway, ye go ahead and smell the wind—it's clean, ain't no stench of unnaturalness."

Caxton nodded, but her brow stayed furrowed. She said nothing more. When Simon appeared, lugging two huge ceramic jugs of moonshine, she set out down the hill and the two men followed. Patience and her disciples had already hurried down with their own burdens, moving with the speed of youth.

At the bottom of the hill lay the Hollow, a patch of clear ground where the brush had all been carefully cleared away to make room for a dozen little cottages, some of which could be called shotgun shacks if you were feeling uncharitable. Behind the shacks sat ten or so single-wide trailers up on cinder blocks.

"Smells like chrysanthemums," Simon said, pulling Caxton back from her reverie. The three of them were approaching the center of the village, where picnic tables had been set up in long lines. Tiki torches ringed the common, their flames just a little more red than they should be. The smell came from the oil they burned.

"Special recipe," Caxton said, nodding at the nearest torch. "Supposedly it's better than citronella at keeping mosquitoes away."

"Does it work?" Simon asked.

"Does citronella?" Caxton replied. "I always thought that stuff was a scam. Anyway, this mix smells better. You can put those jugs down over there," she said, pointing at a spot near the edge of the common that was already heaped with coolers and a half keg of beer. "Oh, boy. Here they come. Remember to be nice, Simon. You're a guest here."

The doors of the cottages opened one by one, and the witchbillies streamed out to get their first look at Astarte Arkeley's son.

[1715]

The pistol sat heavy in Justinia's hand, a beautiful construction of oiled wood and blued steel. She had come to love the smooth, curved grip and the complicated matchlock, the octagonal barrel etched with a floral motif. It was a nobleman's weapon and it had cost every last farthing she'd tucked away over years of gambling and selling her virtue. It was the last thing she would ever buy.

In the week since Vincombe had refused to slaughter her, she'd had many thoughts like that. *This is the last candy I will ever taste,* she would tell herself. *This is the final time I will pluck my eyebrows. Or clean my teeth. Or powder my wig.*

It was not so much the melancholy of loss as a kind of final bookkeeping. She was putting away the things of life, folding them neatly into a chest she would then throw into the river. Things she had cared about once, but no longer. Things she was happy to give away.

Vincombe's curse was inside of her. She could feel it coiling like an asp around the stem of her brain. It wanted her to take her own life. That was the only way the curse could work. It made her see things differently. Every time she passed an open window, she thought of the immense freedom a bird must feel as it launches itself into the sky. Every time she ate a meal she wondered what rat poison must taste like. These things made her giggle.

Then she had seen the pistol in the window of a pawnshop not three lanes away. It had glinted in the morning sun, and it was like a beacon fire had been lit, just for her.

Vincombe had not returned to her since the fateful night. Despite the usual demand she had not run a game, or entertained a gentleman caller, since then. She had largely stopped eating or sleeping.

More things to put away. More things to let go.

The pawnbroker had been reluctant to sell the pistol to a woman. He assumed she was going to kill an unfaithful lover or a husband *who refused to leave his wife. She'd had to spread her legs to convince him.*

This is the last time I will let a man touch me, she thought.

She would never be married. Or have children of her own.

She had to put the pistol down, because mirth overwhelmed her and made her press her hands against her mouth, wipe tears of laughter away from her eyes. Such things had never been in the cards of Justinia Malvern.

The pawnbroker had shown her how to load the pistol with a bit of wadding and just the right amount of powder. She inserted the lead ball— smaller than she'd expected, but heavier, too—and rammed it down with a little rod that had its own sheath underneath the barrel. Such a cunning design. She thought the pistol was the most beautiful thing she'd ever seen.

Lifting it to her mouth, she licked the end of the barrel to see how it would taste. The oil on the metal was unpalatable, and for a brief moment her mind cleared and she thought—What am I doing? Why this, why now?

No. She would not place the barrel in her mouth like a man's member. That was undignified.

She wanted to see it coming. So she lifted the pistol higher, until she could squint with one eye and look directly down the barrel at the waiting ball. It was black in there, as black as a pip. My ace, she thought. My ace of spades, hidden away to be brought forth when needed.

What a wonderful cheat to play on the world. On death. On life.

She did not blink as she pulled the trigger.

9.

The seventeenth century had been a hard time for witches. Pushed out of Europe by centuries of persecution, they had flocked to America looking for a new start, just like so many other marginal religious groups. They were a misunderstood lot. They were not Satanists, nor did they worship graven images in the woods, and very, very few of them ever flew on broomsticks. The vast majority were, in fact, devout Christians who just knew a bit more than their neighbors about herbal cures and simple, harmless charms. That was enough, unfortunately, to get them demonized by the Puritans and the Pilgrims, blamed for every manner of thing that went wrong in the fledgling colony of Massachusetts. In this way they were quite similar to the Quakers.

The Puritans hanged every Quaker they could get their hands on. Some managed to escape, first to Rhode Island, then to Pennsylvania, where they established a commonwealth, a place where all religions would be tolerated—to a degree. After the hysteria that gripped Salem and nearby towns at the end of the century, the witches flooded into Pennsylvania in search of that tolerance, and if they were not welcomed there with open arms, they were at least no longer hounded to death by the authorities.

Still, it wasn't exactly the paradise they'd hoped for. The Quakers constantly tried to convert them, and while technically witchcraft wasn't even a crime on the books, the people were happy to take matters into their own hands whenever a two-headed calf was born or a child got lost in the woods. In 1749, a mob nearly tore down a courthouse when a judge refused to convict a man known to practice witchcraft. In the more rural part of Pennsylvania, witches were dragged out of their beds and lynched right up until the beginning of the nineteenth century.

The witches responded as they always had. They moved on. Yet not so far this time. They disappeared into the ridges of central Pennsylvania, ground so rocky and hard to till that nobody else wanted it. There they continued the old ways, carrying out ceremonies in the woods, performing their rituals behind closed doors. Their craft blended well with the folk magic brought to Pennsylvania by German immigrants—the hex signs they painted over their doors, the herbal lore found in that great book of medicine, *The Long Lost Friend*. They learned as well from the local Native Americans, so that in time their wisest practitioners became known as Pow-Wows, like Urie Polder.

There had never been very many of them, and only a dozen or so families still existed in Caxton's time, all of them with elaborate genealogical charts to show they'd descended from Giles Corey or Dorcas Good or Rebecca Nurse, the famous victims of Salem. Their numbers were bolstered by the occasional hippie or New Age mystic who wandered into their sphere, though such people rarely stayed long. There was no Internet connection in the Hollow, no cell phone towers or even a local newspaper, and the New Age types needed to feel connected to the larger world.

The true witchbillies, the survivors of the old families, never left. They knew how little there was for them out in the wider world.

As they came out for the full-moon dinner that night, Caxton tried to imagine how Simon would see them. He must think they'd stepped straight out of a time warp.

The men dressed like Amish farmers and wore fringes of beard under their chins. The women kept their black dresses buttoned all the way up to the neck and down to the wrist, and their long skirts swept the dust of the common. The children dressed in more colorful clothes, but as modestly as Patience Polder, who was the closest thing the Hollow had to a fashion guru.

They looked very prim and proper. Except, of course, for the ones who didn't.

Mixed in with the soberly dressed residents of the Hollow were women who draped themselves in silk shawls and tied kerchiefs around their heads like gypsy fortune-tellers. Some of the children wore T-shirts and shorts, while others had tie-dyed every garment they wore. There was one man who wore a long black cloak with a red lining and smeared kohl around his eyes, like a Goth pretending to be a movie vampire. One woman wore as little clothing as the law would allow but had covered all of her exposed skin in cabalistic tattoos.

Regardless of how they dressed, they descended on Simon like a flock of crows on a half-decayed badger. Visitors to the Hollow were incredibly rare and always the subject of much interest. The children wanted to sit in his lap or begged him to come play with them. The adults asked him a million questions about his family, very few of which he could answer. He did know that his mother was descended from both Sarah Osborne and Tituba, the Caribbean slave who had supposedly taught the girls of Salem how to do magic. He also knew that Astarte had become a Theosophist toward the end of her life, studying the teachings of Madame Blavatsky and Annie Besant. Apparently he had not realized that his father, Jameson, had also been a witchbilly, though of a decayed strain from North Carolina that had turned away from the old path.

The interest wasn't entirely in his bloodstock, however. Or at least not directly. One of the women took his arm and smiled into his face until he looked at her. "We're going to dance in the woods later, when the moon comes up. You'll have to join us, of course," she said. She batted her eyelashes and added, "It's a full moon, so we'll go skyclad."

Simon frowned, trying to work out what she was saying. "Naked, you mean." His mouth fluttered as if he was trying to decide whether to grin sheepishly or lasciviously. "You're going to do a Wiccan ritual?"

She laughed fetchingly. "It's what you do for fun when you don't even have basic cable," she told him.

She let him go with a smoldering look. Caxton pulled him away from the throng to make sure he got a good seat at the dinner table. "I don't get this," he told her. "That woman was wearing so many clothes I couldn't even see her wrists. But I think she was coming on to me."

Caxton had to laugh, despite herself. "You didn't notice anything about the sex ratio here?" She gestured around at the gathered witchbillies. For every man around the picnic tables there were six women. "Trust me, she was definitely coming on to you. Some of them get desperate enough to come on to *me*."

"But the clothes—they're dressed like the Amish. My mom dressed modestly, but she wore stuff that had been designed in the twentieth century, not the seventeenth." He shook his head. "They look like farmers, not witches. Or like they all belong to the same cult. Except—some of them don't wear the Amish stuff, and—and—and you're dressed like freaking Lara Croft."

"Who?" Caxton asked.

"The Tomb Raider."

Caxton stared down at her own clothes. It was summer, so she was wearing a tank top and cargo shorts. It was what she always wore.

Simon shook his head in perplexity. "They don't mind you wearing that? Or—her?" He nodded at the tattooed woman, who had on one of the smallest tube tops Caxton had ever seen. The tattooed woman—her name was Glynnis, and she was a student of the Kabbalah, Caxton knew—stared back at Simon with pantherish eyes.

Caxton nodded in understanding. "You're thinking that most of them are dressed *modestly*," she said.

"Um, yeah," Simon agreed.

"No. They're dressed *humbly*. There's a difference. Modesty is when you dress a certain way because you're afraid men will be overcome by lust if they see what you've got. Humility means thinking nobody wants to see it."

"Okay," Simon said. He was having trouble not watching the tattooed woman arch her back.

"That's the principle, anyway. It means you can dress however you want here, and nobody minds. Come on. Aren't you hungry? It's time to eat."

10.

About half of the witchbillies were vegetarians, some of them pure vegans, some who just refused to eat meat. The rest seemed to take great relish in piling up chicken and pork bones on their paper plates. The wild corn couldn't be eaten off the cob—it was nothing like the sweet corn Caxton had grown up eating—but it made excellent popcorn, which soon filled huge baskets all over the tables. There were loaves of fresh bread, leavened and unleavened, and pitchers of cream to pour over fresh berries. Caxton counted at least seven different varieties of potato salad, the traditional side dish of German immigrants everywhere, coleslaw with or without raisins, cornbread smeared with honey or molasses, buttermilk biscuits, baked beans, bean salad, bean casseroles, and bean barley soup. This on top of fried chicken, chicken fried steaks, pork ribs slathered with barbecue sauce, pierogies and dumplings and sauerkraut.

"Not exactly the healthiest meal I've ever seen," Simon pointed out.

"It's all organic, at least," Caxton told him. "This is farmer's food. It's supposed to give you enough calories to work all day in the fields." She made a plate for herself—mostly greens, with a single piece of fried chicken for protein—and stepped away from the table. "I'll leave you to enjoy your dinner," she told Simon. He looked like he might protest at being left alone, but two women came and sat down on either side of him and started piling food up in front of him and asking him so many questions he couldn't get away.

Caxton never sat with the others during the full-moon dinners. It just wasn't her way. It would be too easy to get caught up in the spirited discussions the witchbillies engaged in, endless debates over the proper way to harvest mandrake roots or what a given passage in the Bible had to say about necromancy. Then there were the endless squabbles and gossip over who was sleeping with whom and who wasn't doing their fair share of work around the Hollow.

It was the background noise of a working community, and Caxton didn't begrudge them their chatter. But it was also a distraction, and she weeded those out of her life wherever she found them.

So instead she wandered over to the fire pit, where Urie Polder was cooking a dozen fish at once. He needed no spatula, instead turning the fish with his wooden fingers. Apparently they didn't feel the heat.

"He seems a good fella, ahum," Urie said when she approached.

Caxton bit into her chicken thigh and said nothing. She looked out over a table covered in pies and Bundt cakes—just in case the witchbillies didn't get enough to eat—and out into the gathering shadows beyond the common. The sun was almost down.

Some of the Hollow's younger children were out there—the ones too young to sit through a meal without throwing a tantrum. They chased after things Caxton couldn't see. Fairies and elves, or at least illusions of fairies and elves that their mothers had bewitched them to see. They grabbed at the imaginary creatures with chubby fingers and laughed when their hands closed on nothing. The sprites kept them close enough to the common that Urie could keep an eye on them.

Caxton finished her meal and threw away her plate. Wiping her hands on her shorts, she announced, "I'm going to take another look at the cordon."

"You don't trust me, as I've said it's fine?" Urie asked, looking a little hurt.

"You know it isn't that."

"If my Vesta were still here, she'd have summat to say to you 'bout tryin' to enjoy what you got before you lose it, ahum."

Caxton ignored him. Vesta Polder was dead because Caxton hadn't been fast enough to save her. She hadn't been focused enough.

"We'll send the dogs out after full dark," Urie suggested.

Caxton nodded. Yes, they should do that. Vampires and their half-dead servants were unnatural creatures. Any animal more complex than a maggot could sense that. When a vampire came near, cows stopped giving milk. Cats went and hid under beds. Dogs, most usefully, started to howl, and wouldn't stop until the vampire moved on. The Hollow was home to several dozen hounds of various breeds, all of whom were allowed to roam at night as a kind of early warning system.

"Just humor me. I won't feel comfortable until I'm sure the trap is properly set," Caxton said.

Urie Polder shrugged, his wooden arm lifting high. They had this argument so often he barely even tried anymore. "Alright, then. You go on. I'll make certain the boy don't get into any mischief, ahum. Leastwise, none that the ladies don't concoct for him."

Caxton squeezed his human shoulder, then turned to head into the dark, away from the people in the Hollow and the safety of numbers. She didn't get very far, though. Before she even reached the road she heard someone pounding on the picnic tables for attention. Others took up the drumbeat and soon the Hollow was ringing with laughter.

She turned back to see what had gotten them so worked up, and saw Patience standing at the head of the table.

The girl was blushing again. She was wringing her hands in front of her and she wouldn't look up to make eye contact with anyone.

In the entire time Caxton had known the girl, Patience had

never looked so flustered. Normally it was the people around her who freaked out at what *she* said.

"I'd like to take this time," the girl said, feeling her way through the words, "to make an announcement. I'm very happy."

She bit her lower lip. Around her, her teenaged acolytes hugged themselves in excitement or bit their knuckles. They knew what was coming.

"I'm happier, I think, than I've ever been."

Caxton frowned as she headed back toward the common and the light from the tiki torches. She had no idea what Patience was about to say.

"You see," the girl stumbled on, "I met someone today. I met the man who is going to be my husband."

Not a soul breathed in the Hollow. Even the children too young to understand what was going on must have sensed that something important was happening. Every eye fixed on Patience's glowing face as she simpered and giggled. Then she did, finally, look up, to make eye contact with one man sitting at the table.

Every one of the witchbillies turned to follow her gaze. To look right at Simon, where he sat with a plastic fork and a bowl of coleslaw. Realization dawned on him very slowly, visibly, as he turned white and dropped his fork.

"Oh, fuck, no," he wheezed.

11.

Simon jumped up from the table and held his hands up in front of him, as if he expected the witchbillies to seize him and force him to marry Patience on the spot, at gunpoint if necessary. The people gathered around the picnic tables all started talking at once, trying to reassure him.

"But it's such an honor—"

"—she's been waiting for you her whole life, and—"

"No use fighting, friend." This with a friendly chuckle. "What she's foretold—"

The boy's face turned red with anger. "You are all fucking nuts. Nuts! I did not come here looking to marry some—some—prepubescent girl, much less the creepy prophet of some bizarre cult. I'm going to bring the police down here and they'll—they'll *raid* you. They will *raid* this place."

Caxton grunted in annoyance and rushed forward to grab Simon's arm. She hauled him away from the common. It wasn't hard. Flustered as he was, he lacked the strength to resist.

She took him up the road that led back up to the top of the ridge, where he'd left his car. When they reached the front of Urie Polder's house, however, she kept walking, though she let go of him. It was his choice whether to follow her or not.

"I don't know what you think you're going to achieve, Caxton," he called out, stomping after her as she headed into the tall grass beyond Urie's garden. "I don't know what sick fantasy you have about me becoming one of your cult groupies, but—"

"They are not a cult," she said. She used the voice she'd honed when she used to be a cop. Calm, firm, and unyielding.

"Communal living. Naked dancing in the woods. Probably piles of guns sitting around all over the place. Oh my God. I had some cider with my dinner. I drank the cider. What did they put in the cider? Am I drugged? Did you drug me?"

She slapped him.

Just once, across the cheek. It was enough to shut him up.

"The cider was just cider. Now. Come with me. I'm going to show you something."

She walked off again without stopping to wait for him to recover. He followed her as she made her way down a winding path to a stand of trees on the slope of the ridge. Each tree was circled by a length of chain, and hanging from each chain was what looked like a piece of tattered white muslin. Yet as they approached, the scraps of cloth began to stir. There was no breeze up on the ridge. Even the cicadas had stopped their thrumming song as Caxton took another step closer to the trees.

The piece of cloth nearest to her lifted in a way that looked almost like someone was manipulating it with a hidden wire. But there was no one there, and no wire. The cloth began to shift and stretch as it lifted. Then it began to take on the shape of a reaching hand.

It was dark up on the ridge. The moon hadn't risen yet, and the stars, while plentiful so far from city lights, gave little illumination. The scrap of cloth was only so visible because of its lack of color. In the dim gloaming, it almost seemed to glow with its own light.

If she hadn't known better, Caxton could have believed it was just an optical illusion. It had that feeling, that half-real sense of something seen out of the corner of your eye that can't possibly exist. It could have been just a trick of the light.

The night air grew thick, as if it was clotting around Caxton's head. It became difficult to breathe.

Laura.

No one had spoken her name. It was all in her head. Yet she knew that voice so well. It was Simon's father's voice.

Laura.

"No," Simon said behind her. "No, Dad. No! You're dead!"

His shrieking broke the spell. She hauled him backward, away from the trees. Her breath came back in a deep inhalation and she wiped sweat off her forehead. She turned and found Simon staring at the trees as if—

Well. As if he'd seen a ghost.

"Teleplasm," she explained, though he hadn't asked. "It's what's left behind when a spirit has pierced the veil of the living world and—"

"Nobody says teleplasm anymore," Simon interrupted,

speaking softly. "It's ectoplasm. Or better yet, 'material psychic residue.'" He was still staring at the tree. The piece of teleplasm hung limp and lifeless once more. "I heard—he called my name, and asked me to—" Simon shook his head. He lifted his shoulders and turned away so he wasn't facing the teleplasm anymore. "Ghosts." He shook his head. "They're not spirits, you know."

Caxton raised an eyebrow and waited for him to go on.

"The latest theory is that they're not dead people—that they're not human at all. Instead they're some kind of parasitic organism that feeds on human psychic energy. They're mindless animals that somehow evolved a way to tap into our fears telepathically." He closed his eyes and ran one hand over his sweat-slicked face. "God. That voice—it sounded just like my dad."

Caxton nodded. She remembered his uneasiness around the witchbillies, but she knew that wasn't from lack of experience with the supernatural. "That's right. You studied teratology in college. The study of monsters."

"What does that have to do with anything?"

Caxton didn't answer him directly. "A ghost can't hurt you, not really. You can walk away from it at any time. It's tougher than it should be, though, isn't it? You *want* to believe what it's saying. The person that voice belongs to is dead, you know that, but you *want* to hear their voice again. Some primitive part of you wants to believe it's real, that they're back." She shrugged. "Vampires are even more susceptible than we are. Maybe because they're more innately psychic than we are. A vampire wandering past these trees would get sucked in. Caught. Hopefully long enough that I could get the drop on them. Urie Polder and I have traps like this all over the ridge. We have other defenses, too." She led him away from the line of trees and over to where a wooden post had been driven into the ground. A bird's skull had been nailed to the top of the post, with a complicated hex sign painted in very fine strokes between its eye sockets.

"That's just freaky," Simon said.

"There's a post like this every fifty feet in a wide perimeter around the valley. If you didn't know they were here, you probably wouldn't see them. But anytime something unnatural—a vampire, or a half-dead—crosses the perimeter, these things start shrieking. It's an old vampire spell. What they call an orison. It was used on me once, and I assure you, it's not a sound you ever want to hear."

"Magic?" Simon asked. "It's bullshit."

"It's real enough."

He shook his head. "Sure. But it's unreliable. Too easy to counter. Any vampire worth her salt could just wave her hand and that skull would turn to powder. And if I'm right in thinking I know which vampire you're after—"

"There's only one left," Caxton insisted.

Simon bent to study the bird skull more closely. "Justinia Malvern is a master at the orisons. She won't fall for this."

"Maybe not. Her half-deads would, though. And she's way too smart to just walk in here without some backup."

"You really think she's going to come after you?" Simon stared at her in the darkness for a while. "You're counting on it."

"She's always had a certain fascination with me," Caxton told him. "She likes to play sadistic little games with people. Your father learned that—" She saw him stiffen at the thought, so she relented a little. "Well. I learned that the hard way, myself. She wants to turn me into a vampire, just like her. Or at least kill me while trying." Caxton sighed. "I guess when you're three hundred years old and spend most of your time trapped in a coffin, you get your kicks where you can. I'm hoping that'll be enough to draw her here. To where I can shoot her. But that's the thing. I'm not counting on it. Because I know she's smarter than that."

Hot blood everywhere. Great lashings of it, like a punch bowl full of the stuff spilled all over her. So wonderfully warm. The squelching horrible screaming pain was difficult to ignore, but—red—everything was red——and then black.

She heard her heart stop beating. She heard the perfect silence.

And then. And then. So much.

Her heart did not start beating again, no, but it convulsed all the same. It contracted with a rumbling growl. A desperate hunger.

She opened her—eye. The other wasn't there. It felt like the hole left behind by a pulled tooth. She understood this was proper, but she couldn't exactly remember why.

She stared up at her own ceiling. Flecks of blood still hung from the plaster. One droplet formed—she could see it with such exquisite clarity—and then fell.

Her body moved with incredible speed. Her head snaked to one side and her mouth—why did her mouth feel so strange?—opened wide. The droplet fell on the perfect center of her tongue.

She went mad for a while then.

She would not fully regain her mental faculties for another sixty-five years.

12.

Simon looked confused.

"Most vampires, I know how to get to them. You cut your finger and flick a drop of blood at them, and it's like a shark feeding frenzy. They stop thinking about anything but how good your blood would taste. That makes them stupid—pure, bloodthirsty predators. I've killed a lot of vampires that way. But Malvern's smarter than the rest. I don't know how she does it, but she's got some way to overcome her instincts. The first time I met her, your father tried that trick on her, and she managed to just walk away. The last time I saw her, she had a chance to kill me. She had a chance to do anything she wanted to me. Instead she tried to use me—she tried to convince me I had killed *her*. She resisted her natural urge to kill me so she could fake her death—and it worked. Right now, the police think she's dead."

"She *is* dead," Simon insisted. "I mean, everybody thinks she's dead. Everybody except you and Urie Polder."

Caxton grinned without merriment. "That's exactly how she wants it. We were getting too close to her—I almost had her a couple of times. She knows how dangerous I am. There's one trick she can pull, though, which will take me completely out of the picture."

"Oh? She has a way to kill you?"

"Close enough. She can wait for me to die of old age."

He looked confused.

"The smart thing for her to do right now is lie low," Caxton explained. "She's effectively immortal. As long as she doesn't show herself in public the police will eventually forget about her. People will think vampires are extinct, and they'll stop being afraid of them. If I'm not around to remind them how to fight vampires, they'll never be ready for her when she pops back up. Twenty years from now—a hundred—it's all the same to her. An eyeblink compared to the eternity she can live. She's done it before, and she's always come back . . . eventually."

Simon looked terrified by the prospect. Good.

"But . . . she needs blood," Simon pointed out.

"No. She wants blood, desperately. But she can live forever even if she never drinks another drop. She's strong enough to handle the cravings, to control herself, for a long time. She's strong enough to put aside whatever satisfaction she might get from killing me in exchange for her own safety. Now, if I had my freedom and unlimited resources, I could spend the rest of my life trying to figure out where she's hiding. I could scour every dark corner and musty old shed in Pennsylvania. I could spend years doing it. But that's no longer an option for me. If I show my face outside of this ridge, I'll get scooped up by the Feds right away. So instead I've built this very elaborate vampire trap—and I've laid my own plans for the future."

"Oh," Simon said. "I think I know where you're going with this, and—"

Caxton wouldn't let him derail her. "I know how to kill vampires better than anyone now living. I'm going to spend the rest of my life teaching the people in the Hollow how it's done. I'm going to teach Patience Polder every one of my tricks. After I'm dead, she'll teach others. Maybe her own children. And they'll teach theirs. The point is, no matter how long Malvern goes to ground for, when she wakes up there'll be somebody waiting with a gun pointed right at her heart."

"And you think that I can—that those children will be mine with Patience, and—"

"You studied monsters in college. You're a scientist who knows all about monsters. Don't you see how that makes you perfect for this? You match up your technical knowledge with Patience's gifts, and you'd make a hell of a team."

"Count me out," Simon said. "That's not what I want for my life."

"It's not?" Caxton asked. She was a little surprised.

"The last thing I want is to have anything more to do with vampires," Simon told her. "That should be pretty obvious."

"A vampire killed your entire family," Caxton said. "You don't want revenge?"

Simon rubbed at his eyes with the balls of his thumbs. "My *father* killed my entire family. My *father* killed my mother, and my sister, and even my stupid redneck uncle."

"No," Caxton said. "Your father killed himself. His body came back as a vampire and did all those things."

"That means nothing! Do you have any idea what it's like to lose everybody you've ever cared about?"

"Yes, I do," Caxton said.

He stared at her. "I've spent the last two years in intensive psychotherapy. Just so I could function. I nearly flunked out of school. I can't find a job. I don't sleep more than a couple of hours a night. Every time I close my eyes I see—I see fangs. And those red eyes."

"Help me kill Malvern, and nobody else has to go through that."

"I don't care! If she leaves me alone, she can live to be ten thousand and two, for all I fucking care," Simon said. And then he turned on his heel and headed back toward the house. Maybe he intended to spend the rest of the night in his car rather than continue the conversation.

Caxton stood out on the dark ridge and wondered what she'd said wrong.

13.

Eventually Simon got his car to start. There were more than a few shade tree mechanics in the Hollow—in rural Pennsylvania people knew their cars—but he refused any sort of help. He just sat there with his window rolled up despite the heat, turning the key again and again as the engine snarled and sputtered.

Caxton stood next to the driver's-side door and waited, thinking he would eventually change his mind and come back to the house to spend the night. After an hour had passed she recognized the stubborn streak he'd inherited from his father. She knew better than to try to butt heads with an Arkeley, honestly, but she was a patient woman.

When even she had grown tired of waiting, though, she made a hand signal behind her back. Urie Polder went to the back of the car and kicked at the dirt there, disturbing a complicated pattern of thorns he had laid behind the car while Simon wasn't looking.

The car started on the next try. It sounded fine.

Caxton knocked on Simon's window until he rolled it down.

"I am so out of here," he barked. "Don't try to stop me."

"I understand you need to go," she told him. "I don't blame you. Just—here. Take this." She handed him a piece of paper. "This is the hardware I need."

He stared at the paper for a long time, as if his eyes could set it on fire. Eventually he grabbed it from her. "You have a lot of nerve, Caxton. Trading on my debt to you like this—it's *not* cool."

She nodded in assent. "I never had any intention of making you do anything. I honestly thought you would want revenge. If that's not the case, okay. But please. I need your help. I need you to get that stuff and bring it here. I can't go get it myself." She folded her arms on the sill of his window, bringing their faces closer together. "I saved your life, Simon, because I had access to all kinds of fun toys. Including Teflon bullets and high-powered guns. Right now I have none of that. I have a couple pistols and hunting rifles I could scrounge together. If Malvern showed up tonight, I honestly don't know if I could stop her. You bring me the stuff on that list and maybe I'll have a chance. Okay?"

"Whatever," he said, and pressed the button to raise his window. She had to yank her arms back to keep from getting them caught.

A moment later and he was gone, rolling down the long gravel road in a plume of dust. Caxton watched him go until she couldn't see his lights anymore.

Then she went back to the porch, to sit by her pile of guns where she could watch the whole side of the ridge. And wait.

Urie Polder came by a little later with a thermos of coffee. Some nights he would sit with her a spell, less for the sake of watching with her than for the cool breeze that came over the ridge in the evening. Most times they didn't talk to each other—both of them were more comfortable with silence. This time, however, he asked, "You think that boy'll come back?"

Caxton shrugged. "Maybe. It may not matter. He may serve my purposes just as well by staying out there in the world."

If that confused Polder, he gave no sign of it.

Caxton yawned. She reached for the coffee and poured herself another cup. It was going to be a long night. "We scared the hell out of him. He's not going to keep this to himself. Oh, I don't think he'll go to the police. He's too good a kid at heart to turn on me like that. But he'll start talking, to somebody. Anybody who will listen. He'll tell them all about the crazy cult of witchbillies out in the ridges, and how they're obsessed with killing vampires."

"Ahum," Polder said.

Caxton nodded. "Eventually, that information will get back to Malvern. Somebody will tell somebody who will say something where somebody else can hear it. Malvern pays attention to this kind of thing—she'll learn about my plans soon enough."

"And that's what you want? For her to know everything you got in store?"

Caxton let herself smile. "It's exactly what I want. She can't let it happen—she can't let an entire new generation of vampire hunters get trained and raised for the sole purpose of destroying her. She'll have to take action to stop it. Which means—"

"Which means she has to come here, ahum."

Urie Polder looked frightened at the thought. Caxton couldn't blame him. If Malvern came to the Hollow, there would be death, and maybe a lot of it.

Caxton found that acceptable.

[1721]

Justinia had learned not to smile. Not when she wanted to put someone at their ease. The teeth tended to scare people.

But there were so many subtler ways to toy with them.

"Please, ma'am, I do not wish to die," the little girl said. Tears streaked through the dirt on her cheek as Justinia held her face to the earthen floor of the little cottage. The flames that were already consuming the barn out back—and the bodies inside—danced in each of the little girl's tears.

Amazing what one eye could see when it had been changed.

Justinia could see the little girl's blood. Not a drop of it had been shed yet, but even through that thin, fragile skin she could see the blood moving, throbbing through the tiny body. She could see the girl's heart pumping in her chest, as if her flesh were made of glass.

The thing in Justinia's rib cage that was no longer a heart trembled in sympathy. How badly she wanted to rip this little creature open and suckle at her veins.

"Ye wish to live?" Justinia asked. Normally her voice came out in a slurred growl, the words torn and rent as they passed over her wickedly sharp teeth. She had learned, however, to force her voice to sound soft and kindly.

"I'd like to see my brother again, and my parents," the girl squeaked.

Justinia had to admire her composure. Usually when the hunt got to this point, the children could do nothing but scream.

She was not unaware that she had once been the same age as this girl. That they had a great deal in common. In fact, she relished the jest of it.

"But ye will see them, my dear. In heaven."

That was enough. The look in the girl's face changed. This was the delicious moment that Justinia had sought, the moment when her prey realized the natural order of things. That she was going to die. That it was going to hurt a great deal. And that no one, no one at all, was going to come and save her.

"Nooooo," she moaned. "Noooooo." Just like a cow. Like the livestock she had become. A food animal.

Justinia laughed—and smiled. All the better to show her great, big teeth.

Enough.

The word appeared in Justinia's head as if it had been written across the back of her skull in letters of fire. She winced backward, releasing her hold on the girl. The girl still had the presence of mind to leap to her feet and run for the door.

Vincombe waited for her there.

"Damn ye," Justinia grunted. "Ye followed me."

Vincombe ignored her and squatted down to catch the girl and look deeply into her eyes. "It's alright, now, child," he said. "I'm your father. I'm perfectly fine. And you're safe now. Trust me."

Justinia watched the girl go limp in Vincombe's arms. She actually sighed a little in pleasure as he twisted her head until her neck snapped.

"We are meant to be hunters. Not demons," he said. Then he tossed the body to Justinia. "Drink. Then come find me outside. It's time we talked."

Justinia did not waste a drop. It was getting difficult to conceal her murders these days. The local authorities knew something was up—too many bodies had been discovered in the river, bloodless and mutilated. Questions had been asked. Justinia had been forced to flee Manchester, the city of her awakening, and instead haunt the darker night out in the countryside.

When she'd finished, she walked out into the light of the burning barn. Vincombe waited for her inside the flames. They did not harm him. She approached, and found that her skin shriveled as she got too close. The fire couldn't kill her, she knew that from past experience—but it could cause her unbearable pain.

Yet he simply stood there in the conflagration and stared at her.

"How?" she demanded.

He refused to answer her question. "Ye didn't fear death. I thought, perhaps, that finally someone understood my work," he told her. "That

I had been given someone to help me. A new angel of death, to lighten my burden."

She snarled at him.

They had met only rarely since her transformation, and never for more than a single night. She didn't know where he slept during the day. If she ever found out, she would find a way to destroy him. He wasn't her father. He wasn't anything to her, except competition.

But now—now as she watched him stand in the flames that would not consume him—now she wondered if maybe he did not have more to give her.

"Ye tease them," he said, and there was a sorrow in his voice that she would never understand. "Ye make them fear you before you do what is necessary. This isn't a game."

Justinia closed her eye and saw the cards falling toward the table. Lucky cards, ill-favored cards. Aces and deuces, diamonds and clubs. How could he not understand? All of life was a game. A wager, placed against death. And death always won.

"Ye may justify your actions as you please," she said. "We were given these powers to use at our pleasure."

"God granted me the right to take lives, lives that are ready to be culled. Lives that have lost meaning, the lives of men who have forgotten their souls, though their bodies are still strong and—"

"God?" Justinia demanded. "Ye think God made us like this?"

He came out of the flames then, so fast and so strong she had no time to defend herself. He grasped her around the waist in arms like iron bars, twisted her around, thrust her face toward the flames.

"Ye didn't fear death," he said. "Do ye not fear hell, either?"

She felt the skin of her nose dry out, felt it stretch painfully. She felt her chin burning like a brand. Her eye began to boil in its socket.

"I'll teach you," he said, and his voice was harsh and breathless. It was a voice she knew, the voice of the men who had paid to lie with her. The voice they used when they called her a whore. When they announced how they would possess her, how they would show her to her proper place. "I'll teach ye to fear hell."

"Yes," she said, because she knew what men wanted when they used that voice. "Yes. I've been such a naughty girl. Teach me, master."

And while you're at it, *she thought,* teach me to stand in fire and not be burned. Teach me how to hypnotize a child by simply looking into her eyes. Teach me everything you know.

When he finally pulled her out of the flames the skin and flesh on her head had burned down to the skull. Her one eye had gone milky and dull, and she could see nothing. Her tongue was gone and she could not speak.

In the morning, when she slept, all would be healed. This new body could heal any wound. But in the meantime, she could still listen. She could still hear him as he whispered secrets in her ears.

And she forced herself to remember every word. To fix them in her mind, as eternal and changeless as scripture. That was the night she began to learn the orisons.

He let her sleep, and heal, when dawn began to break. She did not expect to see him the next night when she rose from her coffin, but he was there. He had more to teach her, and by then she understood the game. If she made him believe that she wanted to be a good little angel of death, that she wanted to be his protégé, he would teach her everything she wanted to know.

Eventually he began to even trust her. "It's time ye met the others," he said.

"There are others?" she demanded. "Others like ye?"

Because she knew there could be no others like herself.

14.

A little bell rang as Clara pushed open the door of a diner in Bridgeville, one of the suburbs of Pittsburgh. She'd been driving for hours to get here, but she wasn't tired. If Glauer had what he claimed, it would be more than worth it.

Her eyes had been trained by working for the police for so

long. She took in all the little details right away. The diner was deserted except for one waitress who was mopping up a spill of coffee on the counter. At the very back of the dining room, as far away from the parking lot as you could get, Glauer sat hunched over a table. A half-eaten plate of pancakes sat in front of him, as well as three empty coffee cups. He'd been waiting awhile.

The two of them had to meet in secret like criminals even though they were both decorated police officers. Fetlock had a passionate disregard for personal privacy, and since he was still their boss he was allowed to pry into their lives as much as he liked. He routinely tapped their phones and kept tabs on where they went and what they got up to.

Fetlock had a good enough reason for that paranoia, Clara supposed. After all, his employees were conspiring against him.

Clara sat down across from Glauer without a word. They went through their old ritual of putting their cell phones on the table. Clara popped the battery out of her phone and set it down next to the salt and pepper shakers. Glauer's phone had already been sabotaged in the same way.

It was a creepy world they lived in. Fetlock could listen to their conversations through their phones even if the phones were turned off and hidden in their pockets. They had to be careful.

"It's good to see you," Clara said once they'd both sighed and relaxed a little.

"You been alright? Bruises healed up?" Glauer asked.

"I'm good," Clara said. She gave him a warm smile. "How are your investigations going?"

Glauer shrugged. "You mean my official stuff, right? We're closing in on a guy who provides chemical supplies to meth labs. Technically he doesn't do anything illegal. Just runs a wholesale scientific supply warehouse. We might have to run a sting, send somebody in undercover and get him to implicate itself. It's a long job."

Clara nodded. When Justinia Malvern was—allegedly—

killed during a prison riot, their old outfit, the special subjects unit, was closed down. Disbanded. Fetlock had found other things for the two of them to do. Glauer had become a kind of detective at large, while Clara had been sent off to school to become a forensic analyst. Both of them still got their paychecks from Fetlock, but he didn't want them to screw up his manhunt for Laura Caxton.

He couldn't stop them from talking to each other, though.

"You said you had something," Clara said, and bit her lip. As always when they met she wondered if she should ask Glauer about his family, about his notoriously unsuccessful love life. She often worried she didn't spend enough time shooting the shit with him. Acting like she was his friend, instead of jumping right in to what she really wanted from him.

He didn't seem to mind. She thought maybe he was just as desperate as she was to find Caxton. Though for very different reasons.

"Simon Arkeley," Glauer said, and laid a manila file folder on the diner table.

Clara's eyes lit up. "The only survivor," she said. "The only one who made it out alive from the Jameson Arkeley case."

Glauer nodded and tapped the folder. "He's—"

He stopped abruptly as the waitress came over to take Clara's order. "Just a Diet Coke, thanks," she said.

The waitress tried to stifle a yawn as she went back to the counter.

"Simon," Clara said. "I've heard he's a little unstable. Not that I blame him after what happened to his family."

Glauer nodded. "He spent the last two years in heavy therapy. Even went away for a while, for a rest at a private mental hospital in Colorado. I guess he wanted to get as far from Pennsylvania as he could. Away from where it all happened. For the last six months he's been seeing a therapist three times a week."

"Poor kid," Clara said with a frown.

Glauer nodded. "I feel for him. It can't have been easy."

"You think he's in contact with Laura, though? I would think she was the last person he'd want to see." Clara shivered, though it was warm enough in the diner. "Laura . . . well, she killed his father. And his sister. They were vampires, but—she tried to save his uncle but was too late. She tried to save his mom, and . . ."

"I was with her that night. It was bad. Real bad." Glauer pushed the manila folder to one side. "No. No, I don't think he'd want to see her at all. But."

He took another folder from beside him on the seat and put it before her. She thumbed it open as the waitress brought her drink. Inside the folder was a dossier on Urie Polder. It was strangely incomplete. Polder had no social security number. He paid his taxes every year, on time, but used money orders instead of personal checks. He didn't seem to have a bank account, or a credit card, or even a telephone number. There was one report in the folder that stood out, a memorandum from the Department of Alcohol, Tobacco and Firearms that listed Polder as a potential cult leader, but offered no proof of that statement. Funny how a dossier like that could twist things around. It made Polder look like some kind of homegrown terrorist. She'd met him a couple of times, however, and she knew he was a sweet, if slightly creepy, old man. Completely harmless. "Now, he's someone I'd like to talk to."

Glauer nodded. "He disappeared shortly after Caxton broke out of prison. Moved house, no forwarding address provided. Took his daughter with him. Child Services for Centre County would really like to ask him about her schooling, but of course, they can't find him either. We've suspected for a long time that Caxton went underground with Polder, but neither of them has so much as blipped on the radar screen since they disappeared."

Clara nodded. "Okay. I knew most of this already. So what's

the connection? How do you get from Simon Arkeley to Urie Polder?" Which, of course, meant getting to Laura.

"That," Glauer said, leaning back in his seat, "took some actual good old-fashioned police work. I asked my hairstylist."

15.

Clara smiled, but she didn't say anything. She let Glauer tell it in his own words.

"I've been keeping an eye on Simon. Not even thinking he would lead me to Caxton—I just wanted to make sure the kid was okay. I always felt . . . responsible for what happened to his sister. I was supposed to be guarding her when she went vamp on us. I just . . . I feel bad about that."

Clara reached across the table and gave Glauer's hand a warm squeeze. He was such a good man, and he gave himself so little credit.

The big cop looked away from her face as he went on. "Simon's been keeping his nose clean, of course. Finished up his schoolwork and got his diploma. Moved on, it looked like. Started applying to graduate schools. Bought a car. Then, one day, he started shopping at some pretty shady places. Botanicas—you know what a botanica is? I didn't. It's a place you can go and get magic herbs and fancy candles that drive away evil spirits. Stuff they use in Mexico, and Haiti, and Brazil. Most of them are just scamming their customers, promising that a jar of consecrated graveyard dirt will drive off the evil eye, whatever, and the dirt came from a ditch in back of the store. Simon went to one of these places in Wilkes-Barre, that's almost a hundred miles from where he lives. He knew the right place to go. After he left, carrying a bunch of bags, I went in and asked to know what he bought. The old lady who ran the place told me to go to hell. Wouldn't talk to me at all. I figured maybe that was as far as I needed to go in prying into Simon's life. But then I thought of something."

"What did you do?"

"I got his credit card statements. You wouldn't believe how trusting people can be, even these days. If you call up a bank and say you're with the U.S. Marshals, they give you whatever you want. So I went through the statements for the day in question and I found a list of everything he bought at the botanica. It was all itemized. Problem was, I had no idea what any of it meant or what it was good for. He bought a bunch of roots and plant parts. Weird stuff, too, exotic plants that don't grow much north of the equator. I couldn't even pronounce most of the names, but one stuck out. John the Conqueror root."

"That sounds—weird," Clara said.

Glauer nodded. "But so what, right? The kid gets a cold, he takes some funny plants as medicine. Lots of people do that. Unh-uh. Not that simple. John the Conqueror root isn't an alternative therapy for pimples. They used to write blues songs about the stuff and what it could do to you if you shaved it into your oatmeal. I started asking around. The lady who does my hair knew what it was for. She's Haitian. When I first asked her she clammed up real fast. Said that was nothing a white guy needed to worry about. Then she asked me if I was having trouble in the bedroom."

Glauer blushed and looked down at his uneaten pancakes.

"I'm sure that's not a problem for you," Clara said.

"Damn straight. Er—you know what I mean. Anyway. I told her, yeah, I was, you know. She said one of the uses of John the Conqueror root is restoring sexual potency. But you can't just eat it, or anything. It needs to be prepared properly. You need a guy who can work the right spells on it and so on. I asked her if she knew anybody like that and she said no. She didn't know any conjure doctors."

"Conjure—that's—"

"That's one of the things Caxton used to call Urie Polder. A conjure doctor. So we've got this kid, Simon, buying shady materials he has no use for. And we know he is very peripherally connected with somebody who does have a use for them. I'm thinking that connection got a little less peripheral recently. And the only reason I can imagine why Simon would have anything to do with Urie Polder—"

"—Is if Laura had asked him to," Clara said.

For a long time the two cops just stared at each other. Then Clara picked up her Diet Coke and sipped at it. "This could be nothing. Or, if we watch Simon closely enough, he could lead us right to her."

Glauer nodded. He'd said his piece.

"Okay," Clara said. "Okay. This is—this is good. That was some first-rate old-fashioned detective work."

Glauer shrugged.

Clara hugged herself. She wanted to giggle, but she didn't dare. This was the first real lead in two years. This was it, she could feel it. She dug some money out of her wallet and threw it on the table. "Your pancakes are on me." She started to get up, gathered up her cell phone and its battery. But he lifted one hand to stop her.

"Hold on," he said.

"There's something else?"

He seemed to be wrestling with something. Glauer didn't look like the kind of man who had a lot of deep thoughts, but she knew appearances could be deceiving.

"What are you going to do? When you find her?" he asked.

Clara opened her mouth to speak but couldn't find the words. "Just—talk to her," she said, finally.

"You know she doesn't want to be found."

Clara's heart sagged in her chest. "I know. I know that, but. But. But!"

"But what?"

"I need to tell her about that half-dead I saw. She needs to know about that."

"The half-dead you *think* you saw," Glauer clarified. "You've been a cop long enough to know that's different from evidence. And anyway, what will that mean to Caxton? She already believes Malvern is still alive."

"Come on! You've been working this case with me for years. You want to find her as much as I do."

"I want to know she's okay. I want her to know that anything I can do, all she has to do is ask. I can achieve that by telling Simon as much. I don't have to put her at risk just to let her know that."

Clara stared daggers at him, but he didn't flinch. Was he really going to make her say it? "I need to tell her I still love her."

He nodded. Accepting that. She knew him well enough to know he wouldn't fight her on that. But then he said something that he must have known would hurt her. "Two years ago she made a choice. She could have gone back to her cell and waited for us to lock her away again. Instead she ran. Even knowing that it would make her a fugitive. An outlaw. Maybe she still loves you, but she chose the vampires instead."

"She had to." Clara's cheeks were burning. "You know that, you asshole. You know she couldn't just stop, not until Malvern was really, really dead. It's who she is."

Glauer shrugged. "I didn't say she made the wrong choice."

Clara grabbed her phone and fled the diner, not looking back. If the waitress wondered why she hurried off in such a huff, she didn't care.

[1729]

Justinia shrank back in terror from the thing in the coffin. "What in the devil's name is that?" she demanded, horrified because she already knew.

It was what she would one day become.

The body in the coffin had been human once. Then it had been more than human. For a while. It had pointed ears. It had the rows of wicked teeth. It had been like her. But it looked nothing like her otherwise. Its paper-thin skin sagged on its bones. Its white flesh was mottled with sores and blemishes. Its mouth hung permanently open, in the eternal rictus grin of a skull that has surrendered to time.

There were twelve coffins in Vincombe's lair. Each held a dead thing, more rotten and decayed than the last. No, not a dead thing, because she knew they were still alive, if trapped in those faltering carcasses. She could hear their thoughts like whispers in her mind, like the sound of cards shuffling together for one last hand at the end of a long night's dissipation.

"These are your ancestors, Justinia. Your family. This one is Bolingen. He created me to replace him when he grew old. Beyond him lies Margaret, who was like a mother to him. And so on. For more than a thousand years, the creatures in these coffins have served as the angels of death. They understood duty. They knew purpose."

"They're disgusting," Justinia spat.

"They are wise. I come to them when I need their counsel."

Justinia shook her head in negation. Wise counsel? She could hear what they were thinking. What they were saying, over and over. Blood I must have blood blood give me blood where is the blood bring me blood.

It was the only thought in any of those rotting heads.

If Vincombe thought they still believed in his self-appointed role, his sacred duty, then he was fooling himself. Unless he couldn't hear their actual thoughts. Unless . . .

"If ye will not accept the purpose I laid out for you," Vincombe said,

"then there is still something thou canst do. Something to justify your existence. Ye will feed them. Ye will gather blood, and bring it here. It is done like this."

He crouched over Margaret's coffin. She stirred within, though her muscles were so decayed she could barely lift her head an inch. Vincombe smiled down at the ancient mummy and then opened his mouth wide. His chest and stomach seized as he forced himself to vomit up the blood he'd drunk that night. It splattered across Margaret's face, only a little of it getting in her mouth, though she twisted and rattled around trying to drink more.

With loving hands, Vincombe cleaned her, sweeping every drop of the regurgitated blood into her gaping mouth.

"This will be your purpose," he said, shaking. Spent. "When I must lie me down in eternal wakefulness—for so must we all, one day—you will come and you will feed me. Just as others will come to feed you, in your time."

Justinia's eye went wide. He couldn't be suggesting—but—ah, yes.

For the first time she saw the wrinkles around his eyes. The slenderness of his arms and legs, as if his muscles were beginning to wither away.

Vincombe was getting old.

She was too consumed by her own plotting and scheming to think that it would happen to her as well. Someday.

For now—this was information she could use.

"I humbly accept this burden," she said, because it was what he wanted to hear.

16.

Clara hurried out into the parking lot, heading straight for her Mazda. If Glauer followed her, she decided, she would refuse to talk to him at all. It didn't matter if he apologized for what he'd said, or even if he promised to help her find Laura. You just didn't get to talk to people like that, not ever, and—

She nearly missed the van.

She had never been a true cop. She had started out as a police photographer and just recently become a forensic specialist. So she didn't have the kind of instincts most cops developed, the kind of observational skills that became second nature after a while. But she had been a damned good photographer in her day, and the van was ugly enough to offend her sensibilities. It was a big black number with a scene of wolves howling at the moon airbrushed on its side, and not well. It was enough to make her turn up her lip in disgust. The kind of vehicle she and her friends in high school would have called a Molester Mobile.

It was sitting near the exit of the parking lot, and it might have belonged to a cook or a baker working in the back of the restaurant. But that didn't explain why the van's sliding side door was open, or why its engine was on.

She tried to do two things at once. She turned around quickly, intending to shout for help. She might not be talking to Glauer just then, but he was still a cop and the kind of guy who could intimidate the hell out of any would-be rapist. The second thing she tried to do was reach for her sidearm.

Bony hands stopped her in both endeavors. One wrapped around her mouth and she tasted dry, dead fingers as they slipped between her teeth. Another hand grabbed her wrist before she could even unbuckle her holster.

"Don't move. Don't say anything," her attacker said, behind her. He had a high-pitched giggling voice she knew all too well. "We're not going to kill you—yet."

We, he said. Suggesting that there were others nearby. She had walked into a very nasty trap. And she knew exactly who had laid it for her, and just how bad things could get, and just how fast.

"That's right. We're going to take a little ride. Stay quiet and I won't hurt you very much. Heh."

Clara thought of two more things to do. This time she was more successful.

She twisted her wrist inside the skeletal grip that kept her hand away from her holster. The assailant's fingers slipped down over the thicker part of her hand and lost their viselike grasp. Instantly her hand was free.

The other thing she did was to bite down very hard on the fingers in her mouth.

During her time studying to be a forensic analyst, she had been required to take at least one self-defense class. She had signed up for all four that were offered, and gotten straight A's.

The assailant behind her screamed. Human teeth could, under stress conditions, bite right through the small bones of human fingers. Half-dead fingers were far less sturdy. The joints in her mouth separated at the knuckles and her mouth was full of dry, bloodless flesh. She desperately wanted to spit it all out—but not quite yet.

The quick-release catch on her holster came open with a pop and she filled her hand instantly with her Glock. Spinning around on her heel, she fired point-blank into the attacker's chest.

He went down in a heap. A slim male, mid-twenties, wearing a hooded sweatshirt. Just like the one she'd chased out of the convenience store, the one who got smashed by the semi. This one was in bad shape, but there was no way Fetlock could deny he was a half-dead.

All he would have to do was take one look at the bastard's face.

Or lack thereof.

Cooked spaghetti was the first thing that always came to mind when Clara saw one of these things. The second thing that came to mind was that she never wanted to eat spaghetti again. Half-deads were unnatural creatures, tormented by their own undead existence. They expressed that anguish by scratching at their own faces with broken fingernails until all the skin came off. What she was looking at was exposed muscle tissue, drained of blood, stretched thin over the man's skull. His eyes swam like rotten oysters in a mass of twitching, stringy flesh. His lipless mouth stretched sideways in a grimace that showed off all his teeth.

He screamed for mercy, clutching his mutilated hand to his wounded chest. His voice was so high and squeaky it hurt her ears. She kicked him in the face and he shut up. That was something else they'd taught her at the academy. Always wear sensible shoes.

He'd said there were others. She took a step back toward the diner, scanning the parking lot, looking for any sign of another attacker. Behind her she heard a little bell ring and she nearly discharged her weapon in panic.

It wasn't a half-dead behind her, though. It was Glauer. He didn't say a word. He just moved to cover her with his own weapon.

"There'll be more," she said. "I don't know how many."

She peered through the dark at the van, trying to see if there were any of them inside. She thought there might be someone in the driver's seat, but it was hard to tell.

"Okay. Move forward, slowly. Our target's that van."

"Got it," Glauer said, quietly.

They took it one step at a time, back to back, covering each other, keeping perfect firing arcs that covered the entire parking lot, just as they'd been trained.

It didn't occur to Clara to look up.

"Anything?" Glauer asked.

"No, I—"

Her response was cut short as something sailed through the air toward her, moving far too fast for her to jump out of the way. Time seemed to slow down, so she had a perfect chance to see a big sharp kitchen knife come toward her, tumbling as it flew. She tried to turn sideways and managed to catch the knife in her hip. It went right through her skirt and pierced her skin, then fell away to clatter on the ground.

She couldn't help herself. She cried out and fell to one knee.

Glauer was already on it. He spun, his handgun gripped in both hands, and fired at a dark shape on the roof of the diner. The shape exploded in a cloud of bone fragments and screams. Instantly three more shadows detached themselves from the side of the diner, over by the Dumpsters, and raced toward the van.

Glauer fired twice more, winging one of them and nearly taking its arm off. Clara tried to bring her own weapon up, but before she could aim the half-deads jumped in the van and it went squealing off into the night.

"Are you hurt?" Glauer demanded. "I'll call for an ambulance, we'll—"

"No fucking way are we sitting here waiting for backup," Clara said. She hauled herself back up to both feet. She could stand on her injured leg, and that was good enough. She grabbed her car keys out of her pocket and ran toward the Mazda. "Come on," she said. "I've seen the way you drive. We're taking my car."

17.

"This is a bad idea," Glauer insisted, as she threw the Mazda into gear and sent it hurtling out onto the road.

"Seat belt," she said.

He did as he was told.

She was bleeding all over her seat. The gash in her hip wasn't deep, but it felt big. No time to do anything about that. She stamped on the accelerator and tore after the van, which she could just barely see ahead of her on the road. Its lights were off, but its paint job was darker than the dusty two-lane, so it looked like a massive shadow trying to escape the moonlight.

"Fetlock will have a hissy fit when he hears about this," Glauer told her.

"Maybe he'll have a stroke and we'll get a new job. Would you please call this in already? It's illegal in this state to use a cell phone while driving, or I'd do it myself."

Glauer grunted unhappily, perhaps at being reminded of how to do his own job. He pulled his cell phone from his pocket, then had to fumble with it for a while since he had removed the battery. Eventually he got it working. "This is Special Deputy Glauer with the U.S. Marshals. I am currently in vehicular pursuit of a late-model van, black with a painted mural on the side, headed northeast on the Washington Pike. Requesting all available assistance."

Ahead of them the road wound through a brightly lit shopping mall. Clara could see the van better now and had eaten up most of its lead. She was only a few dozen car lengths behind. The half-dead driving the van was pushing it to its limits, but the top speed of a van could never beat the top speed of the Mazda. They would catch up, and very quickly.

The problem was—what then? Clara had never taken a class on vehicular pursuit. She had no idea how you were supposed to make an unresponsive subject pull over. Maybe she should have let Glauer drive after all.

She gritted her teeth. The wound in her hip was starting to hurt. But she was damned if she was going to let them get away now. Laura wouldn't have given in to that kind of self-doubt. She shoved her foot to the floor and willed the car to go faster.

Apparently the half-deads knew they couldn't get away—not without playing dirty. Ahead of her the back door of the van swung open and flapped back and forth like the wing of a wounded bat. Inside she could see the half-deads grabbing on to anything they could to keep from falling out. One of them leaned out the back and threw something into the air.

It came arcing toward the Mazda's windshield and Clara flinched sideways as if to avoid it, but she managed not to swerve as it smacked into her car. "What the hell was that?" she asked. She'd been too focused on the road to get a good look.

Glauer didn't answer right away.

"What are they throwing?" Clara demanded again.

"It was—it was an arm," he said.

Clara's eyes went wide.

"Back at the diner I shot one of them in the arm. You know how they just come to pieces when you shoot them. He must have torn his wounded arm free and thrown it at us," he said. He sounded like he was about to lose his lunch.

"Keep it together," Clara said. "We need to—"

She stopped as a leg still wearing a hiking boot smacked against the windshield and a long crack shot through the glass.

"No fucking way," she said. A silently shrieking head came sailing through the air toward her and she involuntarily swerved to avoid it. "Glauer—they're tearing each other apart in there!"

"I guess . . . they have nothing else to throw at us," he told her.

"Do something!"

The big cop turned to look at her, but she didn't dare look away from the road long enough to make eye contact. "Like what?" he demanded.

"Lean out the window and shoot at them, duh," she said, bracing herself as another leg bounced off the roof of the Miata.

"Are you kidding? This is a heavily populated area. It's a shopping center on a Saturday night—there will be hundreds of civilians around us," he said.

She flicked her eyes sideways and saw they were passing by a huge fabric store. There were plenty of cars in its lot—he was right. Any stray bullets he fired could potentially end up in that store, or the sports bar across the street. Damn it, she thought. Laura would have done it anyway. She would have been very careful with her shots, but she would have taken them.

Jameson would have just blasted away and not cared. Then again, Jameson Arkeley had ended up turning himself into a vampire, all the better to fight them. And that had not ended well.

"Fine," Clara said. A once-human arm hit the road and the Mazda bounced as they rolled over it. "Fine, don't shoot—but think of something else. How long did they say it would take our backup to arrive?"

"Ten minutes," Glauer told her. "Tops."

Clara shook her head. "Too long. We need one of these bastards intact so we can beat some information out of him. In ten minutes they'll be all over the road. Or the driver will just pull into some side road with no street lamps and we'll lose him. What else can we do? Come on, you're a real cop. You must know something about car chases."

He was silent for a second. Then, in the tone of a man at the very end of his rope, he said, "PIT maneuver."

"What?"

"PIT maneuver. It stands for 'precision intervention technique,' though I was told the acronym originally came from 'push in tire.' It's how you stop a fleeing car. When absolutely nothing else will work."

Clara ducked involuntarily as an entire human torso came at her. It bounced off the side pillar of the Mazda, where the windshield met the side window. The thump it made deafened her for a second. "Is it dangerous?" she asked.

"Yeah. Very dangerous. This car's too low, and the van's center of gravity is too high. But it'll work. I just don't know if we'll come out intact."

"Screw it," Clara said. "Laura wouldn't think twice."

"I was afraid you'd say that. Okay. Pull up parallel to the van, with your front left wheel even with his rear right wheel. Match their speed as best you can."

Clara did as she was told. The van tried to veer away, but the Mazda was far more maneuverable and she matched its motions. The half-dead hanging from the back of the van, the one who had been throwing body parts, reached out and tried to grab the Mazda. He lost half his fingers in the process. They went skittering and bouncing along the roof and side of the car, reminding Clara of the sound a tree branch makes when you don't quite clear it. The half-dead pulled back in agony—but then returned with a severed arm, which he used like a club to try to smash in Clara's window.

"What now?" Clara demanded. "Tell me what to do!"

"Establish contact with the side of the van, lightly as possible— you don't want to wreck us with a bad sideswipe. Then, just when you make contact, swing the wheel hard to steer right into the tire."

"That van has to weigh four times as much as this car," Clara said. "That's crazy, we can't possibly hope to—"

"Now!" Glauer said, as the Mazda touched the side of the van with a horrible squeal. Then he grabbed the steering wheel and shoved it over, hard.

[1739]

"It's alright," she told Vincombe. "Shh. Just lay back."

"I . . . can still . . . walk," he insisted, as she pushed him back into his coffin. "I can . . . go out. My work . . ."

"Your work is done, master," she said, and gave him a warm smile. She'd been practicing it for weeks.

"No," he breathed. But he could not resist her hands. She held him down against the silk lining of the coffin and eventually he relaxed.

Eventually he succumbed to the great weariness that must be dragging him down. Every night he needed more blood just to stay on his feet. Every night it was such a chore, bringing enough victims to him. Enough to satisfy his hunger. And every time she had to come up with some pretext as to why God wanted the victim to die. Why it was a good thing, a noble thing that he drink from their veins.

She was bloody tired of it.

"God will reward ye," she said. "For ye have done His work."

"Yes . . ." he said, finally. And his eyes drifted closed.

He was as thin as a fence post. His skin hung on him like a suit of clothing grown too big for his dwindling frame. Once he'd seemed enormous to her. Stronger than a lion. More fierce than a tiger.

No more.

"Yes. Rest yourself. Dawn will come soon, and ye will sleep."

"Justinia . . . remember . . ."

"I remember everything. Master," she said. She could not keep the sneer out of her voice, but he didn't seem to notice. "I remember everything ye taught me. All of the orisons. All of the secrets. I remember how to stand in a fire without being burned. I remember how to draw the dead back from hell, and make them serve me, if I have tasted their blood. I remember how to hold men with my eye, and take away their minds."

"And . . . the purpose . . ."

She placed one finger on her chin. "Purpose? Maybe I have forgotten one thing."

His eyes snapped open again. But it was too late.

She had hidden a mallet in his lair while he was resting. A big ten-pound hammer, meant for breaking up houses. As he reared up in his coffin, reaching for her, she shattered his arms. Then his kneecaps.

His vampiric body could heal any injury—if it was given enough blood to fuel the transformation. But he had no way of getting blood now. It would take a long time for his bones to set themselves.

Until then he could do nothing but watch her, while she went down the line of coffins he'd protected for so long. Bolingen first. His creator. She pried open the bones of Bolingen's chest—he was so decrepit she could do it with her bare hands—and plucked his heart out like a fruit from a tree.

Bolingen screamed, a noise she heard more inside her head than out. Vincombe gasped in sympathy.

She squeezed the heart in her hand until it burst.

Margaret next. Then Hoccleve, who had been Margaret's father figure. His heart exploded in a puff of dust when she smashed it with the mallet. One by one she destroyed them all.

"There is not so much blood in this world," she said when she had returned to Vincombe's coffin, "that even one drop is left over to be shared. It is all for me," she told him, the man she had thought was Death. The man who thought God gave him the gift of a new body, a new purpose. "I'm afraid ye need to go as well."

"Ye . . . will . . . age too," Vincombe gasped out. He was rolling from side to side in his coffin. He looked pathetic, like a turtle overturned on a beach, desperately trying to regain its legs.

She tortured him for years before she let him truly die.

18.

A lot of things happened all at once.

The Mazda hit the van right in its wheel well and the car's lower front end screamed and deformed as it crumpled, one headlight exploding in a shower of glass as the two vehicles tried to fuse themselves together. The Mazda was too old to have airbags, so Clara was thrown forward against the steering wheel as her car came to a very abrupt—and not very soft—stop. The engine roared and then died, and Glauer's head cracked against the windshield hard enough to sound like a gunshot.

For all that, the van got the worse end of the impact. It swung around on the road directly in front of the Mazda, its tires screeching and its back end fishtailing wildly. It was top-heavy and boxy and the driver must not have known to steer into the skid, because suddenly both wheels on the right side were off the ground and the van started to tip over. It fought a losing war with physics as all the energy of its previous velocity added to the energy of the collision sent it tumbling down the highway, rolling three times before it came to a stop. The noise and the vibrations were colossal and made Clara's head buzz as she was thrown around in her seat belt like a rag doll.

Eventually things stopped moving, and she looked over at Glauer in the passenger seat. A line of blood crossed his forehead where he'd hit the windshield, but his eyes were tracking.

"I'm okay," he said, a little too loud in the silence that followed the impact.

"Good," Clara said. She felt like hell herself. The steering wheel had caught her across the chest and she could already feel bruises rising there. Her neck felt like someone had tried to shoot her head out of a slingshot, and she was terrified she might have whiplash.

"We need—to—go grab the half-deads, see what—what they have to say for themselves," she said, clamping her eyes shut to cope with a sudden wave of dizziness.

"Yeah," Glauer said. "Yeah."

"Just give me one second to, to—"

A wave of sleep washed over Clara and nearly dragged her under.

Crap. That was one of the signs of concussion, wasn't it? But she hadn't hit her head. Had she? She couldn't really remember.

"Local cops are inbound," Glauer said, very softly. It was an invitation. A very seductive offer. They could just sit still. Wait for the paramedics to arrive, and let the local cops clean up the mess. "Less than five minutes."

"Yeah," Clara said.

"Caxton wouldn't, though . . . she would . . ."

"She'd already be punching a half-dead to bits," Clara agreed.

They stared at each other for a second. Daring each other to give up. Daring each other not to.

Clara's memories of Laura won. She unbuckled her seat belt and shoved her door open, then staggered out onto the blacktop. She would not let the half-deads get away. Not this time.

Thus resolved, however, she faced a new problem. She couldn't see where the van had ended up. She had a very bad moment where she thought it must have landed on its wheels—and simply driven away. That they'd achieved nothing.

But then she saw it, or what was left of it. It had flipped into a drainage culvert on the side of the highway, upside-down and nose first. Its wheels were still spinning wildly as they tried to grab at the air. The rear door had been torn off, but she could see only darkness in its exposed cabin.

She reached down for her weapon and brought it up to a high ready position. Behind her she heard Glauer opening the Mazda's trunk. Laura had kept a shotgun back there and Clara had never bothered to take it out.

They advanced carefully on the wrecked van, covering each other every step of the way. There was no sign of any half-deads around the vehicle, but they were crafty little bastards and you never turned your back on them unless you wanted to catch a butcher knife in your kidneys.

When Clara reached the back of the van, she pointed her weapon inside, then put one foot on the ceiling of the cabin, which was now its floor. No bony hand shot out to grab her ankle, so she threw a hand signal to Glauer and jumped inside. She could feel him behind her, his shotgun poised to blast anything that moved.

He needn't have bothered. There were no half-deads in the cabin.

Just pieces of them.

Lots and lots of pieces. Arms and legs and rib cages. Organs and exposed bones, everywhere. No blood, of course, but the human body is full of other fluids, too, and these were splashed all over the walls of the van and dripped from the upholstery. Clara counted three heads. The eyeballs still rolled in the sockets and the teeth clattered together as if to bite at her, but they couldn't reach.

A severed hand tried to crawl up the tilted bottom of the cabin, pulling itself along by its finger bones. Clara stamped on it until it stopped moving.

"Wow," Glauer said behind her.

"Yeah."

"What about the driver?"

Clara's eyes went wide. She hadn't considered him. The front section of the cabin was badly crumpled and the two front seats stuck up at odd angles. The windshield of the van was just gone. The force of the impact had broken the steering wheel off its pillar. She found the lower half of the driver right away—his legs were trapped under the collapsed dashboard. The upper half, though, was nowhere to be found.

"He must have been thrown clear. Quick!"

Clara jumped back out of the van and followed its trajectory with her eyes. On the far side of the drainage culvert lay the parking lot of a grocery store, its lights so bright they ruined her night vision. She blinked as her eyes adjusted, then scrambled up the sloped side of the ditch and over the top, gasping for breath as her abused body refused to believe what she was demanding of it. She could hear her heart pounding as she clutched her weapon tight in both hands.

The driver—or at least, his top half—was crawling toward the lights of the market. His guts spooled out behind him, leaving a clear trail of how far he'd gone in just the few seconds since the impact. Pulling himself along on his hands, he kept glancing back toward Clara, as if he honestly thought he could get away.

He must have flown fifty feet when the van crashed. He'd

covered another twenty feet under his own power. After being chopped in half.

"Stop, now!" Clara shouted, but he ignored her and kept crawling.

She started running toward him, but she kept slipping on the slope of the ditch. Eventually she managed to get clear and made a beeline right for him, shouting as she ran. "Stop or I'll shoot your arms off! You're wanted for questioning. Stop immediately!"

"Questions? I don't think so," the half-dead yelled back at her. Then it rolled over on its back and reached up to its face with both hands.

She was still twenty feet away. Too far to stop him.

At first Clara thought he was just going to scratch at whatever remained of his face. The way half-deads always did.

But then she realized she was wrong, that he had something completely different in mind. And she started dashing toward him as fast as she possibly could, even knowing she would be too late.

With a sickening persistence, the half-dead grabbed his own lower jaw in both hands and tugged and yanked and pulled until it snapped off.

You couldn't get a lot of answers out of a suspect who couldn't talk.

[1745]

Alone at last, and it was glorious.

No distractions. No obligations. She moved all the time, staying ahead of her pursuers. She covered her tracks well. Justinia used the orisons when she needed to, but relied more often on human stupidity to hide herself from those who would destroy her.

In Nottinghamshire there lived a man who fancied himself a great hunter of vampires. This because he had stumbled on a coffin in the bright light of day, and plucked out a still-living heart. He became a local hero, and was even given a stipend by the Crown for his good works. Justinia tore his arms off and let him bleed to death in a village square while terrified farmers watched. A waste of good blood, perhaps, but that night she visited half the houses in the village and reminded the people inside of what they were: a foodstuff for more powerful creatures.

In Leeds she was nearly caught by a mob with torches and long knives. They chased her up to the top of a church. Up on the lead roof they held her at bay, thinking that if they could keep her penned in until dawn they could destroy her.

She fought like a demon. They threw themselves on top of her, seemingly heedless of their own lives. She clawed and bit and tore them to pieces, their stink all over her, their blood flowing in runnels down the lead roof of the church, pooling in its gutters. When it was over she stood alone. She went to the belfry and rang the church bell over and over, laughing, calling, "Bring more, bring more! I'd have a sweet course to end my supper!" No one else came. She slept that day in the church's crypt, daring them to come find her. Drunk on their blood. When night came once more she had sobered enough to make a quick and quiet exit from the town.

A witch met her on the road in Scotland two years later. The old woman offered no threat, nor asked Justinia to spare her life. There was something odd about the air that night. Even the crickets seemed to hold their breath. Justinia longed to take the witch's blood, but for once reason got the better of her.

"Ye're not what you seem, are ye?" she asked.

The witch said nothing. But her eyes never left Justinia's face, and her lips never stopped moving. She was whispering something, some chant or spell.

Justinia fled into the woods. She would never find out just what trap had been set for her, but from then on, she avoided any human who could work magic, and perhaps match her orisons.

As for the rest of the human race—they were fair game.

The blood. The blood was everything. Food and fuel. Joy and felicity. It filled her empty veins, suffused her skin with a pink glow. It made her strong, made her invulnerable even to musket balls and steel rapiers. It made her body sing, made her brain fizz in her skull.

She did not notice at first when it stopped working as well.

Had she been paying attention, she would have realized that she was taking more risks. Haunting more and more houses every night, wandering farther from her coffin as she sought out travelers on the roads and shepherds sleeping amid their folds. There had been a time when one victim in a night was enough to quench her thirst. Now it was two or more, or she would feel starved and mad the following night. Soon enough she had to have three men die at her hands every time she rose from her coffin, just to feel the strength she'd come to take for granted.

When the blood hit her tongue, when it jetted hot and red all about her, such questions of logistics and mathematics seemed quite abstract.

There came a time, however, when she could deny it no longer.

Her perfect, immortal body was starting to falter.

19.

The local cops arrived only a few minutes later in a great wash of red and blue light and the howl of sirens. Dozens of uniformed officers descended on the drainage culvert, weapons drawn and covering anything that moved.

Glauer waved his USMS ID over his head—holding it high in case any of the locals got trigger-happy and shot at him—and called out that all was clear. The local sheriff suggested he go get stuffed, that he wasn't going to declare the scene clear until his own people were damned sure it was clear. "Which means you got so much as a squirrel down there with evil intentions, you better let me know."

"Ah," Clara said. "Our reputation precedes us."

Back before Laura got arrested, the three of them had been the core of the SSU, the special subjects unit of the Pennsylvania State Police. Back then vampires had been all over the news—especially after what happened at Gettysburg—and they had received every manner of cooperation the local cops could provide, whether that be manpower, forensics labs, or just a place to sleep all day after a long night's vampire hunting.

The cooperation had been freely given by smiling men who looked good on camera. It had been a prestigious thing to help the SSU.

Then the bodies started piling up.

Sometimes the only way to fight vampires—and it had been so ever since the Middle Ages—was to throw armed people at them until they couldn't stand up or fight back. Jameson Arkeley had known that, and he had been personally responsible for dozens of local cops getting killed. He'd accepted those losses, because the vampires went down, too.

Laura Caxton had been a little gentler on the local manpower. At first. In Bellefonte, when she'd tracked down Jameson Arkeley himself, she had overseen an operation that left that local copshop almost unmanned.

The smiling men who looked good on camera had stopped shaking their hands after that. The SSU had the highest loss rate of seconded personnel of any working group in the history of the Pennsylvania State Police. Soon when you heard the SSU were coming to your town, you made a point of giving all your favorite people the day off.

Even now—when vampires were supposed to be extinct—the locals were afraid of them. They weren't too thrilled about Clara and Glauer, either. They formed a perfect perimeter around the upside-down van and the two Feds, officers covering each other to both the right and the left, ready to shoot with or without a direct order. The sheriff stayed just outside of that circle, standing on the hood of his own vehicle where he could see what happened.

Clara and Glauer knew the drill. They sat down in the tall, dusty weeds of the culvert and kept their hands visible. In a vampire investigation, even federal agents were subjects of interest until they were officially cleared. More than once, a cop who should have been somebody's best friend, even somebody's partner, had turned out instead to be a half-dead wearing his uniform. Or even worse, it could be a half-dead who still *looked* like their friend. It could happen that fast, the victim of a vampire being called back from death to serve his master.

Inch by inch the circle of local cops closed in on them. Taking their time, the uniforms kicked at the weeds, drew beads on suspicious shadows, and generally exhibited the kind of paranoia that could keep a cop alive.

Good for them.

It gave Clara and Glauer a chance to talk, anyway.

"Fetlock won't like it. You know him—he's been taking credit for years now for eliminating the vampire threat. If we turn up real, solid evidence that Justinia Malvern is still alive and active, he'll—"

"He'll shit bricks. Then he'll tell us we were wrong. That our eyes were playing tricks on us," Clara said. "That there can't be any more vampires, because he knows for a fact that the last vampire died in that prison. And what Fetlock knows to be a fact must be true." She scrubbed at her face with both hands. Then stopped abruptly, because it was the kind of thing a half-dead would do. One of the local cops might have heard that half-deads were sometimes called the Faceless, and would get the wrong idea. Carefully, she put her hands back up in the air.

"We do have it, though."

"Have what?" Clara asked.

"Real proof. Solid evidence. Those were half-deads, no question about it. Maybe there's some sicko out there with a fetish for zombies, and maybe he might dress up like a half-dead sometimes. Paint his face and so on. But nobody human could pull himself to pieces like this." He nodded at the van, which was still full of body parts. "And even if he did, the pieces wouldn't keep wriggling."

"And wherever there are half-deads, there are vampires. Yeah."

"So Malvern is back, and active. Even though we haven't seen one sign of her in two years. Even though she hasn't so much as left a single victim where we might find them."

"That just means she's been careful."

Glauer nodded. "Which she's known for. So. With all that established, we have one burning question we really need to address."

"Oh?" Clara asked. She shifted her weight around—her butt was falling asleep. It turned out to be a mistake, as it agitated the bruises all over her body and opened a few cuts that had finally stopped bleeding. Adrenaline had gotten her this far, but she knew that very soon she was going to crash. "What question is that?"

"What we're going to do about it."

Clara sighed. She inclined her head toward Glauer's shirt pocket. His cell phone was there, with its battery in place. And as long as the phone had power, Fetlock could listen in on their conversation.

"Only one thing we can do about it," she said. "We tell Fetlock everything. Lay out all the evidence, give him what we know. And let him make a decision about what to do next."

Glauer grunted in response. Then he took his phone out of his pocket and ejected the battery. "What's the real answer?" he asked.

"We find Laura. We find her, and we help her end this thing. We find her and we do everything we can to help her kill Malvern, once and for all."

20.

At that particular moment, Laura Caxton desperately needed help.

Patience Polder had asked her about the birds and the bees.

"I understand this is not your . . . particular field of expertise," Patience said. "That is, the ways of men and women on their marriage night."

Behind her, one of her acolytes—the red-headed girl with braces, whose name was Tamar—laughed behind her hand. Her cheeks turned the color of her hair.

"Yet you must know something of what happens. You must have heard stories from your friends, and other women of your same age. You know, women who—well. I don't wish to say normal women, which would suggest that—"

"Straight women. You're asking if I have any straight female friends who got married. And yeah, pretty much all of them. Pretty much all of my friends from high school. A couple of them already have kids. A couple of them are already divorced."

"So you must have heard whether the bridegrooms still carry their helpmeets over the threshold. I always found that custom so romantic. The bride so transported by the ecstasy of her new life that her feet must not be allowed to touch the ground, lest she lose some of the joy, lest she stop feeling as if she was walking on air . . ."

Patience had spoken of very little other than marriage since Simon Arkeley had come to the Hollow. That didn't mean she slacked off in her duties—just that she turned every chore into an opportunity to further discuss the blissful state of marital union.

It made Caxton slightly ill. Still, when Patience had asked

if Caxton was coming on one of her "herb walks," Caxton had agreed without question. Every few days Patience Polder took a long, meandering walk through the woods around the Hollow—up and down both sides of the ridge, down into the shadows at the bottom of the valley. She took along a basket, a pair of dainty pruning shears, and an incredible knowledge of plants and their proper uses.

For Patience it was a chance to gather magical herbs and plants to use in her rituals, and also a time to teach her disciples about the local flora. For Caxton, it was a chance to check the perimeter with the best tracker in Pennsylvania. Patience didn't miss anything. If a tree branch was broken or a stand of flowers stepped on anywhere in the Hollow, Patience would find it. It was one more guarantee that no one was sneaking closer to the house on the ridge.

"The wedding gown is white, of course, and most will tell you this is a token of the bride's virginity. In fact, she wears white for the same reason this small flower does," Patience said, kneeling down in the mossy forest floor and breathing gently on the white petals of a wildflower. The petals stirred in her exhalation and one, more delicate than the others, fell away from its stalk. Patience let it fall to drape across the ball of her thumb. She waited a long minute while the others just stared at her hand. Patience seemed totally unaware of the passing time. Caxton came close to tapping one foot to get things moving again, but the disciples wouldn't have heard of it.

Eventually Patience turned her hand to the side, and the flower petal fell away. In its place it left a red mark on her thumb, the same size and shape exactly as the petal.

One of the acolytes gasped. Becky, the fat, pimply one who thought her mother was a fraud, who, when she'd come to the Hollow, had told everyone at dinner one night that magic was bullshit and it didn't work. Caxton had had high hopes for that one. Then Becky had entered Patience's orbit and soon she was the most zealous of her devotees. The one who hung on her every word, and would defend her pronouncements with physical violence if necessary.

On the plus side, Patience had recommended some kind of oil that totally cleared up Becky's acne.

"Poison aster," Becky said, and Patience nodded. "It's poison aster. So the bride wears white because . . . she's poisonous?"

Patience laughed. Not at Becky—she was no sadistic teacher with a fetish for mocking her students. No, when Patience laughed at you she made it feel as if she was sharing the joke you just told. "Because, silly, she can't be touched. In some cultures it means death to touch a bride's hand before the ceremony is complete. But we must never consider the bride to be dangerous herself. Instead, like the flower of this small plant, she is utterly fragile, her joy and her virtue so delicate they must be protected no matter the cost."

Caxton shook her head and stopped paying attention. The girl was getting insufferable. If Simon had actually been there, he probably would have—well, he would have run away in panic. Just like he had before.

Yet Patience hadn't taken offense at Simon's response. Not at all. She knew from long experience that people who lacked the second sight—those poor mortals who could only see the present, not the future—often rejected her prophecies on an emotional level. Even if they knew she was right, in the long run. And Simon didn't even have a reason to believe that Patience *could* predict the future.

To her, his cold feet were just that. A momentary lapse in what was to be a long and grand career of being her man. *She* had no doubts that the two of them would be very happy together . . . eventually.

Caxton hoped she was right. If Malvern did go to ground— literally—it could be generations before she rose again. She could sleep in the earth as long as she wanted. Long enough for humans to forget there had ever been such a thing as vampires, unless—

"Don't step there!" Becky said, suddenly, and Caxton nearly fell over in her surprise.

"What? What? Why? Am I about to step on some dittany-of-Crete or something? Maybe a choice mushroom?"

"Miss Caxton, please, just take a step back. Without disturbing the soil just before you, if you please," Patience said.

There was a look on her face that Caxton didn't like. A look of focus that had completely displaced the dreamy romanticism.

"Well done, Becky," Patience said.

The girl blushed so hard Caxton wondered if maybe Becky belonged in her, Caxton's, ah, well, um, particular field of expertise. It would explain why she'd taken to Patience so quickly. "Is somebody going to tell me what's going on?"

"Does anyone in the Hollow wear those?" Patience asked. "You were a policewoman at one time. I imagine you always make a note of people's footwear."

Caxton slowly lowered her eyes to the ground as she realized what they were talking about. The herb walk had been following a path of trodden-down grass that wound through the woods of the Hollow, a trail so wild that it might as well be an animal track. No one but Patience could have followed it. Yet there were clear, muddy footprints all over the flattened grass at Caxton's feet.

She knelt beside the prints and studied them carefully. They were the kind of prints left by rubber-soled tennis shoes. Sneakers. "No," she said. "No, I don't think so." Most of the Hollow's residents went in for hobnailed work boots—or open-tied sandals, or bare feet altogether. Sneakers weren't really appropriate for the rural setting.

"What does it mean?" Tamar asked.

"It means there are strangers on the ridges," Patience announced. Not, however, in the voice she used when she foretold the future. Just her usual commanding intonation. "Tamar, draw a protective hex sign around this print. I want very much to know who left it. Charlotte, Sunshine, and Claire-Ann, you three go and fetch me all the sage you can find, and some flowers of the hawthorn if any are yet in bloom, and something alive. Something small, preferably, like a field mouse. I don't want this casting to make too big a mess."

"What are you going to do?" Caxton asked.

"Try to see if the intruder left any of himself behind. Any psychic residue I might be able to read, you know."

"Sure."

"It'll take some time. And it's disturbing to watch," Patience told her.

"That's okay. I've got a strong stomach."

The girl surprised Caxton then, by actually looking a little irritated. Normally nothing could faze the great Patience Polder. Her zenlike countenance never cracked. But Caxton was pretty sure she saw Patience's eyes flash, just for a moment.

"We will have to—we must remove—for this ceremony we—"

"You're going to go skyclad," Caxton interpreted.

It was Patience's turn to blush. What a red-letter day.

So the girls were going to get naked. And they didn't want Caxton around. She had a feeling she knew why—it was, after all, her field of expertise—but now wasn't the time to make a stink.

No. Now was the time to talk to Urie Polder about a certain something he'd been holding on to for years.

21.

She made it back up the side of the ridge in record time. Caxton had been all over these heights so many times she knew every step of the way, knew, usually, where the gravel of the road was going to slip under her feet, knew where the mud on the side of the road would be too deep to cross. She slipped between tree trunks that looked so close together a bird couldn't have flown between them, hauled herself up a slope of scree because she knew which rocks wouldn't give way when she put her weight on them.

In ten minutes she was up to the house, breathing heavy and a little scratched up but not complaining. She raced to the porch and checked her pile of guns. All loaded, all ready to go, just like she'd left them. She shoved one of the pistols down the back of her waistband and yanked open the screen door.

"Polder!" she called. "Polder! Are you here?"

She could just hear the high-pitched whine of talk radio coming up from the basement of the house. She ran to the door and saw light emerging from the edges of its frame. There were very few places anywhere on the ridge where Caxton wasn't supposed to go, but this was one of them. Whatever Urie Polder got up to down in his basement, he didn't want anyone seeing him at it. He'd been very clear on that.

She knocked on the door, but apparently Urie Polder was too preoccupied to hear her—or maybe he'd just turned the radio up too high. He was starting to go a little deaf, after all.

Caxton pounded harder and kept calling his name, but there was no answer.

There was also no more time. If there were intruders in the woods, and they'd managed to get past all of Caxton's safeguards, then they could come for her at any time. Come for every man, woman, and child in the Hollow. The vampires could—

No. Not just "vampires." She wasn't just facing some random blood-munches. There was only one left.

The worst of the lot.

Malvern. The vampire who had taken away Caxton's girlfriend Deanna. The monster who took away Jameson Arkeley. The bitch who drove a wedge between her and Clara, and made sure Caxton would never have a life.

"Urie Polder," Caxton shouted, yanking open the door, "I hope you're decent, because I'm coming down there right now." She had half expected the door to magically resist any effort to open it, but no, it swung right open. Somehow that made it seem much more wrong.

"Polder!" she shouted, one last time. There was no response.

She headed down the stairs, past ancient and rusted tools hung up on the walls, past Mason jars full of nails and boxes full of old, oil-stained rags. Nothing all that creepy. Her own dad's basement had looked like that.

However, her dad's basement didn't have the world's largest hex sign painted on its floor.

Tourists in central Pennsylvania often bought "hex signs" from little craft shops in Amish country. They would take the brightly painted signs home and put them over their garages or in their living rooms. The better sort of tourist might actually take the trouble to find out what the weird combinations of birds and trees and stars on their hex sign actually meant. They would probably get some simplified description of which symbol brought good luck, which one health, and so on.

They would most likely not be told that the people who painted the original hex signs in America were immigrants from Germany, and that in German, the word *hex* simply means "witch."

The hex sign on Urie Polder's floor was twenty feet across. It was the real thing. No bright paint, no cheerful little birds in rows. Oh, there were birds, but they looked about ready to scratch somebody's eye out. This hex sign showed trees blowing in strong winds, and a man pushing a plow while a team of oxen strained forward. Surrounding the figures were words in Latin and Hebrew, five- and seven- and eleven-pointed stars, symbols of the zodiac and of the planets and of alchemical metals. Around the edge of the hex sign were Bible passages written out in ancient Greek. Plenty of other symbols decorated the hex sign as well, most of which Caxton didn't even recognize.

There was three hundred years of history in that circle. The history of people who'd come to Pennsylvania seeking opportunity and found coal mines and black lung. Of people who'd come for the state's religious tolerance—only to watch the rest of the world move on without them until they looked like freaks. This was the history of a country where magic was supposed to be forgotten, where science was big business and big business was the only thing that mattered. And also of a country where people still read their horoscopes and went to storefront psychics to have their fortunes read and buried statues of saints in their yards when they wanted to sell their houses.

Sitting in the exact center of it was Urie Polder. He was not, thank God, skyclad. But he did have his shirt off, and she could see where his wooden arm attached to his shoulder. The wound that took his arm must have been horrifying to look at. Even now the skin there was red and irritated, torn to shreds that hung down in painful-looking flaps. The wooden arm wasn't strapped to his body but instead sent out thick roots that burrowed into his flesh, presumably anchoring the artificial arm to his real, normal, bones.

He was facing away from her when she entered the basement. The radio was on loud enough to mask her footfalls—some right-wing pundit talking about how kids should be required to say the Lord's Prayer every time they recited the Pledge of Allegiance, since they were basically the same thing. Caxton went over to the radio and switched it off.

Urie Polder's head snapped around and he looked at her with bewildered eyes. He was breathing heavily and she realized she'd startled him. "I didn't feel you come in, ahum," he said.

Not, I didn't *hear* you come in. Caxton understood the difference. "Your wards didn't pick me up?"

He frowned, which was all the answer she needed. Then he reached for his white T-shirt and pulled it on over his wounded shoulder.

"She's here. Or—or very close."

"You sure about that?"

"Patience's girls found footprints out in the woods. They're casting some kind of spell over them now. But that already means somebody crossed our best line of defense—the teleplasm cordon—without setting it off. And if I can walk into your . . . your inner sanctum, here, without you being aware that somebody's coming down the stairs, then—"

"They's walking light, ahum," Polder said, with a nod. He didn't seem particularly concerned.

"It can't be anybody else. Can it?" she asked.

Polder shrugged. "There's always some way 'round magic. Even my magic. Could be anyone or anybody, if'n they knew the right countercharms. I haveta say, it don't feel like her."

"No?"

"Now a vampire, when she walks, she leaves a trace. A kinda foulness in the dirt. Makes things hard to grow where she set her feet. I don't feel that just now."

Caxton shrugged. "Alright, so it was a half-dead. One of her half-deads."

"That's as may be."

"It doesn't matter. We need to assume it is her, that she's found us. Right?"

Polder didn't disagree.

She wanted to get back to work. To make more preparations, to focus herself more on the task at hand. Yet there was something weird about Urie Polder's basement. A sense of peace that she didn't really feel, but which was . . . imposed on her. No, not that. It wasn't so intrusive. But something about the big hex sign made her feel calm when she looked at it. "This sign," she said. "It's doing something to my head."

Urie Polder laughed. "Nothin' so sinister. This is my safe place. Ain't much can get through these lines. Oh, it won't stop bullets, or a rampagin' monster. But the cares of the day, ahum. My worries. They stay outside, flutterin' at the edges, wantin' to get in, but they cain't."

"That must be nice," Caxton said, though she was thinking how dangerous such a thing might be. People who didn't have magic used drugs to feel that way. She shook her head. "Magic. I used to hear stories when I was a kid. My dad—he was a county sheriff—told me stories about things he'd seen out on dark country roads. But we never really believed, you know?" She thought of whom she was talking to. "No, you wouldn't know about that. Outside this Hollow, people believe in science. Here it's different."

"I've always been a big booster of science, ahum."

"Really?"

Urie Polder shrugged. "Science makes a certain sense, don't it? It always works. It's repeatable. Magic don't work that way. Anybody who practices magic, they know that frustration that comes when a charm that functioned a thousand times suddenly stops workin'. And you cain't say why."

Caxton grimaced. "I'm kind of counting on your magic, for what's coming."

"More fool you." But he was smiling.

"How does magic even work?" she asked.

"I would dearly like to know. Nobody has any notion, to tell it true." Polder rubbed at his face with his wooden fingers. "'Tis like a cookbook handed down from mother to son for generations. The recipes inside, you know they worked for somewhat.

And you can try 'em yourself, and maybe you get what you wanted. But nobody knows where those recipes came from. Nobody knows why they work. You just gotta trust that they do. And if they don't work for you, ain't no recourse."

"You seem to make it work pretty reliably."

Polder nodded. "Not that it didn't cost me." He lifted his wooden shoulder, let it fall again. "There's them that can do it better than t'others, that's all. My Patience has got a real gift. Down the Hollow, there's Heather and Glynnis, they've got some real juju. But you add us all up together, we hain't a pinkie finger's power between us, compared to the likes of Astarte Arkeley, or my Vesta, God rest her."

Caxton nodded in agreement. She'd never met Astarte Arkeley while she was alive, only talked to her on the phone, but from what she'd heard Astarte had been a powerful mystic. She *had* known Vesta Polder. Vesta had been a good friend to Caxton, even if the witch had scared her shitless. To Jameson Arkeley she'd been more than just a friend, at least when she was alive. Vesta been a great ally against the vampires, and then Jameson had murdered her. He'd been after everyone he ever loved, back when he was human. He'd killed his own wife— and his mistress.

For the first time, she realized the connection there.

Jameson hadn't chosen his wife—or his lover—because they were beautiful or they could cook well or some other normal reason. He'd picked them because they were witches. His brother had supposedly been talented, too, though not even on Urie Polder's level. And his children had both been initiated into magical circles, born into a tradition. He'd seen to that.

He had been trying to put together the same trap she was building now. Jameson Arkeley, that old son of a bitch. He'd been way ahead of her. He hadn't loved the witchbillies, he'd *collected* them. Made them care about each other, made them bond together as a force that could fight vampires.

When he became a vampire himself the first thing he'd done was to kill all the people he had brought together. She'd assumed at the time he was just trying to cut ties to his own humanity—that he had gone after his own family because he couldn't bear to think of what he'd become. But he'd always been smarter than that.

He had been trying to wipe out a dangerous threat. The witchbilly families—the Polders and the Arkeleys—had been among the few people in the world who could bring him down. So they had to go.

"They're afraid of you," Caxton said. "The vampires are afraid of magic."

"I told you nobody knew who wrote that cookbook," Polder said. "But I know why it was set down. To give us a chance 'gainst 'em, ahum."

"Sure. Before there were guns, we needed some way to fight back against the vampires. So that's why magic was invented in the first place."

"The knot's pulled tighter than that."

"What do you mean?" she asked.

"Who you think wrote that cookbook, first?"

She got his meaning immediately. "The spells you use are just like her orisons," she breathed. "Oh my God."

"Every bit o' magic I got, every charm, every enchantin'. It takes us years to learn, and costs us dear. All so we can do as they do with no effort whatsoever."

"Wow. Oh, wow," Caxton said. "Like Prometheus stealing fire from the gods. Your ancestors stole magic from the vampires." She thought of something. "Justinia Malvern is a master of the orisons. The other vampires I've met, even old Alva Griest, always said she was a hundred times better at the orisons than they were. You don't stand a chance against Malvern, do you?"

It was a cruel thing to say, and even Urie Polder—calm,

quiet, Zen monk–like Urie Polder—rocked with the sting of her words. His face darkened for a moment as if he might respond with a cruelty of his own.

But the hex sign on his basement floor worked its magic, and the anger drained from his face.

"I'll do my best, you just see if I don't," he said with a sad smile.

"I'm—sorry," Caxton said, though she had a hard time summoning up the sentiment. "Look, anyway, we have other lines of defense."

"Aye."

"The cave," Caxton said, rubbing at the bridge of her nose. "It's ready. Right? Ready as it'll ever be. That's where it'll end. I have a . . . a feeling."

"You developin' the gift, now of all times?"

She shook her head. "Just a hunch." She had another one, too. "Listen," she said. "Years ago. The first time I met you—Arkeley brought me to meet you, and you showed me what was in your barn. That night Vesta read the cards for me, and gave me a little charm to protect against the vampires. You remember?"

"Ahum."

"She didn't do it for free. When she asked to be paid, Arkeley gave you something, a little bag—"

"Still got it," Polder said. He rose to his feet and went over to a workbench up against the far wall. There was a ghost skin on the bench, a shimmering, iridescent piece of what might have been—but definitely was not—leather. It was hard to look at. Polder ignored it and reached into a drawer underneath. He fetched the little bag, then emptied its contents into her cupped hands. One after another they fell out of the bag, triangular and white.

Thirty-two in all. Thirty-two fangs. Jameson Arkeley had personally pulled them out of the jawbone of the vampire Congreve with a pair of pliers. Congreve had been the first vampire Caxton ever met. The first one she'd helped to kill.

"Back when he brought you these, Vesta said you would find some use for them. But you never did. You just put them away for when we would really need them. You've been waiting for this, haven't you? Just like me?"

"Yes'um. And I know exactly what to do with 'em. Don't you worry now, girl. It'll be ready in time."

[1772]

Running from a mob of would-be vampire killers, she laughed and leapt from rooftop to rooftop, easily evading their bullets and their swords. It was a pleasing diversion, for once to be the hunted instead of the hunter. Especially because she knew they could never win. She jumped from the top of an inn to sail gracefully across a lane, already anticipating the cat-like landing on the roof of the stable across the street.

Below her the horses went mad, stamping in their stalls, bucking at their gates, trying to escape, to run free. Perhaps they distracted her with their annoying noises, perhaps she merely misjudged the distance. She had no depth perception, after all.

Either way—she fell.

She kept laughing all the way down, as the cobbles rushed up at her. So what if she collided with the earth? Her body would heal itself. Even as her thighbone snapped on impact, she was laughing.

Inside her leg she felt the bone fragments start to knit back together, to re-form themselves. She leapt back to her feet—

—and fell again. The leg hadn't fully healed. She felt new bones snapping. She stopped laughing then.

She managed to get away that night. But it was a close thing. Her perfect vampire body had betrayed her. She did not want to think about what that meant.

The next night, when she rose from her coffin, she reached automatically for her gown. Yet before she could put it on she turned and glanced at the looking glass in the corner. She had not studied her reflection for years. She had no vanity in her. Yet this night, she could not help but look. Like a man scratching at the bite of an insect, she could not help herself.

Justinia looked in the mirror and saw death there. It was not as pleasant an experience as she'd once believed it would be.

Where was the girl who had not been afraid?

She was old now. Her breasts were empty sacks sagging on her chest. The lines on her face were like cracks in a porcelain mask. Her arms, once graceful and strong, had become sticks hung with sagging pennons of white flesh.

Blood. All she needed was more blood—a few more victims, surely, would be enough to restore her. She should go out and hunt, and sup deep of the life that thronged around her in this city. So many beating hearts out there, so much blood—

It was never going to be enough.

She closed her eye and sobbed until rusty tracks of blood rolled down her cheek and splashed on her knees. Once she had been unafraid. She had embraced the cosmic gamble, the inevitability of death, the rest and comfort it would bring. It was what had drawn Vincombe to her. Convinced him she was worthy of this gift.

He'd been a fool. But so had she.

She had not feared death, because life had not been sweet. Now, with all the power of her new body, with all her strength, she had something to lose. To never go out by night again, to never stroll beneath the moon, surrounded by the smell of blood, by the veins that throbbed and glowed in the darkness around her—to never again leap and run in the forest, where she was a more fearsome beast than any tiger. To never taste the blood again.

It was terrifying.

She opened her eye and looked at herself again. Perhaps, she thought, the ravages of time would so sicken her she would regain her fearlessness. Perhaps she would accept that all the cards had been played and it was time for an end. Then she would tear out her own heart and scream, *but only for a moment, and then the overwhelming rush of blackness, of oblivion—*

But in the mirror she saw not blackness, but the perfect creamy white of her own face. And there, in the center of it, her one, red eye.

One red pip on a field of white.

The ace of hearts.

One of the strongest cards in the deck. As long as your hand contained the ace of hearts, no wager was truly lost, she considered. There was always a new trick to play.

One ace . . .

She could go on. She could go on forever. Not as she had been, not as strong. But there was hope, one ace alone was enough for hope. There was a future, a continuation. If she must fear death, that did not mean she could not cheat it.

Yet she knew, for the first time in her life, that she would not have the strength to beat this game alone. She knew she would need help. After all, if one ace meant hope, how much more advantage it was to have a pair. . . .

22.

When Glauer came out of Fetlock's office he was white as a sheet. Clara was sitting in one of the uncomfortable chairs outside the door, waiting her turn. She shot Glauer a meaningful glance. He caught her eye for a moment, then just looked away.

"Specialist Hsu? He's ready for you now."

Clara looked up suddenly, as if she couldn't remember where she was. Fetlock's assistant—they didn't call them secretaries anymore—gave her a sympathetic smile. Clara tried to return it with a cocky grin. She knew she failed. Then she got up, smoothed out her skirt, and walked into the lion's den.

Fetlock's office was not so much decorated as enshrined. It was not big, but he kept it uncluttered—just a desk, with a laptop computer and a single telephone. Two chairs. One whole wall of the room, however, was taken up with a massive glass-fronted display case. The inside was lined with flocked red wallpaper. A very old, very moldy leather duster hung inside, as well as a mangy cowboy hat and a leather holster. Relics of some ancient cowboy out west, one of the first U.S. Marshals. Fetlock loved to tell people stories about the old days, when the Marshals were pretty much the only law enforcement west of the Mississippi.

Clara had never been able to figure it out. If there was any American citizen living in the twenty-first century who had less cowboy in him than Marshal Fetlock, she had yet to meet him.

He sat behind the desk looking like he was there to conduct an employee review. Like a dismal little bureaucrat. Maybe a tax lawyer. He had his hands steepled in front of his face and on the desk before him lay Clara's permanent dossier.

"You were hurt again," he said.

She took the chair in front of the desk and sat down, trying not to sigh.

"Hurt in the line of duty. Most cops accept that's going to happen from time to time. They expect commendations for it. Of course—you aren't actually a cop."

Clara frowned but said nothing.

"You're a forensic specialist. Not like Quincy, mind you. Not like *CSI Miami*. Like in the real world. Where you're supposed to examine crime scenes, then take evidence back to the lab for analysis. The most dangerous thing you're supposed to do is handle blood evidence."

She couldn't help herself. "In a vampire case, there's rarely any blood evidence to work with. You need to get in there, in the middle of things, while the evidence still exists, and—"

She stopped because he had lowered his hands to the surface of the desk. He didn't ask her to shut up. He didn't need to.

He scared her in a way vampires didn't. In a dull, ugly little way.

"Laceration to the hip. Contusions to the chest and face. You crashed your own car to stop a suspect from getting away. Even real cops—and I mean field agents, active-duty people—don't get those kind of injuries very often. This is the second time in a week for you. Hsu—may I call you Clara?"

He waited, as if he actually cared what she said in response.

You can call me Specialist Hsu, you pencil-necked desk drone, she wanted to say. Instead, because this was her job, this was where her paycheck came from, she said, "Sure."

"Clara. I'm worried about you. Honestly, humanly, compassionately worried for your safety. I wonder if you're trying to get hurt."

She couldn't help herself. She laughed.

He waited until she was done.

"I've seen it before. Adrenaline junkies are common enough in any field of law enforcement. Here in the Marshals Service, it's a real occupational hazard." He nodded toward his display case. "We forget we're not all Wyatt Earp. We get addicted to the thrill of the chase, the real, honest, down-in-the-dirt work. Taking out bad guys. So we put ourselves in more and more desperate situations. We forget to call for backup. We discharge our weapons far more often than the policies and guidelines suggest."

"Sir, honestly, I—"

"It happens to the best of us," he said, with a sad little sigh. "Look at Caxton. It happened to her and now . . . look at her. Look at what has become of her."

"Sir. With all due respect, last night we uncovered some real evidence of a continued—a renewed—vampire presence in Pennsylvania. We—"

He might as well not have heard her. "There's only one cure, sadly. Removal from active duty. Putting the afflicted on desk jobs where they can't hurt themselves."

Christ, no. Not now. "Sir—"

"Of course, we can't do that in your case."

"Oh."

She sat back in her chair. Watched him smile at her for a while.

"No. Since, technically, you're already assigned to a desk job. At least, a lab job. There's not really a lot I can do to make your job less dangerous. I doubt you have the necessary clerical skills for actual paper-pushing."

"No," she admitted. "I've never done that kind of work."

"So I can't reassign you," Fetlock said. He raised his hands in the air, then let them settle on the desk again.

Relief washed through Clara like a cold shower. She closed her eyes and just said *thank you* for a while. Not to anyone in particular. Just—*thank you*.

Prematurely, as it turned out.

"No. My only option at this point is to fire you."

She sat up so fast her knees collided painfully with his desk.

"As of now you are no longer an employee in the USMS," he told her. "I'll need you to turn in your ID and any Service equipment or materials you have in your possession. I'll give you until the end of the day to get your files in order for your replacement. I don't need to tell you—well, actually, I'm legally required to tell you—that you'll be observed at all times until you leave your lab for good, and that any office supplies we find on your person after the close of work today will be considered stolen property. There's the question of your pension and your severance package, which I'll be happy to go over with you, if you like, and—"

"You son of a bitch! Malvern is alive!"

He looked at her expectantly.

"We fought half-deads last night. She's not just alive, she's active. She's here now, killing people. Maybe she wants to finish Laura off before she goes underground, or maybe she just intends to start her rampage all over again. People are going to die, lots of people are going to die, and—and—"

"I know," he said when she'd sputtered to a stop.

"What?"

"I know what you found, and I agree. It's proof positive that Malvern is alive and active. I'm putting a team together right now to handle it."

"But—you—" For the last two years Fetlock had maintained in public and private that Malvern had died in the prison riot. That vampires were extinct. It had become sort of a private joke between Clara and Glauer—that Fetlock wouldn't believe Malvern was still alive until she'd actually torn his head off and sucked the blood out of his stump, and that even then he would ask her for identification.

"Despite what Caxton might have led you to believe, I'm no fool," Fetlock told her. "The evidence you recovered last night is good. It's solid. I'm convinced."

"But—then—you need me. You need me on this case. You really need Caxton, but since you can't have her, you need me to—"

"I need you to stay as far away from this as possible," he said. "For one very good reason. Where Malvern shows up, Caxton can't be far away. And I can't trust you, Clara, not for a second, where Caxton is involved. The romantic relationship the two of you once shared is enough to cloud your judgment. So my decision stands. Do you want to turn over your phone now, or do you still need to make some official calls? At any rate, I'll take your laminate while I'm thinking about it."

23.

Clara stormed out of the U.S. Marshals Service field office feeling like she couldn't breathe, like she might die at any moment without the slightest warning. Everything gone—her job, her whole reason for getting out of bed in the morning, her phone, goddamn it, he was going to take her phone away. She would have to get a new one, and how would she afford it? How would she pay the rent, or put gas in the car, or—or—

She started crying, tried to stop herself and failed. She shoved the ball of her thumb into her eye socket, grinding away the tears. If Fetlock saw her crying now, if he was watching her from the window of his office, she would never forgive herself.

Fired. Really? Yes. She'd been fired.

She pushed the tears down inside her, shoved all the worries and fears down hard. In their place anger bubbled up. Anger like a hot wind blowing across the top of her brain, anger that made her skin prickle.

Anger at Laura.

You had to go away and leave me with this. You had to go chasing the vampires.

And the vampires are still here!

You should have loved me more. You should have loved me more than you loved fighting Malvern. You should have said no when Arkeley drafted you into his insane crusade. You should have never been a cop. You could have worked at Dunkin' Donuts, and made my coffee for me every morning, and then one day you would have put the sugar in for me before I asked you to, and we would have made eye contact, and you would have said something nice about my hair, and then . . . and then . . .

And then we would have been normal. We would have been happy and boring and none of this would have happened, and I would be heading home now and you would be lying in my bed, waiting for me. Waiting to hear about my nice, normal, boring day as a nice, normal, boring police photographer.

We would have been happy like that.

And when the vampires showed up, when they started killing people, then. Then what? Then it wouldn't have been our problem. It would have been something we read about in the newspaper, something we made jokes about. You would have worried about me, at all those late-night crime scenes, but I would have told you it was fine, that I only ever saw what happened after it was over and it didn't touch me, that it couldn't touch me.

But you had to be a cop. And a fearless vampire hunter. And I had to think that was sexy. I should have walked away back then. I should have run away.

Glauer grabbed her arm and she nearly screamed.

"Come on," he said.

She started to protest, but he wasn't even looking at her face. He pulled her through the parking lot. Past his car. Past the rental car she had parked near the entrance to the lot, as if she'd known she would want to get out in a hurry. He looked both ways across the highway, then dragged her across four empty lanes at a run. On the far side of the street lay an office park, a collection of dentist's and chiropractor's offices. The front of the building was lined with ornamental trees, gray on one side with dust from the road. He took her around the side of the building and through a door into an air-conditioned waiting room full of ancient magazines and bad modern art in cheap frames.

For the first time she found her voice. "What the hell are we doing here?"

"It's safe. We can talk. I come here for my back once a week and the nurses all know me," he told her.

Clara looked over at the reception desk. A nurse wearing scrubs decorated with teddy bears glanced up at her for a second, then pulled a frosted glass partition closed so they were completely alone.

"Your phone?" she asked.

"In my car. Trust me, this is safe."

She dropped, hard, onto a sofa facing the door. She wanted to curl up and just sleep for a long time. Instead she kept her feet on the floor and her hands in her lap. "He fired me," she said, eventually.

"I know," Glauer told her. "He told me he was going to do it." Clara nodded. There were no secrets in Fetlock's office.

Everybody knew everybody else's business. Fetlock felt gossip was damaging to the team culture he wanted to create, so to prevent gossip he made sure everything got said in the open. She had hated that. She had, however, liked getting a paycheck. And getting to keep tabs on the manhunt for Laura Caxton. Those things were gone now.

Something occurred to her. "Your back? You have problems with your back?"

He sighed. "Yeah. Ever since Gettysburg. I got pretty beat up by the vampires there. We all did. Caxton worse than everybody, though she never let it stop her."

Clara nodded. "I'm—sorry. About your back."

"You had to think about that. About what to say," he told her. He was smiling, a little. He didn't often. He was letting her know he didn't take offense. "Caxton used to rely on me for that. To know what to say."

"I remember."

"Funny, huh? A big guy like me. And I was the nice guy. The good cop. But you fight vampires too long and it starts rubbing off on you. They don't think of human beings as people. They're just food. For Caxton, most people fit into two categories. Those people who were going to get in her way and make it hard to fight vampires, and those people who were useful as bait."

Clara winced at the idea, but she couldn't deny it was true.

"Caxton had no time for anything but fighting them. She accepted she was going to get hurt, accepted that some people were going to die. She accepted that her relationship with you was going to fall apart. Those were all necessities."

Clara had no idea what he was driving at, but she didn't care. His voice was so calm and soothing it helped bank the fires of anger and outrage burning in her chest. If he just kept talking for hours, she would be okay with that.

Though—there was something strange there. Glauer, talking so much? He was the strong silent type.

He must be trying to make a point, she realized. And she was too upset to figure out what it might be.

"Of course, she didn't start out that way. I didn't meet her until she came to Gettysburg, and by then she was already wound up pretty tight. But there was still a human being underneath the tough-girl act. You knew her even before then. You must have seen something soft inside her. Something you could hold on to."

So much, Clara thought. She had been—Laura had been kind, and, and, she had cared about people, she'd wanted to save them all. She'd wanted to protect them. Somewhere along the road that had changed. She went from wanting to save people to wanting to kill vampires, period.

"It was Jameson Arkeley who made her tough as nails. He taught her how to put everything else aside and focus. Really focus on kicking ass. She became like him a little more every day."

"She had to," Clara said, finally.

"Did she?" Glauer shrugged. He didn't seem interested in debating the point. "You still have a chance," he said. "I think Fetlock was right to fire you."

She sat up very straight and stared at his face. He looked back with no expression at all. She wanted to slap him.

"Arkeley fought vampires until he became a monster himself. Caxton fought them until she was a criminal. Now you're shrugging off injuries. Now you're chasing half-deads across half the state, intending to beat answers out of them any way you can. Now it's your turn, and you're turning into something you might end up hating."

"Maybe I think she'll—maybe Laura will love me again if I'm more like her."

"No. That won't make her love you. It might, after a very long time, get you some grudging respect out of her. The way she got just a little out of Arkeley. But he never loved her for becoming like he was. He never loved anybody. He was just glad there would be somebody to keep fighting after he was gone."

Clara nodded. He was right, of course. She'd seen the way Laura and Arkeley had been around each other. She'd been jealous of it, God help her.

Glauer took a pad of paper out of one pocket and a pen from another. He scrawled something on the paper, then tore off the sheet and laid it down on the seat beside him.

"What is that?" Clara asked.

"Simon Arkeley's home address. You walk out of here now, and if you want, you can pick it up on the way. Or you can leave it lying there and go have a decent life. I'm going to regret even giving you this choice, I know. But you need to decide for yourself. Stop, now. Let the cops handle the vampires, and go do whatever you want. Whatever you enjoy. Be a forensic expert if you want, just do it somewhere else."

"Or?"

"Or pick up this piece of paper."

She stood up. Pushed her bangs out of her face. "This isn't fair. You can't make me decide just like that."

"I'm not making you do anything," he told her.

She walked out of the office then without looking him in the eye at all. She didn't say good-bye or tell him to go fuck himself, though she kind of wanted to. She didn't do anything on her way out.

Except pick up the sheet of paper.

[1779]

His name was Thomas Easling, and he was the slave of a shrew of a wife.

To Justinia he looked like the future. Like life itself.

He was not a pretty man. He tended to fat, and as she watched him age—for this was a very long game she was playing, and it took years to

*be sure she had the right man—his jowls hung low, giving him the air
of a melancholy bulldog.*

*Had he been just a sad sack, a gentleman loser, she might have rejected
him and chosen another. But in that sighing face there were two eyes that
burned with something else. The fires of hell—a banked and glowing
hatred. A longing to rend and destroy.*

*One night she perched on the roof of his house and closed her eye and
listened to the disputation going on inside.*

*It was about money, of course. Money. How the living obsessed over
it, as if it could buy anything of value. Apparently Thomas Easling had
spent too much money on a gift for a colleague at the merchant house
where he toiled. He'd intended to grease his way to a promotion, but instead the colleague had simply returned the gift in the form of a bottle of
wine. And Easling's wife, a devout Methodist, didn't even drink.*

*What followed was less of an argument than an enumeration of all
the ways he had failed her. He made not so much as a reply, other than
to agree with her points, one and another.*

*Eventually it came to an end. The wife stormed out of the house,
intent on going to the local wineshop. She intended to sell the bottle for
whatever she could get.*

It was what Justinia had been waiting for.

*She slipped in through the window of the second floor of the house.
She found herself, as she'd expected, in Easling's bedchamber. Like
many married couples of that time the two of them had separate rooms.
Probably if they'd been forced to share a bed they would have slaughtered
each other long since.*

*Justinia could hear Easling coming up the stairs. She must move
quickly. Slipping out of her gown, she chanted the words of an orison
that Vincombe had taught her. In her own shape she could hardly tempt
a man, even one so hateful of women as Easling. Yet as the spell took
effect she felt herself changing. Her skin filled out, her breasts inflating
on her chest like biscuits rising in an oven. A pinkish tone colored in her
white flesh. Hair sprouted from her head, long, luxurious red hair that
tickled her shoulders.*

She had been a whore long enough to know what a man like Easling truly wanted. When the door opened and he stepped inside, he was greeted not with a succubus or an angel, but a damsel in distress. With stout ropes—as illusory as her hair—she lay bound spread-eagled on the bed. A thick cloth had been tied around her mouth as a gag.

She looked up at Easling with two eyes that pleaded silently for him to remember his best morals, to recall every sermon he'd ever sat through in church.

The look on his face was worth it. Surprise gave way to a moment of horror. And then his face changed once more. His lips curled up at the corners. His eyes narrowed. His brows drew together as if he could not believe his luck.

Then he closed the door behind him and removed his belt. Doubling it in his hand, he approached her. There were so many questions in his eyes, but he was not the kind of man to look a gift horse in the mouth.

24.

Clara hadn't been there the night Simon Arkeley's mother died. Glauer and Laura had. They'd been just a little too late to stop it. Instead they had walked into an ambush and nearly been killed. A lot of cops had died that night, and for nothing.

It happened in Bellefonte, a little town just outside the main campus of Penn State. A place that Clara had always associated with well-preserved Victorian houses, with parades and gazebos and quaint small-town charm. Astarte Arkeley had lived in one of the darker and creepier houses in Bellefonte, a place the local kids probably shunned as the house of a witch.

They wouldn't have been far off. Astarte had made her living as a medium, holding séances for people so desperate to talk to their dead loved ones that they were willing to believe it was possible. From what Laura had told Clara, maybe it was.

Standing in the front yard of the house, Clara felt the hair standing up on the back of her neck like it was trying to run away.

It was an abandoned place. A place where nobody should live. The grass out front was unmowed and studded with weeds. The paint on the front of the house had started to peel in the summer sun. A couple of windows on the side of the house had been broken by thrown rocks. Maybe junkies would crash inside, maybe bums would sleep in there on rotten floorboards, but no self-respecting adult would call it home.

Simon Arkeley's car was sitting in the driveway. This was the address Glauer had dug up. Simon's LKA, his last known address.

When Clara knocked on the door, she still had no idea what she was going to say or do if he actually answered. Fortunately she didn't have to figure it out. She knocked and knocked and pushed the doorbell button over and over, even though she couldn't hear any bells ringing inside. She went to a window overlooking the porch and peered through the rain-streaked glass, trying to see if anyone was inside. She saw no signs of life. Maybe Simon was out—maybe he had gone for a walk, or to the store, or who knew where. Maybe she should sit on one of the moldy rattan chairs on the porch and wait for him to come home. Or maybe she should just leave.

Then she heard a crash from inside. The sound of glass breaking. She had enough of a cop's instincts to reach for her weapon at that sound. Of course, there was no gun at her hip now. Fetlock had taken it from her.

She heard a whispered curse from inside, from just beyond the window, and then running footsteps, headed away from her. Whoever was inside clearly meant to escape out the back. If Glauer had been with her, he would already be back there, waiting to catch whoever it was. Of course, Glauer wasn't with her. He'd washed his hands of her.

She ran around the side of the house, keeping her head down below the level of the windows. There was a small garden in back with a sundial and a trellis for climbing roses. Right now all it held was a few strands of ivy, the leaves dry and dusty in the summer heat. It wasn't great cover, but it would do. Clara crouched behind the trellis and waited, watching the back door.

It opened with the merest creak, an inch at a time. Simon poked his head out and took a good look around. She remembered him—just barely—from Laura's trial. He had given testimony against her, though he kept telling the judge over and over that Laura had saved him, that she had saved his life. The judge had been unimpressed.

Simon stepped out through the door and headed down through the garden, walking in the stiff-legged exaggerated way of somebody who doesn't know how to move silently but really, really wants to try. The garden ended in a high fence of wooden pickets that separated Astarte's lot from the garden of the house on the other side. It wasn't the kind of fence that was easily climbed, and Simon didn't look like the kind of kid who had enjoyed gym class in school. Clara watched him grunt and try to heave himself over it for a while before she finally took pity on him.

"Freeze," she said, and stepped out from behind the trellis.

He took one long, confused look at her, and ran back into the house. The door flapped all the way open and then started swinging back behind him. Clara rushed forward and hauled it open, then ran inside.

Which was pretty stupid, of course. She would tell herself that later.

Simon was waiting for her inside, just to one side of the door. He was holding an old cast-iron skillet over his head, gripping its handle with both hands. He brought it down on her head as she came rushing in. He could have cracked her skull open, but he wasn't committed to actually killing her. So instead he hit her just hard enough to make everything go white with pain.

She dropped to one knee on the floor of the house's kitchen, staring very intently at the grimy linoleum tile that covered the floor. She forced herself to breathe, to deal with the pain. She couldn't hear much over her own heartbeat, but she got a sense that he was running away from her again.

Get up, she told herself.

This was exactly what Glauer had been talking about. A normal person, a sane person, would stay down. Or flee.

Get up. You aren't really hurt. It's just pain, and pain is all in your head.

That nearly made her laugh. Of course it was all in her head—that was where he'd hit her. Giddiness, of course, was one of the symptoms of a nasty concussion.

Stand up.

She managed to get both feet under her. The whole world swayed while she stood perfectly, totally still. Or maybe it was the other way around.

Move! Get after him!

She realized then it wasn't her own voice she heard in her head, telling her to do things. It was Laura's voice. She wondered if Laura had heard Arkeley barking at her like that, even after Arkeley was dead.

It would have been hard to disobey that voice. She didn't even try. She rushed after the kid, heading deeper into the house. The kitchen door opened into a short hallway under the main stairs, and beyond that lay the front parlor. She saw a lot of broken furniture. Shards of glass littered the floor. She thought about the crash she'd heard, back when she was still thinking she could just knock on the door and he would answer. He must have gone to the window to see who it was, then tripped on the pieces of a broken armchair or something.

The place was trashed. Did he really live here? It looked like there'd been a hell of a fight here at some point.

Then she noticed that the broken furniture was covered in dust. The fight had been a long time ago.

"Fucking just go away!" Simon shouted at her from overhead. She looked up at the stairs leading to the second floor. A trail of blood ran down from the top, staining the stair runner half the way down. She rushed forward to check it out, to see if he had wounded himself somehow. Maybe he was suicidal. But no, the blood was old. Really old, dried and crusted and left to sit for weeks, maybe far longer.

She was a forensic expert—determining that only took a second.

It was long enough. He came at her again with his frying pan, perhaps intending to finish the job he'd started. The heavy black pan swung through the air, aimed right at her face.

Clara grabbed for it. Had she been a split second slower or faster, it might have smashed every bone in her hand. Instead she caught it just right, grabbing one greasy edge of the pan in such a way that she only needed to twist it around and he was forced to let go of its handle. She swung it behind her and let it clatter like a thunderbolt on the floor.

He stared at her like he couldn't understand what she'd just done. Like she'd mastered some bizarre martial art he'd never heard of. Pan fu or something.

She didn't waste time thanking God for making her so lucky. She just slugged him in the jaw until he fell over, then kicked him a few times when he was down for good measure.

25.

Well, that had gotten things off on a bad foot, she decided.

She had really only intended to *talk* to Simon. Not beat the crap out of him. She had no idea how to properly subdue an antagonistic subject, and it showed. That course hadn't been required at the academy, not for forensic specialists—just basic self-defense. Clara had been in a few fights in high school, and she'd had to scrap a little when she'd been held hostage during the prison riot. But she had never in her life struck someone with malice before.

Yet when Simon went down, it had felt proper—right—to kick him. He had made himself her enemy, and that was how you treated enemies.

When had she started thinking that way? The very idea terrified her, now that she'd calmed down. She thought about what Glauer had said. Then she pushed that thought away, because she had more important things to do just then than psychoanalyze herself.

Simon never lost consciousness. In the movies one good tap to the back of the skull usually knocked out the bad guys. But human heads were actually built to resist just that kind of impact—it was why the skull was so thick, and why there were so many muscles in the neck. He did, however, stop fighting back as she hauled him back into the kitchen and then heaved him into a chair. He was, luckily, a skinny little runt or she would never have had the strength to do that.

Rummaging in the kitchen drawers, she found a roll of duct tape and used that to secure him to the chair. It was dark in the kitchen—the power was out, probably turned off years ago—so she dug up some candles, too, and lit them so he could see who she was.

In the silent refrigerator she found a warm bottle of soda. It wasn't even diet, she saw with disgust. She poured herself a glass and sat down in a chair across from him and waited for him to ask the obvious questions.

"Who are you?" he asked, his head rolling back and forth, just a little. He was going to have a nasty bruise on his jaw. It looked like his eyes were tracking, though.

"Clara Hsu," she said. "Laura Caxton's girlfriend."

"S-s-seriously?" Then he laughed. "Actually, yeah. Never

mind. You're just as big a bitch as she is. I believe you. Did she send you to get me to marry that little girl?"

Clara very much wanted to know what the hell he was talking about, but she didn't want to give away how little she knew. "No," she said. "Laura and I lost contact a while ago. I actually came to ask if you knew how to get her a message. I definitely didn't mean for this to happen."

"I get it," he said, and laughed again. A little more bitterly this time.

"Get what?" Clara asked.

"This is a setup. A trap. You work for the Feds, like my dad did. What was that asshole's name? Forelock?"

"Marshal Fetlock," she said. "But no. I don't work for him. Not anymore."

"Sure, whatever. You think I can take you to—I mean, you think I have some idea of where Caxton is. Which, for the record, I don't. I know you want to arrest her again. And honestly? I would love to mess up her year. But she did save my life, you know. Like, a couple of times."

"She saved mine more," Clara told him. "Simon, you can verify it if you want. I've been fired. I don't work for Fetlock, or any other cop."

"So maybe if you hand them Caxton on a silver platter, you get your job back," he said. Damn it, the kid was smart. Way too smart for this. He raised his head until it was almost fully upright and stared at her with pain-dulled eyes. "I want to see my lawyer, right now. I won't say another word until I see my lawyer."

Clara's hands squeezed into fists. She had the urge—the very strong urge—to hit him again. To do whatever it took to make him talk.

Laura had given in to that urge once. She had tortured a sociopath named Dylan Carboy until he gave up what she wanted to know. And she had gone to jail for that.

Fighting every natural instinct she had, Clara forced herself to calm down. She straightened out her hands and wiped her sweaty palms on the legs of her jeans. "I'm not a cop," she said again. "Let me tell you something, Simon. I'm taking a huge risk here. I broke into your house. You hit me—with intent to kill—and I fought back. Now I've subdued you. I really don't know which of us is in more trouble. We would probably both go to jail if we pressed charges on each other. Okay?"

"Okay, what?"

She gritted her teeth. "I just implicated myself in a crime. Right? A cop wouldn't do that."

"Sure."

She stood up from her chair and poured herself some more soda. "You want some of this?"

"I doubt you're the kind who would drug me for information," he granted her, "but I think I'll pass just in case."

"What the fuck ever." She drank in silence for a while. The soda was cloying and it made her teeth hurt. She felt it coating her tongue. Her head was really starting to ache from where he'd hit her with the frying pan. In a very short while she was going to have to lie down. Or maybe check herself into an emergency room, if she had a concussion. It was notoriously hard to tell, especially when you were diagnosing yourself. For the moment, though, adrenaline kept her going.

"You seriously live here?" she asked.

"I can't afford anything else. I inherited this place from my mom."

"It's a hole," Clara told him.

"Is this where you break down my resistance by insulting me?"

"Seriously, whatever—but all the furniture's busted up, there's no power, and there's a huge bloodstain on the stairs." She saw him wince when she said that. "What?"

"It's . . . my mom's blood. From when she died."

Clara felt her eyes protrude from their sockets in shock. "No way. No fucking way. Dude! From two years ago? Doesn't that freak you out?"

Simon lowered his head to his chest. "Every single time I see it. But when I try to clean it up I just start crying again."

"Seriously?"

He sniffed, hard. In the candlelight it had been hard to tell, but she saw now that tears had rolled down his cheeks and splashed on his shirt. "It's been . . . tough," he said. "My whole . . . family. Just—just all at once. I was seeing a shrink for a long time, but I couldn't afford to keep going. I can't really afford anything anymore."

"Oh my God. You poor kid," Clara said. "Don't you have a job?"

"No. I'm living off of my credit cards. There was some life insurance, I mean, my parents had some insurance, but most of the settlement is gone."

And then—he just cried. For a long time he said nothing, no matter what she said or did. He just sat there, crying, completely shut down. It was like he'd turned into an infant and had lost the power of speech altogether.

Crap, she thought. Glauer had definitely been right, hadn't he? And Fetlock, too. She'd become just like Laura. Instantly floodgates of compassion opened up in her again, and she could barely control the force of her sympathy. She'd hurt this kid—really hurt him. The guilt and horror threatened to overwhelm her. "Jeez. I kind of want to give you a hug right now."

"If you come over here I'll start screaming."

Clara knew he was telling the truth. "Okay. I'll stay over here. But really, I feel for you. I do. I know what it's like to lose somebody you care about."

"You mean Caxton? Nobody killed *her.*"

"No. They just dragged her away to jail. And then she broke out and I haven't seen or heard from her since. Maybe it's not the same. But it really hurts."

"You really got fired?" he asked, sniffling.

"Yeah. Just yesterday. It sucks."

He nodded. "I was working, for a while, as a medical lab assistant. Just, you know. Washing out beakers and test tubes. Sweeping up. But every time—every time I opened the lab fridge and saw the blood samples, I would have to go and get drunk. And it was a lab that handled a lot of blood samples. So they fired me, too."

"It feels like the worst kind of rejection," Clara told him. "Like you failed at being a human being, you know?"

"I do," he said.

There were tears on her own cheeks then.

"I'm so, so sorry about hitting you. I just didn't know what else to do. I need to see Laura so badly," she said, not caring if it was the right thing to say or not. "I'm—I'm not going to hug you. Not if you don't want me to. But I want to come over there and cut you out of that duct tape. Is that okay?"

"Sure," he said. "And maybe—maybe we'll talk about the hug."

[1780]

"I've done it," Easling said, his breath coming in fast spurts as his fat body heaved in guilt. Blood stained his hands and whiskey stank in the air between them. "Justinia, I've done it, I've . . . I've killed her, it was easy, just like you said it would be, simplicity itself, easier than I thought, easier than—than—my God, I've wanted this so long, I've dreamed of it! And now it's done, it's done and I—I don't feel guilt. Not a bit of it, I refuse to—to feel any—"

With one white finger across his lips she hushed him. He'd done well. The knife that had butchered that shrew of a wife lay forgotten behind him in the doorway. She could see the blood glowing on it as if it had caught fire. How badly she wanted that blood . . . but Easling had not yet seen her true form. He'd never watched her lap up the spilt blood of a victim. Seeing that now might turn him from the path she'd laid out so carefully.

One did not give up the game until all the betting was done, until the last card had been played. One more trump remained.

In silence she held his eyes. When he looked at her he saw only the beautiful redhead she'd created for him, with two good eyes in her comely head. It didn't matter. The curse could be passed on regardless.

He calmed as she stared into his soul. His body quieted and his breathing became regular and gentle. He was as a man asleep and dreaming, and she let him have a moment of peace, of forgetfulness.

I will never leave ye, *she told him without words. She let the thought slip through his head like smoke through the chimney of a lantern, leaving nothing but soot behind.* I will protect ye from all who design against ye. I will teach ye so much. In return I ask only a little. And to seal our compact, I give ye this gift.

When the curse entered him he sighed like a man relieved of a great sickness. When Vincombe had given it to her, she had felt almost nothing at all, but for Easling it was a kind of grace and a sexual thrill at the same time. His own blood rushed to his cheeks and his forehead, and she had to fight herself not to take him then, not to slaughter him and drink deep.

No. Not now. Not when there was so much more to be gained.

Now, *she went on.* Now, ye must do a little something for me. Not so very much. It won't hurt. I promise.

His chin bobbed up and down as he assented. Then he turned away from her, breaking her gaze. She fell back across the bed in utter exhaustion. It had drained her to pass on the curse. But it was done. She let the orison go, let her body take on its true shape. It was alright. He wasn't looking at her—and when he did again, when he rose and looked upon her next, the orison wouldn't have worked on him anymore, anyway.

He rose to his feet and staggered to the doorway. He was so drunk he put up no resistance at all. Grunting as he stooped, he took up the knife again. The same one he'd used to kill his wife. He did not hesitate or flinch as he drove its point deep into the long artery in his thigh. He waggled the blade back and forth for a while, then pulled it free and let it clatter once more to the floor.

Outside in the street the life of Manchester went on. Wagons rumbled past over boards laid down across potholes. A dog growled at rats in the alley, while newspaper boys shouted out teasing hints of the great events of the day. In recent years the people of the city had grown complacent, forgetful of the monsters in their midst. Justinia had lacked the energy to keep them properly afraid.

It would not be very much longer until they remembered, and cowered as they should. Until she had her new knight in pale armor at her side, to help her, to bring to her the blood she required.

Easling collapsed in the doorway, his back against its jamb. He made low sobbing sounds she did not attempt to understand. His blood flowed out in a great pool across the wooden floor.

Eventually he closed his eyes, and she dared to slither off the bed. To crawl across the floor like a snake, with her tongue flicking at his spilled life. She had to get it all up while it was still warm.

26.

Clara was waiting in the driveway when Glauer pulled up to the Arkeley house.

He got out of his car and just stood there, as if waiting for her to explain why she'd chosen this path—and why she'd called him, why she'd forced him to come along on this crazy ride with her. He'd given her a chance to walk away. She had refused it, and now they were both committed.

There'd never been any question he would help her. He was still Glauer, after all, and he fought vampires just like Clara. Just like Caxton.

Clara had been very worried, however, that he would judge her. Condemn her for making the wrong choice and putting both their lives in danger. Not that he would ever say anything—but he had other, subtler ways to show disapproval. She had been dreading the moment when he sighed, for instance. Or when he looked at her the same way her father had looked at her when she came out to him. All it would take would be for Glauer to frown at her once and she would shrivel in embarrassment, in guilt.

He didn't sigh. He didn't give her a look of disappointment. He didn't even frown. And that was good enough. He'd given her a choice, and she'd taken it, and that was as far as he was going to go, emotionally.

She nearly wept in gratitude.

"What are you doing out here in this heat, waiting for me?" he asked. It sounded more like concern than a judgment.

"I wanted to make sure you could find the place okay. And the doorbell doesn't work," she explained.

"I don't think I'll ever forget how to get to this place," Glauer told her. He took a long look one way up the street, then the other, as if he was worried he'd been followed. It was unlikely. He was driving his own personal car and was wearing his off-duty clothes, including a baseball cap pulled down low over a huge pair of mirrored sunglasses. He still looked like a cop, of course—no disguise was going to cover up his broad shoulders or his bristly mustache. But at least no one would be able to identify him by sight. Clara knew he hadn't needed to be warned to leave his phone at home, or to avoid police attention on the way over.

When he'd satisfied himself he was unobserved, he looked up at the house for the first time. She couldn't see his eyes behind his sunglasses, so she couldn't be sure what he was feeling. He'd told her once before that the night of Astarte Arkeley's death was the night he'd realized Laura wasn't human anymore. That she'd become a kind of monster herself. "Though," he'd said at the time, "I was pretty damned glad *this* monster was on our side."

Now the house was like a shrine to that night, and that death. Clara almost didn't want to force him to go inside and relive those memories.

Almost. But this was too important to ruin by worrying too much about one man's feelings.

"You got what I asked for?" Clara asked.

"Basically. Let's get out of the street," he said, and took her arm and steered her toward the house's broad porch. Inside she had some candles burning in the parlor. In the three days it had taken to contact Glauer by mail—the only safe way, since Fetlock had no power over the post office—she had done a pretty good job of cleaning the place up, if she said so herself. The broken furniture was cleared away, replaced with a card table and folding chairs she'd found in the basement. She'd tried to scrub the blood stain off the stairs, but Simon made little moaning sounds every time she started filling up buckets or pulling on rubber gloves. So instead she had covered over the stairs with old bed linens. The two of them never went upstairs anyway. That was where Jameson Arkeley had murdered his own wife, and the very thought of going up there made Simon turn pale and look like he was going to pass out. It just gave Clara the creeps.

In the three days she'd spent with him, she had grown to realize just how profoundly damaged Simon was. He could seem perfectly normal for hours at a time. When he was out of the house the illusion was almost perfect. Yet eventually, always, something would trigger an attack of his nerves, and he would break down in a puddle of tears and snot on an instant's notice. He would start by trembling violently and repeatedly insisting that no, he was okay, that this time he would be alright. That he could fight his way through the shakes. So far he'd been wrong every time.

Then there were the times he just shut down. Clara would

be having a perfectly normal conversation with him and he just wouldn't answer a question. Or she would think he'd finished what he meant to say, because he stopped talking. But in fact he was just off in his own little world. Clara found that much harder to deal with than the melodramatic breakdowns, because she could just about imagine what that other world was like. He was replaying in his head the last time he saw his father. The thing his father had become, anyway, looming over him with a mouthful of fangs, speaking to him in that grunting, slavering voice that vampires had. Telling him he had a choice to make. To become a vampire himself, or die there and then. The same choice his father had given his mother just before he killed her.

And then Laura had come in blasting away, and Simon's father went away, too.

Clara shivered just thinking about it. "Do me a favor," she said. "Don't mention the word *blood*. *Vampire* is okay, and *teeth*. But not *fangs*. And definitely don't talk to him about what happened upstairs."

Glauer took off his sunglasses and stared at her. "Seriously?" he asked. "This is—this is what you're doing now?"

"Just trust me. I've made real progress on the case."

"There is no case. You don't work cases anymore."

"Then just humor me," she said, her eyes flashing.

He held up both hands for peace. She went in the other room and brought Simon out to meet him. The two men didn't make eye contact as they shook hands, but they seemed civil enough. Clara sat them down around the card table.

"Now. Glauer. I asked if you could bring me some files. Did you get a chance to snag them before you came here?"

"Not exactly," he said. Then he shut up, withdrawing, the way Simon did sometimes. Yet Clara knew this was for a very different reason. She hadn't just asked him to pick up a few pieces of paper for her. She'd asked him to steal documents pertaining to an open investigation. To remove them from their proper place and give them to someone who no longer worked in law enforcement.

That was a lot for a solid cop like Glauer to handle.

"Just . . . just tell me what you can give me," she said.

"I can give you the gist of things. That's all."

Clara nodded, trying to look patient. Like he could have all the time in the world to go on. Even though if he didn't get to the point soon, she was going to rake her fingernails across his face in frustration.

"Okay. So you asked about lab results on the bodies—the partial bodies—of the half-deads we fought in Bridgeville. I imagine you won't be surprised when I tell you all the tests came back inconclusive. No fingerprints, no facial recognition, of course. And no bl— That is, no hemolytic fluid to type or sample."

That was standard for half-dead investigations, Clara knew. They weren't like living people. They were decaying corpses given brief animation by the power of the vampire who slew them. There just wasn't that much left of them. "Okay, but what about hair and fiber analysis? Shoe tread patterns, eyewear, dental records, distinguishing scars, features, piercings, tattoos?" Clara had, herself, written most of the book on how to identify walking corpses.

Unfortunately, nobody else ever bothered to read it. Vampires were extinct, after all—that was the official party line. "They did some fiber matching on the hoodie the driver wore, and the jeans that one of the guys we put down in the diner parking lot had on. They got matches but nothing interesting. Cheap clothes you could buy at any discount store. In fact—the sweatshirt and the jeans came from the same store. Which suggests to me that maybe the clothes were bought after the subjects were killed."

Clara put her hand over her mouth. "Now, there's a thought," she said. "But it makes perfect sense. Malvern's smart enough to know what we can do with a couple of fibers. She'd know better than to let us find where she's getting her minions."

"Why's she being so secretive?" Simon asked. "So now we know she has dead people to play with. It's not like we didn't know she's a killer."

"If we could find out where she gets her victims, we could lay a trap for her," Clara explained. "Or at least track her movements. But she's still one step ahead of us. She gets her half-deads by preying on people who are off the grid, people who—"

"Migrant workers," Simon said.

Clara was surprised. "Yeah," she said. "Yeah—that was what she did the last time she was at large. She preyed on people who didn't have family here, people who could disappear and not leave much of a trace. It took us far too long to figure it out." She raised one eyebrow. "You look like you know something. Tell me."

"Nothing concrete. But I know somebody you might want to meet. Somebody who keeps track of all the people society pretends don't exist."

[1782]

Only a few steps out of their door, Justinia stumbled and nearly fell on her face. She threw out her arms and grabbed the stone wall to her side. Pressing her body against it, she clung on for dear life. Her legs would barely hold her up.

Ahead of her in the alley Easling looked back in terror.

How she'd grown to hate his smooth and unblemished face.

"I am perfectly well, thank ye," she said. "We must feed. Please— please lead the way, sir."

"You don't look very well," Easling said. The expression of concern and compassion in his red eyes made her want to rake at them with her claws. He'd been a fat and unappealing specimen in life. The changes of death—the colorless skin, the hairlessness, the way his new teeth

protruded from his lips—made him too ugly to look upon. She would gladly have destroyed this thing, her miscreation. If she did not need him so very much.

Looking down at her own hands, she saw that she had passed a certain Rubicon. She no longer resembled a withered crone. Her skin was no longer just thin and pockmarked. It was rotting, visibly decaying. She had come to the look of a corpse.

She had known this would happen. She'd watched it happen to Vincombe. Seen all the others that came before him, and knew it was her fate.

Rage filled her and gave her strength. She released the wall and staggered forward under her own power. She would not succumb, not yet. Blood would restore her. Enough blood and she would be whole and hale again. Enough blood . . .

Was there enough blood in the world to hold back the ravages of time?

"We must feed," she said.

"Return to your coffin. Rest. I'll bring you tasty morsels. I'll bring you a troupe of dancers, their vitality glowing within them," Easling promised. "I'll bring you anything you ask. Please. My love."

With her one shriveled eye she studied him as an entomologist might study a pinned beetle. What cruel mother had warped him so? Or had it simply been that vituperative wife of his? Some woman had twisted him, that was clear. When she'd been beautiful he'd desired to punish her, to hurl abuse upon her illusionary form. Now he saw what she really was, he worshipped at her feet.

"I can still hunt," she insisted. "The time has not yet come when I cannot kill for my own sustenance." She pushed past him into the lane. Heaven help the first man I meet, she thought.

Heaven help me, if he's too strong to take.

It was something like a prayer. Something too much. She shoved the pitiful mewling down with fists of anger and stalked forward, smelling for blood, her eye dancing across the cobbles, looking for the glow of it. That cheery red, that burned like welcome coals on a winter's night. When she found her victim it was little more than a boy, some apprentice cobbler working late in his shop. She barely remembered spying him, barely recalled how she'd opened the locked door—had Easling helped her? She had been too far gone to push her companion away. Now here her prey was, this human wretch. He screamed. Sometimes they screamed.

Sometimes they feared death.

Life is just a game, she'd thought. Life is a hand of cards. You cannot choose which cards you are dealt, only how they are played. It had seemed so fair back then. When Vincombe had been hunting her. When she had only a mortal life to lose.

For the first time in her entire existence, Justinia Malvern felt sorry for one of her victims. She eased the boy's pain, snapping his neck while she supped at his arteries. He had been so frightened. So horrified that the world worked this way.

I do not fear death, *she thought.* I who am death itself. I do not fear death. *She thought it over and over again, a meditation, a rosary of her innermost belief.* I do not fear death. I do not fear death. I do not fear death.

But oh! I am so frightened now, for I grow old. . . .

27.

Patience Polder screamed in the night, and a shiver ran down Caxton's neck. She bolted upright in her chair and grabbed for her pistols.

Behind her, inside the house, Caxton heard Urie Polder stumbling around and then the yellow flicker of a kerosene lamp burst through the window behind her, destroying her night vision. Upstairs Patience had stopped screaming, but Caxton still wasn't sure what to do. If there was something inside the house, already preying on the girl, then Caxton's move was to rush inside, guns blazing. But it could be a diversion, meant to cover a frontal assault on the house. If she went inside she could be trapped in there, besieged by an army of half-deads, unable to escape if—

"Come in here, trooper, and quick," Urie Polder called.

Caxton grunted in frustration, but she pushed open the screen door and ran up the stairs of the house. She found both Polders in Patience's room. The father, shirtless and wild-eyed, knelt by his daughter's bed, holding the lantern high. Patience was white as a sheet, sitting upright in bed and clutching the thick fabric of her nightgown as if she desperately wanted something to hold on to.

"Tell me," Caxton said. She had a pistol in either hand. The right hand covered the doorway and the stairs beyond, while the left, weaker hand kept guard over the window.

"I woke to see a face in my window," Patience explained. She knew better than to waste time talking about how scared she'd been. "A masked face. I thought they'd come for me. Yet when I screamed it disappeared."

"Coulda just been some manner of dream, ahum," Urie Polder said, stroking his daughter's hair with his wooden fingers.

"Could have, sure," Caxton said. She kept her eyes on the window. It was wide open, and the darkness outside was absolute—Justinia Malvern herself could be standing out there and it would be impossible to see her in the glare of the lantern. "Urie, close and lock that window. It won't keep them out for long, but it'll give us some warning. Patience, set up some kind of protective barrier. A ward or something. We can't afford to lose you."

The Polders knew better than to expect anything like empathy or tact from their houseguest. They did as they were told, staying close to each other for comfort. Caxton took a quick look down the stairs, then rushed down to the porch and checked her stash of guns. Nothing had been disturbed.

A masked face, she thought. Masked. A half-dead might wear a mask to hide its disfigurement. She'd never heard of one doing so before, though. They *liked* scaring people. Liked creeping everyone out with their horrible visages. Maybe this one didn't want to let on that it was a vampire's minion. Maybe it had been sent to pass a message to Patience, and had believed the mask would keep her from screaming. Well. If that was the case it had failed in its mission.

Maybe it was just supposed to make sure Caxton would stick close to the house.

Caxton jumped over the railing of the porch and into a thicket of bushes at the side of the house. She ducked low for cover, then moved quickly around to the back, to the ground just below Patience's window. She couldn't see any tracks there, but she didn't expect to—it was far too dark to make out footprints in the grass. She used the toe of her boot to feel around in the soil for the holes a ladder would have left, but found nothing.

Damn. She did not want this bastard to just get away, to flee into the night leaving no clues behind. She wanted to chase it, wanted to hunt it through the trees atop the ridge. Wanted to track it down and then pull off its fingers until it told her what she wanted to know.

But Malvern would know that, of course. She might have set this all up as a trap. She might have a hundred half-deads hiding in the trees, just waiting for Caxton to step away from the light and security of the house.

Caxton shook her head to clear it. She couldn't lose her cool like this. Couldn't start imagining potential conspiracies, jumping at every shadow. There were just too many possibilities.

She crouched low, her guns pointed at the ground. She closed her eyes and listened. Strained every fiber of her being into just hearing what was around her.

The crickets were going crazy, like they did every night in the summer. Their chirping chorus swelled and broke and swelled again like an ocean of sound. Somewhere she heard an owl hooting in the woods. Down in the Hollow someone was listening to a transistor radio.

Not so far off, much closer in fact, a twig snapped. As if some-one had stepped on it.

She spun around in that direction, tempted to open fire with a wild salvo of shots just in case she hit something. But the chances of that were too low. Keeping her head down, she duckwalked toward the sound, stretching her eyelids wide to try to soak up as much starlight as she could. The noise had come from a stand of trees just on the other side of Urie Polder's vegetable garden. As she passed by the rows of cucumbers and summer squash, she saw broken stalks and a tomato that had been pulped when somebody stepped on it.

Pouring on speed, she headed into the trees, in the direction the sound had first come from. She pushed her back up against a tree trunk and listened again, forced herself to stop breathing and just listen.

She was certain she heard muffled footfalls from deeper in the trees. But nothing else. No sadistic tittering, no noise of an army of half-deads lying in wait.

She hurried onward, following the footfalls as best she could. But by the time she emerged into a clearing in the trees, a quarter mile from the house, she already knew she'd lost her quarry. It just took too long when she had to stop every hundred yards or so and listen. The half-dead she was chasing was gone, already past the perimeter of teleplasm, past the protective circle of bird skulls she'd planted. She knew better than to follow it further, out into a part of the ridge she hadn't properly fenced off.

Instead she looped back, looking for any sign of its pas-sage. She found it quickly enough. One of the bird skulls had been smashed to bone splinters, broken beyond recognition. It must have been done quickly and by someone who knew what they were doing—it had been destroyed before it could get off any kind of signal. It should have started shrieking at the first touch.

Which meant that Malvern already knew about her first line of defense—and knew how to bypass it.

"Crap," she said to the darkness.

She did not receive a reply.

28.

Clara squinted through the windshield. "Seriously? There's somebody still doing business back here?"

Simon had brought them to a ghost mall in Chester County, a sprawl of concrete and asphalt and weeds. Once it had been a strip mall like any other in Pennsylvania, but the recession had hit the place hard. The storefronts were all dark, their once brightly painted signs faded by sun and rain until it was hard to tell what they had sold in their heyday. It looked like there had been a vitamin store, and maybe a Radio Shack, once. Now through the plate-glass windows Clara could see empty modular shelving and piles of debris where acoustic tiles had rotted away from the ceilings and fallen in heaps on the dusty floors.

Glauer pulled into the parking lot without comment. It was hard to tell where the painted lines of the lot had once been, but it didn't really matter. He pulled up in front of a line of stores and killed the engines.

"It's in the back. Kind of hard to find—there's an old grocery store that hides it from view from the street," Simon said, pushing open his door.

Clara traded a suspicious glance with Glauer, but then she shrugged and climbed out into the summer heat. "You should probably stay here," she said. "You look too much like a cop to fool anybody."

He didn't take offense at the comment. "Fine. Be careful."

"Sure," she said.

Simon was already marching across the parking lot, headed around a corner toward a pile of twisted and spray-painted shopping carts. She walked past the front of the abandoned grocery store, its plate-glass windows smeared with paint so no one could see inside. Just past the padlocked doors she saw the one store that was still open in the forgotten mall, though it looked only marginally more lively than the ghosts around it.

CUATROS VIENTOS, the sign over the door said. The front windows were covered in brown kraft paper, on which someone had scrawled various advertisements in Spanish: ¡*Artículos religiosos!* ¡*Consejos Espirituales!* ¡*Maldiciones Eliminado!*

Simon pulled open the door and a little bell rang. Clara followed him in to the smell of incense burning and the light of several dozen candles that shed more illumination than the sputtering fluorescents overhead.

The inside of the botanica looked surprisingly like any dollar store Clara had ever been inside. The shelves were dusty and cramped, with many items just thrown in big bins for shoppers to paw through. There were a few signs this wasn't a normal store, though. One wall was covered by a hanging Navajo blanket, while a glass-fronted display case protected glass bottles full of dried chicken feet and chopped-up pieces of cactus floating in alcohol and what Clara was relatively certain were not, in fact, authentic shrunken heads. Though she couldn't be sure.

"Mr. Simon, back so soon?" the proprietor asked. She was a middle-aged Hispanic woman with long and frizzy magenta hair. She wore dozens of crystals around her neck on silver chains, and her hands were covered in turquoise rings. Her eyes were sharp as razors as she looked Clara up and down. "Who's your friend?"

"This is Clara," Simon said. "She's cool."

"Is she, now?" the proprietress asked. She stared at Clara's shoes for a long time before waving long fingernails in the air and then sweeping back behind her counter in a flourish of skirts.

"This is Nerea," Simon said, introducing her to Clara. "She helped me out when I needed some stuff recently. She's good people."

"Pleased to meet you," Clara said.

"You're a cop," Nerea said, with a nod. "I see. Mr. Simon, I did not expect you to betray me. Not the son of your mother. But the world is full of evil combinations. Is this a raid? I only ask because I'd like to get my cigarettes before you take me to the station, and I don't want you thinking I'm reaching for a gun or something."

Clara's mouth fell open. "No—no, it's not—I mean, I'm not—" How could the woman have known? How could anybody know? She'd spent so much of her life trying to convince her fellow police that she *was* a real cop, that they should take her seriously. Now that she wasn't a cop anymore, everyone in the world seemed to see it right away.

"She *was* a cop," Simon admitted, wringing his hands together. "But not anymore. I mean, she was fired."

"There are two occupations one can never give up, not in a true sense," Nerea said, her mouth pursing as if she had just bitten into a ripe lemon. "The priesthood, and *la policía*. Why are you here, cop?"

Clara looked to Simon, but he was staring at the floor. She turned back to Nerea and tried to think of what to say.

Something about this woman made her think of Vesta Polder. The witch who had helped Laura for a while, before the vampires got to her. Maybe it was all the rings on her fingers. Finally she just lifted her hands in surrender. "You must be psychic, right? Or something. So why don't you tell me why I'm here?"

Nerea's eyes narrowed. Then she nodded curtly and drummed her fingernails on the top of the glass display case. "Clever. Alright. Give me a moment." She closed her eyes and started muttering something that might have been a chant. Then she reached for one of her candles and, without opening her eyes, blew it out. The last trailing ribbon of smoke from the extinguished wick broke in two and wreathed around her face.

Then she opened her eyes again and laughed. It was not a mirthful or particularly warm laugh. If Clara had been feeling less generous she might have described it as a cackle.

"Vampires. Vampires! They are extinct, the television says. But you have their stink all over you. Vampires . . . and you have lost a loved one. Someone who is still alive, though she might as well be dead. Oh. You're gay."

"I . . . am. Does that change things?"

Nerea shrugged. "In the town where I come from, in Guatemala, we used to say that homosexuals were closer to the old gods, because they were neither man nor woman, and so were less tied to the ways of this earth." She shrugged again. "Of course, that was only gay men, and specifically transvestites."

"Most cross-dressers are actually straight," Clara said.

"Yes, dear, I know," Nerea told her, batting a pair of amazing false eyelashes. They had to be an inch and a half long. "But in my town we only had one, and he was *flaming*."

Clara opened her mouth to protest again, but then a flash of intuition told her to take a good look at Nerea's neck. She was surprised she'd missed the prominent Adam's apple before.

Ah, she thought.

"Now. I can see you're not here to cause me harm. Good. You want to find this lost person. This person who is not actually dead, though in many ways—"

Clara interrupted before Nerea could say anything more about Laura. "Actually," she said, trying to remember the correct pronunciation of the word Simon had taught her, "I wanted to ask about *los desaparecidos*."

Nerea's face went pale under all her makeup. She said something Clara couldn't catch, a curse or maybe a quick prayer in Spanish. Then she went to the wall and carefully took down the Navajo blanket.

"You really wish to know? Most people would like to pretend this isn't happening," Nerea said, glancing back over her shoulder at Clara.

"I need to know," Clara said. Malvern was using the migrant worker population to swell the ranks of her army. If Nerea knew anything about that, if she had any way of tracing the victims, Clara had to hear it. Any lead was worth investigating now.

Behind the blanket, the entire wall was covered in sheets of paper stapled to the drywall. Each was a cheap photocopy of a "missing" poster, though none of them looked official. They were handwritten and full of pleas for help and desperate plaints of love and loss. Each had a black-and-white picture of a young man or woman, many of them smiling. The photocopying process had turned their eyes into solid pools of black.

There were hundreds of them.

[1783]

"Try to sit up. Just a little more," Easling said. "That's it. You're doing fine."

"Confound ye, man!" Justinia creaked. Her voice sounded like the tiny warblings of a plover. It hurt to move. It hurt to open her mouth.

"Just a little more. There isn't much. I don't want to waste it." He leaned forward over her and let stringy blood fall from his mouth onto her still-sharp teeth. With every drop she felt life stirring inside of her, felt new strength. But not enough.

"I'm ready for the rest," she told him when he drew back.

"That's all there is," he said, and his eyes were sympathetic. A vampire's red eyes should never look like that. She cursed him silently a thousand times. She needed him, she'd accepted that—she could not continue without his mercies. But couldn't he be a little crueler? She thought

of what she'd done to Vincombe. Nasty, perhaps—but it was what it took to be a killer. A hunter.

Her eye struggled to track him as he moved about their rooms. His hands moved around so much it was distracting. "They're after me, you understand. There's a hue and cry up for the vampire that's been spotted in the corn market—it's not easy. It's never been this difficult before to find victims. And they have so many guns. So many. Muskets everywhere you look, and soldiers marching . . . the troops are back, they've come back from America, and—"

"They won this latest war. Very good," Justinia rasped. Already the stolen strength of the blood was leaving her, consumed by her need. She settled back onto the silk lining of her coffin. It was so much easier not to move now. She'd been restless for years, but now—now she could sleep. She could sleep as much as she liked. "The Crown's men will never be defeated."

"Ah," Easling said.

It would have taken too much energy to demand why he looked so ill at ease, so she simply waited for him to explain.

"They—that is to say . . . they rather. Well. Let the end down."

None of it mattered, of course. History was a game for mortals. But she had to admit she was intrigued. "The colonies—"

"They've won their freedom. They, well . . . It's been coming for a while now, no real surprise, but the peace is signed and—and—no, Justinia, don't let it disturb you so! Don't struggle so much, my dear."

"America is free," she said. She was not as perturbed as she expected. "Imagine how much easier we could live there," she told him. "On the frontiers of that vast land. We could feast on red Indians and drink our fill of Bostonian blood." She cackled a little. The sound she made could not be properly described as laughter. "Yes," she said. "I see it so plain."

"Let's not make any grandiose plans just now," he told her.

Her eye shot open. "Damn ye, Easling. I need more blood. I must have it. Ye must bring me living victims. It should not be so hard. I gave ye the strength, the power! Use it, for the devil's sake, while ye still can!"

"Yes, of course, it's only—"

"Excuses! Whining, that's all I have from ye! No wonder your wife was so dissatisfied, man. Get me blood!"

"I've told you, it's really not safe just now, and dawn is only a few hours away at any rate, so—"

"Now! Blood! Bring me blood!"

She harried him until he went out again, pleased with her control over this pathetic creature. Soon, she knew, he would return, with the blood she needed—the blood—the blood—just thinking about it was enough to hypnotize her. To daze her senses. The blood—the blood—*it became a booming chant inside her mind.*

The blood. The blood.

She was so preoccupied she did not notice when he failed to return that night.

Or the next.

It would be many, many years before she learned how he'd been caught, pinned under a mob of bayonets, pierced in a hundred places by musket balls. Dragged into the marketplace and there, on a stake driven next to the pillory, set aflame. His screams were heard all over the city, amid the cheers of the people liberated from their local monster. It was enough to soothe the hurt, a little, of their national shame.

She could only hear her own thoughts. The need that echoed inside her skull, constantly and forever. Blood. Blood. More blood.

When the door of their rooms opened again it was not Easling who came for her, but living men.

29.

"They came here from Mexico, from Honduras, from Ecuador. Things in Ecuador are very bad right now," Nerea said. "All they wanted was to work. To make a little money. Then they vanished and left no sign behind of where they went."

They were very young, mostly, the people in the pictures.

Few of them could be over twenty-five. In the pictures they looked hopeful and energetic. Clara choked up a little when she realized that every one of them was dead.

Half-dead, anyway.

She was certain that these were the people Malvern had killed to sate her need for blood. These were the anonymous victims, the ones Fetlock had been unable to turn up over the last two years. Malvern needed the blood just to stay mobile. If she didn't have a victim every night, she would weaken and decay until she wouldn't be able to rise from her coffin, until she would be little more than a dried-up corpse with pointy teeth.

Clara studied the pictures and the names, one after another. So many that the posters had been tacked on top of each other, obscuring the ones beneath.

"I . . . I wasn't expecting there to be so many," she said. "How is it that I haven't heard any of these names? So many people just can't vanish into thin air without generating police reports, can they?"

Simon was staring at one of the pictures in particular. It showed a young woman with light-colored hair. She looked a little like Raleigh, Simon's sister. Who had followed her father into vampirism and death.

Clara grabbed his shoulder and rubbed it a little.

He looked away from the poster. "They come here for a season, at most, before moving on to follow the jobs. They live in shared no-lease apartments with no telephones. They don't have credit cards, or social security numbers, or driver's licenses. They're completely off the grid. Typically they work hard and they don't make enough money to get in trouble. What little money they do have gets sent back to Mexico or South America, to their families. All done by wire, perfectly anonymously."

Clara nodded. "Malvern could take as many of them as she wanted and we would never hear about it. Though—they *do* have families, after all. You'd think somebody would let us know this was going on."

"Are you kidding? People who live like this," Simon said, gesturing at the wall, "are more afraid of the police than they are of vampires. By far. If they do have family living here, contacting the police—even to report a disappearance—would get the entire family deported."

"But their families back home, south of the border—they can't just let their loved ones vanish without doing anything, can they? How could anybody live with that?"

"They don't just give up, no," Nerea said. "That's where this wall comes from." She lit a cigarette and blew smoke toward an open window at the back of the shop. None of it actually made it far enough to get outside. "They make up those posters and send them to every botanica and groceria and Latino-owned shop in the state. They call us all the time asking if we've heard anything. It breaks my little heart, I assure you, every single time. They always sound so hopeful, as if any day now their son or their wife or their nephew will check in and everything will be fine."

"Do—do any of them ever turn up again like that?"

"No," Nerea said, and blew smoke again.

"Malvern can't be responsible for all of these disappearances," Simon said. "A lot of migrants just disappear anyway. Either they never make it across the border—it's not easy, no matter what Rush Limbaugh thinks—or they get sick here but they're too afraid to go to the hospital. They know they'll get deported when they're asked for ID. It's a very dangerous life, even without vampires to add to the mix." He shrugged in defeat. "But . . . I'm guessing most of them are hers."

"Jesus. So many. So many in just two years."

"Two years? What are you talking about?" Nerea asked.

Clara frowned. "The vampire's only been active for two years now. If some of these disappeared before then, it couldn't have been Malvern that—"

"Honey," Nerea said, her face a carefully arranged mask of dispassion, "the oldest poster up there is three months ago. That's when this started."

Clara couldn't help herself. A nasty shiver went through her. She did a quick calculation in her head, based on the number of posters she saw. To fill the wall so fast Malvern must have been taking two or three victims *every night* for three months. And there would be others, others whose faces didn't make it onto the wall. Maybe a lot of others.

She had known that Malvern preyed on the migrant population. That was horrible enough. But this—this said something else. It said Malvern wasn't just drinking blood to sustain herself. It said she was drinking so much blood, raising so many half-deads, that she had to be preparing for something. Something apocalyptic.

"If these people were white, if they were citizens, this would be all over the TV," Simon said, trembling with anger. "If the police knew about this—"

"They would do everything in their power to track down Malvern and put an end to these disappearances," Clara insisted. "Trust me. Cops aren't as racist as the media make them look. Murder is murder, and we always take it seriously."

"Apparently not seriously enough," Nerea scoffed, "to come in here and ask me about what's going on."

"I'm here now, damn it," Clara insisted.

"And you're going to do something about this?" Nerea asked. "You're going to find this vampire you claim is killing so many people? No offense, my darling, but you're just a little slip of a girl. You're what, five foot six? Five foot five?"

"Five-five," Clara said, sneering. "It's not just me who's after the vampire, though. So shut up." She took a notepad and a pen out of her pocket and started jotting down the names of the *desaparecidos*.

"What do you think you're doing?" Nerea demanded, and started toward Clara to grab the notepad away from her.

"I need to figure out where these people were killed," Clara said. "Where they were last seen, where they lived—anything. Then I can plot all the locations on a map, and it'll give me a rough idea where Malvern is hiding."

"No. No. Absolutely no," Nerea insisted. "It's bad enough I let a police person even see this wall. The families would never forgive me if I let you have their names. Don't you understand?"

"I promise—I swear!—I have no interest in deporting anybody! I'm not even in Immigration and Naturalization. I mean, I never was. I was a forensic specialist!"

"Forget it! *La Migra* would get the names, one way or another. That's what they do—they find you trying to put your children in school, or trying to get vaccinations for your baby. And then your whole family is on a boat back to your home country. And the death squads, and the fifty percent unemployment, and the poverty and the sickness you fled. You put that pad away, *puta,* or I will summon up some big nastiness and drive you right out of this shop. I'll put a ghost on your trail you'll never shake off."

There was a light in Nerea's eyes that made Clara feel queasy inside. She'd seen its like in the eyes of Vesta Polder and Vesta's daughter, Patience, and she got the definite impression that Nerea could do exactly what she threatened.

"Okay," Clara said, softly, and put the pad and the pen away. "I'm sorry. I'm . . . sorry. I only want to help."

"You've got what you came here for," Nerea said, stubbing out her cigarette in an ashtray shaped like a painted skull. "Get out of my shop."

Clara wanted to know more, wanted to ask a million questions, but she just nodded and left. Simon followed at her heels like a puppy dog.

"What's our next move?" he asked.

Clara shook her head. *His* next move, she knew, was to go home and try to get sane again. She was definitely not going to bring him in on this investigation. This totally nonsanctioned, non-police investigation. What she was going to do herself was an open question. A pretty good one, too.

She knew one more thing, though, than she had before. One thing that scared the living shit out of her.

"Three months," she said. "All in three months. Yeah. If it had been going on for two years, there's no way the police could have missed it. I don't care how far off the grid those people are." She thought about the half-dead who'd jumped her in Altoona, and the van full of them in Bridgeville. "It doesn't make sense. The smart thing for Malvern to do right now is to lie low. Minimize her blood intake and just hide out. Wait for us all to forget she ever existed, and then come back when it's safe. But she's not doing that. She's taking chances right now. Big chances that put her at risk."

"Yeah?" Simon asked, as if she'd been talking to him.

Clara walked over to the car, where Glauer was waiting to hear what they'd found. She reached for the handle of the passenger-side door. Then she dropped her hand, because she needed to stand still for a second while the whole world rolled around her.

"It means she's about to go public. It means she's going to do something so nasty and huge and bloody that the whole world will get to hear about it. And she's going to do it now, in the next couple of nights, while we're still not ready for her." She turned and looked Simon directly in the eye.

"There's no more time," she said. "You have to take me to Laura. Right now."

30.

Clara braced herself against the dashboard, pushed her feet down into the leg well of the passenger seat, even though Glauer kept their speed to a sedate forty-five, even on the back-country roads where pickup trucks thundered past them on the gravel shoulder. Glauer was right, of course—there was no reason for them to draw attention to themselves. Absolutely no good would come of them being picked up by the cops now. If that happened, Fetlock would hear about it instantly. And he would have far too many questions. Questions about what Glauer and Clara were even doing in the same car.

He'd really want to know about their passenger. In the back-seat, Simon Arkeley sprawled across the available space with no seat belt on, staring resolutely out the windows, only stirring when he needed to give them directions.

He took them south, through Amish country. Into the ridges that corrugated central Pennsylvania like a furrowed brow. Soon Clara was seeing the billboards on the side of the road that didn't advertise cigarettes or family restaurants, but eternal salvation—the ones that implored her to save her soul before she lost her life. Those billboards had always creeped her out with their none-too-subtle messages:

HOT ENOUGH FOR YA? TRY HELL!

DID YOU TAKE A WRONG TURN? ONLY ONE ROAD LEADS TO GOD

YE ARE ALL SINNERS! REPENT NOW!

There was almost no traffic on those roads, except for the occasional horse and buggy, each emblazoned with an orange reflective triangle to tell motorists to slow down. The farmers in the buggies stared at them with suspicion, but that was alright. There was nearly no police presence at all in Amish country— the farmers resented any attempt by the government to meddle in their affairs, and they voted reliably every year not to fund an actual police department. If they actually needed help, they relied on the county sheriff, or whatever units of the state police happened to be nearby at the time.

"I don't get it," Clara said, as she had a dozen times before. "If I was Laura, on the run, this is *exactly* where I would come. It's so obvious. You're telling me Fetlock didn't think of this, too?"

Glauer shrugged. "These ridges all look so close together, but they're deceptive. There's a lot of country down here, and not many roads. You can hide an awful lot in the hollows between them. Somebody who didn't want to be found could pick a lot of worse places to hide."

Laura could have been living an hour away from Clara the whole time. She stared forward through the windshield. Ahead of her fields of corn shimmered in the heat of the day, while the air conditioner pushed an icy breeze into her face. "Are we at least getting close?" she asked.

"Kind of," Simon told her. "We're only a couple miles away. But it'll take about an hour more to get there."

He didn't explain what that meant, but she found out soon enough. They took a side road that led over one of the ridges, the car's engine chugging as it crested through the thin air. On the far side the road narrowed down to one lane, and that barely paved. Glauer grunted as he dropped the car into low gear and rumbled down the side of the hill again. At the bottom, in a shady hollow, he had the choice to turn right or left. Both roads looked the same—one lane of unpainted blacktop.

"Which way?" he asked.

"It doesn't actually matter," Simon said.

Glauer put the car in park and turned around to face the kid.

"Tell me you mean that this road joins up again in a bit. That left and right go to the same place."

"No," Simon said, looking sheepish. "Just—just pick one. I could explain, but I don't think you'd really believe me."

"How about me? I believe in lots of things," Clara said.

Simon squirmed inside his shirt. "Look, it's magic, alright? I don't like it any more than you do. But it's magic."

"Magic," Clara and Glauer said in unison.

"You asked earlier how Laura could hide back here. Why nobody ever thought to look for her in these ridges. Well, I'm pretty sure they did. Probably lots of times. But the Polders aren't crazy about visitors. So they kind of mess up reality over here."

For a second nobody said anything. Clara tried to catch Glauer's eye, but the big cop seemed to be lost in thought.

Eventually Glauer smoothed down his mustache with his fingers. Then he reached across Clara to open the glove box. He took out a GPS unit and switched it on, then held it patiently while it found the necessary satellites.

"Huh," he said, finally.

"Care to share?" Clara asked.

He handed her the GPS. It showed the road they'd just taken over the ridge, but not anything beyond their current location. The fork in the road didn't appear on the screen—there weren't even any dashed lines to show seasonal or unpaved roads in the vicinity. As far as the GPS was concerned they'd reached a dead end.

Clara stared through the windshield, severely annoyed. "It doesn't look magical. It looks like two fucking roads, and we have to pick one."

"Yeah," Simon said. "It's pretty subtle. If you come here with bad intent—and no, don't ask me how a magic spell can read your intentions like that, it's not my area of expertise—but if you do, then you'll think you're supposed to turn one way. And the road will twist and turn through some very pretty views for a while, and you'll end up back on top of the ridge. If you come here for the right reasons, then you'll pick the right direction." He shrank down in his seat. "So you just—just pick one."

It was Glauer who came up with the solution, though. "Simon. You said that Caxton asked you to come back. She invited you. So which direction would you pick?"

Simon hemmed and hawed for a while. "Left, I guess."

"Good enough." Glauer put the car back in gear and turned left.

The road led into a stand of trees that quickly became a dense grove. It twisted around until Clara was certain they were headed back to where they'd started, and she began to worry that the spell would keep them away. But eventually the trees fell away from the sides of the road and they crossed a rushing stream and up ahead, in the shadows of the trees, Clara saw signs of human habitation. A row of mailboxes, rusting on top of a wooden fence. A tractor abandoned in a ditch on the side of the road, weeds sprouting from its engine compartment and the split leather of its seat. Up ahead she saw trailers parked on cinder blocks, and a couple of tiny bungalows.

She'd seen a hundred little hamlets like this in Pennsylvania. They sprang up around every fishing hole and picturesque waterfall, in clusters around the state parks and tourist caves. This one looked a little different, though. It took her a while to realize why. "I don't see any satellite dishes," she said.

"What's that?" Simon asked her.

Glauer nodded. "She's right. It's weird."

Clara tried to explain. "Places like this can't get cable TV—they're just too far from the trunk lines. So you always see huge satellite dishes on their roofs. Sometimes you see places that still have outhouses and wells, but they've always got huge satellite dishes to get TV reception. But not here. No telephone lines, either."

"Huh," Simon said. "I never noticed that. But if you think

that's weird, you haven't met these people yet. Get yourselves ready, if you can."

"We've met weird people before," Clara said.

Yet even she gasped when a woman walked out into the middle of the road and held up a hand for them to stop. She had a shaved head and wore only the briefest of shorts and a bra for a top. Every square inch of her exposed flesh was covered in tattoos.

She didn't look very welcoming.

Glauer stopped the car and waited. The woman just stood there, looking in at them, not smiling.

Simon rolled down his window. "Hi," he called, leaning out into the heat. "Hi—you're Glynnis, right?"

The woman came striding over, not exactly hurrying. She peered at Simon for a while as if trying to remember his face, then shot a look at Clara and Glauer in the front seats. "Simon, nobody said you could bring guests."

"Caxton will want to see these two," the boy protested.

"I kind of doubt that." Glynnis ran a finger along the roof of the car, as if checking it for dust. Clara felt the air around her thicken and warm up. Maybe it was just because Simon had opened his window and let all the air-conditioning out. Yeah, it might have been that. "I guess it's her call, though," Glynnis said, finally. "Yeah, okay. You go ahead and drive up to the big house. She'll be there expecting you."

"She's really here?" Clara blurted out.

Glynnis stared at her with pure hatred. She said nothing to Clara, though. Instead she leaned down toward the boy and said, "Simon, you remember how to get there?"

"There's only one road," the boy said.

"Yeah. So you stay on it, and don't try anything." Then she nodded and stepped back to let them pass.

"Friendly folk back here in rural PA," Glauer said, as he started the car again.

"They're not all like that," Simon promised.

Clara didn't care.

She was going to see Laura again. In just a few minutes. She felt like she might have a heart attack on the spot.

31.

Glauer drove up the side of a ridge to a house perched at its top. The house didn't look like anything special—the paint was peeling, bits of the gingerbread had broken off, the screen doors were torn and patched with duct tape. Compared to the shacks down in the Hollow, though, it was a mansion, an enchanted castle, a fortress on a hill. Glauer pulled into a driveway that ran around the side of the house and killed the engine.

"This is safe, right?" he asked, and flicked the power locks on the doors before Clara could jump out of the car and run inside and find Laura. "Those weirdoes down there aren't going to try anything, are they?"

Simon shook his head. "No, they're harmless. Just—look out for the little girl."

The big cop turned and stared at him.

"I mean, she's not going to hurt you. But if she offers to read your future or, or, or something, just. Just don't take her up on it."

"Uh-huh," Glauer said.

"And the guy with the wooden arm. He's in charge," Simon added. "He kind of creeps me out."

"Sure." Glauer sighed and looked over at Clara. For way too long. "Too late now to say this, but—"

"So just don't," Clara told him.

He nodded and flicked the locks open. Clara shoved her way out of the car and ran around to the front door of the house. She rubbed her hands on her jeans because her palms were suddenly sweaty.

The door swung open, but it wasn't Laura who emerged. It was Patience Polder. Clara had met the girl before, though it had been years earlier. The girl had grown into young womanhood and lost all her baby fat. Her face would have been pretty if she smiled, but her expression was severe. She wore a long, modestly cut white dress and a lace bonnet that covered some of her hair. She looked at Clara with eyes that held an almost infinite sadness, but very little compassion. Three other girls trooped out after her, their hobnail boots crunching on the wooden boards of the porch. They were dressed in similar clothes, though in different drab colors.

"Okay," Clara said. "Hi, Patience. Is Laura home?"

The girl in white studied Clara's face for a long time. The girls beside her tried to do the same, but they couldn't match that probing stare.

"I want you to know," Patience said, finally, "that we don't blame you for what's going to happen. Your motives, at least, are pure."

Clara felt her cheeks grow hot. "Now, what the hell is that supposed to—"

"Seriously!" Simon called out, running up to stand next to her. "Do. Not. Ask."

"Ooookay," Clara said. "Um, can I talk to Laura?"

"Yes," Patience said, but didn't move from where she stood. Slowly she turned to face Simon. Her expression softened and she gave him a trembling little smile that made Clara cringe. She knew what that look meant. Patience must have a crush on Simon or something but she was trying her best not to show it. Trying—and failing.

"Hi, Patience," Simon said. He folded his arms tightly across his chest and looked up at the second floor of the house. It was just as clear to Clara that he wasn't looking up there to see if anyone was in the upper windows. He just wanted to look away from Patience's eyes.

There was clearly a lot going on there. Deep emotions and a complicated history.

Clara did not give one shit.

She got tired of waiting and pushed past the girls, pushed open the screen door and stepped inside a parlor with dusty wallpaper and a really loud ticking clock. There was probably some incredibly important rule about not just shoving your way into the Polder house, but she didn't care. She headed through the house and into a kitchen and looked around but didn't see anybody. For a moment she just stood there, watching sunlight come in over the kitchen sink and light up twists of dust in the air. The house was creepily quiet, so quiet the clock sounded like a pounding heartbeat just behind her head.

Then she heard someone come clomping down the stairs. She knew that sound. She knew the shoes that made that sound. She knew the rhythm of those footfalls oh, so very well.

This is it, Clara thought. *This is the moment when I turn around and it's just like the first time. Like when I made her kiss me the first time. It will all still be there, all the feelings I tried so hard to get rid of, all the love. She'll come to me and take me up in her arms and kiss me, just—just kiss me, once, and I'll feel in that kiss all the time we've been apart and why it doesn't matter at all.*

She turned around slowly and Laura was there. For real. Laura's dark hair had grown out a little, so it hung around her ears. There were a few more lines around her eyes, and a lot more muscles in her arms. She looked sexy as freaking hell.

Clara imagined a million things she could say and rejected them all, in the time it took her to open her mouth. When she did speak—when she could—all that came out was one word.

"Hi."

Laura nodded at her. Then she took a step toward Clara. She was visibly trembling when she spoke. "You little fucking idiot," she said. "This is the worst thing you have ever done to me, coming here."

[1804]

Sometimes, Justinia thought she had gone to hell.

Time and travel had not been kind. She had been transported a great distance by sea, sealed up in her coffin and jostled about so violently that her head had nearly come loose from her neck. It had taken the better part of a decade to repair that damage, now that she had no blood to help heal her—even after she reached her final destination and her coffin was pried open so she could be put on display.

Her one eye had grown dim, and she could make out only fuzzy shapes around her, but they were evil, threatening shapes. The skeletons of enormous reptiles loomed over her, claws stretched toward her face, massive jaws craned open to swallow her whole. Yet they were frozen in place, for it seemed that time had stopped, here in this eternal prison. Everything had stopped, except her thoughts.

Inside her brain she had a kind of life still. A grasping, desperate need that would not die. The refrain of blood, blood, blood was a kind of psychic heartbeat. Her need, her inexorable thirst, would not let her die. There was no hope in this place, no possibility of hope, no succor, but as well no release.

At least . . . not until he began to visit her.

His name was Josiah Caryl Chess. He introduced himself to her like a proper gentleman. He explained that he had purchased her bones at an auction, the previous owner having no idea just what a marvel he'd possessed. She'd been found in Easling's rooms and the men who took her had assumed she was dead. A grisly trophy of Easling's depredations. They had understood she was not strictly human, and therefore they did not just bury her—instead they had placed her up for sale.

"When I realized what I was looking at, it was all I could do not to

cry out in joy," Chess said. "That would never have done, would it? They would have raised the reserve price. I got you for a song, my dear. Such a prize."

The last known vampire, intact in her original coffin! He spoke honeyed words about how much he treasured her. About what a great acquisition she was, and how she would make him the envy of every fossil hunter the world round. He spoke all kinds of flatteries, enough to make her want to smile, should such a thing remain possible for her. And then he carved into her shoulder with a scalpel and a tiny trowel. Taking samples, he said, for proper scientific study.

"Sometimes I think you're still in there," he said with a chuckle. "Sometimes I see flickers of life. What secrets are you keeping from me, darling?"

This with another patronizing laugh.

Later he came back and carefully removed her gown, the better to examine all of her parts, he said. It did not escape her that he spent longer examining certain parts than others.

Could she but move a single finger, or close her own prized open jaws, she would have devoured him entirely then and there. There was no pain in his ministrations—she was far beyond the point of feeling physical pain—but the indignity was beyond the pale. She would rend him, tear him down to the sinews and the thews, she thought. She would—she would—

Her supply of energy was so low, the fires of her life so banked, that a single thought could stretch out over long nights, words creeping through the dried-up catacombs of her mind like blind maggots crawling after sustenance.

She would kill him. Of this she had no doubt. No matter how long it took.

In the end it took more than twenty years. Like a babe learning how to walk, she had to take fumbling, uncertain steps at first. She had to learn whole new realms of discipline, learn how to marshal her energies, to conserve the low, guttering flame of her existence—and then channel that precious heat into a single message, a single thought she let slip out into the room like a tendril of smoke, evanescent and teasing. She could only hope it would be enough, that he would be receptive enough to this most subtle of communications.

It was while he was carving out one of her finger bones, removing her dry flesh shred by shred. He had a jeweler's loupe screwed into one eye, and he was bent so close to her that she felt the heat of his blood like summer's sun shining down on her. She had never properly seen his face. She knew nothing of him he had not told her—or shown her. Yet he had touched every part of her, as intimate as any lover.

Chess is not my game, *she whispered to him. If he could not hear her now, if his mortal brain was too thick and brutish to receive the words—but if—but if—*

But perhaps ye'll teach me to play.

He fell backward as if she'd struck him. His loupe fell to the floor in a trill of broken glass. He stared up at her with true horror in his features. And that alone was enough of a victory to send a thrill through her dry bones.

But the fact that he did not run away, that he did not flee, was worth far more.

I have ye, *she thought, careful not to let the words loose outside her own skull.*

32.

"Laura!" Clara shrieked. She wanted to slap Laura's face or just yell at her for saying something like that, but she couldn't catch her breath. The whole room seemed to spin as Laura stormed out onto the porch. Clara managed to follow her and saw her grabbing up guns. "Laura—"

"Don't talk to me. I've spent two years building the perfect trap and you just ruined it." Laura hurried down the porch steps and onto the road that led down to the Hollow.

Clara might have kept following her if a wooden hand hadn't clamped down on her shoulder. She shouted in surprise, then whirled around to find Urie Polder standing there. The look on his face was perfectly impassive but his eyes searched hers as if he was trying to read her mind.

"Can you do that?" Clara asked.

"Do what?"

"I guess not." She shuddered and pulled away from him. The wooden arm had always bothered her in a way she just couldn't get past. "Look. We came here for a good reason. Not just because I wanted to see her."

"I figured as much, ahum."

"If she won't listen to me, at least I can tell you. We've found clear evidence that Justinia Malvern isn't just alive, but currently active. She's been taking victims—multiple victims, every night. Which means she's ramping up for some kind of major push. Obviously that means she's looking for Laura—for Caxton— and so you're all in danger. We've seen aggressive half-dead activity as well, which means she won't be coming alone. Based on her previous tactics, we know she won't just make a frontal assault. Most likely she'll try to lure Caxton out into the open before she pounces."

"Well, thanks for that," Polder said, nodding.

"I'm totally serious here," Clara insisted, because he didn't seem upset enough. "We expect the strike to come within the next week. Maybe even the next few nights."

"Sounds about right, ahum."

Clara shook her head. "I know you have no reason to trust me."

"Sure I do," he told her. He sat down on a bench swing that hung suspended from the roof of the porch by chains. He kicked a little to get it moving. "You're one of hers, and that's as good a recommend as I can think up."

"So—so—what are you—why aren't you running around

making preparations, then? There must be a million things to do to get ready."

"There was. They're all done. We knew about everything you said already." He shrugged and his creepy wooden arm lifted in the air. "There's been some half-deads around here, last couple of nights. One startled my Patience by lookin' in her bedroom window last night, even. They found some way past the safe-guards. Yes, they're bound to attack just about any time. Won't do nothin' 'til tonight, though. Not while their queen bee's still sleepin'. Miss Malvern's going to want first crack at Caxton, and everyone knows it. 'Bout the only thing predictable she's like to do. You thirsty, girl? I've got some sun tea brewin' on the back porch, if you'd be partial to a glass, ahum."

Clara could only stare at him.

"Wait," she said.

He said nothing, just looked out over the trees that covered the ridge.

"Seriously?"

"Ahum."

"You already knew this. You were already ready for it. My coming here doesn't help you at all."

"Complicates a few things. But it was nice of you, all the same, to think of us in our time of danger, ahum."

"Crap," Clara said, and raced off the porch and down into the trees.

It wasn't hard to find Laura. There was only one path down to the Hollow. Laura was hurrying down the hill, her strides long to eat up the ground. Clara couldn't match those strides, so she had to break into a sprint to come even with her. She was out of breath when she finally caught up.

"I'm so sorry," she said, trying to catch her breath and explain at the same time.

"I haven't contacted you in two years. Did you really think I wanted to see you now?" Laura wouldn't even look at her.

She just kept walking, and Clara had to jog backward to keep pace with her and see her face. "I really didn't mean to cause a problem. Glauer and I will leave right away, before it gets dark. I know my being here is a burden on you."

"All of my plans are based around the concept that when Malvern attacks I don't have to worry about anyone else. If you're here, she'll grab you up and use you against me. Just like she always has."

"I . . . know," Clara said. "I've been trying to turn myself into somebody who isn't a liability. But I guess we're not there now. I'm so sorry, Laura."

Laura stopped walking then and finally looked at her. Clara blushed as those hard eyes scanned her face.

"Glauer said something recently, something I didn't want to hear," Clara said. "He said you had to choose between me and the vampires. And that you picked the vampires. And that maybe that was the right choice."

Laura said nothing at all.

"It's true. What you're doing here is important. I never meant to interfere. I'll go now. It was—well. I was going to say it was nice seeing you. But between how embarrassed I am for wasting your time, and how pissed off I am that you think you're allowed to talk to me like that, it wasn't very nice at all."

She started back up the path but stopped when Laura called her name.

"I'm sorry," Laura said. It sounded like she was dragging the apology out of herself. Like the words caused her physical pain. "I'm sorry. Too. I've just worked so hard, for so long."

"I know."

"I can't afford to let anybody fuck that up."

"Yeah."

"I don't want to ever see you here again," Laura went on.

"I kind of got that." Clara started walking again, figuring they were done. Laura did not call her name again.

Clara didn't walk very far, though. Before she'd taken more than a dozen steps, she heard a sound like a lawn-mower engine starting up, echoing over the ridges. She hadn't seen any lawns down in the Hollow, and couldn't figure what it might be. It grew louder, however, as she listened for it, louder and more insistent, until it was chopping up the air. She glanced up just as a helicopter shot by overhead, the roar of its engines enough to deafen her, its rotorwash enough to shake the trees all around her and send leaves raining down around her feet.

Then she heard the sirens and saw the flashing lights, as a dozen police vehicles came racing into the Hollow.

[1836]

He made a place for Justinia in his front parlor, eventually, in a marble casket lined with red satin. She imagined his wife must have objected to this, but then she was rarely seen around the plantation anymore.

Sometimes he fed her himself. Sometimes, when he needed to punish one of his slaves, he sent them in to give her what she required. They were so terrified, every time, and that was delicious, but it was the energy the blood gave her she savored the most. It gave her the power to wrap herself in illusion, to make herself resemble the creature he wanted, and that was almost as enjoyable for her as it was for him. She could almost forget, when he kissed her breasts, her belly, between her legs, that it was dry and flaking skin he caressed, that she had come to resemble the hateful thing she'd always been inside.

Sometimes she forgot she was a killer, even. Sometimes she forgot her sins. And then she was merely the mistress, the lover, the paramour. When he would trail one finger into her mouth, and let her nibble a bit, and take what she needed, it was a little bit like love.

There were worse things in the world than being a kept woman. Especially when those worse things included rotting away, alone and forgotten, in a wooden box in a room full of dinosaur bones. That, it emerged, had been his passion before he found her. He'd been energized by this new theory of evolution and the stony fossils that were dug up out of the ground to prove it. He was a creature of wild imagination, Josiah Chess, able to look at the skeleton of some titanic beast and imagine what it must have been in life, all scales and teeth and flashing eyes.

It was not so great a leap to show him the woman he wanted to see, with red hair and creamy flesh and round, full breasts.

She watched him grow old, while she stayed young. If only in imagination. Sometimes in a game the cards ran hot for quite a while before luck eventually had to change.

There came a time, though, when a new man came along. A younger, stronger man. Josiah's blood had grown thin with time. He'd lost his ruddy complexion, and anemia is a terrible thing for the old to have to bear. But his son Zachariah grew stronger with time, his shoulders broader. His heart beat so strongly in his chest, until she saw it shining like a light in the dark.

Josiah didn't know about his son's visits to the parlor. After the master of the house had gone to sleep, weakened by his exertions, she would receive another gentleman caller. Sometimes. At first he was as frightened of her as the slaves. But with time, and familiarity, all things can change.

She did not know what year it was when he started asking her for his heart's desire. When they started plotting together. But it was not so long after that, the night when Josiah came to her and she saw how wrinkled and feeble he'd become. The night he lifted one emaciated finger to her lips and she cooed for him the last time.

In the morning they found him, dry as a husk, his flesh torn in a hundred places, his eyes staring in horror at nothing at all. Zachariah gave him a proper burial and had some of his slaves tried and convicted for the murder.

"Now you're mine," he said, the night after it was done, crawling into the casket with her, curling against her naked bones. "Mine, forever."

"Oh, yes," she promised. Thinking that she would have to drive off

Zachariah's wife just as she'd done for his mother. But not quite yet. Not until she bore him a son. A good strong son with a heart like a lamp.

Sometimes the cards just keep getting hotter.

If she kept this up, if she played it right, she might be able to walk again someday. Walk under her own power—and hunt again.

33.

"Crap!" Caxton shouted. She turned and looked at Clara, for a moment thinking to blame her former lover for this. But she knew better. As angry as she might be at Clara for coming to the ridge and upsetting her carefully laid plans, she couldn't truly believe that Clara would lead the cops right to her door.

"Who are they? Local? State police?" Clara asked, craning her neck to see better through the tree branches.

"Get your head down," Caxton whispered, and pushed Clara down into the undergrowth. She moved forward herself to get a better view, but didn't much like what she saw.

Eight unmarked police cars had wheeled into the Hollow, forming a protective ring around the main clearing at the center of the little town. The same open space where the community took its meals on warm nights. Now it was obscured by a cloud of dust as men in blue ballistic vests and windbreakers poured out of the cars, their weapons out and held at a high ready. Behind them four more vehicles pulled into the ring the cars had made. Two of them were armored cars, one crowned by the antennas and radio dishes of a mobile command center, one a reinforced paddy wagon, a prisoner transport. The other two vehicles were Jeeps full of cops in full SWAT gear, armored and masked and carrying heavy carbines.

"Jesus, they must be expecting another Waco here," Caxton breathed. She ducked down as the helicopter made another pass over the Hollow, shredding her thoughts with its noise and the waves of air pressure it beat down all around her.

From her position Caxton could see the people of the Hollow taking up defensive positions of their own, as if preparing for a firefight. They hid behind the trailers, their backs up against the metal walls. Some of the men had guns—hunting rifles, mostly, but she counted four handguns she hadn't known about. She'd done more than one census on the firearms in the Hollow, but apparently some of the men had been holding out on her.

The women, dressed in their plain and simple clothes, bonnets on their heads, were unarmed. They could be far more dangerous, though. Two of them were busy drawing an elaborate hex sign in the gravel behind one of the bungalows. Caxton had spent years with them, but she still didn't know exactly what they hoped to accomplish. Heather, the single mother who had flirted with Simon, sat in full lotus on top of one of the trailers, her hands pressed together in an attitude of prayer. She was highly exposed up there and would probably be the first one to get shot if things went wrong.

No—Caxton had to revise that impression. The first one to get shot would be Glynnis. Because Glynnis, she of the shaved head and full-body tattoos, was about to unleash hell on the clearing.

The woman's eyes were closed as she strode deliberately toward the ring of policemen. She kept her hands down at her sides like a gunslinger walking into a shoot-out. Across her back a ripple of light spread through her tattoos, as if they were coming to life while Caxton watched. The air around Glynnis rippled as if she were generating an enormous amount of heat.

"What the hell do they think they're going to accomplish?" Clara asked. At least she kept her voice down.

"What I trained them for. Except—"

"You trained them to fight a police raid on this level?"

Caxton frowned. "Except, I trained them to fight vampires.

Not cops." She shook her head. "These are not the world's most stable people. They're defending their way of life, Clara. They might not see a big difference there."

"You've got to stop them!"

Caxton might have answered, but just then a bullhorn wailed and she winced at the feedback. She recognized the amplified voice that spoke next.

"Federal agents!" Fetlock called. "Everyone will surrender now or my men will open fire. We have authorization to use lethal force!"

"That son of a bitch!" Caxton barked. "Goddamn it. He followed you right here." She couldn't resist. Rage bubbled up in her chest and she said, "Thanks so much for your lovely visit, Clara."

"No," Clara insisted. "He couldn't have followed us. We were really careful!"

"Really? How careful? Because that guy is a U.S. Marshal who has spent years searching for me. I'm the one who got away. Did you think he wouldn't try very hard? He has access to satellites, Clara. He has some of the best trackers in the world on his payroll—he has experts on wiretapping, on computer surveillance, on covert ops. He's got packs of bloodhounds. He's got the entire U.S. government on his side. But you—you and Glauer—were really, really careful."

"Do you think I didn't know all that? I used to work for that asshole. I know how he operates, and I'm telling you, we took all the necessary precautions to—"

"Shut up," Caxton said. "Look—there."

Down in the Hollow, Glynnis was ready to attack.

The tattoos on her exposed skin writhed and seethed with light. She was no more than a dozen paces from the ring of cops when she stopped walking. She lifted both arms to the sky, then brought her hands down again in one flowing motion. She stopped with her arms held parallel to the ground, her hands turned up so her palms faced the police cars.

Nothing visible passed between her and the raiders. Yet Caxton felt the energy being released from Glynnis's hands. It made her teeth ache. The air seemed to curdle in front of Glynnis and then cops started screaming.

One after another they dropped their weapons—or threw them away from themselves as if they'd suddenly realized they were holding poisonous snakes. Some of the cops wrestled with their own ballistic vests, desperately trying to unbuckle them as if the vests were on fire. One cop who had been leaning against the side of a car screamed as if the vehicle had grown white hot and burned him everywhere he made contact with it.

"This is my home," Glynnis said in a clear, steady voice. She wasn't shouting, but Caxton felt like she could be heard for miles. "You will not come here uninvited. You will not take us away from here. You will do nothing in this place without my permission."

Caxton could see some of the cops nodding, as if they agreed with everything she said. As if they had suddenly realized she was in charge here, not them, and they'd better do what she said.

"Damn," Caxton admitted, "she's good. I don't think Urie Polder could do this better."

"What are you going to do about this?" Clara demanded. "Are you going to let her get herself killed?"

Caxton gave it a moment's thought. She had toughened herself these last two years. Squeezed what little humanity she had left, choked it until it succumbed. She had known there would be casualties when the time came. "She knows what she's doing."

Fetlock's bullhorn wailed again, which seemed to shock the cops out of their hypnotic daze. "This is your last warning! Stand down or you will be shot!"

Glynnis didn't seem to hear him at all. She didn't flinch, didn't shift so much as an inch from where she stood. The tattoos on her back and arms blazed with light. One of the police cars pinged and rocked back and forth on its tires as steam burst from its radiator. The cops nearby rushed to get away from it as if they expected it to explode.

"Stop her," Clara said.

Caxton shook her head. "I don't think I could. You want to run down there and grab her arm? You'd probably lose all the skin off your hand."

"You have to do something!" Clara begged.

"Fire at will," Fetlock said.

The cops in the windbreakers were too busy panicking to respond. The SWAT teams, however, didn't seem to have been fazed at all by the supernatural attack. They formed up in neat rows, down on one knee in perfect firing postures. One of them opened up with his weapon, and then two more.

The bullets whizzed all around Glynnis. Caxton knew what the men in the SWAT teams were capable of—she knew how much they trained for things like this. There was no way that all of them were missing her. At least some of the bullets had to be striking Glynnis. But she didn't take a step back. She didn't move a muscle.

"Jesus," Caxton said, in an admiring tone.

"Enough!" Clara shouted, and ran past Caxton. Clara hurtled down the last hundred yards of the ridge and right up to the edge of the clearing. Caxton's heart jumped in her chest, despite herself. The little idiot was going to get herself shot. She felt a desperate urge to run after Clara, a palpable need to protect the woman who had once been her lover—

But. But, no. No, she couldn't afford to be captured now. She couldn't let Fetlock take her, not when Malvern was so close. She closed the distance between them, but made sure she stayed well back in the cover of the trees.

"Glynnis!" Clara shouted. "Glynnis, just surrender! Drop to the ground with your hands above your head!"

Glynnis must not have been expecting that, because she turned her face a fraction of an inch to the side before she caught herself. Before she remembered she couldn't afford to be distracted.

It was just enough to shatter her concentration. And with that, the enchantment that protected her failed.

Bullets tore through her chest and neck. Blood slicked down her front, obscuring her tattoos. For a split second longer she stayed upright, her palms still stretched out toward the cops. But it couldn't last. Before Clara even started to scream, Glynnis fell in a heap in the dust, stone cold dead.

34.

Clara couldn't help herself. She screamed like a little girl.

She had just killed Glynnis. She wanted to drop to her knees and sob, let out all the guilt and horror she felt.

Unfortunately time failed, just then, to stand still. One SWAT team rushed forward, weapons up at their shoulders, ready to shoot anyone who moved. The cops in the blue windbreakers moved to cover them from behind the cars.

It was clear to Clara that at any moment a real firefight would break out—a free-for-all, in which many people would be shot and killed. Over behind the trailers the menfolk of the Hollow readied their guns. The women had almost finished their elaborate hex sign, though there was no suggestion yet of what its purpose might be. Up on top of the trailer the other woman, the hippie woman, remained in perfect repose, hands on her knees with her fingers poised in some complicated gesture.

Clara had to do something. She had to stop this. She still couldn't move.

She choked down her scream and looked at Laura. It was like she'd never seen the other woman before. Laura's face bore no emotion whatsoever. Just cold, unfeeling calculation. She was working out the odds in her head, trying to figure out who would come out on top in the storm of lead that was about to erupt.

"Stop them," Clara said. She didn't plead. Begging wasn't going to help here. She merely uttered the words as an instruction.

"I can't let Fetlock take me right now," Laura said. It sounded almost like an apology, but only a mere sop. A quick explanation offered to someone too stupid to understand what was really happening.

With a steady, practiced motion, Laura worked a round into the chamber of her Glock handgun. She was ready to fight her way through this.

That made Clara angry. And that was what finally broke her paralysis. "There are kids here! Where are they right now? In those houses over there? Ducking under their kitchen tables, waiting to find out if their parents are going to live through the next few minutes?"

"They're safe. That hex sign the women are drawing will protect them. It'll keep stray rounds from traveling too far," Laura explained.

"It won't keep their fathers alive."

Laura had no response to that. What could she possibly have said?

Clara had no weapon of her own. She couldn't just shoot Laura. She wondered, briefly, if she could have done so, given the opportunity. She reached out to grab Laura's arm, but the other woman shrugged her off.

"You shouldn't be seeing this," Laura said. "You shouldn't be here. If I had to go out in a blaze of glory, I wanted to do it alone."

"Glory? You call this glory? Glynnis is dead, Laura. Dead! You were the one who wanted to protect people! That was why you started fighting vampires. Remember? And now a woman is dead, for no reason at all. It wasn't a half-dead that killed her. It wasn't Justinia fucking Malvern. It was a SWAT trooper sent to bring you to justice."

"You think that's going to stop me?" Laura shook her head. "This isn't about protecting people, not anymore."

"It's—it's not?"

"No. It's about killing the vampires. If you need a better reason, then you've already failed. The vampires are evil. They have to be killed. That's it. And whatever it takes to kill the vampires, you do it."

Clara stared at Laura in horror. "I can't let you do this," she said. Then she opened her mouth to scream, to shout for Fetlock and tell him where Caxton was. It would mean attracting the SWAT teams, and probably getting shot in the crossfire herself. But it would save the rest of the people of the Hollow, and maybe that was worth it.

Before she could make a sound, though, Laura—Caxton—had her gun up and pointed right at Clara's face. "Give away my position and I will shoot you," Caxton said.

And it destroyed Clara—utterly ruined her—to think that Caxton meant it.

"I'm . . . sorry," Caxton said.

Clara didn't believe it at all. Slowly she raised her hands. She knew better than to make the slightest sound.

Up on top of her trailer, the hippie woman lifted her hands a few inches above the level of her knees. A sudden breeze rippled through her hair. The SWAT teams, who were only a few dozen feet from the trailers, suddenly looked like they were fighting their way through a hurricane. The many straps on their uniforms snapped and shook. They had to lean forward into every step, and as Clara watched, one of them had to turn his face away as if he wasn't strong enough to push on any farther.

"New target," Fetlock called over the bullhorn. Where was he? But Clara knew—he had to be inside the mobile command center. Fetlock wasn't a field agent. He would never be out on the front lines with a gun in his own hand. He was an administrator. "Seven o'clock high. Fire at will."

"No, not again," Clara moaned.

"Keep quiet or I'll—"

Caxton fell abruptly silent. Clara turned her head slowly to see why.

And hope flooded through her, desperate, half-believing hope. Glauer had come down the trail from the house on the ridge. He must have been making his way down the whole time, moving with glacial slowness so he didn't make a sound. He had a double-barreled shotgun in his hands and now both barrels were pressed against the back of Caxton's head.

"You, too, Glauer?" Caxton asked.

Glauer didn't waste time on apologies. "I know you're faster than me, and I know you're deadly. But I've got my finger on both triggers right now, and I will unload the second I think you're trying something," he told her. "Laura Caxton, you are under arrest."

[1861]

Obediah Chess laid her across the bed, across white sheets that looked ivory against her pale skin. Or at least, the skin that he saw when he looked at her.

The blood he gave her, the little drop or two she received every night, was enough to let her practice her orisons. But it was no longer enough to let her lift her head, or even so much as a finger. She could only lie there and receive him, a china doll. Unlike his father, he was a gentle lover. Like his grandfather, he possessed a gift of wild imagination. Sometimes it ran away with him.

Have ye done as I asked? she inquired, speaking directly to his mind. Speech was so difficult these days. The older she grew the more blood she needed even for the simple things, and there was never enough. Have ye spoken with the ladies in town? We must find ye a wife.

"Someone to bear me an heir, you mean," he said. His brow was dark with trouble and he stared out a window at the black night beyond. "I know your game. I know it and I don't care. Eventually you'll kill me and take my son into your bed. I understand. It's the family curse, by now. By God, it's my blessing."

Ye're . . . frightened of . . . something, *she said.*

He came to her and brushed her hair—hair that existed only in his mind's eye—with silver brushes. It soothed him to take care of her this way. He really was her favorite of the Chess lineage.

"A wind is coming. A wind to blow away everything my forefathers built," he told her. "You needn't trouble yourself with particulars, my darling. But there's war in the land. A war I fear Virginia will never win. Lincoln will punish us, I have no doubt. We could lose everything. When I was in town they said the Union bastards were closing in. They've been hunting up and down the country, teasing out our boys wherever they're hiding. It's only a matter of time before they start seizing the plantations, all of our treasure, our land."

Soldiers? Coming here? Ye must protect me.

"And so I shall. Have no fear." He took up her hand and pressed it to his lips. His own fingers were covered in tiny scars where she'd supped from his strength every night. She could feel how rough they were. "I will defend you with my last breath. Or perhaps . . ."

Ye've been thinking on this. Ye have some plan in mind.

"Not so much a plan as a wild surmise. A crazy notion that sounds foolish when I speak it aloud. No, it would never do, I—"

If ye can't speak it aloud, only whisper it in my ear.

"Yes—yes, perhaps—perhaps then it won't sound so lunatic. Yes . . . listen, my love . . ."

She still had the strength to smile when she heard what he had to say.

35.

"You're making a mistake," Caxton said. She didn't move, didn't even turn her head to look at Glauer. "You know that, right? With me in custody, Malvern won't be afraid anymore. She's definitely not afraid of you."

"I don't have a choice," Glauer said.

Caxton sighed. She knew he was telling the truth. He always did. And she understood exactly why he was doing this. Because it was the right thing to do. The way he saw it. She had appreciated this virtue in him once. She had made him her second in command, back when she had run the special subjects unit of the state police. Back when the world still wanted her to fight vampires.

"Do you have a cell phone, Caxton?" he asked. The pressure of the shotgun barrels on the back of her head never wavered.

"Why the hell would I do something stupid like that? They can track cell phones, you know. Fetlock tracks yours all the time."

"I'm aware of that. Which is why I left mine at home this morning. I'm starting to regret that. We need to get through to Fetlock, right now, and stop this."

"Laura, just—just be cool, okay?" Clara wavered into Caxton's field of view. Caxton had trusted Clara once, too. Amazing how everything you believed in could turn into a liability so fast. But she should have guessed. Jameson Arkeley had tried to teach her that lesson. Then he'd become an undead example of it in action.

The moment she'd seen Clara in the house, she should have run for the woods. Abort everything and start over fresh somewhere else. She'd done it before. But she'd spent so long building the perfect trap. That had been a mistake as well. Ever thinking she could rest, that she was getting to a point where she was safe. She should have known. As long as there was one vampire left, there was no such thing as safety.

"I guess we'll have to do this the weird way," Glauer said. "Mr. Polder?"

Caxton turned to look at the hexenmeister. Urie Polder looked confused for a moment. Then he nodded, as if he'd worked it out. "I guess there's no point in more killin', not now."

"We can't give up," Caxton insisted. "You can't let them take me!"

"Miss Laura, you be peaceful, now," Polder said. "I am sorry. But there's a lotta people down here that might get hurt. Folks with families."

No. Not Urie, too. Urie had just as much reason to hate vampires as Caxton did. She couldn't believe he would turn on her like this.

"I'll take care of things, ahum." He lifted his twig fingers to his face and closed his eyes. For a moment she heard whispers in her head, whispering voices that weren't meant for her, so she couldn't understand what they said. Out in the clearing, nothing much changed—but she could see the message had been received. The men of the Hollow lowered their weapons. Up on top of the trailers, Heather let go of the psychic wind she'd summoned.

The SWAT teams had nearly been knocked flat by that wind. Now they rose shakily to their feet, looking ready for whatever came next.

Heather shifted from her lotus position and lowered her hands. "Marshal Fetlock!" she called. "We would like to surrender now. We have Caxton and are prepared to hand her over."

There was a trace of disappointment in Heather's voice, but not enough to appease Caxton.

"Every last one of you. No backbone at all," she muttered.

"Did you forget already? Did you forget what a vampire can do?"

"No," Glauer told her. "I'll never forget. I saw it at Gettysburg. I saw what happened to Jameson Arkeley. And now I've seen what they did to you." The shotgun barrels pressed a little harder against the back of her head. "Slowly draw your weapons—all of them—and drop them on the ground. Clara, you gather them up."

Caxton did as she was told. She knew Glauer had already located all her weapons—it was a skill they called visual frisking, when you studied somebody's clothes to see all the unnatural lumps and bulges that were concealed weapons. He was pretty good at it, since she'd trained him herself. She put the safety on her Glock, then dropped it carefully in front of her. From the back of her waistband she drew her other pistol, a Beretta, and did the same. Then the knife in her left sock, and the pepper spray in her pocket. "That's everything."

"Good," Glauer said, while Clara took her weapons away. That felt like the most serious betrayal of all, for some reason. Like if she'd been a lion and they had pulled out all her teeth and claws. "Everybody hold tight until we're ready."

"Got it," Clara said.

Out in the clearing the SWAT teams stayed ready, in case this was a trap. Fetlock got on his bullhorn again and called out, "All units stay on mission. Shoot anything that looks suspicious. Bring Caxton out slowly, where I can see her."

Glauer marched her forward, into the clearing. She didn't take much prodding. She knew she was sunk. She lifted her hands carefully over her head. Normally she would have put them behind her head with her fingers laced together, but she didn't want Glauer thinking she was grabbing for the shotgun. He walked her between two trailers, then told her to stop when they were still ten yards from the advanced position of the SWAT teams. A dozen guns were pointed at her all at once.

"All this for one subject?" she asked.

Nobody answered her.

"Is that you, Glauer? I'll expect a full report," Fetlock blared. "Alright. Hand her off to Sergeant Howell."

One of the SWAT troopers moved forward, his carbine pointed right at Caxton's face. He used his free hand to grab her by the neck and shove her head down, then let his weapon fall on its strap so he could cuff her hands behind her back. "Down on the ground, on your face," he ordered. She complied. He searched her thoroughly, then shackled her feet, too. She did not try to get up.

Four more SWAT troopers came forward. They lifted her at her upper arms and her thighs and carried her forward, her face still looking down at the ground. She didn't resist, nor did she try to go limp. They had ways of dealing with people who resisted, even passively, and she did not want to get capsicum swabbed into her eyes. She'd been exposed to pepper spray often enough in her life already. They carried her for some distance, then she heard the doors of the paddy wagon clang open, and they threw her inside. Steel benches ran along either side of the back compartment of the wagon, with attachment points for various kinds of chains and shackles, but they didn't put her in a seat, they just laid her on the floor on her stomach and left her there as if they were afraid to touch her any more than that. They did not slam the doors shut behind her.

For a very long time nothing seemed to happen. She couldn't see anything, even when she dared to look up. The back of the paddy wagon was pointed at the road out of the Hollow, and there was nothing out there but the dust the cops had raised on their way in. It still hadn't settled. How much time had passed since they arrived? A few minutes at most. It felt a lot longer.

All around her she heard radios bleating and men talking in low tones. She knew what was going on only because she recognized what it felt like. This was the calm after a major operation, the time when cops were just milling around, still expecting a drugged-up lunatic to take another shot, still ready for anything, but also knowing that nothing was likely to happen. The moment when peace had been restored but nobody really believed it. A lot of things had to happen in that time. Perimeters had to be established and secured and double-checked to make sure they were secure, and then approved by superior officers. Casualties had to be counted, assessed, tended to, and removed from the scene. (*Glynnis,* she thought. *Now Glynnis had proved to have some guts.*) Every detail had to be squared away, recorded, and then relayed back to headquarters so people there knew their people in the field were safe.

Only then, after all that, would Fetlock even dare to step outside his mobile command center. She knew exactly where he would go first. So she was not surprised when he walked around to the back of the paddy wagon and stared down at her.

She expected him to gloat. He did not. This was a major get for him—she'd been a fugitive for two years, and her capture would remove a major blot from his record. But he didn't look particularly happy. He looked like he was still waiting for something else. Maybe he wanted her to cry, or show some sign that he'd truly beaten her. Or maybe it was something more.

"I'm secured," she told him, as if she were still a cop. As if he wanted her report. "Are you going to take me back to jail now?" she asked. She didn't feel like she had the energy left to make a threat or bluster at all.

"Not yet," he said, and nothing more. He nodded at someone she couldn't see, and the doors of the paddy wagon were shut, leaving her in the dark.

Something was wrong. Something was going on.

She had no idea what it could be.

36.

The defense of the Hollow collapsed all at once. The men dropped their guns and the women drew back toward their homes, where their children were waiting. The windbreaker cops moved quickly through the tiny village, this time letting the SWAT troopers cover them. Witchbillies were rounded up with textbook efficiency, their hands bound behind them with plastic cuffs. They were marched into the clearing and their names checked off against a comprehensive list.

"Say what you like about Fetlock—and I'll add some choice expletives myself. But he knows how to keep his own hide intact," Clara observed, while she waited to find out what her own fate would be. She had come out of the trees with Urie Polder as soon as the immediate threat had passed. Now she was sitting with Glauer, their backs up against the mobile command center, their hands always in clear view. None of the cops were actively covering them with weapons, but that could just have been professional courtesy, or simply that all available law-enforcement units had better things to do.

The windbreakers moved quickly through the bungalows and trailers, gathering up the women with their children. Families were allowed to stay together but everyone had to be accounted for. That was just standard practice. The Hollow had presented an armed resistance to the police raid. You didn't leave any potentially dangerous holdouts in their homes—somebody could always do something stupid, and a cop could get hurt.

Every gun in the Hollow was gathered up, logged, and checked off another list. Rounds were ejected from chambers (and logged on their own forms), plastic trigger blocks were inserted, and then the guns were sealed in plastic evidence bags. They were piled up inside the mobile command center in a padlocked cabinet. Other potential weapons—everything bigger than a paring knife—were identified and similarly stockpiled safely away.

The one casualty of the raid, Glynnis, was put in a body bag and hurried away so nobody could see her. So her death couldn't inspire anyone to decide to start the fight all over again. Clara was grateful for this. She knew she wasn't completely to blame for Glynnis's death. The woman had been resisting arrest against two highly armed and alerted SWAT teams. It wasn't like she'd been an innocent bystander who got caught in the crossfire. And Clara had had no idea that calling out to her would break her concentration, or what would happen then.

Still.

It was going to be a long time, if ever, before she forgave herself. That woman had been alive. She'd had a life, a community, probably friends and family. And now she was dead. If Clara had kept her mouth shut, things might have turned out differently.

She tried to distract herself by wondering how this had all gone down. There were no answers immediately available, so she turned to Glauer to see if he had any ideas. As the witchbillies were herded into the circle of cop cars, Glauer just watched it all, occasionally nodding to himself as if he were confirming some deeply held intuition.

"What is it?" Clara asked when she couldn't stand it anymore.

"Huh?"

She sighed in exasperation. "You're thinking something. I know you well enough to see your brain working."

He shrugged. "We led Fetlock here, right? Pretty good scheming on his part. When we fought those half-deads, when we had real evidence, he made his move. He fired you. Yanked me off the case." He shrugged again. "He knew what direction we would jump. Straight toward Caxton."

"Yeah," Clara said, her cheeks burning. They'd acted so predictably. And as a result Caxton had lost her freedom. Having seen what Caxton had become, Clara figured that was probably a good thing. But she really didn't like how she'd been used.

"Sure, that all makes sense," Glauer went on. "But one thing keeps bugging me. His intel is too good."

"What?"

Glauer nodded at a man standing a dozen yards away who was working his way down a printed checklist. Other cops were piling up various weird objects in front of him—cattle bones inscribed with tiny hex signs. Bundles of feathers. Sticks made out of dried sage, gathered tightly together and tied with twine.

"He knew exactly what he would find here. He's got a list of names, names of everybody in this village. Even though these are people who live off the grid. Half of them probably don't have birth certificates. But he knows their names. How?"

"What are you suggesting?"

Glauer shrugged one more time. Then he clucked his tongue. "We didn't give him those names. He needed us to bring him here, but he already knew enough to—"

"All will be explained," Fetlock said.

Clara jumped awkwardly to her feet, keeping her hands out in front of her. She had not seen the Fed coming toward them—it was as if he'd just appeared out of thin air. "Marshal," she said.

"Ms. Hsu." Fetlock wasn't looking at her. He was too busy scanning the clearing, visually inventorying the various efforts he'd organized, perhaps. "Officer Glauer. I'd like you to come with me—I'm about to interview Urie Polder. If you're useful to me in that interview, I promise, I'll let you in on the big secret."

Clara turned to Glauer and they exchanged a puzzled look. That wasn't like Fetlock at all. He never let anybody have the whole story.

As if reading their thoughts, Fetlock went on. "You both still have a role to play here. That's why I haven't arrested you yet. And it's why I'm willing to be frank. Now. Come along. We have a lot to do before the sun goes down."

[1863]

Reb or Yank—it made little difference to Justinia.

She had profited well from the Chess boys, and never once had they complained of their lot. She had felt something akin to affection swell inside her breast for Obediah, her latest swain, as he took up the curse and became her knight protector. With burning eyes and skin the color of the moon he had stalked the war-torn fields, bringing back to her that which she required, and for two years she had regained a little strength, grown a little bolder. Thought, perhaps, that the future might not be so entirely bleak.

But war has a way of upsetting dreams, and bringing reality back to those who flee it. She was unable to sit up enough to watch Obediah hang, or the insults the Yankee boys imposed on his body. She did not see them take him away.

But she knew it was over.

She was discovered in time and brought away from the ruined house, startled as they moved her to see how far her mansion had fallen into disrepair. She had heard the guns, of course, and the screams of dying men. She had not realized Virginia itself could be wounded so—the fields untended, the woods allowed to grow gnarled and thick where once they'd been cleared away for agriculture. They took her to a little plain room and a soft bed, and there they made their schemes. She was barely aware what the Union spy asked of her, barely conscious when they brought their soldiers in, one after another, each more hideously wounded than the last in body or in mind. She knew they wanted to use her strength to end their war.

It meant so very little to her.

Time had changed its complexion for Justinia Malvern, nearly two hundred years after her birth. Years flashed by like the phases of the moon. A thought once begun could reach its conclusions after a full decade had passed. She was losing a war with eternity—not the way that mortal humans lost it, in some sudden flash of pain and light and then sudden darkness. No, this was a war of attrition.

With each day there was a little less of her. A little less of her beauty, a little less of her sharp mind.

If she was going to live forever she would have to stop relying on the kindness of lovers. If she was to be immortal, she needed to start thinking. Start plotting on her own.

And she was determined that she would be immortal.

She was not without resources, even at that late date. She could command the dead—her own dead, the victims of her knights, even. She could raise them from the soil and make them do her bidding. It was simply an act of will, an imposition of desires on minds no longer able to defend themselves. And if she still possessed one quality, Justinia Malvern had an iron will.

She called on her half-deads. A wagon was summoned. A daring escape by nighttime, and she was gone.

She would not learn what happened to the army of vampires for another century. She never bothered to inquire. It didn't matter. They'd each given her some little quantity of their blood. Their strength.

As the wagon headed west and her coffin jounced and rattled in the back, she savored the taste of them. Savored her schemes and her imaginings. Yes, a new life, a life out on the frontier, where gunslingers mowed each other down in the high streets and the bodies were dragged off in smears of blood, spurs still spinning on their boot heels. A new life. A new life.

Any kind of life at all.

37.

Fetlock led the two of them toward the trailers that surrounded the clearing. Outside one of them stood a sentry in full body armor—one of the SWAT troopers from the raid. He had his face mask off and Clara saw he was a young man, barely more than a teenager, with a wispy mustache. He also had two different-colored eyes. One was a piercing pale blue, but it wasn't as arresting as it might have been, since his other eye was golden. Not hazel. Not a human eye at all. It had the golden color and the vertical slit pupil one expected in the eye of a snake.

"Trooper Darnell," Fetlock said, holding out a hand for the man to shake, "these are Clara Hsu and Special Deputy Glauer. For the moment, at least, he's still a special deputy. Ms. Hsu used to be one of my employees, but she has since left the Marshals Service. They'll be with us on this interview."

Darnell nodded but didn't say a word. His carbine hung from his shoulder, the barrel pointed at the ground, but Clara knew he could swivel it up to a firing position at a moment's notice. He looked like the kind of guy who practiced such moves—snake eye notwithstanding.

Fetlock turned to Clara and Glauer. "Trooper Darnell is an excellent field officer, but he has served me in quite a different capacity recently. I trust him implicitly, and I intend to make him a full member of the special subjects unit with all the commensurate ranks and privileges. Now. Come inside—our subjects are already secured and prepped. Hopefully they're feeling communicative."

Darnell threw a hand signal and two more SWAT troopers came over to flank the door. They weren't acting like guards outside a temporary holding facility, but more like raiders preparing to breach a hostile structure. Clara was more confused than ever.

When Fetlock opened the door of the trailer, nobody jumped out at them with homicidal intentions. The Fed went inside, followed by the rest of them. Clara let her eyes adjust to the gloom inside the unlighted trailer and then looked around. It was a cramped space decorated only sparsely, with a dream catcher hanging on one wall and a shelf full of books taking up most of the living area. The tiny kitchenette was designed to fold up into the wall when not in use. It was folded down now, revealing a narrow table flanked by two benches. Urie and Patience Polder sat on one bench facing the door, crammed together in the narrow space. Patience's hands were bound behind her with a plastic restraint cuff. Urie Polder had been secured with actual handcuffs, one cuff cinched down as tight as it allowed to hold his bone-thin wooden arm. The Polders looked fatigued but unhurt. They did not look up as Fetlock approached them.

Darnell stayed near the door, facing everyone in the small space. Fetlock squeezed into the unoccupied bench, facing the Polders, then gestured for Clara and Glauer to come stand next to him. It was a warm day outside and the air inside the trailer was stifling. Clara could hear the roof of the trailer ping in the sunshine.

"Mr. Polder," Fetlock said, folding his own hands in front of him on the table, "you've violated a number of laws, and I'm afraid I can't offer you much leniency. The charges against you are minor, for the most part. Tax evasion, possession of illegal weapons in the third degree, child endangerment, harboring a fugitive, resisting arrest . . . but they add up to a pretty damning pattern. There will have to be jail time. Your daughter, on the other hand, is a minor. It's possible I can convince the district attorney to show clemency in her case."

It was Patience who responded. She hadn't seemed to pay attention while Fetlock was talking, but suddenly she gasped and looked up with frightened eyes. "Father, that man by the door—"

"I feel it, baby girl, ahum," Urie Polder responded. Then he laughed.

It was not a particularly mirthful sound he made. It was more the laugh of a man who sees that his leg is caught in a bear trap in the moment before the pain registers. "A man in a mask. We all just assumed you meant some manner of half-dead. S'pose I shoulda asked what sort of mask."

Patience was staring at Darnell.

"What is it?" Clara asked, even though she knew it wasn't her place to speak. She squatted down next to Patience and looked the girl in the eye. "Do you know that man?"

"A few nights ago, a man came to my window and peered inside while I was sleeping," Patience told her. "He wore a mask over his face. A—a gas mask, I believe they are called. It was that man. I'm quite sure of it."

Darnell didn't move or react. Clara turned to look at Urie Polder. "They've been spying on you? But how did they get through your spells? Simon said there was no way anyone could get into this valley without your approval."

"Lest they had their own counterspell, ahum," Urie Polder assented. "That man there, he's got the eye of a snake, you see it?"

"Yes," Clara replied. "I—of course I see it."

"Only 'cause he wants ya to." Polder shook his head sadly. "I'll bet he can hide it, as he likes. He's got some strong virtue in him, that one, ahum. You. Fella. Where'd you get that serpent eye?"

Darnell surprised Clara by speaking in almost exactly the same accent and dialect as Urie Polder. "They's plenty o' Pow-Wows in this state, you know which rocks to turn over ya can find 'em," Darnell said. "My pappy was Alphonse Darnell, you know that name?"

"Ahum," Urie Polder replied. The look on his face said he wished he didn't.

Darnell nodded, briefly. "Took me out as a child, took me to see an old woman who lived down the bottom of a hollow much like this one. Told her I needed to learn the old ways. She plucked the eye right from my head, gave me this one. Hurt so much I turned away from that profession of Pow-Wowing, never wanted to learn more. But already I could see the things others don't."

Clara was starting to understand, though she didn't get the

details very well—nor did she particularly want to. "His eye can see through your spells."

"See through just about anything unnatural, ahum," Urie Polder confirmed. He turned to look at Fetlock for the first time. "How long you been spying, sir?"

"Long enough. Trooper Darnell has been living on your ridges for almost a month, evading your wards and learning your ways. Still. Ms. Caxton nearly caught him one night. I have to admit I'm impressed. I've seen Darnell sneak up on a deer in a forest clearing so smoothly the animal didn't know he was there. Not until he had his hands around the deer's throat."

Clara fought down a wave of nausea. She too had to admit she was impressed—by Fetlock. As long as she'd known him the Fed had never had any use for magic or the more esoteric bits of vampire lore, considering science a far more useful tool in tracking his subjects. Caxton must have been counting on that attitude, though, when she came to Urie Polder for protection—she must have believed that Urie Polder's magic would protect her from Fetlock's more modern forms of policework. So Fetlock had made the necessary leap and found himself a magician of his own. "If you had a man inserted here the whole time," she asked, "then why did you need me to lead you here?"

"I didn't," Fetlock told her.

"No? But—wait a minute, no, you followed us in—you followed us . . ."

Fetlock frowned at her, as if to suggest this wasn't the time for such a discussion. But then he shrugged and answered. "Trooper Darnell was able to bypass the magical protections around this place, but he couldn't disable them. I knew exactly where Caxton was this whole time, but I couldn't raid this place without setting off every alarm in the Hollow. The witchbillies would have been ready for me and we would have had a bloodbath on our hands. No, I had to wait for Caxton to lower her defenses. To be so distracted she couldn't prepare for my attack."

"And we . . . gave you that opportunity," Clara said.

"Hardly," Fetlock said, rolling his eyes. "No. Caxton didn't want you here. She did everything she could to keep you away. But there was one person she needed, one person she would let inside. When he came to her she lowered all her barriers and made it possible for me to stage this raid."

"Who are you talking about?" She glanced sideways at Glauer.

"Simon Arkeley," Fetlock told her.

38.

"Simon?" Clara gasped. "You knew Laura would approach Simon?"

"I know everything Simon does. I implanted him with an RFID device so I can monitor his movements at all times."

"What's an RFID?" Urie Polder asked.

"It stands for Radio Frequency Identification," Clara explained. "In this case it would be a tiny metallic chip, about the size of a grain of rice. You can inject it through a needle under somebody's skin, and they'd probably never even notice it was there. It doesn't have any working parts on its own, it's just a little scrap of magnetic material that can hold a few bits of data. But that data can be read remotely by another machine that knows to look for it. Most commercial RFID chips only have a range of a few feet, but apparently the Feds have some way of reading them at longer distances."

"I'm able to track him by satellite," Fetlock agreed.

"How did you do it?" Clara asked.

"The chip was implanted when he was in the hospital, recovering from the wounds his father gave him. After Caxton pulled him out of the Centralia mine. He was told it was an injection of morphine to help with the pain, and never guessed what was really happening."

"No way," Clara said, despite herself. "That's just . . . evil."

No—worse than that. It was calculating. Cold-blooded.

Fetlock didn't bat an eyelash at her accusation. "I've had updates about his movements every day since. Pretty boring stuff, really, until one day when his blip disappeared from our screens—the first time he came here. It seems even satellites can't see through the magical fog over this valley. It took us far too long to realize what was happening. We assumed it had to be an equipment malfunction, or that he had discovered the chip and removed it himself. It was Trooper Darnell who figured out what had actually happened and brought it to my attention. After that, well, I grew much more interested in keeping tabs."

Clara ran her hands through her hair. "But—but why? Why Simon? Why do this in the first place? He's just a kid. He's not even—I mean, he's kind of crazy. What made you think Caxton would ever reach out to him?"

"He's a survivor," Fetlock explained. "Vampires have a tendency to go after the ones who got away. They like to tidy up loose ends. Ever since I became involved in vampire cases, I've been putting chips in every survivor I could find. Just as a precaution. This time it turned out to be worth it."

Clara had nothing to say to that. She was too stunned.

It was Glauer who asked the obvious question. "Isn't that illegal? That's more intrusive than wiretapping, even."

"Quite," Fetlock admitted. "But we're well past the point of legal niceties now. If it means stopping Malvern, even I can learn to bend a little."

"But—surely you don't want to taint this capture. If the court finds you used illegal methods to bring her back, it could cause all kinds of problems for you, and—and—"

Fetlock wasn't looking at her. He was ignoring her words. He had sat back on the bench and folded his hands in his lap.

As if he was just waiting patiently for her to finish, so he could get back to what he really wanted to talk about.

"Unless—you didn't come here for Caxton," Clara said, piecing it together.

Glauer cleared his throat. Trying to get her attention.

She ignored him. "If you didn't come here for Caxton, then . . . why?"

Fetlock waited until she was done. Then he looked Urie Polder straight in the eye. "I've been forthcoming here. More so than I usually would. Because I need your help, Mr. Polder. In exchange for that help, I can make sure your daughter has a decent life. If you refuse, I can send her away for a long time. Juvenile detention facilities aren't as bad as adult prisons, they say. She'll be given a proper education, and even be taught a few useful skills to help her find work when she's released at eighteen. She could learn meat cutting. Or HVAC repair. There's always a need for skilled machinists. Maybe that's all you want for her."

"Down my part of the world," Urie Polder said, flexing his wooden shoulder, "folk don't threaten each other's children. T'aint done, ahum."

"Your part of the world no longer exists," Fetlock pointed out. "I've just conquered it."

"Father," Patience said, "don't listen to this man. He—"

"Hush now, girl," Urie Polder said. "Alright, Mr. Fetlock, you put the scare into me. Now tell me what you want."

"My name," Fetlock said, straightening his tie, "is Marshal Fetlock. That's how you are supposed to address me."

Urie Polder's eyes narrowed. He strained briefly against his handcuffs. Either in a vain effort to intimidate, or simply because they were uncomfortable. He let out a long exhalation of breath that was not quite a sigh. "Marshal Fetlock, what in blazes do you want?"

"There are certain wards and protections set up in a ring around this valley," Fetlock said, without so much as a nod of thanks. "You and Caxton spent quite a bit of time on them. Trooper Darnell was only able to circumvent them due to his unique gifts—and because they weren't specifically meant to keep him out. They were meant to keep away vampires and half-deads."

"Unnatural folk in general, ahum."

"I need to weaken those wards. Not remove them entirely— that I could do without you. But if they just disappeared, that would send the wrong message. It would look altogether too much like a trap. What I want is to make it look as if they haven't been properly maintained. As if they aren't as robust as they once were. I want a vampire to be able to get through them with only a little trouble."

"A vampire. Like Miss Malvern," Polder said, nodding.

"You came here to draw Malvern out!" Clara said, nearly shouting.

Fetlock turned to face her at last. "I should have thought my purposes were abundantly clear. I didn't come here just for Caxton," he said. "I came because I knew I could get all of Malvern's favorite people in one place at one time. You and Glauer. Caxton and myself. The Polders. Everyone on earth who represents any kind of actual threat to her. She's unlikely to have such a chance again—she's almost certain to strike here tonight. And we'll be ready for her. I have enough guns and enough men to handle anything she can bring to bear."

"This—all of this—killing Glynnis, threatening children, firing me, everything," Clara said, because as much as she understood it, she didn't want it to be real. "This raid was just meant as a trap for Malvern? You locked up Caxton in that paddy wagon just to tempt Malvern into attacking?"

"Caxton isn't the only one who knows how to bait a hook," he told her.

[1881]

When the Vaquero found her she wore black lace, like a lady of Spain. She lay on velvet pillows in a cave where water never stopped dripping, where stalactites grew down to touch stalagmites and form stately columns. Half-deads attended to her needs, but they withdrew discreetly when he came to her.

They called her the Mesa Ghost in town. The Mexicans called her la Llorona or la Malinche after old legends, or la Chingita when they feared her most and needed to curse her name.

They called her all kinds of things, but they never stopped coming.

The Vaquero was a hard man, scarred and gray, with one eye that was always bloodshot. He was missing teeth. He was missing two fingers from his left hand. His right hand stayed on the hilt of a knife he wore at his belt.

"Come forth," she whispered to him. The cave amplified her tiny voice. She had chosen this place carefully to minimize her weaknesses. "Come to me, lover." And she laughed. Sometimes they did come to her that way, the jaded cowboys too worn out for human whores, or too desperate for a fuck to care about the price. She used her orisons to give them what they were looking for, but always slightly twisted, slightly depraved. A man looking for his long-lost sweetheart, some girl he'd left on a railroad siding in Chicago before heading west, would find her in the cave—but oh, the things she would say, the secrets she would whisper, about how her innocence was gone, about the things she'd done in his absence. A man looking for the perfection of a Parisian beauty would find a cancan girl waiting for him, but only too late see the scars and lesions on her inner thighs.

She liked to play little games with them, to keep herself sharp.

But the Vaquero had not come for love. Nor for money—she could see it in his eyes. His haunted eyes.

"You got a true form I can see?" he asked, as he approached. Never quite so close that she might lunge over and take what she wanted from him. "I like plain dealing, is all."

She closed her eye and relaxed her spell. She felt him flinch when he saw what he was truly speaking to, but she chose not to take offense.

Justinia knew what she looked like these days, when there was no one there to see her, no distorted mirror of a man's private fantasies to shape her countenance.

"Speak your desire," she told the Vaquero.

"Desires? I got none of them. A man with desires in this desert is a dead man," he told her. "The way you stay alive is to conquer yerself."

"Interesting," she purred. "But ye came here for a reason."

He shook his head. "Damned if I know my own self what it was. Mebbe to kill you, do one good deed to atone for a lifetime of sinning. Mebbe it was to fuck you after all, like them cowboys said I could. Maybe one and then the other."

"Hopefully the latter shall come first, and the first shall be much later," she said.

"Don't try to confuse my mind. I heard tell you can do that, too." The Vaquero edged closer to her. He was careful. He was alert. She thought it might be enjoyable to charm him, to mesmerize him with her shriveled eye, but he wouldn't meet her gaze.

"The Indians say you's always been here," he went on. "But I say that ain't true. Got word from an old veteran he saw you back east, during the War Between the States. Don't know what to make of that. You sound continental, like you's from Europe. Everyone agrees on a little of the story—that you prey on those what come by here. Every rider through these canyons hears your siren call, and more than will admit it come to answer. You take a little of their soul away and in return they get what they want, though by the ashen faces I saw in town, mebbe they don't want it so much afterward. You're some kind of demon, and you're definitely a vampire, like in them old stories."

He fell silent as if he could only speak so many words in a given day and he had used up his quota. His knife had protruded an inch from its sheath as his hand played with its hilt.

Justinia was not then so much afraid of this man as wary. Respectful of his strength. She'd never met its equal before in a living man, though there had been a few women, witches mostly. . . . She found herself wishing he would relax, calm down, so she could make a shocking proposition. But he was full of some manner of stimulant—either pure adrenaline or too much coffee or some Indian drug—and he held himself like a bear trap ready to be sprung, like a pair of jaws ready to bite down on the instant.

"Ye've lied to me," she said. "I see ye have a desire, after all." When he quailed she turned her head from side to side. She had the strength for that. "Oh, ye'll not fuck me, nor do ye want power. But ye're lost. And like all lost men, ye desire to be found."

"I . . . done things," he admitted. "Things not sanctioned by the Bible."

"Tell me. I like stories," Justinia breathed. "Don't worry. I'll forgive ye for all your sins."

"That's a sorry kind of absolution you offer."

"Better than none. A man like ye—no priest can shrieve you now, can they? Ye've sinned mortally. I see it in thy blood."

He shuddered and sighed and shook. And then he nodded.

And she knew she had him.

He sat with her all through that night, grunting out his tale of heartbreak. Of a little girl in a dusty town, whose eyes were still as bright as the dawn, and of stray bullets, and of a man who never touched a gun again. A man who'd been wandering since, searching out killers, oath breakers, monsters—anyone more evil than himself.

It did not take an intellect of Justinia's caliber to know what would happen when he laid his head on her shoulder and wept bitter tears into her dress. She reached up one skeletal hand as if to comfort him.

His knife was already in her flesh, twisting through vital organs. The tip of the knife tore her liver apart, lobe by lobe.

That made her laugh. "I haven't used that in centuries," she whispered. And then she sank her fangs deep into his neck.

It was the most blood she'd dared to take in a very long time, and she grew drunk on it, intoxicated by his strength and his power. For years afterward she slept with his bones, remembering the man, reliving that wonderful taste.

39.

"No . . . no," Clara said. "No. You can't do this." She couldn't believe it—not from Fetlock.

He was going to sacrifice Caxton's life, just to draw Malvern out of hiding.

"I'm not looking for your input at this time, Ms. Hsu," Fetlock said, rising from the table. "Mr. Polder, I'd prefer to give you some time to think this over. Unfortunately that's not an option. We must be ready before nightfall, or I can't guarantee that my trap will take Malvern."

"You think you can guarantee that if he complies?" Clara demanded. "Listen, the reason we came here—the thing we wanted to warn Caxton about—you don't know how many half-deads she has. How much blood she's been drinking. Malvern isn't playing around. She's not just going to walk into a trap and let you kill her. Don't you understand? People have been trying to do that for three hundred years, and none of them have succeeded. She is not going to fall for this!"

"I have a number of surprises up my own sleeve," Fetlock said. His eyes flashed with impatience. "You are not helping me right now, Ms. Hsu. If you wish to come out of this without being charged for any number of crimes, I suggest you *start* helping me. You and Special Deputy Glauer can do that by going outside right now and walking around the clearing, making yourselves as visible as possible. I'm certain that Malvern is watching this place around the clock, and relatively certain that her spies already know you're here. I'd like to be completely sure of it."

"No, damn you. I will not play along with this. Not when you have Caxton locked up in that truck—locked up like a hen in a henhouse, waiting for the fox to come! Let her out of there. Let her out of the paddy wagon and I'll—I'll help you. Let her out and give her a gun. It's the only real chance we have. Caxton is the only one here who really knows how to fight a vampire. She's the only one here who ever killed a vampire!"

"I got a few at Gettysburg," Glauer pointed out.

Clara stared at him. "Please tell me you're on my side here."

Glauer frowned under his mustache. "Don't make this about choice. Not when we don't actually have one. Fetlock is in charge here. There's nothing we can do about that. We play his game because it's the only way. Alright?"

"No, goddamn you, it's not alright!"

"Trooper Darnell," Fetlock said, "please escort these two out of the trailer. Put them somewhere they can be seen from both ridges. I don't think they need to be restrained, but if they give you any trouble, well—use your best judgment."

The snake-eyed cop favored them with a cold smile, then stepped forward to grab at Clara's arms.

"Forget it, I'll go," she said, lifting her arms so he couldn't seize her. As she pushed her way out of the trailer, she heard Fetlock talking again to Urie Polder. Probably asking him again if he would help or not.

Outside in the summer sun, she moved quickly away from the trailer, then realized she had no idea where to go next. Her car was back up at the house, on top of the ridge. She could just retrieve it and drive away, drive as fast as she could and get as much room between her and this place as possible before nightfall. Except she doubted that Fetlock would let that happen. She turned to look back at the trailer and saw Glauer standing right behind her. Darnell waited at the door of the trailer, watching them both. Ready to move in if they tried anything. Like escaping.

"We're prisoners here," Clara said to Glauer.

"Yep. Now, will you calm down?"

"Fuck that!" she shouted. She leaned around him to look at Darnell. His snake eye was gone, and he looked perfectly normal now. "Fuck you, too, lizard face!"

Darnell didn't respond.

"You know, you're doing exactly what Fetlock wants. Right now," Glauer told her. "You're making yourself highly visible."

"Oh, for fuck's sake! Does it even matter? We both know he's right. That Malvern will come here, tonight. Whether or not we're here. Whether or not he weakens the defenses around this place. She'll come for Caxton."

"Yep. The rest is just window dressing."

Clara shoved the balls of her thumbs into her eye sockets and rubbed hard until bright geometric patterns exploded in the back of her vision. She had come here for one simple reason, one—well, maybe it hadn't been so simple, but—but—she had just wanted to see Laura again. She could not have guessed how cockeyed things would get, and just how fast. Nobody could have guessed that. It was not her fault. None of this was her fault.

Except maybe Glynnis's death. But—

"Okay!" she shouted. Then, softer, "Okay."

"Okay what?" Glauer asked.

"Okay, I'm going to calm down. I'm going to start thinking. I'm going to figure out what I need to do in this situation, what the logical thing—or at least the most survivable thing—is, and then I'm going to do it."

"Good start."

Clara shook her head. She stared down at the dirt of the clearing and tried to put the pieces together. "Malvern will come, sometime after dark. She'll have an army of half-deads with her. We've seen no sign that she has any other vampires under her command—she hasn't made any new ones, and the old ones are all dead. So she's the only real threat. A human being can take down a vampire if they know what they're doing."

"It helps if they have a lot of guns."

"Right. I don't. I don't have any weapons at all. But Fetlock does. He's got plenty of guns. Maybe he can actually do what he says. I mean, he's got two highly trained SWAT teams here, and plenty of regular cops. He's got a helicopter. Probably snipers up on the ridges, maybe some special toys to play with. He's taking the situation seriously, and he's read all the case files. So maybe, just maybe, he stands a chance."

"I wouldn't bet on it," Glauer said. "I've seen what vampires do to cops. Too many times. The cops always thought they were ready."

"Yeah," Clara said with a sigh. "I've seen it, too."

"So it's a bad wager. But in this case, we don't even have the ante. We don't get to play. We're going to have to take our chances and hope Fetlock wins."

"Yeah."

Glauer nodded as if he was pleased she'd finally seen reason. Then his eyes started moving. He didn't turn his head, but he rolled his eyes in the direction of Darnell. When he saw that Clara caught what he was trying to communicate, he nodded again, just once, and then looked to the side, toward where the paddy wagon sat in the middle of the clearing like a birthday present ready to be unwrapped.

"If we lose here, we both die, or worse. Even if we win, we get out of here with nothing but our lives. Maybe not even our freedom, if Fetlock decides to prosecute us. Like he did to Caxton, even after she took down Jameson Arkeley and saved Simon."

". . . Right," Clara said, following his argument clearly enough but not exactly sure where he was going.

"Well," Glauer said. "Given all that. What do we do in that situation?"

Clara looked up at him with wide eyes. She knew what he was suggesting—and it wasn't his usual style. It might change the odds, though. It might. "We cheat," she said, and watched him slowly nod.

40.

It was stiflingly hot inside the paddy wagon. There was almost no ventilation, and while the vehicle possessed air-conditioning, nobody had thought to turn it on. Sweat slicked Caxton's skin and made her clothes stick to her. She had to keep rolling back and forth to keep her legs from touching the hot floor, but that expenditure of energy just made her more sweaty and more hot. It was almost pitch black inside as well. She could see nothing, and could hear only the occasional sound from outside as someone went running past, or shouted out some instruction or piece of information. The thick walls of the vehicle kept her from understanding most of what was said. So she had no real idea of what was going on out there, and that was truly annoying. If she was going to make a plan, figure out some way to escape, she desperately needed more data.

It had not occurred to her to just give up. To let Fetlock take her back to prison, there to wait until Justinia Malvern came to kill her—again. She was fully aware that this was her probable fate. But she could still think, she could plan, she could imagine ways to change her current situation.

Eventually someone would have to come to extract her from the paddy wagon. There was a very little slack in the chain that connected her handcuffs to her leg shackles. If she was totally prepared she might be able to twist around and get that slack around a neck or an arm. If she could incapacitate whoever came for her, she would be left unguarded with the door open.

Assuming Fetlock only sent one person to fetch her. Which he wouldn't. The Bureau of Prisons had done this before, and they knew what the risks were. Two guards in full body armor, with excellent neck protection, would do the actual extraction. Meanwhile a whole squad of guards with shotguns and Tasers would be waiting nearby in case she tried something.

Alright. So maybe she could talk her way out of this. If Fetlock came by again—either to gloat or to interrogate her—she could offer him something he desperately needed. Her expertise. She could promise she would tell him everything she'd ever learned about killing vampires, in exchange for her freedom. Not even for letting her go. Just for allowing her a few more weeks in the Hollow, to consolidate her legacy. To get Simon and Patience ready for their generations-long vigil. To teach them what she knew.

There was only one problem. Fetlock would never go for it. He assumed he already knew everything he needed to about killing vampires. Not that he'd ever done it successfully without her help.

Caxton rocked side to side, trying to keep as much of her exposed skin as possible from contacting the searing metal floor of the paddy wagon. The vigorous motion helped keep her blood flowing as well. If she needed to act in a hurry, she couldn't afford to let her legs fall asleep.

It also helped her express a little of her anger.

Clara.

Clara, that silly little girl. Clara, who still believed in love and caring for people and the value of human life. Clara, who had never gotten it, never understood at all that as long as even one vampire still lived, nobody was ever safe. That there was nothing more important than taking down Justinia Malvern—and driving vampires to extinction, once and for all.

Clara. Who had looked so good. Who had changed her hair a little, lost her bangs, but whose eyes were—were—

Clara, who was nothing but a distraction. Even in the dark Caxton squeezed her eyes shut, trying to blank out the image in her head. The image of Clara looking betrayed. Looking to betray in return. But this was all Clara's fault. She just had to come to the Hollow and fuck *everything* up.

Clara—

Someone banged on the doors of the paddy wagon. Then they opened, and brilliant sunlight burst across Caxton's face. If her eyes hadn't already been shut, she would have been blinded. Caxton gasped as fresh air rushed into the confined space and her lungs ate it up like candy.

Slowly she cracked her eyelids to see who had come for her.

It was nobody she recognized. A guy in SWAT armor, holding a plastic water bottle. He had a particularly Pennsylvanian face, she thought. A mix of Eastern European ancestry and pure Appalachian hillbilly. He was grinning at her like she was a twelve-point buck he'd just put in the sights of his hunting rifle.

Standing behind him were six men with guns, and every barrel was trained on her face.

"Are we moving out?" she asked. "I've been waiting here for what feels like hours." There was enough left of her old spirit to want to be obnoxious. "If I'm going to prison, I'd like to get there in time for dinner."

"Oh, not quite as yet," he said. His accent sounded just like Urie Polder's. This did not give her much comfort. "But we figured maybe you'd be taking thirsty by now." He tossed the bottle at her.

She managed to catch it with her chin before it rolled away. It was warm, but not nearly as warm as the floor of the paddy wagon, and for that she was inordinately grateful. "Thanks," she said. "You going to remove my chains so I can actually drink it? Or are you going to hold it for me like a baby bottle?"

He laughed. "Don't thank me. It was your girlfriend convinced Marshal Fetlock you might die of dehydration in there. And we can't have you dyin' on us, not yet anyhow."

Clara had sent the bottle of water? Caxton pushed aside the swell of gratitude that came rushing into her throat.

"You didn't answer my question. How am I supposed to drink this?"

The SWAT trooper shrugged and laughed again. "You're s'posed to be a clever one. You figger it out on your own."

Then he slammed the doors of the paddy wagon in her face and she heard them being locked yet again.

"No!" she shouted, despite herself. "No! Come back! Tell me what's going on!"

Much as she had expected, this failed to achieve anything.

For a while she just lay there, trying not to think about Clara. Mostly she was successful. Then she turned her attention to the bottle of water.

It was a hopeless endeavor. There was no way she could get it open without spilling the whole bottle across the floor. But it was something to focus on. A project. It would help her keep her mind off of other things.

It took her the better part of an hour, but she wanted to do it right. She had to experiment with all the possible angles and all the ways of grasping the bottle without using her hands, since they were still secured behind her back. She managed to twist herself around and brace herself against the benches in the paddy wagon, then push the water bottle up against the unyielding doors. With her teeth, then, she could try to turn the cap. It would take a lot of torsion to break the plastic seal, she knew— probably more force than she could muster. She was so hot and sweaty and tired and had so little strength left. But still.

It was better to try than to despair and accept being so thirsty.

She got her teeth around the cap and twisted her neck around in an uncomfortable motion. She put everything she had left into it—

—and promptly spilled half the bottle all over herself.

The fucking cap hadn't been sealed at all. The bottle had already been opened.

Bastard! she thought. The SWAT trooper had probably spit in the bottle before he gave it to her. She sucked greedily at the water as it flowed across her shirt, trying to get as much as possible into her mouth. She didn't pay much attention to the liberated cap—there was no way she could get it back on the bottle—and let it fall to the floor of the paddy wagon.

Where it landed with a dull metallic clank.

She came very close to losing the rest of the water then. But she managed somehow to drink all that was left before investigating that unusual sound. Then, when she was pretty sure she'd seen what made the noise, she forced herself not to let her hopes carry her away.

But no. It was true.

Wedged inside the plastic cap was a short, stubby cylinder of nickel-plated steel, from one end of which protruded a narrow flange. Caxton recognized it instantly, of course. She'd seen things like it her whole adult life. Had used them more times than she could count.

It was a standard handcuff key.

"Clara," she breathed, terrified of making too much noise, terrified that at any moment the SWAT trooper would come back and see what she had. "Clara—thank you."

[1928]

Electric light—so brilliant, so painful. She'd never seen it before. She raised a hand to cover her face, but they just moved the light around on its stand. Clicking and whirring noises surrounded her. A man stood nearby, dressed in linen, smoking cigarette after cigarette.

Lenses twisted and receded, getting better focus. A man with a clap-

board snapped it in her face. "Living vampire found in California!" he called. "Take seven."

She opened her mouth. Tried to hiss.

"Perfect," someone said. "Make her bite at the camera. Make her roll her eye around like Max Shreck, that's perfect! This is good stuff, kid, good stuff."

"She weren't like this when I found her, just bones, and maggots, and mucky shit."

"Watch your mouth."

"Sorry, mister."

"That's alright, kid—listen—Movietone wants an exclusive on this, you got it? No radio, no newspapermen down here. How's five hundred dollars sound?"

"Pretty swell."

"Thought so. Rudy—get the light closer, it makes her move around more. Damn, she must have been down here a long time to get so strung out. Nathan—Nathan, get me a stick or something, anything. I'm not going to touch her with my goddamned hands, am I? Nah, she's not dangerous." The man with the cigarettes leaned over her, filled her vision. *She reached for him, but he laughed and danced away. "Couldn't suck a kitten dry, not anymore. This is great stuff. Great—"*

His cigarette fell from his mouth. The light was so bright—it blinded her—she could see nothing. It stabbed at her brains.

"Huh, stronger than she looks. Rudy, help me with—damn it. Let go, you old bitch. Let go or I swear I'll—"

The screams started then. Raw red sounds on the cool air. The light kept her from thinking. It kept her from understanding what was going on.

The blood hit the back of her throat like the balm of Gilead.

"Rudy! Rudy, you stupid fuck! Rudy—"

She heard feet pounding all around her. Men running. All of them but one. The one who couldn't get away. The blood, the blood—the blood was in her, new strength, new life. It had been a long time.

She couldn't stay there when it was done. They would be back. Back with their lights and with guns. She crawled from her coffin. Found herself in a dusty cellar. How had she gotten there? There had been a man who collected dinosaur bones—no, that was Josiah Caryl Chess. Another man, much later—a man who collected—who collected oddities, old relics—she had not been able to make him love her, she'd been too weak for that. Time. Time had gone away, she couldn't afford to let that happen again—time—

The stairs nearly undid her. She could only move one arm, and that slowly. She managed to climb the stairs. To slither out into the night. She had to find a new place. A new hiding place, before the sun came.

Consciousness fled from her with every new agony. With every inch she crawled. A dusty road. A car swerved to avoid her, its lights an agony. Had to find—had to—

A horn blared, blasting her ears. So little of her left. So long since she'd had—since she'd—

Blood.

She could smell it on the wind.

She turned her head to the side. Saw that the car had gone off the road and ended in a ditch. The car—the car was full of blood. A man and a woman inside. Not dead yet, though they would be soon. She had to—had to get to them first—

The twentieth century was a bad time for Justinia Malvern.

But she survived.

41.

Glauer sucked on his mustache. "I hope we did the right thing," he said. He'd been uneasy about the scheme the whole time, even if it had been his idea. Clara knew that he could always be counted on to do the right thing—as he saw it—but that he also had a hard time justifying his own actions when they went contrary to the law.

"I just hope we did enough," she whispered back. The two of them were walking back and forth around the clearing, making themselves visible as Fetlock had requested. Putting themselves on display for any half-deads that might be watching. She felt like she'd painted a bull's-eye on her back.

Sunset was barely half an hour away. Still the Hollow was buzzing with activity. The witchbillies had all been herded into their homes and then locked in. Guards with carbines were standing at strategic spots around the tiny village, ready to open fire if anyone tried to sneak out of their own front door. Meanwhile the SWAT troopers were digging in, quite literally digging a trench on one side of the Hollow while they established a hunting blind in the trees partway up one ridge. They were building firing positions, just like soldiers building foxholes and pillboxes in advance of an enemy attack. That was exactly what Fetlock was expecting. A frontal assault of half-deads, most likely coming up the main road—though he was prepared if they came over either ridge, too. The half-deads would try to swarm over the cops in the Hollow, and then Justinia Malvern would make her dramatic entrance, draining any survivors of blood before she went for the main prize. The paddy wagon. It stood in the middle of the clearing just waiting to be torn open so Malvern could get at the vampire hunter within.

Of course Fetlock didn't plan to actually let that happen. His intention was to have his windbreakers engage the half-deads with a withering cross fire, then let Malvern come swooping in right into the sights of half a dozen snipers. Even then he had backup plans. The best sharpshooters he had might not be enough to take down a vampire, and he knew it—vampires were devilishly fast, and snipers were most effective against stationary targets. He claimed to have some surprises hidden in his mobile command center, things he wouldn't tell Clara and Glauer about. He also had his helicopter, though what it could do remained to be seen. "We had helicopters at Gettysburg,"

Glauer had told him, arguing patiently while Fetlock just gloated. "Didn't help much."

"You used them there as support vehicles, mostly for intelligence gathering. Trust that I paid attention when I read your reports, Special Deputy."

Glauer had shrugged and asked no more questions.

So that was the trap, which Clara had to admit sounded formidable. Meanwhile Darnell was up on the ridges making sure it didn't prove too impregnable, that it didn't scare Malvern off before she even got into Fetlock's crosshairs. Fetlock and Urie Polder had figured out a way to make it look like the cops had foolishly ruined their own first line of defense. Rather than just take down the cordon of teleplasm and the perimeter of shrieking bird skulls, Darnell would tear down a few of the teleplasmic sheets as if he had been forced to do so to sneak in when he first started spying on the Hollow (he had actually been able to bypass them easily), then kick dirt over a couple of the skulls as if he'd carelessly disturbed them. They were fragile charms and easily disabled, and it was possible to make it look like he'd done so by accident. As a result of these efforts there would be a clear path for the half-deads to take through the defenses and right into Fetlock's traps, but it wouldn't look like they'd been given an engraved invitation.

By the time the sun set behind the western ridge, everything was in place. As twilight fell across the tree-lined slopes that hemmed them in on either side, Clara felt the muscles of her back stiffen and tense. She watched the last rays of red sunlight cut through the puffy clouds as if she would never see them again.

"Won't happen right away," Glauer told her.

"I know," she replied. It was very unlikely that Malvern would strike exactly at sunset. She had to sleep all day in her coffin. They had no idea where that coffin might be, but it probably wouldn't be within ten miles of the Hollow. So she would have to travel to the trap, which might take ten minutes or it might take hours. And she was far too clever to stick to any expected timetable. She would strike when they least expected it. Which meant they had to expect it to come at any moment.

Glauer and Clara kept wandering back and forth across the clearing, even as it grew so dark they could barely make out each other's faces in the twilight. Even when they started tripping on tree roots and rocks. They had not been given orders to stop.

Every inch of Clara's skin prickled with fear. Every pore of her body exuded greasy fear sweat, though the temperature dropped rapidly as the darkness grew complete. Every instinct she had told her to run away.

"Might not happen tonight," Glauer said, his voice strangely loud in the dimness.

"You know it will," she said.

Still. Fifteen minutes passed in full darkness, and nothing happened.

An hour passed, and nothing happened.

Two hours.

"Oh my God, come on already!" Clara screamed, trying to break the tension. Nearby one of the windbreaker cops grabbed his gun and trained it on her, his eyes wide, his back heaving as he sucked in breath. Apparently she wasn't the only one going crazy with the waiting.

She tried to control herself.

She nearly jumped out of her skin when a radio crackled somewhere behind her. She spun around and saw Fetlock leaning out of the back of the mobile command center. Yellow light painted half his face. He had a walkie-talkie in one hand and he brought it up close to his mouth.

"Unit Nine? Say again," he ordered.

"Unit Nine reporting contact," the walkie-talkie replied. The man on the other end of the connection sounded tense and harried. "We have multiple subjects, moving through the tree line, at locations Whiskey Three and again at Yankee One. Repeat, we have—"

The man fell silent. Clara couldn't move a muscle. All she could do was stand there and watch Fetlock's face. Nothing in it changed.

"Unit Nine, say again," Fetlock ordered.

But Unit Nine didn't repeat his information. Instead he started screaming, a terrible, tinny little sound coming from the walkie-talkie. The sound of a man being torn to pieces while he was still alive.

There was no question. The attack was starting.

42.

The Fed reached down and lowered the volume on his radio, but Clara knew the man up on the ridge was still screaming. She could hear it directly now, floating on the air.

"Everyone stay frosty. Maintain your posts," Fetlock called to the cops in the Hollow. "This is what we planned for. What we've been training for the last month."

There were a few cries of assent, of determination. Most of the cops just kept their heads down. They'd heard the stories. They knew what happened when the police tried to fight vampires.

So did Clara. "Glauer," she said. "Glauer, this is going to get bad."

"I know," he told her. "Now shut up."

She started to protest, but she knew he was right. Worrying about what came next wouldn't change it. Talking about it only made the apprehension worse.

"All sniper units, report in," Fetlock said into his walkie-talkie. One by one, eight men called in to report no contact.

Up on the ridge the screaming stopped. Not as if the man up there had been finished off. Just as if he'd run out of breath and couldn't make any more noise.

"He should bring up the helicopter—get a better visual on the situation—light some flares," Clara muttered. She couldn't help herself. "He should give us guns."

"I know," Glauer said again.

"Ground units, report in," Fetlock said.

One by one the SWAT troopers and the windbreakers started calling in. Just confirming they were still alive.

"Infrared, give me a report," Fetlock said.

"No contact. No movement," the walkie-talkie said.

"IR? Why is he using IR? Half-deads don't radiate heat. He should be using night vision instead, so—"

"I *know*," Glauer insisted.

Then he grabbed her arm. He must have seen something. Something Clara missed. Off to one side of them, a windbreaker cop started turning around, bringing his gun up. Something snatched him out of the dark and pulled him back into the woods, so fast he didn't have a chance to report on it.

A moment later he started screaming. He was not fifteen yards away from where Clara and Glauer stood.

The SWAT troopers opened fire on where he'd been. There was no way they could be sure they weren't shooting their own man, but they must have had orders to shoot anyway. Carbines barked and spat as bullets tore through the dark trees on that side of the Hollow. "Now, lights!" Fetlock called, and a bank of floodlights on top of the mobile command center swiveled in that direction and flared to life.

Clara just had time to see a skinless face peering out from between two tree trunks before it flickered away, too fast to follow. More bullets snapped off in the direction of the half-dead, but it was long gone.

"Ground units, fire at will," Fetlock called.

But there was nothing to shoot.

The man in the woods had stopped screaming almost at once. Clara listened hard for any kind of movement in those trees, peered into the shadows for any human-shaped silhouette. But there was nothing.

"Guerrilla tactics," Glauer said.

"What?" Clara demanded.

"She knows that Fetlock wants a frontal assault. A big pitched battle. She won't give him that. She'll pick us off one by one. This isn't a war. It's a slasher flick."

"You two—shut up or I'll have you cuffed," Fetlock shouted at them. "Ground units fall back. Form a perimeter, keep the man on your left and the man on your right in sight at all times. Do not engage the enemy until you have a clear target. Do not, repeat, do not under any circumstances—"

More screams came from the other side of the Hollow. Clara spun around to look, but there was nothing to see. Guns fired and lights swiveled around, blinding her for a moment. Over the walkie-talkie someone screamed, "It's got my legs! My fucking legs!"

And then: silence.

Once again.

"Goddamn it," Fetlock muttered. "Alright, get that bird in the air—get lights moving, cover the area in a standard sweep pattern, get me information. For fuck's sake, someone get me information! I need contacts, people. Somebody give me a contact!"

"There," Darnell said, peering into the gloom with his snake eye. "There—and there." He pointed. His arm floated sideways and he pointed again. "They's not many of 'em, but they move awful fast. They—"

He stopped because everyone saw the next contact. A half-dead, stripped down to the waist and barefoot, came running into the clearing, shrieking with high-pitched laughter. Its face hung in tatters from its cheeks and chin. It had something bulky strapped around its waist.

"She'll take your blood, every one of you!" the half-dead screamed.

Then Glauer grabbed Clara, picking her up like a sack of potatoes, and threw her behind him. She reflexively struggled against him, even as the half-dead exploded.

It must have been wearing a belt of dynamite on a short fuse. The blast tore through the clearing, lighting up every face, every posture in silhouette. Men screamed and cried out and wept even as the blast echoed and boomed in Clara's ears. Blood was everywhere, blood and—and—oh God, someone's leg, someone's detached leg was right next to her, it might have been the half-dead's, or it might have belonged to a cop, it was too bloody to be sure—

"Squad heads, check your people," Fetlock shouted. "Fall back, form a perimeter. Circle the wagons, people, circle the wagons! Shoot anything that moves, repeat, shoot anything that approaches this clearing!"

Another shrill giggle, and another half-dead came running toward the clearing. Overhead the helicopter's rotor thundered through the still summer night. A lance of light stabbed down at the ground, lighting up the half-dead as bullets riddled his body. He spasmed and danced, but his hand reached for a plunger at his belt and then he disappeared in a cloud of red, and the shock wave banged into the side of a trailer like a rain of hammers.

"Squad leaders, keep your people in sight, fire at will, fire at will!" Fetlock screamed.

"Move it," Glauer shouted, pushing Clara ahead of him as he bulled toward a foxhole. "Move your ass!"

Clara did as she was told, diving into the foxhole as a third bomber detonated at the edge of the clearing. The noise was unbelievable, the screams lost in the booms, the helicopter pounding at the air, pounding and beating until she thought her eardrums would pop. There were six windbreakers in the foxhole, and as she landed in the loose dirt at its bottom six guns were trained on her. One fired but the bullet went wide. Glauer landed next to her, then grabbed the cop who had shot at her, grabbed him and screamed in his face, but she couldn't hear what he said. She couldn't hear anything. She grabbed Glauer's massive arm and tried to pull him off the windbreaker, but he wasn't having it; he was too busy screaming at the man, screaming at him for almost shooting one of his own. There was another explosion and Fetlock shouted something; he sounded panicked; she'd never seen him be anything but calm and cool and collected. This was a disaster, a real cluster fuck. She had no idea what would happen next, but she knew it would be bad, knew it would be—would be—

Silence fell once more, but it was so unreal she failed to believe in it at first. She could just barely hear the helicopter's engine. She peeked over the top of the foxhole and saw its light sweeping along the side of the ridge, lighting up one tree after another. Lighting up animal trails, lighting up old mining equipment that had rusted in place.

The light found a pile of corpses. The bodies of cops, at least half a dozen. They'd been stacked neatly, as if for later retrieval.

Fetlock's walkie-talkie crackled and bleeped. Someone was calling for him, asking for further orders. They repeated the request.

She couldn't see Fetlock from where she crouched in the foxhole, but she could still hear him.

"Stay vigilant," Fetlock said. "This isn't over by a long shot. They're just giving us time to get scared."

"It's working," Clara said. But only under her breath.

[1961]

Where am I? *Malvern thought. She was too weak to project the words beyond the cage of her own skull. She was barely aware of the taste of blood on her shriveled tongue—a taste she'd missed so for lo these many years. She was all but blind, but she could feel the world gently rocking around her.* Am I asea?

She received an answer, though she had not expected one.

"You're on my boat." *A hand moved across her face and a wet towel swiped at the dirt that had crusted over her one desiccated eye.* "You're safe."

She would have panicked, except that the hand didn't smell human. It smelled like her own flesh, though far fresher. As the dirt came away from her face she slowly began to make out the pale round face of a fellow vampire, the red eyes, the pointed ears. The wicked teeth drawn back in a sad smile.

Ye can hear me, so I'm not quite dead.

"No," *the vampire responded, with a soft, sympathetic chuckle.* "Though it was hard to tell at first. I found you buried in a shallow grave. How did you get there?"

There were . . . dogs . . . men with . . . rifles . . . I remember it but unclearly. *Even thinking the words was a trial after so long. For years she'd languished in that makeshift grave, her thoughts, like her body, slowly fossilizing. She had lost so much in that time, piece by piece. Language had been one of the first things to go, so that after a while she could only scream in silence, incoherent howls no living thing could hear. Her sanity had fled not long after.* I crawled into the soil like a cadaver. Covered myself . . .

"You're weak still," *the vampire told her.* "You'd been down there quite a while, with nothing to sustain you. Here. I can spare a little more."

He opened his mouth wide and thick, clotted blood splattered across her face, most of it landing on the back of her throat. Undignified it might have been, but she didn't care. Couldn't care—she needed it so badly. She felt the blood soaking through her like water leaching into porous stone. Felt a trickle of life returning to her limbs.

Who are ye? And why did ye come for me?

"My name is Piter Byron Lares," he told her. It meant nothing to her. "I'm . . . one of the last. Perhaps the last of us still able to walk under his own power. Our once great race has withered and declined so. Here. Let me show you what I do. What I've chosen to do with the time that remains to me."

He put down the towel and cradled her in his arms. So very carefully— more carefully than ever a mother held her babe. He had to take such pains lest Justinia fall to pieces in his grasp.

He walked with a measured step like a priest in a processional. Slowly he brought her to another room, a cramped little space filled with engines and fuel tanks. A row of coffins filled the floor, each of them opened to show the bones inside. No, not just bones. Dim red eyes peered up at her, while paper-thin lips peeled back over triangular teeth as if the vampires in those coffins were jealous of the attention Lares showed her. As if they resented this newcomer in their midst.

"We're dying out," Lares said. "Going extinct. I've heard—from these others, I've heard the old tales. The glorious stories of what we once were. I've devoted my immortality to keeping as many of us as possible alive, for as long as I can. I don't know what will happen when I have to enter my coffin for the last time myself. But I'll hold that day off as long as possible."

One of the coffins was empty. It was clean inside, and smelled like it had never been used. He laid her down on the satin lining and arranged her hands across her chest. Straightened the tattered fabric of her mauve nightgown.

She could feel the thoughts of the other relics, the other dilapidated undead like herself, now that their brains were so close to hers.

. . . too many already . . . not enough blood for us all . . . do you know who I am? I deserve the lion's share . . . blood . . . must have more . . . blood . . . blood . . . blood . . .

"There," Lares said, smiling down at her. "Welcome, Miss Malvern, to our happy little family. I'm sure you'll get on just fine with the others. Now, if you'll excuse me—I have to go out and find some more nourishment for us all. Please, rest and recover your strength. You're perfectly safe here, I promise."

She could barely hear his voice over the chorus of desperate thoughts around her.

. . . blood . . . more . . . blood . . . blood . . . I must have it . . . blood . . .

It was not an unfamiliar refrain.

43.

"All snipers report in," Fetlock called over his walkie-talkie. "Repeat, sniper units report in. Unit one, report. Unit two, report. Repeat—unit two, report," Fetlock said, going down the numbers even though it was abundantly clear all the snipers were dead.

In the clearing the remaining windbreaker cops moved back to back, covering each other with tight firing arcs but staying on their feet in case they needed to run. The foxholes and defensive positions were useless now, when faced with the prospect of more exploding suicidal half-deads.

The main problem with using half-deads as soldiers was that they couldn't operate firearms. Their bodies were just too decayed and weak to handle the recoil, so instead they were limited to knives and blunt objects. As a result vampires typically used their slaves to harass the enemy, or to distract them while the vampires moved in for the kill. That didn't work so well when your enemy knew you were coming and was ready to shoot at the first sign of white skin and red eyes in the dark.

It didn't take much structural integrity to blow yourself up with a stick of dynamite, though—in fact, the flimsiness of the half-deads actually made them more dangerous when they exploded. Their bones would turn into deadly shrapnel. And it wouldn't be hard to convince half-deads to go out with a bang. They despised their twilight existence, longed for death even as they were compelled to do the bidding of their vampiric masters.

Now the stench of death and blood filled the air, while men rolled on the ground and screamed. Their fellow cops did what they could for the wounded, patching and bandaging where such was appropriate, but there was no time and no facilities to really help. If they didn't get to a hospital soon they would die right in the clearing.

"SWAT teams to the rear," Fetlock called, waving toward the road that led out of the Hollow. "I want our path kept open in case we need to retreat. Check all the vehicles, make sure they weren't damaged in the explosions." He was making the best use of the breathing room the attackers had provided, Clara knew, but his orders infuriated her.

"He's going to abort, isn't he?" she asked Glauer. "There were too many of them. More than he expected, and now he's screwed. His carefully laid plans are all falling apart, and he's just going to pull out. Save as many of his people as he can—but leave us and the witchbillies here to hold Malvern's attention."

"Uh-huh," Glauer replied, as if he'd never expected anything more.

Clara remembered how, when she had been held hostage inside a women's prison by Malvern and her cohorts, Fetlock had let her sit and stew for hours—most of a day—because he didn't want to risk any cops in a rescue attempt. He'd sat back and let Caxton do all the fighting then. It was definitely his modus operandi. "That son of a bitch. This is exactly what Caxton tried to teach us about fighting vampires. You don't get to pick your battles!"

"She also taught us how to stay alive as long as possible,"

Glauer replied. He bent over the body of a dead windbreaker cop and pried the gun out of his cold hands. He grunted with distaste as the corpse's fingers refused to let go of the weapon's barrel. Maybe rigor mortis was already setting in—or maybe the man had died in such a state of panic his fingers had locked in a literal death grip. "Arm yourself, Clara. This is going to get ugly pretty fast."

Clara nodded but didn't move from where she stood. She was watching Fetlock intently.

There was still time to turn this around, if he could admit he was wrong.

She strode toward him, not sure if she was going to slap him or just call him a coward. He was so busy shouting orders for his imminent escape that he didn't see her coming—but Darnell did.

The snake-eyed trooper jumped in front of her, carbine held out in front of his body—not with the barrel actually pointing at her, but so that if she threw herself at him she would collide with the gun and not his softer arm. "That's far enough," he said, and she stopped in her tracks. "Get back," he ordered.

She ignored him and called out to Fetlock. "There will be more of them. A lot more than you planned for. I told you, she's been recruiting half-deads for months, she has hundreds of—"

"Whatever she sends, we can handle," Fetlock said. "Now, stop distracting me, Ms. Hsu. I have a battle to command here."

"But you're the wrong general," she insisted.

He glared at her with enough cold fury to make her take a step back.

"Caxton should be in charge here. You have to let her out!" she said. "Caxton is our only chance. You have to free her and give her whatever weapons she wants. You know she's the only one who can stop Malvern!"

Fetlock studiously ignored her. He called out some more orders, shouting for the windbreaker cops to get the vehicles started and running so they could move out at a second's notice.

"Damn you, Fetlock—you know I'm right! She's the one who kills vampires. You just fill out the fucking paperwork afterward! Let her out of that paddy wagon!"

"Not a chance," Fetlock said, finally. He looked up at the ridges, where the helicopter was still circling, still looking for an invisible enemy. "Darnell, if she approaches me again, incapacitate her. Don't actually kill her—she won't be good bait then. But I don't want to hear her screeching little voice again."

Darnell grinned and raised his carbine as if he would knock her down then and there. Clara growled in frustration and moved back. She found Glauer waiting for her by the side of a trailer, crouching low and heavily armed. He threw a pistol to her as she approached, and she nearly dropped it because it was slick with blood.

Snarling, she worked the action and put a round in the chamber.

"You ready for this?" Glauer asked.

"No. Do I get to wait until I am ready?"

"No."

She nodded and pressed her back up against the side of the trailer. And waited for the next attack.

She didn't have to wait very long.

The SWAT troopers moved into the road, keeping perfect fire discipline as they advanced, covering each other in a bounding overwatch as they secured each yard of ground. They were headed back toward the vehicles, perhaps under orders to secure them before Fetlock's forces were bottled in. It was full dark now and the road was merely a slightly paler strip of ground in the darkness. They had red-lens flashlights that preserved their night vision, but the lights could only illuminate small patches of the woods that crowded close on either side of the road.

Still, they were ready for the first assault. A particularly agile half-dead had climbed up into one of those dark trees, and when the SWAT team passed beneath, it fell on them in a flurry of knives and punches. It landed on the back of one trooper, who panicked and dropped his gun. The half-dead's knife couldn't stab through his thick Kevlar armor, but the creature wrenched at the trooper's head as if it would pull it off his neck. The trooper tried desperately to reach behind his neck for the half-dead, all the while shouting for help.

The other SWAT troopers were smart enough to fall back away from him, their guns up but their fire held until they could get a proper shot. They remembered their training and followed protocol to the letter. But it turned out that was a mistake.

As they drew back, some of them stepped off the road and into the trees—where a dozen more half-deads were waiting for them.

How many of those bastards does she have? We were expecting a small army—but there's no end to these things, Clara thought, shocked as she watched a half-dead slit a trooper's throat, even as another trooper opened fire and cut it in two twitching halves. Another trooper went down as a half-dead reached up under his visor and clawed at his eyes.

The windbreaker cops facing the road raised their own weapons and started firing, too scared to realize the danger of hitting one of their own SWAT troopers. The troopers were covered in bullet-resistant armor, but it did little to absorb the kinetic energy of so many rounds hitting them all at once. The half-deads went down, ripped to pieces by the gunshots, but the troopers were knocked around and thrown backward by the impacts as well, which just made them easy prey for the next wave of half-deads waiting in the trees.

Someone shouted—half scream, half warning—and suddenly every weapon in the clearing barked to life. Clara spun around and saw that a small army of half-deads had emerged from the woods on the far side of the clearing, the side away from the road. They had used the attack on the SWAT troopers as a diversion to mask their approach, and now they ran straight for the ring of windbreakers that surrounded Fetlock and his mobile command center.

Right toward Clara and Glauer.

"Take them down!" Fetlock shrieked. "Keep this area clear! Goddamn it, don't let them overrun us!"

His words were wasted. The windbreakers were already fighting for their lives, firing blindly as the half-deads came screaming on. There were dozens of them—scores. Clara couldn't get an accurate count, and anyway, it didn't matter. She lifted her weapon and started firing like all the rest, even as Glauer opened up with his carbine next to her.

Even though she was certain she was about to die.

44.

The stuttering light of the guns shredded Clara's night vision and made it impossible to see half the targets she shot at. She fell back toward Fetlock's position, but they just kept coming. Some of the half-deads came on with glittering eyes or flashing knives, but most of them were just dark smudges, silhouettes against the broken shadows of the trees. One came at her with a pipe wrench held high over its head, and she barely saw it in time to bring up her gun and blow its head off. Another leapt past her with a howl and stabbed wildly at a windbreaker cop with his kitchen knife. The cop fired point-blank into his attacker's chest, again and again, but the half-dead just kept swinging its knife, over and over again, until the cop gasped and fell. Glauer spun around and carved the half-dead in half with a burst of fire, then turned back to face the woods just in time as three more half-deads came at them.

He caught one across its torn face with a three-shot burst, then blew the next one's arm off, sending it spinning and tripping over tree roots. The third one howled and jumped into the air, intending to smash Glauer's skull with a two-by-four. Clara dropped to one knee and shot it through the eye, sending it flipping over backwards before it could bring its weapon home.

"Thanks," Glauer said.

She didn't have time to respond. More of the bastards were coming. She shot one in the mouth, then spun around to face another that was only a dozen yards away. "So many of them," she gasped. "Malvern went for broke here, didn't she? To have killed this many people, without drawing police attention—"

She stopped talking as a meat cleaver came whistling past her ear. Careful not to let go of her pistol, she dodged to one side, then brought up her foot and smashed it down hard on the half-dead's kneecap. The thing screamed as it toppled over, no longer able to stand. Still it crawled toward her, its cleaver swinging for her ankles, until she put a shot through the back of its neck.

"I think she's past the point of caring about police attention. Fetlock handed her the perfect opportunity to wipe out all of us in one night. After this," Glauer said, "there won't be anybody left who knows her tricks."

On every side of them desperate melees played out. Cops struck at half-deads with empty firearms, using them like high-tech bludgeons, or simply beat at them with naked fists. The half-deads were so structurally weak that a good right hook could knock one of their heads off, and if it had all been one-on-one, the cops could easily have defeated Malvern's soldiers. But there were so many of them, and with every passing minute there were fewer cops. Clara emptied her pistol into a half-dead's back, then bent low to scoop up a new gun from a fallen windbreaker's belt. She kicked and swung and shot her way through a knot of the creatures, headed for the side of a trailer so she could at least get her back up against something, so she could see her death when it came for her. Glauer followed her lead, covering her the best he could.

"Everyone, this way!" she shouted, hoping to rally some of the windbreakers. If they could get inside one of the trailers, maybe they could barricade it against attack, maybe they could hold out just a little longer. "It's your only chance! This way!"

A windbreaker cop looked up at her, as if he desperately wanted to believe she knew what she was doing. He reached toward her with one hand, but blood was already spilling from his mouth. He slumped forward and she saw a boning knife sticking out of the back of his skull.

She shivered in horror, but knew she couldn't afford to lose her cool. She shrugged off her fear, at least for a moment. "This way!" she called again.

There was no answer. Either the windbreakers were too busy holding their own, or there was nobody alive left to heed her call. She threw her back against the side of the trailer and looked around for Glauer, terrified she'd lost him in the massacre. Then he appeared in front of her, a huge shadow struggling wildly with a half-dead that had clamped on to his back. With a wave of revulsion Clara saw that it was missing both legs—they ended in ragged stumps—but that its arms were clasped tight around Glauer's waist and it had its teeth in his neck.

She lurched forward and grabbed its head, feeling strips of skin part under her fingers where she touched its face. It laughed maniacally as she pulled its jaws apart, releasing Glauer's flesh. It kept laughing even when she pulled its head off of its neck and threw it deep into the darkness. She had to pry its arms off of Glauer as well.

"Jesus, thanks," Glauer said, panting heavily. He had cuts all over one cheek and his neck, and one sleeve of his shirt had been torn off. There was a bad bloody wound on his elbow, but he was still standing.

"Save the gratitude," she told him. "Look."

He flung himself against the side of the trailer to protect his back, then took in what she'd already seen.

They were surrounded. In every direction, half-deads were approaching them warily, knives clutched in their bony hands. There were at least a dozen of them coming straight at Clara and Glauer. She could still hear the occasional burst of gunfire, but it sounded far away—too far away to offer any hope of reinforcements.

"How you doing for ammo?" Glauer asked.

"No idea, and no time to check. Gotta be getting low, though. You?"

He held up his empty hands. "Bastard took my gun."

"Shit," Clara said.

"We go down fighting, right? No surrender."

"Better than letting Malvern get us."

"Yeah," Glauer agreed. "That one first."

She looked where he was pointing, at a half-dead carrying a machete. It gripped the weapon in both hands and lifted it over its head. She raised her pistol and shot it through the biceps. Its arm came loose at the shoulder, but it didn't drop the blade. She shot it again, this time in the chest. It spun to one side—but then it recovered and took a step toward her. She lined up another shot, aiming for its forehead this time, and—

Her gun clicked impotently in her hand. She was out of bullets.

The half-deads laughed wildly and came running toward them, knowing they no longer had anything to fear. Clara threw the pistol at the closest of them, then dropped into a fighting crouch, her hands balled into fists.

She had been in near-death situations before. Plenty of them. Sometimes an eerie calm came over her. Sometimes she felt like she was standing outside of her own body, observing what was happening with a clinical detachment.

This time she was just scared witless.

"Nice knowing you," Glauer shouted, and then he ran forward to intercept the half-deads as they came rushing in.

"No!" Clara shouted.

Behind her head she heard something wooden snap and break with a noise like a muffled gunshot. She had no idea what made that sound, nor did she care. She did manage to scream as the door of the trailer slammed open.

Urie Polder staggered out. His wooden arm was broken off near the shoulder. His remaining hand lifted toward his face, and in the light that streamed out through the trailer door, Clara saw his palm was full of some kind of glittering powder.

He took a deep breath, then blew hard on the powder, sending it flying outward in a cloud of sparkling light. There couldn't have been more than half an ounce of powder in his hand, but the cloud it made grew and grew, billowing out toward the half-deads.

When the glittering stuff touched them, they started to scream. They dropped their weapons and scratched maniacally at their exposed flesh, tearing off whatever skin remained, scratching until their finger bones tore through ropy pink muscle tissue, scratched until they tore themselves apart. They kept screaming long after they fell down. It seemed they would never stop screaming.

Glauer had been locked in a grapple with one of the half-deads. The powder didn't seem to affect him at all, but his eyes went wide as the creature he held fell to pieces in his grasp. He thrust it away from him, then ran back to the trailer to nod at Urie Polder.

"That should do it, ahum," Polder said.

[1983]

The man was soaking wet and chilled so badly his blood moved like slug-gish pack ice in his veins. He was wounded, his bones bruised and jarred, his face a mask of agony. Yet there was something about this one—something that frightened Justinia to her core, some quality of desperate resolution that she knew would make him a dire enemy.

For one thing, he was holding Lares' heart in his left hand like a black apple, as if he might take a bite out of it at any moment. Lares fell backward and struck the floor of the boat like a hammer coming down, his heels drumming on the floor.

The others, the old ones, dragged themselves from their coffins, think-ing of nothing but depredation, of slaying this human and taking his blood. And oh, what a prize that would be—this creature who had slain their defender.

Justinia felt no grief for Lares. Like all her knight protectors, he'd failed to protect himself. He deserved none of her grief. She only watched with a calculating eye as the others pulled themselves toward the human, and knew this wasn't right—that it couldn't possibly end well.

The man kicked them away, their jaws snapping at the air around his feet. In their weakened condition they could do nothing to stop him. One man prevailing against a half-dozen vampires—it was a disgrace. How low they had all fallen! The man sprayed fuel across the boat's hold, a rank stink that offended Justinia's newly recovered sense of smell. And then he brought fire down on them all, and he left them. His work was done.

The others screamed inside her head.

blood!

without blood we cannot—

—must have his—

I burn! I burn!

get his blood, bring it to me!

They scrabbled over each other, burning hands reaching for each other, reaching for hope, for help that could not come. The flames exploded through the cramped space as they desperately tried to crawl back to their coffins, to some illusion of safety.

Justinia worked her orison, the one Vincombe had taught her. She alone seemed to have the presence of mind to protect herself, to act rationally.

To, perhaps, survive.

The closest coffin was not her own. It belonged to a withered old bat of a vampire, a creature of the Enlightenment so vain he had forced Lares to put a wig on his withered head, even when there was no one to see it. Justinia dragged herself across the floor with one skeletal arm to reach it. Over a score of years in Lares' care she'd regained some tiny shred of strength. It would have to be enough.

She felt bony fingers clutch at her ankle from behind. She spared enough energy to glance back and see another of Lares' charges—one who claimed to have seen Rome fall, if one could credit such a thing—pulling her back toward the flames.

Get blood for me, he thought at her. I need blood.

Get your own, ye pagan thing, she sent back, and kicked him away. She pulled herself into the coffin even as flames licked its sides, even as the ancient decayed flesh of the vampire behind her crackled and spat.

Then she pulled the lid tightly closed on top of her, and squeezed her eye shut, and desperately hoped it had been enough.

The flames roared—and then, quite suddenly, were replaced with a terrible hiss, as if a giant snake had swallowed her coffin whole. She felt the floor give way beneath her, felt water press in on every side as the boat collapsed and sank. Icy cold water jetted in around the edges of the coffin lid, but she could do nothing about that, could only hold the lid with her last remaining ounce of strength, hold it shut as she sank into lightless depths.

It was all she could do. It would have to be enough.

One by one she felt the others dying. She felt their minds wink out like terrible dreams on waking, felt them scream their last. And still she sank. *The sun was coming up in the world above. It was almost dawn. She would not be able to hold on longer when the sun came. The water would rush in, and mayhaps it would scatter her bones. This could be the last trick she ever played, the last spill of cards across the green baize. It could be the end.*

It could be. It could be her death.

For three hundred years, almost, she'd waited for this. She'd looked forward to it sometimes. Sometimes she had fought it tooth and nail. She clutched to the lid, because she could do nothing else. And then—

The sun came up, even if she could not see it, and her mind went away as it did every morning, washed away by the light.

She would never know what happened in that day. How they found her, or how they dragged her bones up from the bottom of the river. The next night she woke to the sound of machines pumping and bleating all around her. To cool air and scratchy starched sheets underneath her. She woke to see men all around her. To see their blood pumping through their bodies. Pumping fast. They were afraid of her.

She wanted to smile but lacked the strength.

A face loomed over her. A face she knew, though she'd seen it only once before. The face of the half-drowned man who had killed Lares.

"My name is Jameson Arkeley," he told her. "The court says I'm not allowed to kill you. That you can't be linked to any crime, so you can't be executed. The court specifically did not say that I have to be nice to you. It didn't say I couldn't torture you for information. It didn't say I couldn't make your life a living hell."

Ask what ye'd know, and I'll speak, *Justinia told him.* Though there'll be a price. *She was more than willing to trade all her secrets for another drop of blood.*

He didn't seem to hear her.

"I don't care who you are or what you used to be," he went on. "A lot of good men died, and you didn't. I hate that. From now on, bitch, you're mine."

His bluster failed to scare her. Because she had seen something in his eyes—a darkness she knew well. A darkness all her men had shared.

Am I? *she wondered.* Am I yours, darling Jameson? Am I to be your lover, then?

Perhaps—perhaps not. But as she looked at the men around her, at the doctors and the policemen who'd come to look on her, she knew. She knew with a certainty—one of them would serve. It seemed that fate had time for one last hand, one more deal of the cards.

45.

Clara spun around, looking for threats—and found none. All of the half-deads in the vicinity were down, their bones still twitching, their screams having turned into plaintive moans. One by one they fell silent.

"Uh—thanks," Clara said. "What the hell was that?"

"Goofer dust," Urie Polder said. "Grave dirt and rattlesnake skin, mostly." As if that explained everything. "This here's Heather's trailer. Lucky she had some on hand. Wish I had a bit more."

"Yeah," Clara said, and turned again to scan the darkness. She couldn't see much, but there were definitely more half-deads out there, moving through the shadows. Except she realized not all of those shadows were enemies.

Some of them were witchbillies. Clearly they'd decided the cops couldn't protect them, and had taken matters into their own hands. Clara could just make out Heather, her hands lifted in complicated gestures that made half-deads explode as she walked past them. She could see a woman in a bonnet holding a slender wooden wand. When she pointed it at a half-dead the creature went rigid and immobile, forced to stand upright in perfect posture with its hands at its sides. That gave a man with a fringe of beard time to blow its head off with a shotgun.

Other witchbillies were searching through the bodies strewn

about the clearing, helping the few surviving windbreaker cops to their feet—or doing what they could in the way of first aid for those unable to stand.

It was over. The battle was over—so abruptly her body couldn't seem to believe it. Her arms kept twitching, reaching for her gun. The cops were routed, and there had been terrible casualties. But it was over. No more half-deads came screaming out of the woods. No more suicide bombers. No more tittering maniacs falling out of trees.

The witchbillies had carried the day. At least for the moment.

"I'm glad you're on our side," Clara said.

"Half-deads are unnatural sorts of bein's," Urie Polder told her. "Our art's well effective against that type of thing. More so than 'gainst your police friends. And none of us is a match for Malvern, ahum."

"Maybe she won't come now. Now that we beat her troops," Clara pointed out. Even as she said it she knew it was just wishful thinking.

"She's already on her way," Polder replied with a sad sigh. "I can feel it."

"You can?"

"I ain't got the second sight, like Patience. But I feel her all the same. The thing that killed my wife . . . I'd know her anywhere."

Clara could only stare at him in terror.

Polder closed his eyes and nodded. "She's passed the teleplasm cordon, ahum. Didn't so much as slow her stride. We got mayhaps ten minutes 'fore she's here. Best get ready."

Clara bit her lower lip and tried not to think about what was coming. She looked Urie Polder up and down and saw as if for the first time the short stump that was all that remained of his wooden arm. "You're hurt," she said.

"Seemed the best way out of them handcuffs, ahum," he told her.

"Jesus, you just—you snapped off your own arm to get free?"

"Hurt a mite. Patience is still inside, still bound. You want to help me out by getting her loose?" Polder asked.

Clara nodded dumbly. She rushed inside and found the teen-aged girl still handcuffed to the trailer's small table. "Don't worry," she said. "We'll get you out of here."

"I'm not worried," Patience said. She looked scared all the same. "I know how I'm going to die, Ms. Hsu. I know exactly when it will happen."

Clara studied the handcuffs as a puzzle she needed to solve. She didn't have a key for the cuffs, so she looked at the table leg they were attached to. It was made of aluminum, and not very thick. She kicked at it a couple of times and it dented, then buckled in the middle. Heaving and straining, she managed to break it away from the table. She pulled the cuff free and Patience stood up, rubbing at her wrist.

"Wait," Clara said. "You've seen what happens here? You know how this is going to end?"

"I do."

"Do I—I mean—how many of us make it out of—"

"Knowing that wouldn't help you," Patience said, calmly. "It would only make you apprehensive. You would constantly be worrying about the terrible things yet to come."

"Christ. But just tell me if Caxton . . . if she . . ."

"No," Patience said, with a determined shake of her head. "No, I won't tell you. Now, come along. They need you out-side."

"Yes, ma'am," Clara growled. Then she stalked out of the trailer, back into the darkness.

Glauer was waiting for her there. He had a new bandage around his elbow, and somewhere he'd found a new weapon, a SWAT carbine. He tossed it to her, and she saw he had another one on a strap over his shoulder.

"No shortage on these now," he said. He peered out across

the clearing at the road that led out of the Hollow. "I took a quick look over there. Not something I want to do again. The SWATs are gone."

"I can't believe they just ran away," Clara said.

Glauer shook his head. "That's not what I meant."

"Oh."

"We have maybe four men—policemen, that is—who can still fight. The witchbillies took some hits themselves, but they're in considerably better shape. I'm going to assume there are more half-deads hiding in the trees, but it looks like they're too scared to attack. Not unless Malvern shows up and orders them directly."

"Urie Polder says she's on her way."

Glauer nodded as if he'd expected nothing less.

"What about Fetlock?"

"Sealed up tight in his mobile command center. He didn't answer when I banged on the side and called his name, but I could hear him moving around in there."

"That son of a bitch," Clara said.

"Just doing what he does best. Protecting his own ass," Glauer told her. "Caxton's still locked inside the paddy wagon. I say our first priority is to get her out of there. Then we load everybody into the other vehicles and make a break for it."

"The road might be trapped. There could be another army of half-deads waiting for us out that way."

"It's still the best chance we've got."

Something occurred to Clara. She tried to ignore it, but she couldn't. "What about Simon?" she asked. "He's still here somewhere."

His face went marginally more pale. "I forgot about him."

"He's probably still up at the house on the ridge," Clara pointed out. "Do we go up and get him?"

Glauer stared at her with his teeth clenched. They had to think about this. They were the good guys. They had to make a decision. And if they made the logical decision, the right decision . . .

"Maybe he's safer where he is," Clara suggested. "If we waste time going to get him—"

"Malvern might show up. And I don't actually want to fight Malvern tonight." Glauer turned his face to the side. She thought he might spit, but he didn't. He couldn't like this at all. "Okay," he said.

"Okay?"

"Okay, we don't leave without him. We can't—not after what Malvern has already done to him and his family. But neither you nor I can be spared to go find him. My arm barely works and I've lost some blood. How's that cut on your shoulder? Why haven't you bandaged it yet?"

Clara frowned, then went over to the nearest police car. She bent over to get a look in its side mirror and saw a nasty cut running from the back of her neck across her shoulder. "Oh, come on," she said. She touched it and her finger came away wet with blood. "I didn't even feel that." The adrenaline must have numbed her to the pain. "I don't even remember which one of those bastards gave it to me."

"About three inches to one side and he would have cut your throat open," Glauer told her. He tore a piece from his ragged shirt and pressed it against her wound. "Hold that there. Keep pressure on it. We don't have time to bandage it properly—it'll have to wait until we get out of here."

"Sure," she said, shaking her head again. Then she checked herself over for additional wounds. There was a superficial cut on her left calf—her pant leg there hung in tatters—but it had already stopped bleeding. "This—was really close," she said.

"Let's not let it get any closer than we have to," Glauer told her. He ran off toward the surviving cops and the witchbillies. "I'll get one of the witchbillies to fetch Simon. You find the key to the paddy wagon," he called back to her over his shoulder.

46.

Easier said than done, of course.

Fetlock might have it. Or Darnell. Clara was certain it wouldn't just be lying around waiting for her to scoop it up.

It occurred to her that maybe they didn't need the key. They could just leave Caxton where she was and drive the paddy wagon away with her in it. She ran over to the paddy wagon and pulled open its driver's-side door. Climbing up into the seat, she looked for the ignition and found the keys were missing. Cursing, she reached under the dashboard, trying to remember how to hot-wire a vehicle. Of course it couldn't be that easy. The fuses and wiring were hidden behind a thick metal panel that had its own lock, to prevent exactly what she had in mind. Of course, the key to that lock was missing, too.

"You stupid fucker," she said.

Then she shrieked, because someone banged on the wall behind her, the wall that separated the paddy wagon's cabin from the prisoner area in the back.

"Clara?" Caxton called. "I thought I heard your voice."

"It's me." She tried to think of how to explain what was happening. Caxton had missed the whole thing, would have only heard the noise of the explosions and the gunfire. And the screams. "They came in force, but we drove them off," she shouted. "Malvern's on her way. I'm going to get you out of here."

"Leave me."

That, of course, would be the sensible thing to do. The utterly logical, coldly calculated choice. Just like it made sense to leave Simon behind, too. "Fuck that," Clara said, and jumped out of the paddy wagon. She had to find that stupid key.

She hurried toward the road, counting the vehicles she passed.

None of them looked like they'd been damaged in the fighting, though a few were sprayed with blood and dirt from the explosions.

In the road she saw what Glauer had meant about the SWAT troopers. They were in pieces. It was difficult to even look at what remained of the bodies. The half-deads must have swarmed over them like a wave of undead flesh. The SWATs had given the half-deads a good fight—there were half-dead bodies everywhere, severed limbs still twitching, eyes still rolling in crushed skulls—but the cops were dead to a man. Their armor had been peeled off of them and some attempt had been made to sort it into neat piles, but mostly the half-deads had focused on killing them and making sure they were definitively dead.

If Darnell was in that mess, he might have the key she needed. She walked over to the side of the road and vomited for a while, then came back and started her search. The first order of business was to find a flashlight so she could actually see what she was looking at. Not that the prospect appealed to her all that much.

She found a SWAT carbine that had a flashlight attachment and switched it on. A cone of red light speared out into the darkness, lighting up a bunch of tree trunks. The eerie light made them look like they were dripping with blood, which was somehow worse than the real blood all over the road. Clara shivered a little, then turned back to the bodies, her light ghosting over the ground, picking out every piece of gravel, making every shadow knife-sharp.

Then something glinted in her light—a pair of eyes. She fought down her fear, thinking she'd just lit up the face of a corpse that had died too quickly to close its eyes. But then the eyes moved and she jumped. Her finger twitched on the carbine's trigger and she sprayed three rounds into the trees.

She saw it moving still, and realized that fear had ruined her aim. The half-dead was still, for lack of a better term, alive. She braced herself for its imminent attack, knowing it would come at her with a knife or a club or just a rock. Instead it tried to run away. It clutched an odd collection of body armor to its chest—some leg protectors, a pair of helmets, and it dodged in a classic serpentine pattern as she tried to follow it with the carbine. She squeezed off another burst, knowing she wasn't aiming properly, that there was almost no chance of hitting the damn thing.

Then a rifle cracked, very close by. The noise was enough to make her soul jump out of her skin. She dropped instantly to the ground, thinking that someone was shooting at her.

That, it turned out, was incorrect. It was Darnell who'd taken the shot—and he'd aimed at the fleeing half-dead. Darnell had been lying in the road, stretched out to look like just another corpse. Waiting for this.

"See if I got 'im," the trooper ordered.

Clara was too wound up to argue. She ran forward into the dark, playing her red light over every body she came across. When she found the half-dead she had to whistle in respect. Darnell's shot had taken the half-dead right in the spine. It lay in a spilled pile of body armor, trying to crawl away on its arms.

She put a boot in the small of its back and pinned it to the road. Then she raised her carbine and aimed for its head.

"You damn well ain't gonna steal my collar," Darnell said, jogging up behind her. "I been trackin' this one too long to let it get away so clean."

Clara looked up because she'd heard someone running toward them. It turned out to be Glauer. "I heard shots," he said.

Clara nodded and gestured at the half-dead under her boot. "You remember Trooper Darnell, of course."

Glauer stared at the snake-eyed trooper. "What's your game here?"

"Intelligence. I got my orders from Marshal Fetlock. Find one of these fools and figger out what it knows. You go ahead and stand back, little lady. It's my turn now to make this dingus talk."

Clara frowned at that, but she removed her boot. The

half-dead immediately started crawling away, but Darnell just bent over it and shoved a hunting knife into its shoulder, ruining its ability to move. "You gonna tell me what I want to know?"

The half-dead mewled like a cat.

Darnell stabbed it again.

Normally Clara would have been disgusted. She would have insisted that Darnell stop at once. But this was one of the half-deads that had killed all the cops in the clearing. This was one of the bastards that had stabbed her and nearly killed Glauer. She decided it had a little pain coming.

Which, she realized, was exactly what Caxton would have said. In her time Caxton had tortured more than her fair share of half-deads for information. It hadn't stopped there, of course. She'd eventually started torturing human beings, as well, and that was why she'd gone to prison.

Down on the ground, the half-dead screamed as the hunting knife bit into its cheek. "Okay! Okay! I'll talk!"

"Better," Darnell said. "Now—how many of you are there out here? How many still alive?"

"Not—many," the half-dead promised in its tinny little high-pitched voice. "You got all but a handful. She told us to fall—to fall back, to retreat. Stop! Please, stop! I'm cooperating!"

"Where'd she get you lot?" Darnell demanded. "I ain't never heard of so many half-deads gathered at one time, and I know all the case files."

"Family reunion," the half-dead said, sobbing a little. "Over by Elizabethtown. My family, my family reunion, we came from, from all over the country to be together. Cousins, grandparents, babies I never got to meet before. She thought it was funny to take us all at once. At the time I didn't see it, but now—"

"She took you all in one night?" Darnell demanded. "Last night?"

"Yes!" the half-dead screamed.

Clara looked to Glauer, and the big cop nodded. If Malvern

could get enough blood, if she could claim enough victims, all the damage of centuries could be erased instantly. Clara had seen it happen during the prison raid. She had watched Malvern's flesh fill in, seen her rise and walk and regain the power of speech. Regain the power and the speed of a freshly risen vampire. It had taken about a dozen victims to make that happen.

There had been scores—maybe a hundred—of half-deads in the attack on the clearing. If she had taken them all in one night, she would be stronger than ever before. She would be bulletproof, and so fast she could probably dodge bullets. She would be able to throw cars around like toys.

"She took a big risk, doin' that," Darnell said. "Profile on her says she's the clever type. That she don't do stupid. You sayin' she just got stupid last night?"

The half-dead screamed again as Darnell broke its wrist. "No! No! She'd never—she's the wisest, most—stop that! Please, I beg you, stop! She has a plan, she said she has a big plan, one final strike and then, and then—"

"What's the plan?" Darnell demanded.

"Kill you all."

Darnell grunted. Maybe at the thought that he was marked for death. Maybe because he'd already assumed as much and wanted new information. "And then? What then? She must know we won't stop. She kills alla us, she's gonna have the army down on her neck."

"Kill you all—and then—then—hibernate. Like a bear. Go underground, hee hee, literally, seal herself up in a tomb. Wait fifty years. Wait a hundred years, until people—until your children forget. Forget what a vampire can do. But first she needs to kill Caxton. Kill the hunter, keep her from passing on her secrets."

"That's what I wanted to know," Darnell said. "Either of you got questions you want answered, 'fore I put this creep out of its misery?"

"I have a few for you, actually," Glauer said.

"That's just fine. Hold on one tick."

Clara looked away as Darnell stomped on the half-dead's skull. It tried to plead for its life, but its words were cut off quite abruptly.

"Now I got to report back to the Marshal," Darnell said. His snake eye burned like a torch in the red light from Clara's carbine.

"Fetlock? That coward locked himself up tight. He's done. Darnell, we can use your help," Glauer pointed out. "We need every man we can get for when Malvern strikes. Which is going to happen any minute now."

"I work for the Marshal."

Glauer shook his head. "I'm telling you, he's buttoned up—"

"Yeah, just like he meant to. You think he aborted on this dustup? You think he's done? He's got surprises still, and—"

Darnell stopped talking because someone had screamed back in the clearing.

Apparently Malvern had arrived.

[1991]

Her fingers drifted across the keyboard, speaking for her now that she lacked the strength to move her tongue and teeth. Letter by letter she spelled out the message, as always delighted by the way the black characters appeared on the screen before her. Like a magical printing press, this device, this new computer they'd given her. It made things so much easier.

> *shall we play our usual game, my dear?*
> *what aspect may i take today?*

Gerald—dear Dr. Armonk, her pet, her plaything, the man of science assigned by the state to study her, the man she'd come to study just as intently, blushed in the dim light of her cell in the abandoned sanitarium. He had a magazine rolled up in his hands, its glossy pages reflecting the overhead lights. He approached her tentatively, as if she would ever refuse him. Spreading the pages open, he licked his lips as he showed her a picture of a woman spread-eagled across a padded bench in a gymnasium. Such simple tastes he had. These new men, these twentieth-century boys! They had cleared away all the old prejudices and blue-nosed moralisms of olden days, whole worlds of erotic possibilities had been opened to them, and yet still, still in their fantasies they wanted the same things as ever.

Justinia closed her eye and worked her orison, giving herself blond hair, full, pouting lips, and massive, impossible bosoms. Across the room she could feel Armonk's heart beating faster. He did so like playing this game with her.

He never touched her when she made herself over into his dream girls. He always stayed well clear of her coffin until he'd finished what he'd come here to do. She often pleaded with him to just let her have a little caress, a single kiss. She begged him to ravish her, to make her feel like a woman again. So far he'd been able to resist, and she had never made the mistake of pushing too hard.

Some games took longer to win than others.

She let her hand drift across the keyboard again.

it's been so long since master jameson came to see me.

"What? Arkeley? That man—that man's a pest. Surely you're glad he's leaving you alone," Armonk insisted as he unbuckled his belt. "With his idle threats and his demands for information. Honestly, I think he's grown bored. He used to bellow at us all the time about how dangerous you are, but you've never hurt anybody since you came here, and no one takes him seriously anymore. The last time I saw him, he was even talking about getting someone else to take over your case. He's been looking for other vampires this whole time and he's never found any. I think he's ready to admit defeat."

Hmm. Interesting.

But that would never do.

Her fingers tapped at the keys. Backspaced to erase what she'd started to write. Moved once again, forming her thoughts, even as Armonk stared at her with those wide, needy eyes.

She had a plan. A rather simple plan, but one that would unfold over a span of many years, and which required certain things to happen at certain times. A plan that depended on certain people acting in predictable ways. Jameson was a major part of that plan. Her sphere of influence was so very narrow now, and if he were to move beyond that sphere, to abandon her for some other interest . . .

No. That would never do.

She needed to make him find her compelling again. To give him new reason to stick close by her side.

lover, i must have your touch. ye are the world to me.

"Justinia, you know how fond I am of you, but——"

ye don't love me. ye've never so much as stolen a kiss.

"Don't say that." He bit his lip. "Please. Don't even suggest such a thing. It's simply not true, and——"

this game grows tiresome.
it takes overmuch of my strength.
i shan't play anymore, not when all the fun is yours.

"No," he said. "No. Please. I implore you. I need this, I . . . I can't live without our . . . without our game," he told her. His heart pounded in his chest. How easy it was to make them afraid. Sometimes it didn't even seem sporting. "Please. Tell me you didn't mean it. Tell me we'll always have——always have this."

Were there really tears in his eyes?

She let the orison slip, just a little. Let her hair turn red, let one of her eyes darken and fade in its socket. Enough to frighten him, but not enough to repulse him.

"Please," he begged, unable to form other words. She'd been his constant lover for almost ten years now. He'd come to believe her flatteries, to believe in her affection. Human beings were so vulnerable to love.

"Please," he said again, but she did not relent.

He did exactly as she'd expected. He had no choice, not if he wanted to keep her. He rushed to her side, wringing his hands, sweating profusely. He leaned over her coffin, leaned so close she could feel the heat of his blood inside of him. Pressed his lips to hers.

She bit down, hard. When he started screaming, when he started flailing back and forth, she used the last reserves of her strength to hold him, to keep him from breaking free. Once the blood started to flow it got much easier.

That should get Jameson's attention, *she thought*. *She expected he would find the time to visit her quite soon.*

47.

It was just too dark. Clara could see nothing of what was happening in the clearing. She could only hear the screams. Then shapes loomed up out of the darkness all around her and she raised her carbine, thinking Malvern must have brought in reinforcements, more half-deads to overwhelm what little resistance remained. She almost fired blindly into the crowd of dark shapes, which would have been a terrible mistake. It wasn't half-deads coming toward her, but witchbillies.

"She's here!" a woman in a bonnet screamed. She held a bawling infant to her chest. "What do we do?"

Glauer stood up on tiptoe, trying to peer into the clearing, trying to see what was going on. "Get to the vehicles—take any car you can. If you can't find a car, just run for it, up the road—you," he said, grabbing a man with a straw hat on his head. "Where's Urie Polder? Where's that woman—what was her name, the one who could do real magic—"

"Heather," Clara provided.

"Right—where are they?"

The man scratched wildly at his beard, his eyes wild in the red light of Clara's carbine. "I can't rightly say—they were—they told us to run this way, they—"

"Damn it, he's going to try to fight her," Glauer said, turning to Clara. He pushed the witchbilly away, sending him toward the parked circle of cop cars, even though that meant heading back toward the clearing, back toward danger. "Clara, there are kids back there. Polder must be holding her off as best he can to give them a chance to escape."

"Yeah," she said. "I take it you're going to go help him."

Glauer nodded. His own eyes were only a little less crazy than the witchbilly's. "But you're not. Get out of here. Help these people get to safety."

"I'm not leaving."

"I don't have time to argue with you," Glauer said. "Darnell, grab her. Get her out of here. I don't care how nasty she fights."

"Sorry, partner. Nothing doing," Darnell said. He slung his hunting rifle over his shoulder and started walking toward the clearing. "I got other orders."

"Goddamn it!" Glauer said, and he grabbed Clara's arm. "You have a chance to survive this. You have a chance to live."

"I'm not leaving," she said again.

He bristled, rising up to his full height. If it came down to blows she would certainly lose. But it would never come to that.

"I'm not leaving without Caxton," she announced. "Do you understand?"

"No, damn it," he told her. "I don't understand that at all. Not after how she treated you. Not after the last two years." She started to speak, but he held up one hand for peace. "But I know you mean it. Come on, then, if you've made your choice."

He hurried after Darnell, and Clara followed close on his heels.

It wasn't far to the clearing. Long before they reached it, though, they saw the chaos that had gripped the Hollow. Witch-billies were running everywhere, some headed for their bunga-lows or trailers, some trying to load up cars with people who didn't want to go, who were screaming for their loved ones. Some of the men had armed themselves as best they could and were clearing bodies out of the foxholes, clearly intending on trying the same strategy that had gotten the windbreaker cops killed. Some of the women were drawing hasty hex signs in the dirt, though their work was ruined every time someone ran through the lines of cornmeal or bitumen they laid out.

In the middle of it stood Patience Polder, her blond hair un-covered now, her fair skin almost glowing in the darkness. She was calling out orders to anyone who would listen. Some of them did, and headed for the cars, or just ran for the road. Most of them ignored her and did what they thought was best.

It had to be hard to keep a level head, when death itself was coming down a mountain, headed straight for you.

It was dark up on the trail that led to the top of Urie Polder's house. The trees screened out all the moonlight and painted the ground an utter and profound black. But as Justinia Malvern ap-proached she shone like a lamp in the gloom. Her skin, far paler than Patience's, seemed illuminated by a spectral lambency as if a spotlight was focused right on her. She was wearing a white gown that flickered as if it were licked by gentle flames, and the enormous wig she wore atop her head shone like spun silver. She wore an eye patch over her empty socket, a black triangle of silk emblazoned with a red heart. Her one remaining eye burned down on the clearing like a laser beam.

She was not touching the ground. Her bare feet pointed

downward and cleared the earth by a good foot and a half. She was floating down the mountain, her hands slightly outstretched at her sides.

There was a smile of utter benevolence, of pure compassion on her lips.

And walking behind her, looking sheepish, was Simon Arkeley.

Simon, Clara thought. *What the fuck are you doing?* She had been right—he must have been up at the house the whole time. When he'd heard the gunfire and the screams, he must have withdrawn, gone into one of his fugue states where he couldn't interact with the world at all. Most likely he had run inside the house and curled up in a fetal position on the first couch or bed he could find.

Malvern must have found him there, cowering away from the anarchy she had unleashed. She could have killed him effort- lessly then. But for some reason, she had spared his life.

The witchbilly Glauer sent to collect him probably hadn't been as lucky.

Clara was so deeply confused that she didn't know which way to jump next.

Glauer raised his weapon and drew a bead on Malvern, even though she was still far out of range.

"She's looking a little better than the last time I saw her," Clara said. "Glauer, if she drank that much blood—if she ate all of those people—"

"She'll be completely bulletproof," he agreed. "I'm out of other ideas, though. I say we shoot her anyway."

Clara shrugged. "Works for me."

Malvern drifted down the mountain path a few more yards, then came to a stop. In the clearing, more than a few of the witchbillies stopped what they were doing to watch her. Pa- tience kept exhorting them to flee, but they seemed transfixed. Vampires had the power to hypnotize their victims, Clara knew.

They could even control people to some extent—a vampire had once forced Glauer to attack Caxton, and he'd been unable to resist. The witchbillies were supposed to have charms against that sort of thing, however, and Clara wondered if they were hypnotized at all, or just so gripped by curiosity as to what would happen next that it had overwhelmed their rational faculties.

Up on the side of the ridge, Simon Arkeley took a few hesitant steps forward until he was standing in front of Malvern. He cleared his throat and started talking, but he was so far away Clara couldn't make out his words.

A trace of irritation passed across Malvern's face. Then she moved like lightning and seized Simon by the throat. Glauer changed his aim and for a second Clara thought he might fire, range be damned, but as quickly as Malvern had grabbed Simon she released him again.

When he spoke again everyone could hear him clearly. His voice didn't sound amplified—not at all like he was speaking through a bullhorn—but his words were perfectly understandable. If a little crazy.

"She just wants Caxton," he said. "She promised me, some of us could live. Patience." He glanced back at Malvern again, but she didn't even look at him. "Patience, she said specifically you and I could leave, and she wouldn't follow us. I think she means it. Patience, we should get out of here. It's not going to be safe."

Patience used no charm to make her reply heard. She just shouted. "She has already cost us too much. I will not obey her commands."

Simon scrubbed at his face with his hands. Was he, in fact, dead? Had she turned him into a half-dead, and he just hadn't gotten a chance yet to scratch his own face off? No, Clara realized. He was just losing his grasp on reality. Not that he'd ever had a very firm grip on that.

"Remember what you said to me? How you and I were going to be . . . to be married? That I was going to be your husband?"

"I remember," Patience said.

"But that means we live. I mean, we have to, right? You and I have to survive so we can make that come true. Your prophecy—"

Patience cut him off with a snarl. "Do not lecture me, Simon, on the proper usage of divination." Clara hadn't heard the girl get angry before—normally she was eerily calm. "I'd rather defy fate and suffer the consequences than give her the satisfaction of watching me crawl away. You come down here now and stand with us, or you are no man."

Simon's face went white as a sheet. White as a ghost. Not quite as white as Malvern's skin, but close. "I can't," he said, a whining rejoinder that made Clara cringe. He shook his head and held up his hands as if to ward off a terrible fate.

It was not, of course, enough.

Malvern seized him with both her hands. For a moment her dress flickered wildly as if it was about to erupt in flames. Then she threw Simon at a tree and he collided so hard that no magical amplification was necessary to make the impact audible down in the clearing.

Darnell was standing right behind Clara. She hadn't heard him moving up to that position, but now he spoke into a walkie-talkie, saying, "I got a clear shot, right about now."

"Take it," Fetlock replied over the radio.

Darnell's hunting rifle fired with a fierce report. Clara jumped sideways as if to avoid being struck in a cross fire, though the bullet was already loosed. Judging by the noise, Darnell must have been firing a .50-caliber round—a lot bigger than most modern rifles could handle. The bullet struck Malvern just left of the center of her chest, exactly over her heart. Darnell was a hell of a shot, Clara decided.

When the round hit Malvern it exploded in a puff of fire and smoke. It didn't look like a normal gunshot hit at all.

"What the hell are you loading?" Glauer asked.

"HEIAP," Darnell replied, pronouncing it "hay-yup." At first Clara thought it was a verbal tic, like the way Urie Polder always said, "Ahum." But in fact it was an acronym for high explosive/incendiary armor piercing. The kind of bullet you'd use against a light tank. Serious military hardware.

Malvern looked down at her chest, and raised one hand to finger a small hole that had appeared in the front of her gown. Then her smile broadened.

"No effect," Darnell said into his walkie-talkie.

But he was wrong. His shot had a definite effect. Once she'd finished enjoying the little joke, Malvern came down the ridge as fast as a freight train.

[2002]

Sometimes all it took was a single glance.

Malvern had known suicidal men before. She'd never known one so miserable as Efrain Zacapa Reyes. He had nothing, no family, no friends. No hopes for life, and no opportunity for death. Arthritis in his feet made every step he took a new exploration of agony, but lack of education meant he was forced to work every day on his feet. His strict Catholic upbringing had taught him that suicide was a mortal sin. Ending his own life would only make things worse for him—he would trade an unbearable but finite existence on earth for an eternity of suffering in hell.

When she met him, he was pondering which might be worse.

He had a job, of sorts, as a menial electrical engineer. He worked a variety of civil service positions—dismantling old and obsolete equipment on public property. Tracing wires through the walls of buildings that were going to be torn down anyway.

Replacing burned-out lightbulbs in crumbling sanatoria.

A great deal of luck conspired to put him in her way. Dr. Hazlitt—

Dr. Armonk's replacement—had left the lid of her coffin open, when it should have been closed. He had also ordered blue lights installed in the place where she slept, because blue lights were less damaging to her skin. Dear, sweet Dr. Hazlitt. Reyes suffered a minor accident himself, another stroke of luck for her. His ladder wasn't quite tall enough to reach the high fixtures in her room. He had to balance on the top step, despite all regulations to the contrary. At one point he stumbled and nearly fell. He managed to catch himself in time, but in the process his gaze fell on her eye, where she was watching him from below.

He looked away quickly. They were not alone—a pair of armed guards stood watching her from the doorway. Had the look they shared lingered, if he had whispered something to her, the guards would have dragged him away at once.

Reyes understood, though, in that single moment of connection, that he had found what he'd been looking for. That his pain and suffering were at an end.

No one in Justinia's experience had ever accepted the curse so willingly. No one had ever embraced it like that, without even a moment's hesitation.

Within a week, Reyes found himself on a different job, dismantling an electrical substation halfway across the state. He stood before the guts of an ancient bank of capacitors. It was his job to safely drain them of any residual charge so they could be torn apart with sledgehammers and sold for scrap.

No one was watching him that time.

He knew what he had to do. He knew what it meant. He would rise. He would not die, and not go to hell, and his pain would be gone. It was almost too good to be true.

Already by that point he had received his instructions. He was to create four more vampires once he had the strength to do so. He was to select them carefully, but he was not to waste any time. Once this small army of knight protectors was assembled, they were to gorge themselves on blood—stuff themselves full of the delicious stuff—and then bring it to her so she could be restored. It was an elegant plan, quite simple. It could all happen before Jameson Arkeley was aware of what Malvern was up to.

It all relied on Efrain Zacapa Reyes. He was going to be important. He was going to be loved. All he had to do was take off his rubber-soled shoes, strip off his insulated gloves, and reach forward to touch an exposed wire. After that it would all come naturally.

Justinia had been quite clear on that.

Back at Arabella Furnace, the place of her incarceration, Jameson was making one of his weekly visits. He watched as Hazlitt ran tests on her muscle tone, or rather her lack of it. He watched as she was fed. He watched her so closely that he saw the faint twitch of a smile cross her lips.

"What are you up to?" he asked.

But he didn't truly suspect. He didn't have any idea yet what lay in store for him. It had been almost twenty years since he'd dragged her out of the river. It had taken that long for Justinia's latest plot to hatch. She would not ruin it now by letting him see her cards before all the wagers were in.

So like any good player, she wiped the smile from her face before it could give her away.

48.

Malvern tore through the crowd of witchbillies. She left a trail of death in her wake, her hands flashing like claws as she ripped through any human being foolish enough to be in her way.

"Go, go, get out of here," Clara shouted, urging the remaining witchbillies to leave any way they could. Most of them got the hint.

One of the last remaining windbreaker cops managed to distract Malvern for all of a second or two, mostly by unloading an entire carbine clip into her face. She waited until he was finished, then impaled him on his own weapon.

Back near the vehicles, only a few dozen yards away, Clara

could do nothing but ready her own weapon and prepare herself for the same fate.

Urie Polder had his own idea about what to do next. He lifted his human arm in the air and started droning something in German. But before he could cast whatever spell it was he had in mind, Darnell grabbed his arm and pushed it down. "Not yet, pops. You think we didn't prepare for this?"

"You got somewhat more, boy?" Polder demanded. "You best spring it now."

The door of Fetlock's mobile command center opened and the Fed jumped out. "Way ahead of you," he said. "Darnell, get her attention."

The snake-eyed trooper nodded and lined up another shot with his rifle. He put a bullet right into Malvern's pointed left ear. There was a puff of smoke and a bit of a flash, but no apparent damage.

"I'm penetrating her armor, that's all," Darnell said.

Armor? What armor? Was he talking about the wig Malvern was wearing? Clara was confused, but she was too busy being terrified to say anything.

"Fire again," Fetlock said.

Darnell's next shot struck Malvern in the throat. With the usual effect—meaning none whatsoever.

Except this time it did seem to annoy her enough to make her turn around. She faced Fetlock and Darnell, a quizzical smile on her lips.

"Miss Malvern," Fetlock shouted. "I have what you want." He lifted the walkie-talkie to his lips and issued a terse order Clara couldn't make out. Then he turned to face Malvern again. "Caxton's this way—if you can get to her."

The vampire smiled broadly, showing all of her horrible teeth. Then she started floating toward Fetlock and the mobile command center—and the paddy wagon behind him. She took her time.

Fetlock's surprise did not. Clara felt something huge sweep over her like a storm front. A moment later she heard the chopping noise of the helicopter as it came in for a pass of the clearing. Instead of buzzing the Hollow and flying off again, however, this time it settled in to hover directly above.

Malvern spared it a momentary glance, but she didn't stop coming.

"Now," Fetlock said into his walkie-talkie.

Malvern opened her mouth as if she would say something. She didn't get the chance.

Clara had not gotten a good look at the helicopter before. She hadn't noticed the rocket pod slung under its fuselage. There was an immense fizzing, whistling noise like a firework being set off. A rocket streaked through the air toward Malvern, so fast Clara couldn't even follow.

A wave of pressure and flame burst through the clearing, rocking the trailers, setting dead bodies alight. The darkness was washed away by sudden light and then the noise hit, a boom loud enough to throw Clara to the ground if she hadn't been headed that way already. "Jesus!" she screamed, but she couldn't even hear the word herself.

When she dared to open her eyes again she saw people sprawled all around her, some of them still moving. Glauer lay next to her on the gravel, flecks of smoldering shrapnel cascading from his back and hair as he propped himself up. He grabbed Clara's arm and pointed toward where Malvern had been.

She wasn't there anymore. For a wonderful, glorious second Clara actually believed that the vampire had been struck by the rocket, that she'd been blown up—vaporized—by the weapon.

Then Glauer moved his finger an inch to the left.

Malvern floated above the ground a dozen feet away from where she'd been when the rocket was fired. Her gown and her wig were on fire, blazing away like they'd been soaked in gasoline. Her pale skin looked unharmed. Not so much as scorched.

Her smile hadn't faded.

"Again!" Fetlock screamed.

Malvern dodged to one side just before the rocket launched. It streaked past her and demolished one of the bungalows on the far side of the clearing. She took a step to the right, as if anticipating the next attack, and a rocket flew straight as an arrow into the trees on the ridge behind her.

The helicopter loosed all its remaining rockets one after another in quick succession, firing in a wide spread to try to catch her as she moved. Malvern threw an arm across her face as they came for her, but otherwise held her ground.

When the shock waves passed, when Clara could see and hear again, she moaned in distress. Malvern's gown and wig had become living garments of fire, but she hadn't so much as been scratched. She closed her one red eye for a moment and the flames died out as an eerie wind twisted all around her. The wig and gown stopped burning almost instantly. They didn't look like they'd even been scorched.

"No," Fetlock said. "No, that's not possible."

Malvern brushed something from the front of her dress. Maybe a piece of ash. Then she turned her face to look upward, at the helicopter.

And then nothing happened.

At least—nothing that Clara could see.

"Damn it," Glauer said. "Damn, damn—Fetlock! Get on that radio and tell your pilot to get out of here! Now, while he still has a chance!"

"She couldn't survive that," Fetlock said, ignoring Glauer. "Nothing can live through a hellfire missile strike. It's impossible."

"Sir," the walkie-talkie said. "Sir, can you confirm? Repeat, can you confirm this new heading? It doesn't seem to make any sense."

That shook Fetlock out of his trance. "What the hell are you talking about?"

"The new heading you gave me. It doesn't seem—no, no sir. I'm not disobeying orders. I'll do it, it just seems—yes, sir."

"Who the hell are you talking to?" Fetlock demanded.

"No," Clara said, because she understood, finally. "Darnell! Shoot her! Make her look away from the chopper!"

But it was too late.

The helicopter's pilot had his new orders. They might have sounded like they came from Fetlock, but in fact, Malvern had simply put them in his head. A vampire could do that. A vampire like Malvern could do it as easily as making eye contact.

The helicopter swung away from its position, leaning over hard on one side as if it were trying to avoid a midair collision. It slid through the air as if the pilot had lost control, picking up speed as it headed straight for the side of the ridge.

It struck the trees with enough force to crumple its rotors instantly. The cockpit section deformed as it smashed through branches and trunks, then flattened as it hit the stony side of the ridge. A moment later its fuel tank ruptured and a new light blossomed over the clearing. For a moment it was bright as day, bright enough to even make Malvern squint.

"No," Fetlock said, and dropped his walkie-talkie on the gravel.

Darnell raised his rifle.

Malvern moved so quickly that he didn't have time to get a shot off. Suddenly she was standing next to him, looming over him as she floated just above the ground. He tried to bring his rifle around, to club at her with its stock, but she flicked it out of his hands with no effort at all.

Then she grasped Darnell's head in both her hands and pulled it cleanly off his body. She tossed the head away from her like a child's ball. Clara heard it roll away, bouncing wetly on the gravel.

His body remained upright for a fraction of a second. Then it slumped to the ground, spurting blood across Malvern's feet.

[2003]

The only problem with Justinia's strategy of employing knight protectors was that she had to listen to them whine.

"I want her," Reyes said, his voice floating across the ether, across miles to reach Justinia in her coffin. Justinia closed her eye and focused on his words. "I want her to . . . to be like me. I want to fuck her."

Justinia looked through his eyes and saw this object of his lust. Human, of course. It had been a long time since Justinia could look on anything human and see its shape, see beauty in its features. When she beheld them now all she saw was their blood.

This one was not unattractive, she supposed. A human female with red hair—well, her own vanity made Justinia partial to gingers. And she was shapely enough, this creature Reyes had come to favor. She was hanging up a sheet inside a barn, pinning it to a long line so it fell down to divide the interior space. Her arms were long and slender. Reyes hid nearby in a stand of trees.

"Her name is Deanna," he told Justinia. "She's a lesbo."

Justinia rolled her eye in distaste at his crude terminology. She'd known enough devotees of Sappho in her own time. It wasn't like they hadn't existed in the seventeenth century. Even then men had obsessed over them. Was it that they were forbidden? Was it the disdain they showed to the men who lusted over them?

"I can take on her shape," Justinia insisted. "I can make myself look exactly as she does. Or I can take on a form even more comely, if it pleases thee."

"You said—you said to find others, to find others ready to take the curse. She's ready. I can feel it. She wants to die! If she's like me, if she becomes like—like us, maybe she would—she would be lonely. Like me. And then—"

A little house lay beyond the barn. As Justinia watched through Reyes's eyes, a light came on over the house's back door and it slipped open. Another woman stepped out. Probably the redhead's lover.

"What's wrong with the dogs?" this newcomer asked. "They're going crazy!"

Deanna lifted her head, looking surprised. She must have been lost in her own thoughts. She looked briefly toward a kennel on the other side of the yard. Then she turned and looked toward the trees where Reyes crouched. For a moment she looked straight at Reyes—and through him, at Justinia.

And Justinia saw that Reyes was right. This woman was ready for the curse. Ready to become a vampire, nearly as ready as Reyes had been himself. It would be simplicity itself to drive her to suicide. "Very well," Justinia said. She had never employed a woman as a knight protector before, but she saw no reason it couldn't work. "Take her at your leisure, Reyes."

"And her—her too," the fledgling vampire said. He sounded as if he was panting there in the bushes. Like a common voyeur.

How grotesque.

"I want them both, and they can—they will do things for me—"

"Yes, yes, very well," Justinia said.

She spared one more glance at the woman standing in the doorway. Taller, stronger, with hair cut as short as a man's. There was something about this one, something that would make it more difficult to impose the curse on her. But it could be done. No human could withstand forever the attentions of a vampire.

"Take them both," she said.

She had no idea that she had just been given her first look at Laura Caxton. At the woman who would become her nemesis. If she had, she surely would have ordered Reyes to kill Caxton on the spot.

But not even the most skilled gambler can say what card will turn up next.

49.

Clara raised her carbine and started to line up a shot, intending to put as much lead as possible into Malvern's back before she ran dry. She had absolutely zero other ideas of what to do next.

"No," Glauer whispered, putting a hand over the receiver of her weapon. "Didn't you see? She's so full of blood she's completely bulletproof at this point. She's rocketproof!"

"We can't let her have Caxton," Clara insisted.

"We don't have a choice," he told her. His face was contorted in horror and disgust. It must have caused him physical pain to admit he couldn't do anything. Glauer was not the quickest man Clara had ever met, nor the bravest. But he had always, always tried to do the right thing.

There was no right thing to do, though. Not here, not now.

Clara could only watch in terror as Malvern turned her attention on Fetlock. The Fed shrieked in fear and tried to run for his mobile command center. He wasn't going to make it, Clara knew. He had no chance.

Before he could get to the doors of the vehicle, Malvern was there, waiting for him. She favored him with a cold smile.

"You can't be this strong," he said, staring into her eye.

"Marshal Fetlock," she said. "I have so much to thank ye for. Thy incompetence has made my existence so easy." She laughed.

Fetlock tried to turn and run away.

Malvern grasped his head between her hands. Just like she'd done with Darnell. This time, though, she didn't kill her victim. Instead she just held Fetlock in place. His legs tried to run, but he could no more escape her grasp than he could sprout wings and fly. She held him without so much as straining a muscle, forcing his face around so he was looking at her again.

"I'm tempted to let ye live," Malvern said. "As long as you're in charge of my case, I have so very little to worry about, do I? But, alas. Ye do keep trying to destroy me. Even when it's clear to everyone ye haven't a chance."

"I'll—I'll do anything you want," Fetlock pleaded. "Anything. I'll get you blood. I'll get you so much blood."

"I've already drunk my fill tonight," Malvern told him.

Glauer tried to pull Clara back to the illusory safety of the trailers. She shook off his hand. "Where's Urie Polder?" she whispered. "Maybe he can do something."

"You think he wouldn't already be doing it if he could? Come on," Glauer insisted. "She'll be after us next. Don't you see? She's eliminating anyone who could possibly be a threat to her. We're on that list."

"Not right now, we're not," Clara said.

She watched as Malvern applied a slight pressure to Fetlock's head. The Fed squealed in pain as blood leaked from his nose.

"My God, it's true," Clara whispered, perhaps only to herself. "She's had so much blood she isn't even thirsty anymore. How many people did she kill?"

No one answered her. She turned to look for Glauer and saw that he was gone. Surely he hadn't run away. That wasn't his style. But where could he have gone?

Malvern lifted Fetlock off his feet so that his body dangled from his neck. His arms and legs flailed at the air, beat at Malvern's chest, but he was utterly helpless.

"Ye can do me one service only," Malvern told the Fed. "Tell me. Tell me where Laura is."

Fetlock's limbs stopped struggling. He lifted one arm to point at the paddy wagon where it sat in the middle of the clearing.

"There. She's in there! She's the one you want! I'm nothing to you!"

"Ah, now that's truth," Malvern agreed.

She closed her hands.

Clara had to look away as Fetlock's head collapsed inward on itself, the bones of his skull creaking and snapping as they were crushed. As his brains spurted out in a cloud of blood. Blood that dripped from Malvern's hands as she let the dead Marshal drop.

Malvern paid him no more heed than a discarded toy. She looked at the paddy wagon as if sizing up how she should proceed, then floated over toward it where it sat alone. She ran one hand along its metal side, then moved to the back, where its massive reinforced doors stood locked up tight.

"Laura," she sang. "Laura. Ye're in there."

The paddy wagon didn't rock on its wheels. Caxton made no sound inside of it. Maybe she just didn't want to give Malvern the satisfaction.

"Oh, I can see ye," Malvern crooned. "I can see your blood, Laura. I can see it like a lamp in the dark of a storm. Right through these metal walls I can see it."

Malvern leaned her face up against the doors of the paddy wagon. Pressed her ear against the metal. A smile of incredible warmth filled her face.

"Oh, Laura, ye must know—of all my hunters, of all mine enemies. Ye were the sweetest. Ye gave me the best sport. I would gladly make ye into mine own image if that would please ye. Would it? We could chase one another down the centuries then. We could dance like this forever. How I'd like that."

Caxton finally responded. The doors of the paddy wagon jumped. She must have thrown her whole weight against them.

Malvern laughed. "Ye won't take my offer, I know. Ye saw what happened to poor, sweet Jameson when he accepted the curse. Not to mention little Raleigh. And Alva Griest, and Reyes, and Scapegrace, what happened to all my protectors. Ye saw what became of your beloved Deanna. Ye know what I have to offer. And ye'll say no."

The doors jumped again. A shrieking noise emerged from inside the paddy wagon—had Caxton finally snapped? Clara couldn't believe it. Had Malvern finally pushed Caxton to the point of madness, until she could do nothing but howl in rage?

"I'll miss ye terribly, my dear. But ye see, fate has ordained that I'm to live forever. The Lord knows there were times I wished it otherwise. But not now. Now I want to live. Now I want to win this game. Time to show your hand. I doubt ye can match what I have."

Malvern lifted a little higher in the air. She reached up and grasped the top of the paddy wagon doors. Her fingers sank into the metal as if it were made of cheese, though it groaned and screamed in defiance. Then, with one quick, graceful motion, she tore the doors right off of their hinges. They were reinforced steel a good inch thick, but she tore them down like a silk curtain.

Beyond lay only darkness. The light of the fires that illuminated the clearing couldn't reach inside. There was no sign of Caxton in there. Had she escaped somehow? Clara's heart nearly burst at the thought. Of course she had. Of course Laura Caxton, world's greatest vampire killer, had somehow escaped once again, had somehow survived, and even now she had some amazing plan, some clever trick that would let her get the best of Malvern and win the day.

"Come out of there, Laura. Ye've nowhere else to go. I can see ye crouching. How like a tiger, lying in wait, in ambush, how like—"

Caxton came flying out of the darkness then, without waiting to hear what else Malvern might say. Her hands and feet were free of the shackles Fetlock had put on them. She was holding something, some kind of weapon. Clara just had time to see that it was a metal pole—a steel rod, something Caxton must have torn out of the inside of the paddy wagon by sheer persistence and desperation.

She shoved its jagged end straight into Malvern's good eye.

[2003]

Justinia's battered frame was not fully healed, not by a long shot. Her muscles were as thin and dry as vines in wintertime and they wrapped around bones easily visible beneath her papery skin. Her tattered night-gown hung on her like a tent. Her face was drawn and spotted and her one good eye looked only half inflated. But the blood Scapegrace and Deanna had brought to her had been enough, just enough, to get her out of her coffin for the first time in over a century. She was standing up, walking even, advancing on Jameson Arkeley with her mouth open. Her teeth were fully recovered—sharp, deadly, and numerous.

"That's right. Come here," Arkeley said. He was propped up on one arm. The other waved her closer. "Come on, you old hag. You want it. You can have it."

He had cut his hand somehow. There was fresh blood on his palm.

Justinia's body wanted this so very much. Every fiber of her newly reconstituted self wanted that blood. It was all she could see, all she could think about.

Vengeance would be hers. After twenty years of imprisonment and degradation, she would destroy the man who had dared to lock her away.

"Come on. Come on and take it," Arkeley rasped.

Malvern glided toward him across the floor.

"You can't resist," Arkeley taunted. "If you were human, maybe, you could handle this. But you're a vampire and you can't resist the smell of blood, can you?"

He was offering himself to her. And she knew why. Should she kill him, she would lose all protection of the law. She would be signing her own warrant of execution. His associates could gun her down without compunction. It didn't matter. Blood mattered. It was all she wanted in the world.

He scuttled toward her, his hand always outstretched, wagging in her face. Her feet urged her forward.

But then she saw the child standing in the doorway. Caxton, the new vampire killer. The pathetic girl who had somehow resisted the curse. Who had somehow survived everything Justinia's knight protectors could do to destroy her.

If it wasn't for this one . . . if Caxton hadn't already destroyed Scapegrace and Deanna . . . if the future didn't demand more. If, if, if.

Jameson's time as a fearless killer of monsters was over. By all rights she should be allowed to savor her victory. But he'd been smart—too smart. He'd trained a replacement. A knight protector of his own.

A thin, translucent eyelid came down over Justinia's eye. It shuddered gently as if she were about to faint.

"Come on," Jameson shouted. His body was shaking too. The little blood still in his body pulsed and trembled with need. "Come on!"

Slowly, Justinia closed her mouth. Painfully. Then she opened it again and a creaking sound like a paper bag being folded up leaked out of her. "Damn ye," she said, the first words she'd spoken in many decades.

She wasn't talking to Jameson. That curse was for the child, Caxton.

Justinia turned around, slinked back to her coffin, and crawled over the lip. Nothing in her long life had ever been so hard. But that life would have been much shorter if she lacked inner strength. If she was not her own mistress. Despite every urge in her body and her soul, she lay back and let her wrinkled head rest on the silk lining.

As the humans started screaming, she closed the lid.

50.

Malvern's head shot backward and she threw up one arm to protect her face, too late to stave off the attack. For a moment her gown, her wig, even her skin flickered and a strange transformation overtook her. The vampire was gone, replaced by a SWAT trooper in full combat armor and helmet.

No, Clara thought. It wasn't a SWAT trooper in that armor. It was still Malvern. What she saw was what Malvern actually looked like at that moment. The radiant being who had come down the ridge, the creature of gowns and wigs and eye patches, was an illusion, an image foisted on Clara's mind by one of Malvern's orisons.

Darnell, with his snake eye, had seen through it. That was what he'd meant when he told Fetlock that his bullets had pierced her armor but not her skin. Clara could see the damage now, the craters in Malvern's chestplate and helmet where Darnell had shot her with his military ammunition. Beneath she could see perfect white skin, unblemished, unbroken.

It made perfect sense, of course. When Jameson Arkeley had faced off against Caxton, he had gone to the trouble of wearing a bulletproof vest. Caxton had been forced to use armor-piercing Teflon bullets on that occasion. Malvern must have been paying attention. She had stripped one of the SWAT troopers of his armor, back at the beginning of the attack on the Hollow, and taken it for her own. Her skin was far better armor than anything humans had designed, but it never hurt to be careful.

Why she had used some of her magical power to hide her appearance, Clara didn't know. Perhaps simple vanity, or a desire to look as terrifying as possible. It had certainly worked in that regard.

The illusion flickered back into place before Caxton had even landed on her feet. Malvern clutched at her eye, but to Clara it didn't look damaged at all. Well, of course not—if she could take a hellfire rocket right in the face without flinching, an improvised steel spear wasn't going to put out that eye. She must have been more startled than hurt.

Which of course had to be what Caxton had counted on.

Caxton didn't slow down. She didn't turn and nod at Clara as she ran past. She had to know that Malvern would be on her trail in a split second. Instead she sprinted as fast as she could for the ridge on the far side of the clearing, the undeveloped ridge opposite the Polder house. As she ran, she shouted over her shoulder, "Now, Urie! Hit her now!"

Clara hadn't seen Urie Polder and Heather moving into position. Neither had Malvern, apparently. Now, even as Malvern began to rise once more to her feet and give chase, Urie and Heather each placed a hand on her shoulder, as if they were trying to get her attention.

"That's suicide," Glauer gasped. Clara turned and saw him behind her, clutching to the side of one of the few undamaged trailers.

Patience Polder stood next to him. "No," she said. "It's a sacrifice."

Clara watched, paralyzed, as Malvern rose to her full height and started to turn around to face the two witchbillies who had accosted her. She raised one arm back in a gesture that, had it been completed, would have disemboweled both of them.

Instead, as Malvern's arm moved backward, gaining momentum, it visibly slowed. It inched through the air, gaining little ground, as if time itself were being distorted.

"What are they doing to her?" Glauer demanded.

"Stealing her power," Patience explained. "Drawing out the magic that sustains her. The more she struggles, the more energy flows into them. Every time she tries to move, every time she exerts so much as a single muscle, they take more from her."

"But that's—that's perfect," Glauer said, and he hefted his carbine. "They've got her dead to rights. We can just go over there and—and destroy her heart, somehow. What's stopping us? Why didn't they just do this sooner?"

"Because in about five seconds, the power will overcome them. This isn't a solution," Patience said. "It's a delaying tactic, that's all. Before you could even reach her it will be too late."

Clara could see what the power drain was doing to Heather. The witchbilly woman's eyes went wide and her mouth fell open. Her free hand shook with a powerful spasm as she fought to keep her other hand touching Malvern. As powerful as Malvern had become, there was no way a human being could absorb all that energy.

She saw the stump of Urie Polder's wooden arm give off a puff of smoke. A moment later it burst into flame. Polder clamped his eyes shut against the pain, but he kept his human hand in contact with Malvern, refusing to give in.

It was clear by that point, however, that it was a losing battle. Malvern's arm had begun to move again—slowly, just an inch at a time. But it was moving. And her eye burned like a torch, an angry red flame that left her intentions obvious.

Meanwhile Caxton had reached the side of the ridge—and hadn't stopped there. She grabbed hold of the edge of a sheet and pulled hard, shaking loose a mass of branches and leaves that had been leaned up against a boulder to camouflage the sheet's presence. When the sheet came away it revealed a dark opening into the ridge. The mouth of a natural cave.

Clara turned to face Glauer and Patience. "What is she doing? What's over there?"

Patience frowned and lifted her shoulders. "The place where the two of them will come together for the last time. Where their final battle will take place."

"You mean Caxton's going to lure Malvern into a cave and fight her there? But why? That makes no sense at all. Are you telling me she's going to go in there and fight Malvern alone? She's not even armed."

"Her weapons will be made ready. Her strategy is her own," Patience said. "Now. If you don't mind, I need to watch my father die. I owe him that much."

Clara's mouth fell open. She spun around again and stared at the tableau by the ripped-open paddy wagon. Heather and Urie Polder were both visibly weakening now, their bodies slumping even as they fought to keep in contact with the vampire. Malvern's arm had reached the top of its swing and her muscles were tensed to complete the attack.

"For Mother's sake, Father," Patience shouted. "For Mother, hold on!"

"For—my—Vesta," Urie Polder grunted. "Ahum!"

But the feedback of the energy he was drawing away from Malvern was too much. First Heather succumbed, dropping to the ground like a sack of potatoes. Smoke wafted off her smoldering dress. With Heather gone, the spell was too much even for a hexenmeister of Urie Polder's strength. His whole body shook as if he were enduring a grand mal seizure. The flames from his wooden stump spread to his shirt and began eating at his beard and hair. He screamed wildly, uncontrollably, as the power burned out his internal organs, until cracks of light appeared on his exposed skin. Until his eyes burst in puffs of steam.

Clara couldn't watch what came next. She couldn't bear to see him die.

So instead she did the one thing she thought she was still capable of. She dashed across the clearing, toward the cave mouth. If Caxton was going to go up against Malvern in there, she wouldn't do it alone.

"Clara!" Glauer called after her from not far behind. "Don't!"

But Clara refused to listen. She didn't even slow her pace when she heard a sudden scream behind her, though she spared one glance over her shoulder. Just enough of a look to see Urie Polder release his hold on Malvern. Just enough to see Malvern move again in a flash of white muscles, just enough to see her fingers strike at Urie Polder's face and chest like the raking claws of an eagle.

Clara had no doubt he was dead before he even fell to his knees. He had been the best that a man could be—brave, wise, and willing to do something utterly stupid if it meant helping others, if it bought the rest of them a second of grace.

As Clara reached the cave mouth and hurried inside, she made a mental note to honor him properly at some later date. Assuming she lived through the night.

[2004]

Sometimes—only sometimes—the cards turned over, and the one trump the gambler needed was lying right there. Sometimes old sins came back not to haunt one, but in the form of blessings.

A hundred vampires. An army of them, waiting in the earth like the bulbs of poisonous flowers, just waiting for the time to sprout. The same army of vampires Justinia had created for the Union army a century and a half before, never used but only hid away from the light of the sun, had risen to plague the good people of Gettysburg.

And arrayed against them was Laura Caxton and whatever scraps of human refuse she could pull together in a single day.

Caxton didn't have a chance.

As Justinia lay in her coffin in some dismal museum's basement, listening with Jameson Arkeley to the reports coming over the police band radio, she could only gloat. If she did nothing, if she let the course of events play themselves out as they were bound to, Caxton would die. The newest thorn in her side would be drawn from her by Alva Griest and his legion of the dead. Justinia had no doubt that Griest and his fellows would be destroyed ere long. They were weakened by their time in the earth and they would be hunted, hemmed in on every side, rooted out during the daylight hours and laid low, one by one.

But not before Caxton perished. How delicious.

Of course, that was if she did nothing.

There was more to be won if she but lifted her hand. She let her weak fingers play across the keys of her computer, her only method of manipulation now.

ye can yet save her, if ye choose to

Jameson slammed the lid of the computer shut, nearly trapping her fingertips. He didn't want to hear it.

Luckily for her, she didn't need to say more. The idea was already planted. The curse was already in Jameson, from long years before. If he but turned his hand against himself now, it would be enough.

And oh how tempting it must be. His mortal body, heir to all the shocks of flesh, was crippled and bent now. One hand was little more than a club. His spine was fused in many places, his muscles withered by disuse. How low the mighty vampire killer had fallen.

Strength could be his. Power unlike any he had ever known. He could race to the little town and fight for Caxton's life. Be her protector. Her savior. Justinia Malvern knew just how seductive it was for a man to be needed. How desperately this man wanted to save the girl he thought of as his spiritual daughter.

He turned and stared at her with desperate eyes as the radio crackled and spat. As reports came in, one after the other, of men cut down, of vampires swarming through the city streets of Gettysburg.

"I could cut out your heart right now," he said, his mouth a hard line. "I could do one good thing, at least. I could end this. I could end our little dance."

He could. Weak as he was, he was still far more sound of limb and wind than Justinia. He could destroy her any time he chose.

But when he rose from his seat, when he went to fetch a scalpel—she was not overly worried.

She'd called plenty of bluffs in her time.

51.

Caxton saw plenty of blood and dead bodies as she ran across the clearing toward the cave. She refused to let it get to her. It didn't matter that Urie Polder was sacrificing his life back there. It didn't matter that Fetlock was dead.

It shouldn't matter that Clara and Glauer were out there, standing around looking helpless. Waiting to die.

It shouldn't matter at all. She'd hardened herself against the possibility. For the last two years she'd worked hard—so damned hard—to divorce herself from everything she used to care about. All the fragments of her old life could be used as weapons against her. Malvern was an expert at manipulating people, at turning loved ones and family members into liabilities. Caxton could not afford to hesitate now, not even for a moment.

She had known, when she started designing this trap, that Malvern would come hard. That she would not pull any punches this time. One of them, if not both, was going to die here, to-night. By planting the rumor that she was going to start a clan of vampire killers, that Patience and Simon Arkeley would breed a whole gaggle of children raised for nothing but Malvern's destruction, she had ensured that Malvern would come and try to nip things in the bud. She had bought herself one solid chance, one single opportunity to end the vampires for good.

But only if everything went according to plan.

Fetlock had nearly ruined that. Had Caxton still been shackled when Malvern arrived, had she been unable to fight, it would have been over. If Fetlock had taken the witchbillies away from the Hollow before nightfall, if he had sent Urie Polder off to jail—everything would have fallen apart.

She had only luck to thank that she was still breathing. That she still had this one last shot at Malvern.

Luck and, of course, Clara. Clara who had slipped her the handcuff key.

She was grateful for that. But not so grateful she would let herself feel a thing when she ran right past Clara, not so grateful that she would slow down even to nod in her former lover's direction.

At the mouth of the cave she pulled aside the makeshift gillie net that had hidden its very existence from view. It was pitch black inside, and she had no way of making a light, but it didn't matter. She'd rehearsed the next part of her plan so many times she could do it blindfolded. She grabbed up the nylon bag that

Urie Polder had left for her just inside the cave mouth. Tearing it open, she found the plunger and quickly attached the leads of the detonation cable. Malvern would be at most a few seconds behind her. She needed to make every one of those seconds count.

There was a place about ten yards inside the cave mouth where she could stand and be safe. Patience had actually proven herself useful for once by pointing it out. Patience had seen all of this, everything that had happened tonight, everything that would happen. She'd been stingy with the details, as was her way, but when Caxton was planting the dynamite Patience had been endlessly forthcoming. Caxton knew exactly how the blast would happen and where all the rocks would fall.

"Caxton?" someone called from just outside the cave.

That was something Patience hadn't mentioned.

"Clara? Is that you? Get the fuck out of here!"

"No," Clara said. She stepped inside the cave mouth, silhouetted by the fires that still burned outside. "No. You don't get to do this alone."

"Clara, I'm warning you—"

Clara came inside the cave and pressed her back up against the wall. She kept her face turned toward the cave mouth, her weapon ready to fire at anything that showed itself.

It was a good position to shoot from, with plenty of cover. It was also right in the middle of the blast zone. "A lot of us have worked for this. A lot of us have sacrificed everything. Not just you. So—so screw you, I'm not leaving. I'll help with this or I'll die trying."

In about three seconds, Caxton thought, *you'll get your chance at that.* She looked up, over Clara's head, and visually checked the twenty sticks of dynamite duct-taped to the ceiling of the cave mouth.

"I don't have time to explain. Just move your ass!" Caxton shouted.

"I'm not going anywhere."

Caxton looked down at the plunger in her hands. All she had to do was push down on the handle. A coil inside the plunger would generate an electrical spark, which would then travel down the length of wire to the blasting caps. The dynamite would explode, bringing down the roof of the cave. Sealing it off from the outside world. Malvern was supposed to be caught in that blast, and buried by the falling rocks.

The explosion wouldn't be enough to kill her. Patience had been clear on that. But it would slow her down while she dug herself out of tons of rubble. It would give Caxton enough time to get deeper into the cave, to the killing floor she'd laid out.

Patience had promised her it would work.

The girl had not mentioned that Caxton would have to drop all that rock on Clara's head to make it happen.

For two years Caxton had worked hard to purge herself of every bit of concern, compassion, and love she had ever felt for another human being. She had trained herself to think of every-one—including herself—as expendable. She gripped the handle of the plunger. There was no time to argue with Clara. Already Malvern would be streaking toward the cave mouth. This was going to take split-second timing.

Her knuckles went white where they clutched the plunger's handle.

Everyone was expendable.

Everyone.

Caxton dropped the plunger and ran forward, into the blast zone. There was just enough light that she could see Clara's eyes go wide. Caxton grabbed her former girlfriend by the arms and pulled, hard. Clara tried to dig in her feet, but Caxton was big-ger than Clara and considerably stronger.

"Come on," Caxton groaned, and shoved Clara inside the cave. "There's no time for this!"

There really wasn't.

Vampires, being unnatural creatures, made the very fabric of reality curdle wherever they went. When they passed by, cows stopped giving milk. Dogs howled. The tiny hairs on the back of Caxton's arms all stood up when one came near.

They were standing up at attention just then, like little soldiers.

"Oh, shit," she said, and turned to see a white streak come racing toward the cave. It was like watching a lightning bolt come straight toward one's face.

It was too late. In half a second Malvern would be inside the cave, in the blast zone. There was no way Caxton could reach the plunger in time, no way she could bring the roof down on Justinia Malvern. The entire plan had failed, and she had lost her one chance. And now she would die because she had refused to kill the woman she loved more than anyone else in the world.

Stupid sucker, she thought. You couldn't be hard enough. You couldn't do it when it really counted.

And yet—there was one thing you could always count on when it came to Patience Polder's visions. They always came true. Not, typically, the way you expected them to. But every one of them was foreordained.

As Malvern hurtled toward the cave mouth, another shape accelerated inward on an intersecting course. A shape that blared with red and blue light and screamed with a cry of sirens. A cop car, a patrol cruiser, came out of the night and slammed into Malvern at top speed.

[2004]

Of all the vampires Malvern had known, of all the mortals to whom she had given the curse, none were more obnoxious to her than Jameson Arkeley.

It had been his purpose, of course, to merely save the day, then allow himself to be destroyed. He had been quite sincere in desiring the power only with the best of intentions. Now that he understood, now that he knew the strength the blood could bring, naturally he had changed his mind. Yet he could never seem to come to an accommodation with that fact. He would not accept that he wanted to live. That he wanted anything, beyond base heroics and cheap nobility of spirit.

Yet want it he did. He wanted the blood, sure as any drunkard wanted drink. Surer than that. There was no drug in the world more enticing, no surcease of sorrow that could compare to the feeling, oh, that precious feeling when the blood hit the back of a dry throat.

She knew it so well. She knew that every night that passed, every night he persisted, his desire grew stronger. Whether he would let himself voice his bloodlust or not.

He had returned for her after saving Caxton and the town of Gettysburg. She'd known that he would. He had threatened her endlessly, even as he demanded information from her, told her in graphic detail over and over how he would tear out her heart when she became useless to him. When he had sufficiently picked her brains.

Justinia knew how to play that game. She promised secrets she did not possess. She tempted him with her knowledge of the orisons, whispered secrets of vampiric lore, much of which she made up on the spot. He knew, of course, that some of what she said was lies. But he could not know how much. In exchange for the few truths she allowed to trickle from her lips, she demanded that he bring her blood. That he make a safe home for her and protect her from all who would destroy her.

And so he had. He found a place no one would ever look for them— at the bottom of a burning coal mine, a place so thick with evil fumes and blistering heat that no one but a vampire could stand it. He made a throne room for himself there, and placed her coffin at its side. He would never see himself as her knight protector, she knew. He would never fall for the cheaper blandishments of her seductions, for the forms she took as she tried to tease out his sexual desires. She made herself look like his wife, Astarte, and that elicited no more than a sneer. She formed herself like Vesta Polder, who had been his mistress. He slammed shut the lid of her coffin and did not open it for many nights.

Justinia took it too far once. She caused herself to resemble Laura Caxton, but a Caxton who liked boys. She made herself naked and writhing in her coffin, begged for his touch in Caxton's voice.

He nearly ripped her heart out that night. His hand closed around it and squeezed. Another few pounds of pressure and he would have crushed it like a grape. Eventually he let go, though the look of disgust on his face remained a long while.

She stopped trying to sway him with orisons after that. Anyway, she'd always been able to seduce with words far better.

"This is what ye are now! Ye must come to some accommodation with your new face," she told him, *while he brooded on his throne. "Lest ye tear your soul in half."* If he didn't, she knew, it was only a matter of time before he turned on her. And she could not resist him now.

"I'll die before I accept what I've become," he said.

But she knew he would not. Or he would have already returned to Caxton, knelt before her, and bared his breast to her.

"Be the angel of death, like my master Vincombe," she suggested. *"Be the conservator of our tradition, like dear Lares."* Give in to your darkest perversions, like Reyes, she did not say. Accept me as erotic mother-figure, like the Chess boys. Let me justify your vengeance, like stupid Easling. *"Ye must find some purpose. Some rationale for all ye've surrendered. All thou hast sacrificed. Ye saved Caxton the one time. Save others, if you like!"*

"Save them? I'm as likely to devour them. I know you understand—every time I come near a human now, all I can think about is ripping their throat out. Drinking their blood. And it will always be like that from now on. I can't leave this place. I can't be human again. Even if somehow I managed to hold back, it wouldn't matter. My family would spurn me if they met me now. Caxton would . . . she would . . ."

"She would destroy ye. Your family would fear your approach. Because ye are different than ye once were."

There were times when Justinia surprised even herself with how clever she might be. As she watched his face, his red eyes hard with anger and self-loathing, she began to see what it would take.

"Of course," she said, picking her words with infinite care, "there's no reason they have to be so different. There's no reason, say, they couldn't accept the curse themselves . . ."

52.

Standing still, with her feet braced, Malvern could have picked up the car and *thrown* it. She could have torn it in half. But she wasn't standing still, and she wasn't braced for the impact. And even vampires have to obey the laws of physics sometimes.

Malvern's headlong course was brought to a very abrupt halt. She was thrown sideways by the impact, away from the cave's mouth, out of Caxton's field of view. The car slewed to one side as if it had struck a steel fence post. It fishtailed into the side of the ridge, hard enough to make dirt and small rocks cascade downward from the roof of the cave. Glass shattered and the siren's pitch changed as the speakers on the roof bar crumpled, changing from an eagle's shriek of vengeance to the mournful blatting of a dying walrus. One of the car's tires exploded with a bang.

The driver's-side door flew open and Glauer rolled out, shaking his head as if he'd suffered a concussion in the impact. Blood leaked from his nose and he held one leg stiffly, as if the knee wouldn't bend.

He stumbled forward, into the cave. Leaned hard against the wall and didn't move. Just breathing, with difficulty.

"Glauer!" Clara shouted. She started running toward him.

Caxton grabbed her around the waist and twisted around, pushing her deeper inside the cave. It was all she could think to do.

"Remember when we were partners?" Glauer asked.

"Sure," Caxton told him.

"No. No." He swallowed convulsively. His eyes kept drifting

shut. Had he hit his head on the dashboard in the collision? He was in bad shape. "No. We were never partners. I worshipped you, Caxton. I thought you were the toughest lady I ever met."

"You took some hits yourself and never complained," Caxton said. She wished she had better words for him. She knew exactly what was going to happen next.

Glauer turned his head to the side to look at something outside of the cave, something Caxton couldn't see. He nodded, once.

"I can only pull this trick once," he said. "Make it count."

Caxton took that as her cue. She grabbed Clara and dragged her back into the cave, back as far as she could get, away from the cave's mouth.

She did look back, just once, to see Glauer still struggling, trying to get up.

And then Malvern roared through him, shredding him into several pieces as she erupted into the cave mouth in pure fury. His blood hit the ground like rain. She didn't even bother to drink any of it.

If the collision with the car had hurt her, Caxton couldn't see the damage. She had her illusory shape again, her wig perfect without a stray hair, her gown glowing with infernal light. Her red eye burned like a malevolent star.

She opened her mouth and showed her fangs, row after row of them. Caxton knew that was an illusion, too, one that came naturally to vampires. They had only thirty-two teeth in their heads, just like human beings. It just looked like they had a lot more because they were so cruel and sharp.

Malvern took a step inside the mouth of the cave. "Enough delays, Laura. Ye cannot harm me now."

"Bullshit," Caxton said, and pushed down the handle of her plunger.

Clara just had time to shout "Gl—" before the ceiling came down.

The explosion was mad, huge, a living, angry thing, a howling darkness. A noise that made Caxton's flesh ripple like water. It blew over her, through her, and she felt rocks the size of her fist, the size of her head, go screaming past her into the dark, felt dust blast across her skin leaving a thousand tiny scratches. But she held her ground, because she knew she would survive. Knew she would not be hurt, really. Patience Polder had promised her as much.

Urie Polder had found the dynamite in an abandoned construction shed near the old strip mine. A full crate of it, just sitting under a sagging roof, getting wet every time it rained and gnawed on by hungry rats. Caxton hadn't believed it could possibly still be potent.

It did a treat now, though. The ceiling came down exactly as promised, burying Malvern under a dozen tons of rock. The cave mouth was sealed off completely, walled off from the rest of the world—just as Patience had foretold it would be. Caxton felt like she'd been buffeted right out of existence, back into primordial void. Everything went black and she went deaf and there was dust in her mouth, dust in her nose and her eyes. She tried to scrub it away with her hands, then reached inside her nylon bag and pulled out a heavy-duty flashlight. When she switched it on its beam revealed nothing but billowing smoke and dust. She started to cough and choke, but she had a gas mask in the bag as well—again, a leftover from the mining days. She pulled it on over her face and swung her beam of light around, looking for any sign of Clara in the debris.

What she found first, though, was Malvern's hand.

It stuck up out of a wall of fallen rocks, the fingers outstretched toward her. So pale and white. No illusions veiled it now. It looked like a human hand sculpted out of alabaster. There were a few age spots where the thumb met the palm. Dark veins ran like snakes beneath the skin, swollen with blood.

"L-L-Lau—" Clara coughed from behind Caxton.

The hand of a vampire. The hand of the enemy who had organized every event, every bad, fucked-up thing in her life for the last five years. She had trouble looking away from it. Especially when the fingers started to move.

"Goddamn it," she said. She turned away from the hand— not without effort—and cast about on the floor until she found Clara. She stripped the mask from her own face and pressed it against Clara's mouth and nose until Clara started sucking in great gasping breaths.

"We have to get out of this mess—it'll take hours for the dust to settle," Caxton said, trying not to breathe too much of it in. "And long before then she'll get free."

"She's not dead?" Clara asked, her voice muffled by the gas mask.

Caxton grabbed the mask back from her and put it over her own face again before she started coughing. "Not even close. Come on, get to your feet."

"I think—I—koff—I got hit by some—debris—"

"I can't carry you. Either you walk or you stay here," Caxton told her.

Clara stared at her with questioning eyes. Caxton refused to respond.

"I guess I'll walk," Clara said, finally.

"Thought so. Come on."

[2005]

Caxton's gun clicked noisily in the throne chamber. She was out of bullets. Jameson threw one arm across his face anyway to protect himself from the death that did not come.

When he realized he'd been tricked, he howled in rage. But Caxton was already gone, headed back up the tunnel of the burning mine. The half-deads raced after her, with Jameson following more slowly behind them.

Justinia had taught Jameson that. He had always been impetuous, ready to race into any trap. She had taught him to send his lackeys first, to let them take the brunt of the danger. Not that it would make any difference.

In her coffin she waited quietly until one of the half-deads returned.

It scrubbed at its face, not tearing at the skin this time but trying to get pepper spray out of its eyes. It looked miserable. Good. The pathetic little failure deserved to hurt. "She got the rest of us—I'm the only one left," the creature squeaked.

It had been human once. Now it was so much less. It was beneath Malvern's contempt.

"I'm sure that the master will prevail," the creature piped. Trying for a confidence that neither of them believed. The half-dead would have made a terrible cardplayer.

"No. It is over," Malvern said. She knew Caxton—and Jameson—well enough to predict how their final confrontation would end. Jameson was a hundred times stronger than Caxton, a dozen times faster. It didn't matter. Caxton would win, somehow. The odds against her didn't matter—she was that most dangerous of players, because she had luck on her side. "Help me up."

The creature put one shoulder under her armpit. She was still so weak. So frail—Jameson had promised her blood, so much blood. In this he had failed her. In many other ways he had done good service for her.

She had always had a healthy respect—and even fear—for witches. Now the two greatest witches in America were dead—Astarte Arkeley and Vesta Polder, laid low by Jameson's own hands. The greatest threat to Justinia's existence, Caxton, still lived, but Justinia wasn't so sure how she felt about that. She had begun to feel a sort of grudging affection for the girl.

And oh, how fun it would be to make her suffer.

There were plans to be made. Quiet times ahead when she would lie low, and think, and scheme.

"What about the master's son?" the half-dead asked. He pointed at the boy chained to a nearby pillar, unconscious with the fumes of this place. "You should take his blood now. You'll need your strength."

"No," Justinia said, after thinking on it for a moment. "No. He and I are old friends. He taught me how to use e-mail. And so many more things."

She bent low over Simon Arkeley's body. Pried open his eyelids with her fingers, stared deep into his slumbering brain. Planted a little of her self in there. Not the curse, not the gift of vampirism. Just a simple orison. From now on she would see everything he saw, hear every word spoken to him, and he would never know it. He would be a perfect spy for her.

"Now get me out of here," she told the half-dead.

"But the master—"

"I do not discuss my orders with the likes of thee," Justinia said, and bared her fangs. After that the little wretch was most compliant.

"Soon, Laura," Justinia said, as they walked together out of the coal mine. "Soon enough."

53.

"We're trapped in here," Clara said, staring at the walls of rock all around her. "We're trapped in here—with *her*."

"Which is exactly what I wanted," Caxton told her. She swept her light along the wall in front of her, a massive beetling brow of limestone. A crack ran along its length, in most places so narrow it would have been difficult to get the point of a knife inside. To the left, however, the crack widened out until it became a low passageway. Caxton grabbed Clara's arm and pulled her inside. They had to bend over nearly double, but the light showed that the passage led to a wider space ahead. Grunting and grimacing, Caxton ducked under a lip of rock and into a tiny room in the rock, a bare chamber with curving walls. It looked like a bubble had been trapped in the stone when it formed. On its far side a slightly more forgiving tunnel opened up.

The cave wasn't part of the strip mine. It had existed long before anyone came to the ridges looking for coal. The original surveyors had explored it extensively—one could still see their blazes chiseled into the walls, if one knew where to look—but had evidently found nothing of value and had left it alone. No one had found a use for it since. There were caves like it all over Pennsylvania—Penn Caverns and Lincoln Caverns were the most famous, flooded labyrinths that had become tourist traps, with legions of suburbanites showing up every year to take boat rides through the weird and otherworldly rock formations. Most were much smaller, with only a few chambers connected by passages too tight to comfortably squeeze through.

Caxton's cave wasn't an enormous system, but it went deep beneath the ridge and it had its sights. It was also exactly the kind of place that a Pow-Wow like Urie Polder knew what to do with.

As Caxton dragged Clara deeper into the caverns, lighting up walls of stalactites and organ pipes with her flashlight, she saw the effect of Polder's spell right away. Clara stumbled forward like a blind woman, even when Caxton pointed out exactly where she should put her feet. She kept reaching out as if to fend off stalactites that weren't there, and tripping over stalagmites she couldn't seem to see.

"Fuck, this is going to be a problem," Caxton said.

"What's going on? I feel like I'm on drugs," Clara said.

"Not drugs. It's a spell. You ran across that spell that kept people from finding the Hollow, right? On your way in—Simon knew the way, or you never would have gotten this far and screwed up all my plans."

"Thanks for that," Clara pouted.

"Oh, give it a rest."

Clara lowered her head. "Alright, so, anyway. Yes. I saw the spell that hides the Hollow. I saw how it doesn't show up on GPS."

"This is basically the same spell. Designed to mislead anyone who comes down here, other than me or Urie Polder. Only it works even better down here. Caves are disorienting at the best of times—there are weird acoustics, you can barely see anything, and they almost, but don't quite, make sense. Passages and rooms, right? Just like a building human beings built. Except these passages double back on each other and go nowhere, or the rooms have ceilings that are twenty feet high on one side but only six inches high on the other. It's damned easy to get lost in a cave, which is why the government seals them off as fast as they can find them. You add a little magic to the mix and you've got a real maze. A perfect death trap."

"You knew you would bring Malvern down here," Clara said.

"Yes. All along. I spent two years hanging up the ghost cordon and the ring of bird skulls, training the witchbillies, hiding the Hollow from prying eyes. All to make Malvern think I wasn't ready for her, that I wanted to keep her *out*. Which of course made her want to get *in*. I wanted her in here, right here, where I could control things. Just her and me, and a fight to the death."

"And now—me."

"Right. Which ruins *everything*."

Clara's lips pursed as if she'd bitten into a lemon. "I was only trying to help. You don't need to be such a bitch about it."

Caxton spun around and stared at her former lover. "If Glauer hadn't sacrificed his life you and I would both be dead, right now. You fucked up, and it took his death—his *death,* Clara—to save us. He was a *soldier.* He knew how to take orders. What are you bringing to the table? A machine gun?"

Clara looked down at the carbine that was slung at her waist.

Caxton fumed. "You see what she's capable of right now? Did you? She's never been stronger. What did you possibly think you could do here?"

Clara bit her lip, but her eyes stayed sharp. She was probably fighting back an emotional reaction, but she didn't let it reach her face. "I don't know," she said.

Caxton turned away with a grunt of annoyance and headed farther into the cave. The killing floor was deeper inside, past a long traverse where they would have to crawl. Caxton knew the path well enough she could negotiate the squeeze without feeling like she was about to be trapped at any second. Getting Clara through it, when she was confused by Urie Polder's spell, would take a lot longer. It might take more time than they had.

"What about you?" Clara demanded. "What are you going to do? How are you going to fight her?"

"I've still got an ace up my sleeve," Caxton said, unwilling to waste breath explaining herself. "Come on. Down on your hands and knees. Try to stay low so you don't scrape your back on the ceiling. There are a couple of places where you'll cut yourself if you're not careful.

Clara did as she was told, though she clearly saw something other than what Caxton described to her. "Is this low enough?" she asked.

"Toward the end you have to scoot forward on your belly," Caxton said, as she crammed herself into the low-hanging fissure. "Just keep moving. We don't have much time."

Clara pushed forward, keeping her eyes on her hands as she moved forward, watching nothing but where her next move would take her. It was probably the best she could manage. Did she think she was in a huge cavern, crawling around for no good reason? Or maybe she saw the walls around her on every side just fine, but couldn't tell which direction she was heading. Caxton had no experience of what it was like to be under the power of the spell, but she imagined it must be terrifying. Yet Clara didn't give in to the natural urge to panic.

Caxton had almost started to respect the other woman. But then Clara spoke again.

"You planned all along to come in here, to face Malvern in this cave," Clara said. "Jesus Christ. You're a fucking monster."

"Why? It's not that I like this cave any more than you do, I just—"

"You let all those people die."

Caxton nearly bashed her head on the roof of the fissure as she turned to glare at Clara. "I beg your pardon," she said.

"The witchbillies—the cops—even Fetlock. I hated Fetlock. The man was just slime. But he did not deserve to die like that."

Caxton steeled herself before responding. "I didn't ask him to come here. I didn't ask him to try to take Malvern on when there was no chance of his succeeding. I definitely didn't ask him to lock me up in that paddy wagon and nearly get me killed. I had to sacrifice some people, yeah. But this isn't about playing nice. It's about killing a goddamned vampire. It's about Justinia Malvern."

"Bullshit," Clara said.

"What? How dare you tell me what this is—"

"This is about you. It needs to be you who finishes her off. You, Laura Caxton, the famous vampire hunter. They made a TV movie about you. They write magazine articles about you— just last month there was one in *Newsweek,* about how you were still evading the law. About how you were still out there some- where, planning, waiting."

"I don't do this to be famous!"

"No, I don't think you do. I think it's because you need to prove something. You needed to prove something to Jameson Arkeley, that you were tough enough that he could count on you. Then he turned, and you got a chance to prove you were even tougher than him. You destroyed my life because you needed to be tough. So tough nobody could love you. So tough you aren't even human anymore."

"Duck your head or you're going to lose it," Caxton growled.

"That's not a denial."

Caxton turned herself around in the tunnel until she was facing Clara. It wasn't easy, and she scraped skin off her palms in the process, leaving microscopic trails of blood on the stone. Trails Malvern would spot as if they glowed in the dark.

"I do this because nobody else will do it right," she insisted. "Every time I try to train somebody else, every time I try to ask for help—from the State Police, from the U.S. Marshals Service, from the witchbillies—hell, from you—they just fuck it up. They do it wrong and lots of people get killed and then I have to go through ten miles of shit to clean up after them. How many times have I paid for Fetlock's mistakes? How many times have I had to rescue your skinny ass?"

"A lot," Clara had to admit. With Caxton's light in her face she looked a lot less confrontational.

"I do this," Caxton said, intending it to be the last word on the matter, "because somebody has to. And if nobody else does it, it doesn't end. I do this because Malvern is fucking evil and the world can't handle evil things. It always underestimates them. It always thinks that if it just pretends the bad things don't exist, then they'll just go away. The world functions by denial and wishful thinking, and that's why the world runs red with blood. I do it so people can keep being stupid and not have to pay for it. So people can be weak and it's not a death sentence. I do it," she said, "because nobody else can."

[2006]

After Jameson's death, Justinia haunted the woods of Pennsylvania, hunting only as much as she dared. She could walk under her own power now. She could take her own victims. That in itself was a glorious thing after so long, after so many decades of being constrained to her own coffin. Of being a dead thing that would not sleep.

It was not enough.

She couldn't take as much blood as she wanted. Every death left evidence behind. Every killing was an arrow pointed directly at her heart. There were others now, other hunters. Inept, incompetent—this Fetlock, for instance, this government man, was so poor at his work that it was child's play to avoid his attention. The others, Hsu and Glauer, were more problematic. Laura had trained them and they knew all the tricks. They would eventually find her, if she was careless.

Justinia Malvern knew exactly what she should do next. She should flee, head for places where they'd never heard of her. Where no one knew her secrets.

Yes, that would have been the wise thing to do.

But she didn't go west. She stayed very close indeed.

She lingered in Pennsylvania, taking only exactly as much blood as she needed to subsist. All her old associates and protectors were dead, but their phantoms came to advise her all the same.

"Thou needst to find new purpose," Vincombe warned her. "Ye're forgetting what thou art. A killer, not a player of games."

She ignored his voice as it spoke to her every night. As her depredations took her back, again and again, to the same place. To a stand of woods overlooking a certain fence. A certain zone patrolled by dogs and lit up by searchlights that hurt her eyes.

"There's easier blood to be had in more pleasing climes," Easling counseled. Easling, who had lived for comfort.

She waved him away as she watched armed guards stand watch on a high wall. Like men-at-arms guarding a castle, standing in defense of the princess locked away inside a strong tower.

"You can find others who'll love you, as we did. And was that not a worthy thing? Did it not please you, even a bit?" the Chess boys asked.

She snarled at them and they vanished like the ghosts they were.

"You're the last of us," Lares insisted. He looked so sad when she saw him in her mind's eye. "You have to keep yourself safe, or we'll be lost forever."

He was too insubstantial to demand much of her attention. Justinia focused instead on the gates of the prison. On looking for a way in. For one of her talents it should not be too hard, she thought.

"She'll kill you," Jameson said.

That and nothing more. And maybe he was right.

She should leave. If she couldn't do that, she should go and lie low. Let time be her weapon, as it had been with Jameson when he was human. Let the girl grow old inside those prison walls. Let her grow bent and scarred and withered, until she could no longer fight. Until she was no longer a threat.

But no. Justinia wouldn't do that. As much as she longed to live forever, as much as she wanted to bathe in blood, there was one thing she could not do, and that was let Laura Caxton get away.

They had not yet finished their game.

54.

Clara had to stop arguing with Caxton because she suddenly couldn't breathe.

It was just a spell. She kept reminding herself of that fact. What she saw, what she felt, everything her body was telling her was wrong.

Her body refused to listen. Her breath raced in and out of her lungs. Her back started to sweat, as she felt the stone around her closing in. Ahead of her the tunnel, barely illuminated by Caxton's light, narrowed down to be no more than a foot wide, and less than that from floor to ceiling. There was no way she could fit her shoulders through that passage. She didn't even want to imagine trying.

When she turned her head to look back, though, she nearly screamed. Behind her there was no passage at all, just a blank wall of rock.

Clara bit her lip and tried to master herself. She had come that way. She knew for a fact the passage back there was open and led to the round bubble room. This was just an illusion, just a trick . . . repeating that to herself, over and over, seemed to help a little.

"Come on," Caxton said. "The worst bit's just ahead. We're almost there."

Then Caxton scuttled forward on her belly, shoving herself forward with her hands and feet, right through the impossibly narrow part of the tunnel. It looked absurd. It looked like Caxton shrank as Clara watched, her body diminishing as she moved forward with the light. When Caxton pushed through the narrow space she looked like she was no more than half her original size.

It's just a trick, Clara repeated. *This is Urie Polder's spell, and I'm not stuck. I'm not wedged in here under an entire mountain of rock. The ceiling is not going to cave in. I'm not going to get snagged on a spar of limestone and be caught here until I die of dehydration. I am not going to freak out, I am not going to—*

Caxton's light disappeared around a corner, leaving Clara in total darkness.

Clara did scream a little then. But she shoved one hand over her mouth and refused to make much more noise than a field mouse caught in a rat trap.

The light came back after a second. An enormous hand reached through the narrow tunnel ahead, a giant white hand with fingers as thick as Clara's arms. It grabbed at her and hauled her forward, toward the foot-wide aperture, and Clara was certain she would be yanked through, her bones broken until she fit. She threw her arms out to brace herself and felt the rock all around her, and that was even worse than just seeing it. She could feel how solid it was, how massive and unforgiving and—and then—

And then she was through. She didn't even scrape her skin on the stone as she was hauled through the aperture. She saw that it was Caxton's hand, Caxton's perfectly normal-sized hand, that had grabbed and pulled her, and she squeezed her eyes shut until she stopped wanting to panic and die on the spot.

The tunnel opened up into a massive cavern, far bigger than anything Clara expected to find under the ridge. It looked like the entire ridge was hollow inside, most of the space taken up by this incredible chamber. Stalactites hung down overhead, hundreds of feet long, as narrow at their tips as ice picks. A broad, rushing river wound through the floor, between out-croppings of stone that looked like cathedrals or candles on a birthday cake or grinning devils with sharp pitchforks. Clara stared down into the water of the underground river and saw it had to be thirty feet deep. The current moved past at an in-credible pace—Clara was certain if she set foot in that water she would be carried away, washed down into the bowels of the earth, sucked down forever into measureless caves and smashed endlessly against submerged rocks until she was nothing but blood and paste.

Then she saw the fish and she jumped back in all-new ter-ror. They were gigantic, as big as sharks, and white as vampires. Backward-pointing tentacles fringed their mouths, but that wasn't the most terrifying thing about them. They had no eyes at all. Their faces were nothing more than enormous grinning jaws, their teeth as wicked and sharp as Malvern's had ever been.

If she fell in that water, Clara wondered whether the current or the fish would kill her first. It would be a close race.

"Just jump over this little creek," Caxton said, waving her flashlight across the surface of the water so it glared like a sil-ver mirror struck by a lighthouse's actinic beam. "We're headed over there, to the left. There's a natural chamber there where we're going to set up our ambush."

"But—we have to cross the water?" Clara asked.

Caxton stared at her. "You can just step over it here. You don't even need to jump." She pointed at a place where the river bent around a massive stand of stalagmites, roaring and foaming as it turned. The water seethed and snapped like a living thing.

Clara shook her head. "How wide is it?" she asked. It looked like it had to be twenty feet to the other side. At least twenty feet. "I know what I'm seeing right now. How wide is it really?"

Caxton groaned in displeasure. "Right there? About a foot and a half."

"And those fish? How big are they, actually?"

"Those tiny little things?" Caxton asked. She laughed and stabbed her light toward them. They didn't respond at all, but Clara could see them even better in the light and they didn't look like fish anymore. They looked like prehistoric monsters, the kind of sea creatures that would jump up and drag antelopes down to their doom. "Your average goldfish could take one of those in a fight. I don't have time for this, Clara. It's not real. You know that."

"I know it. I also know what I'm looking at right now."

"Screw it. You come with me now, or I leave you behind. With no light. I don't have time to baby you. If you get killed down here, it's because you had to go racing after me when I specifically told you I didn't want you here."

Clara gritted her teeth. She wanted to tell Caxton to go fuck herself.

It wasn't really the time for that, though.

Caxton jumped over the river then. She seemed to hang in the air for long seconds as she arced over the water, one foot stretched out to reach the far shore. It looked like she would make the jump easily.

Then a cold wind blew through Clara's head, and she doubled over in pain. She heard a voice like a bullhorn sounding off right inside her brain.

Laura, the voice said, *I am not well pleased by your hospitality.*

Caxton stumbled in midair and landed with one foot in the river. The white eyeless fish swarmed around her ankle as if they would devour her whole. She casually pulled her foot out of the water and shook it off to dry it.

"Damn," Caxton said.

"I assume you heard that," Clara said, shouting across the river to be heard over the roaring current.

"What, Malvern? Yeah. I heard her. And I know what that means. She's already dug herself out. We have zero time left. Come now, or stay there and die. I don't care which." Caxton turned away from the river with her flashlight, leaving the massive cavern in near-total darkness.

Clara closed her eyes and jumped. Every muscle in her body tensed as she hurtled over the massive river, then refused to relax when she landed on the far side—completely clear of the water. She had to force herself to stand up straight. When she opened her eyes and looked behind her, she saw the river had been no more than a thin trickle, less than six inches deep.

She did not ask Caxton to wait for her, but followed close on her heels.

[2006]

Much of the prison was on fire. The inmates raged and rioted in the courtyard, while outside the police hammered at the gates with a battering ram. It had never looked more like a medieval castle under siege.

Up on the wall, Justinia watched her double fighting with Laura Caxton and wished it could be her.

Oh, such a foolish desire, she knew. The whole point of this scheme had been to have Caxton kill the doppelgänger. The warden of the prison—a particularly vile little human—had been made to look just like Justinia, or at least enough to pass a quick inspection. Justinia had torn the woman's eye out with her own fingers. Dressed her in the mauve nightgown that Justinia had worn for so many years. Told her that her only chance to live through the night was to defeat Laura Caxton in single combat.

She would be no match for Caxton, of course. And once the warden was dead, Fetlock and his cronies would believe that Justinia had been defeated. They would give up their crusade against her.

But not Caxton. No. Caxton would know better. Caxton would see through the deception. And then she would be faced with a dilemma. She would have the perfect—the only—opportunity to escape the prison in that moment. She would have the perfect motive to do so, as she would be the only human left who would believe Justinia was still alive. Her only other option would be to return to her little cell like a good girl and finish out her sentence.

If she did so, Justinia had decided, she would leave Caxton alone forever. She would flee to the west and lie low for a hundred or a thousand years, and wait for a new nemesis to show him- or herself.

But if Caxton followed Justinia over the wall, well. Then the game would be back on. The cards would all be shuffled, and a new hand dealt.

Justinia knew she should make her own escape with all due speed. The plan would be foiled if anyone saw her up on the wall. But she could not help herself—she wanted to watch for just a little longer. To see Caxton prevail. To know what choice Caxton made, to extend the chase, or to give up.

Come, Laura, *she thought.* Do not disappoint me now.

55.

"It'll only take her a few minutes to find this place," Caxton said. "Even with Urie Polder's spell in place, she'll make good time. We need to be ready."

She led Clara into the killing chamber, her light playing along its walls. Beside her Clara's body stiffened and Caxton felt her shiver. The spell didn't extend to this part of the cave. Maybe she was just feeling its effects wear off.

Or maybe she saw what Caxton had seen the first time she'd entered this cavern. It was impressive, she had to admit. Beautiful, maybe, if you could still feel that kind of thing.

The cave system ended here, in an enormous natural geode, twenty feet across. A bubble in the rock, lined all over its inside walls with purple and blue crystals that glittered in the light. They hung down from the ceiling in a thousand massive dripping stalactites, and made the floor uneven except where they had been meticulously cleared away.

Maybe to Clara it was like climbing inside a massive sapphire. Maybe it was like finding a treasure cave with no guardian genie. Maybe it was just dazzling, literally dazzling, to watch the light fracture and spread, beaming all over the small space, reflecting and refracting in a prismatic spray. Maybe it was like something out of a fairy tale to Clara.

To Caxton it was the perfect trap.

Uneven footing. Only one entrance. Plenty of natural cover. Justinia Malvern would have no choice but to come roaring through the narrow gap in the wall, the single access point from the long creek cavern. Caxton had already figured out the best place to stand when that happened. The best place from which to take her shot. Maybe the only shot she would get.

"Go over there," Caxton said, pointing to a spot out of the way. "Hide, if you can. Stay out of my way. You can handle that, can't you?"

Clara frowned at her. "I've got a gun. I can provide covering fire."

Caxton shook her head. "You've seen how well that works. She wouldn't even be distracted by the bullets in your carbine. No. She's all mine."

"Of course she is," Clara said.

Caxton closed her eyes and rubbed the bridge of her nose. She suddenly felt very, very tired. The last two years were catching up with her all at once. All those nights with little sleep, all those days spent working so hard.

"The plan," she said, sighing deeply, "was for me to be here, alone with her, at the end. That was how it was supposed to happen. The two of us sealed in here. Forever."

Clara's eyes grew bright in the broken light. "Forever? But what about after you kill her? How are you supposed to get out again?"

Caxton shrugged.

"I . . . see," Clara said. "You aren't. You never intended to leave here."

Caxton was too tired to explain. She let Clara work it out for herself.

"You still have the curse in you. From the time Reyes . . . from when he put it in your head," Clara said. "He wanted to turn you into a vampire. He put the curse in you, but that wasn't enough. You had to kill yourself. That's the only way a vampire can rise. You had to commit suicide, and he did his best to drive you to that, but it didn't work. But the curse doesn't wear off, does it?"

"No."

"So if you die here, if you kill yourself, you'll come back as a vampire." Clara put a hand over her mouth. Then she shook her head. "But if Malvern kills you in here, that's not suicide," Clara pointed out.

"Are you sure? The vampire's victims don't just kill themselves because they're depressed, Clara. The curse drives them to it. It makes them think death would be wonderful, an amazing release. Or maybe they know what's waiting for them on the other side and they can't wait for it to happen. It's not the act of slicing your wrists or taking too many pills that seals the deal. It's the desire to die."

"And you want to die?"

"I . . . don't know," Caxton said. "Sometimes. Sometimes it feels like it would be okay. Like going to sleep." She shook her head. "I've known would-be vampires who attacked armed cops just so the cops would shoot them. Does that count as suicide? What about going up against an invulnerable vampire? That sounds pretty suicidal to me. I don't know, Clara. I don't know what will happen when I die. But I figured I should be alone, buried in a tomb like this when it happens."

"No," Clara said. "No. No, you didn't just come here to die. No. I refuse to believe that. You're not just going to let her kill you."

"Jameson Arkeley did it. He accepted the curse so he could fight other vampires. It worked pretty well, too. Until he tasted blood. Then he became one of them. If I take the curse now and I become a vampire, stuck down here with Malvern, I can destroy her. I'll have the strength to do it. And because there wasn't supposed to be any source of blood down here, I wouldn't fall into the same trap as Arkeley."

"Except now . . . I'm here. A, um, a source of blood."

Caxton nodded. She was too tired to deny it.

"Wow. I fucked up everything for you."

"Maybe," Caxton said. It was the kindest thing she could think to say. The most compassion she could spare for the woman who was now fated to die along with her, deep beneath the earth. "Maybe. There's one chance." She opened her nylon bag and took out her weapon. The one Urie Polder had readied for her.

"That's a shotgun," Clara said.

"Yeah."

Clara frowned. "But you taught me never to use a shotgun against a vampire. Never. It was one of the first things you taught me. They're too inaccurate. You need precision if you're going to hit the heart."

Caxton examined the firearm. It was an old beat-up ten gauge, its barrel thicker than her thumb. She cracked it open and found a brown and brass cartridge already loaded. There were three more shells taped to the stock. Once upon a time she had taken on a brood of vampires with no more than thirteen bullets handy. Now she had four.

"Depends on what you're loading. These shells are . . ."

Clara stared at her. Caxton shook her head and stared back.

"What?" Caxton demanded.

"You kind of trailed off there," Clara said, looking concerned. "You were telling me about your shotgun shells, and then you never finished your sentence."

"I didn't?" Caxton asked. "I guess . . . I. Um, I guess that . . ."

So tired, suddenly. Why was she so tired? She should be amped up. Ready for the fight to come. Instead she would have really, really appreciated the chance to take a nap first. Maybe Malvern would be willing to give her a time-out. The thought made her laugh.

"Something funny now?" Clara demanded.

"No, no . . . nothing. Just."

"Just what?" Clara asked.

Laura. Just rest. There's no danger right now. Ye may rest, as you wish, Malvern said, her thoughts boring right through the stone walls.

"Jesus!" Clara screamed. "She—"

Caxton didn't hear what she said next. Everything went soft, and warm, and rosy. There was no sound at all. Her eyelids fluttered closed, and she slept.

56.

The next morning Laura was finally getting some sleep when sunlight flooded into the room and burned her cheek. She tried to roll away from it, but the heat and light followed her. She clenched her eyes tight and grabbed hard at her pillow.

Something soft and feathery brushed across her mouth. Laura nearly screamed as she bolted upright, her eyelids flashing open.

"Time to get up, beautiful," Clara said. She had a white rose in her small hand and she'd been running its delicate petals across Laura's lips.

Laura took a deep breath and forced a smile. After a tense moment Clara's face turned up with a wry grin. Clara had already showered and her wet hair hung in spiky bangs across her forehead. She was wearing her uniform shirt and not much else, except for a pair of tortoiseshell glasses with one lens blacked out.

"Too much, so early?" Clara asked. Her visible eye was bright with mischief. She held out the rose and Laura took it. Then Clara picked up a glass of orange juice from the bedside table and held that out, too.

Laura forced herself to calm down, to push away the darkness of the night. There had been bad dreams, as always. She was, over time, learning ways to forget them when she woke up. Clara had learned ways to help.

"Your eye," Laura said, as she drained half the juice.

"The doctor says it's just mild conjunctivitis. It'll clear up in a couple of days. In the meantime I didn't want you to see me look all scary. Anyway, I always thought glasses were kind of sexy." She sat down on the bed next to Laura and leaned her head back against Laura's chest. "What do you think? Am I turning you on?"

Laura withheld comment. "Is that today's?" she asked, pointing at a copy of the *Harrisburg Patriot-News* on the bedside table.

"Mm-hmm," Clara purred. "Are you seriously going to tell me you're thinking about current events right now?"

"I just wanted to check something." Laura picked up the paper and looked at the masthead. OCTOBER 1, 2004, she read. Then her eye caught on the headline. NEW VAMPIRE ATTACKS IN OHIO, POLICE BAFFLED.

Before she could read any more, Clara grabbed the paper away from her and threw it across the room. "Jesus, they won't shut up about those vampires!" she laughed. "Seriously, I am so glad you didn't take that case. I would worry about you so much if you were still hanging out with that old fart Arkeley."

"Sure," Laura said. "It would have been really stupid of me to try to fight vampires. I'm just a highway patrol trooper."

"Besides, Arkeley wanted all of your time. I would never have gotten to date you properly." Clara turned around so her breasts were pressed up against Laura's stomach. She reached up and took away the glass of orange juice, placing it down carefully on the table. Then she licked her lips and started moving in for a kiss.

Caxton belted her across the face as hard as she could. It was like punching a statue, but Clara recoiled from the blow. Caxton got a foot up between them and kicked Clara right out of the bed.

"Did you seriously expect me to fall for this, Malvern?"

Clara—the thing that looked like Clara, anyway—rose from the floor as smoothly and gracefully as a snake rising from a basket. She glared at Caxton with one red eye, the other still hidden by those ridiculous glasses.

"I wanted to show ye some moment of peace, before the end, 'tis all," she said.

"I'm asleep right now. I'm dreaming this." Caxton remembered that in 2004 she had always left her sidearm hanging in the kitchen closet. Would it be there if she ran for it now? Would it have any effect in a dream? "Just like when Reyes made me dream I was in the steel mill. He was trying to make me suicidal so I would accept the curse. Is that what this is about? You still think I'll become one of your brood if you ask the right way?"

Malvern/Clara shrugged prettily. "No. I've let that hope die."

"Then what are we doing here, damn it?"

The vampire in Clara's shape went to the window and drew back the curtains. Yellow sunlight burst into the room, bathing her pale skin. She stretched in it like a cat basking in warmth. It might have been the first time in three hundred years Malvern had actually seen the sun, even in a dream.

"This," she said, "is a card ye never played. In this little fancy, ye told Jameson ye would not aid him. When he tried to recruit ye, ye told him to bugger himself. Look how it turned out. Not so bad, really?"

"Vampires all over Ohio, apparently. At least he drove you out of the state."

"And out of your life. Oh, thy girl Deanna is still dead, in this place, and I fear that's my blame to carry. But ye have the better of the bargain, methinks." Sighing with pleasure, the vampire ran her hands up and down her borrowed body. "So sweet, this one. So sweet and slender and full of little graces. Ye could have been happy, Laura. Instead you chose to make me thy life's work."

Caxton glanced at the door of the kitchen. "How do I wake up from this?" she demanded. "How do I get out of here?"

"When I release ye, and not before," Malvern said without turning.

[2008]

Through Simon Arkeley's eyes, Justinia looked into Laura's face once more. How she had missed the girl!

"She's officially dead," Laura was saying. "She's also effectively immortal. She wants to stay that way. The smart thing to do, the smartest thing, would be to just lie low. Stay in her coffin, not make any fuss or bother. Not kill anybody. She can wait in that coffin as long as she wants. She could wait until I'm old and gray and unable to fight anymore, and come for me then. Or she could just wait until I die of old age. Until everybody's forgotten what a vampire was, much less how to fight one. Then she could come back and start killing people all over again."

Justinia could feel Simon's soul curdling at the prospect. How fragile she had made him. An imperfect instrument. But for this service, he was priceless.

"She's smart enough to think of that. To put aside whatever satisfaction she might get from killing me in exchange for her own safety. Now, if I had my freedom and unlimited resources, I could spend the rest of my life trying to figure out where she's hiding. I could scour every dark corner and musty old shed in Pennsylvania. I could spend years doing it. But that's no longer an option for me. If I show my face outside of this ridge, I'll get scooped up by the Feds right away. So instead I've built this very elaborate vampire trap—and I've laid my own plans for the future."

"Oh," Simon said. "I think I know where you're going with this, and—"

Caxton wouldn't let him derail her. "I know how to kill vampires better than anyone now living. I'm going to spend the rest of my life teaching the people in the Hollow how it's done. I'm going to teach Patience Polder every one of my tricks. After I'm dead, she'll teach others. Maybe her own children. And they'll teach theirs. The point is, no matter how long Malvern goes to ground for, when she wakes up there'll be somebody waiting with a gun pointed right at her heart."

Justinia opened her eye. There was a smile on her face.

"Oh, well played, child," she said.

The half-deads gathered around her coffin looked down at her with surprised expressions. Perhaps they thought she was speaking to them.

Justinia did not care.

"She's laid the perfect trap, hasn't she? And she knows I'll not resist it. What skill she has for this game. I think I love her, in my own horrible way." She couldn't resist the urge to chuckle. For far too long her existence had been one of suffering and despair, punctuated only by the rush of the blood down her throat. What new passion for living Laura had provided! Vincombe had told her to find a purpose, a reason to be immortal.

Laura had given it to her.

"We must make preparations now," she said. The half-deads looked at each other, wondering what she would demand next. She had treated them cruelly, as was their lot, and they expected no reward. "There's so much to do. I'll spring her trap, oh, yes. I shall indeed. But if she's to be so crafty, she can't object, can she, if I choose to cheat?" Through Simon's eyes she had seen all of Laura's defenses. The cordon of ghosts, and the ring of bird skulls she'd set as alarms. The people of the Hollow, and the power they possessed, their magic.

It was a good scheme. It would have defeated any other vampire. But Justinia knew the one thing Laura could not plan for. The one thing that could ruin all her hopes.

"Go out, tonight. Go and find me Clara Hsu. Watch her, but do not disturb her. Not yet."

57.

"We could not talk, ye and I, another way," Malvern said, running Clara's knuckles along the line of Caxton's jaw. "When I sprang ye from your prison in that car, ye attacked me straightaway. I've no doubt ye'll do the same when this dream has ended."

"You can count on it," Caxton told the vampire.

"So it behooves me little to release ye now, does it? When there is so much left to say. Do ye know how much ye've entertained me these last few years? I've met enough vampire hunters in my time. I've slaughtered a brace of 'em, my own self, and caused others to be brought low. None has ever caused me so much grief—or provided such sport—as thou hast."

Caxton slipped toward the bedroom door while Clara/Malvern stared out the window at the sun. The kitchen closet was only a few yards away. If she could dash in there, get her gun, and start blasting before Malvern even saw her, then—

The vampire turned around and smiled at her. "I've come to respect ye. Do ye know how rare it is for me to say that to a mortal? I like your brains. I like your spirit, Laura. So many choices ye've made, so many sacrifices, and ye never flinched. Ye never turned away, when even a brave man would falter. But of course, that's some of it, eh? Ye're no man. Ye're a woman, same as me. Oh, ye may dress like a man, and talk as salty as they do. But underneath ye've a girl's heart. Women, in my experience, think with their hearts. Do ye not agree?"

"That's kind of sexist," Caxton said, leaning casually against the door frame.

"Not at all. Women think with their hearts, but men think with their pricks." Malvern shrugged Clara's shoulders with an elegant grace that Clara had never possessed. "I've yet to meet any creature that really used its brain for what God intended. Are ye going somewhere?"

Caxton had taken a step backward, through the door. She smiled and shrugged. Malvern chuckled, a low and unnerving sound.

"Make your move," the vampire said.

Caxton dashed backward, always keeping her eye on Malvern/Clara. The vampire didn't seem to move at all as Caxton rushed into the kitchen and threw open the closet door. She half-expected to find its contents changed, by dream logic, into a cavern of snakes or maybe a burst of fire. Instead her coat hung there, her highway trooper's coat. Her Smokey Bear hat hung on its usual peg. And her sidearm, tucked neatly in its holster, hung exactly where she'd always left it.

She grabbed up the Beretta, thumbed off its safety, and started to turn toward the bedroom door.

Before she could even lift the weapon Clara was on her, all flashing teeth and burning eye, her fingers digging through Caxton's flesh, her fangs sinking through veins and arteries to suck blood from Caxton's body, and Caxton screamed, knowing she was dead, knowing she was—

—she was standing before an empty grave. The cemetery was a vast expanse of rolling yellow hills, the dead grass sparkling with frost even so late in the morning. Most of the snow had melted or been removed from the plots. The dead lay in neat array all around Caxton, hidden under endless lanes lined with obelisks and family crypts. Smaller, more modest gravestones stuck up in neat rows.

The stone directly before her was a simple affair of unfinished granite. Chiseled into its surface was a minimal inscription:

JAMESON ARKELEY
MAY 12, 1941—OCTOBER 3, 2004

It did not say "Beloved Father," or "Rest in Peace," because those things would have been lies, and the people who had erected that stone knew Arkeley would have wanted the truth, even now.

Caxton remembered this day. She remembered feeling foolish even coming to the ceremony. After all, at the time Arkeley hadn't even been dead. Not technically. The stone was a cenotaph, a memorial for a man who had refused to die.

Standing just behind the stone was Vesta Polder, dressed all in black with a veil over her face. It bunched in the wintry breeze, obscuring one of her eyes. Other people stood to either side of her, looking down at their feet or away at the distant trees. None of them would look at Caxton.

The scene seemed frozen in time, though still the breeze plucked at Caxton's clothes and ruffled the dead yellow grass.

"Let me guess," Caxton said. "This is another point where I could have chosen a different life. Where I could have given up."

Vesta Polder smiled at her. Or rather, Malvern smiled through Vesta Polder's face. "Perhaps, though I imagine thy devotion was never greater to the cause than just here. Thy own mentor turned evil and loosed upon the world. Ye could not say no, not at this time."

"I felt responsible for what he'd become. He did it to save me, after all."

"Are ye so sure?" Malvern asked. Her eye twinkled. "Trapped in a broken body, made frail by time and circumstance. So much left undone, and no strength left to do it. He had contemplated suicide long before ye gave him compelling reason to do it. Do not forget I was with him at the end. I was privy to his doubts. And his failings."

Caxton felt blood rushing to her face. "He was a good man. Maybe he was an asshole sometimes, but he was a good—a good man." Her hands balled into fists. "He kept fighting. He didn't care if people hated him for it. He didn't care how much it cost him, he kept fighting, right up until the end, right up until—"

"Until he failed," Malvern said.

Caxton turned her head away, unwilling to let Malvern see the anguish that contorted her features.

"He did fail, Laura. They all do. And look at what his failure cost. His failure, and thine. Take a look."

"No," Caxton said, refusing to turn her head back.

Malvern shot out one of Vesta Polder's arms and grabbed Caxton's chin. She couldn't resist that pressure. She was only human, and in this dream Vesta Polder had all of Malvern's strength.

The vampire twisted Caxton's head around so she could see all the people standing behind the tombstone. All the people who had been there that day—and some who had not. There was a little crowd of them.

Angus Arkeley, Jameson's brother and the first to go. His face under his trucker cap was pale with blood loss. Astarte, Jameson's wife, whom Caxton had not been able to save. One of her wrists was torn open and it still drooled blood. Urie Polder, his skin burned to a crisp. Vesta herself, her face now torn away, her body used as a weapon against Caxton. Glauer and Fetlock, their bodies so mangleigh she could barely look at them. Raleigh Arkeley, Jameson's daughter, transformed into a vampire but with a hole where her heart should have been. At the end stood Deanna.

Deanna, whom Caxton had loved with all her heart. Her old girlfriend. Transformed, like Raleigh, into a pale and vicious parody of herself. Her body was pierced in a hundred places by broken glass.

Caxton couldn't help but cry out when she saw Deanna.

"You killed all of them," Caxton whimpered. "It doesn't matter who pulled the trigger, or . . . or who tore them up, or burned them, or—or whatever. You're directly responsible for all of their deaths."

"I am," Malvern admitted, still using Vesta Polder's mouth, even though now the lips had been torn away. "I take no shame in that. But can ye really say, Laura, ye are not at least a bit responsible for this?"

"Damn you! If I hadn't fought against you—"

"These people might still be alive," Malvern pointed out.

"Others would have died. A lot of other people would have died!"

"But no one you knew. No one you loved."

Caxton fought desperately to control her emotions. She had spent two years hardening herself to this, to the cost of her actions. It just wasn't fair that Malvern could tear her open now and let all that pain come out. It wasn't fair! "Damn it, I saved some of them! Some of the people who were there the day we mourned Jameson. I saved some of them. I saved Simon, and—"

"Turn around," Malvern said.

Knowing it was a bad idea, but having no choice, Caxton did as she was told.

Standing behind her were three people dressed in funeral black. They looked appropriately sad for a funeral, but they were alright. They were unharmed, alive, and safe and—at least they were alive.

Simon Arkeley, Patience Polder, and Clara. Clara, looking cute even in funeral clothes. Clara, with her bangs and her little nose and her slim hips, Clara who—

"They'll be dead before sunrise," Malvern pointed out. "After I kill thee, I must go and see to them as well. Do you understand why? Because they are your potential replacements, Laura. They have reason to hunt me down. And they know a little of your tricks. You've taught them somewhat. Enough to make them dangerous. I'd be a fool to let them live."

"Fuck you," Caxton howled. "It's not going to happen that way! I'll beat you—I led you right into my trap and I will destroy you, you bitch! I will—"

Caxton stopped speaking, because pain had gripped her chest, searing agony she couldn't comprehend. Her body curled up and she dropped to the frigid soil, suddenly lacking the strength to even stand.

Vesta Polder leaned over her. Except this was a Vesta Polder with only one eye. The other socket was full of darkness, a blackness as profound as the gulf between the stars.

"What—are you—doing?" Caxton grunted through clenched teeth.

"Stopping your heart. I've shown ye what you might have gained by turning away from this path. I've shown ye what it costs to be human. Now let me show ye what could have been yours if ye'd not been so proud."

Caxton had a good idea of what was coming next. She couldn't have stopped it, though, not for all the strength of will she possessed. The dream couldn't end until Malvern allowed it to end. She could only go along for the ride.

The darkness in Malvern's missing eye grew and spread. It filled up all of Caxton's vision. She felt her body blow away on the breeze like so much dust, felt even her consciousness leach away and disappear. Soon she was no more than a speck of ego floating in a cosmic void, an observer, passionless, devoid of even critical judgment. She could do nothing but watch the scene that was presented to her next.

[2008]

It was foolhardy to come so close, but Justinia had lost much of her natural caution. This game demanded taking certain risks.

And sometimes she just wished to see things for herself.

She stood atop a mercantile store, a place that sold woolens and yarn, in a town called Bridgeville. She had a spyglass through which she could observe as, below, a van full of her half-deads careened off the highway and into a ditch. Inside the van the last survivors would be tearing each other to pieces, on her orders. It would not do to leave too many of them intact, lest they be caught and interrogated.

One of them would hold off, though. One, the driver of the van, would wait until the proper moment.

It was not long in coming. Back on the highway, the little red car rocked on its tires, its front end crumpled and ruined. One of its headlamps flared briefly, then died. The doors of the car popped open and two of Justinia's old enemies clambered out. Hsu and Glauer, Laura's little assistants.

She knew what they would do next, but she watched with the kind of patience only a three-hundred-year-old corpse can muster. They approached the van, weapons drawn. They discovered the ruin of bodies inside. Found the driver, but not in time to question him.

Hsu and Glauer had never been in any real danger. No, that would have been a complication for Justinia's plan. This all had to be done a certain way, to a nicety, if it was to work at all.

She needed all of her enemies in one place. The whole raft of them— Urie Polder and his clutch of witches; Marshal Fetlock and his great apparatus of the law; Caxton, oh, yes, Laura Caxton.

Now the last two players had to be invited to the table. Hsu and Glauer. The two people Caxton cared for the most in all the world. Their presence would throw Caxton off her game, distract her when she needed most to focus. Oh, yes, Malvern would ensure that Hsu and Glauer would come.

Hsu and Glauer were clever for humans. It would not be enough to invite them directly, she knew. She had instead to suggest, to give them clues. To make them feel like they had a lead on her, that they were close to finding her.

And all the while they just played directly into her hand.

When it was done, when the last half-dead pulled his own jawbone free of his torn and rotting face, Justinia finally removed herself to safety, to an abandoned storefront not far away. The windows had been boarded *up, the doors all sealed. She slipped inside through a broken window at the basement level. Inside more half-deads awaited, along with Justinia's victims of the night. A pair of teenagers who had been foolish enough to think they could break into her lair and find some privacy there for their dalliances.*

They were tied and gagged now. They wriggled so in their bonds, whimpered in their fear. They knew that death was coming for them. As much fun as it might have provided, she did not make them wait.

58.

The details were hard to make out at first. She was in a very dark place, a place full of shadows. It might have been an abandoned shopping mall, or maybe the halls of a high school. Only a trickle of light filtered in through frosted windows to spill across linoleum tile floors.

Then a flashlight beam split the gloom, as bright as a laser beam in that dark place. A second beam roamed across one wall, moving so fast it added no details to the scene.

Someone spoke in a whisper, a sound so small even a mouse would have had a hard time making out the words. But Caxton heard them with no difficulty.

"Keep your gun pointed down at the floor. You'll probably shoot me by mistake, waving it around like that."

Caxton knew that voice. Just as well as she knew the voice that answered.

"I'd be doing the world a favor, Arkeley. You're sure they're here?"

Jameson Arkeley let his light play across the ceiling. He looked tired, exhausted even. He was bent over like an old man. But he was alive—human, and still alive. His crinkly eyes studied the acoustic ceiling tiles. "I'm sure," he said.

"Because the last three places we looked didn't have anything but dust and cobwebs," Clara replied. "I'm sure you felt at home, but I ruined a perfectly good jacket."

Clara. She was wearing a leather jacket. She had a gun in her hand—a Beretta. Caxton's Beretta. And she was working with Arkeley. Working with him to hunt down vampires.

"The half-dead I tortured this morning was very helpful," Arkeley said.

"Was that before or after breakfast? Or during?"

It didn't make any sense. Nothing like this had ever happened.

It might have, Malvern told Caxton. *It could have been. If ye'd been less stubborn.*

What are you talking about? Why would Clara be there, and not me, if—

Oh, hell no.

Malvern laughed inside Caxton's head. *Watch. Watch what might have been.*

Clara pointed her light at a door set into the wall ahead of her. A door with an inset glass window. When the light touched the window, Caxton felt her body coming back, re-forming around her point of consciousness. Except it wasn't her body. Not the way she remembered it.

This body was stronger. So much stronger. Its hands were white claws. It was hairless, with pointed ears, and red eyes.

And it was desperate for blood.

No. No. Don't make me see this, Caxton begged.

Ye have no choice.

Clara took a step toward the door. Another. She raised her weapon and aimed it at the glass window.

Caxton's body moved then, far faster than she'd ever imagined possible. There was an exultation in it. A nearly sexual rush of pleasure in the way her body moved, its speed, its power. She burst through the door like it was made of paper. Shot out into the corridor like a white bullet. But she didn't attack Clara, as she'd feared. She flew right past Clara—and straight toward Jameson Arkeley.

Her claws grasped him, that weak old man. The feeble cripple—she could feel his heart beating next to hers as she clutched him to her. Beating so fast, the blood in him pumping through his extremities. It was intoxicating. It was unbearable. She brought her head back and grinned, exposing her sharp, sharp teeth.

"What are you waiting for? You little idiot, shoot her!" Jameson howled.

Clara brought the Beretta around, gripping it with two hands. Her flashlight fell to the floor in slow motion, drifting down toward the tiles like a feather.

"Shoot her!" Arkeley screamed.

Clara's hands trembled as she aimed the gun.

"I can't," she said. "That's Laura. It's—it's Laura, I'm sure of it."

"Laura's been dead for months," Arkeley protested. "You know it! You saw her die at Arabella Furnace. You saw what Deanna did to her! Don't make the same mistake!"

But Clara didn't shoot.

Caxton buried her teeth in Arkeley's neck. The blood came fast and hot, spurting into her mouth, across her white skin. Arkeley died a moment later, but not before he had time to say one last thing.

"I always knew you were too weak for the job," he said.

Caxton didn't let it get to her. She dropped his corpse when she'd had her fill. If she wanted to, she knew, she could bring him back as a half-dead now. Make him say whatever she wanted him to say, while he peeled skin off his own face.

But that wasn't why she was here tonight. She wasn't here to kill. She was here to give new life.

"Clara," she said, and to her own ears her voice was a growl, a low rasp of menace. "Clara, it's over now. You don't have any options left."

Clara's whole body shook. She said nothing.

Behind her, through the broken door, two more vampires streamed out into the hall. Malvern and Deanna. They did not surge forward to attack. They stood behind Clara, ready to grab her and hold her down if that was what it took. If Caxton couldn't convince her.

"We can be together again," Caxton growled. She took a step toward Clara. Another. Clara raised her gun again, but Caxton just grabbed it out of her hand and threw it away. "We can be lovers if you say yes. We never had a chance before. I never got to make love to you. But now I can."

"Caxton," Clara said. There was something wrong with her voice.

"We'll be a family. You and me. Deanna and Malvern. They're willing to share me. They'll be your lovers, too. Lovers and sisters and a mother, that's a family, right? You just have to say yes. I know you're scared. I was scared, too."

"Caxton, fuck, come on, Caxton! Come on, snap out of it!" Clara said.

Caxton didn't know what she was talking about. Behind Clara, Malvern stiffened, though, as if she understood. What was happening? This dream didn't make as much sense as the others. It wasn't as solid, either. The edges seemed all blurry. The light was wrong.

It didn't matter. Caxton wasn't in control of her own voice. She was reading from a script Malvern had written. She had no choice but to continue. "It's good, Clara. It feels so good. And it's forever. We can be together forever."

She was close enough to kiss Clara now. Close enough to pass on the curse.

Clara slapped her across the face.

It shouldn't have hurt. It definitely shouldn't have thrown

Caxton's head to the side. Vampires were stronger than that. Much stronger.

Clara slapped her again.

"Wake up, you fucking moron! Wake up! She's here!"

The light changed again, radically this time. Clara's face hovered in front of her still, but behind Clara the vampires were gone, the hallway was gone, there was only darkness, darkness and something blue, something—

"Wake up!"

Caxton gasped for breath and stared up at the ceiling of the cave, of the killing floor, at the blue and green quartz crystals up there. At the cave—at the cave, the place under the ridge, the place—

The dream was over.

"Shit," Caxton said.

Malvern was crawling across the ceiling. Not the Malvern of her dream. The Malvern of reality, the Malvern who had killed everyone in the Hollow, the Malvern who was trapped inside the cave with them now. This Malvern had given up any pretense of illusion. She was dressed in nothing but a few tatters of burnt body armor. Her one red eye burned with blood.

And she was climbing on the ceiling like a spider.

"Shit!" Caxton said again. She was lying on the floor, with Clara looming over her, ready to slap her again. Malvern was about to drop on them both.

Caxton reached down and felt the nylon bag she'd brought with her. She found the shotgun and brought it up so fast she didn't have time to aim, but it didn't matter, she had to shoot—she understood now, understood what Malvern had been trying to do—

The shotgun erupted in her hands, the recoil worse than she remembered. The shell smashed through the crystals on the ceiling only inches from where Malvern hung, shards of broken quartz showering down across Clara's shoulders and hair.

Shit—one of the four precious shells, and she'd missed!

Malvern laughed.

Damn it, Malvern hadn't wanted to talk to her at all. The dream hadn't been about convincing Caxton to become a vampire. It had just been a distraction. It had just bought time for Malvern to find her way through Urie Polder's spell, find her way to the geode, to the killing room.

Shit, Caxton thought, *shit shit shit,* as she tore one of the remaining shells from the stock of the gun and rammed it into the barrel. Shit! She hadn't planned on this, she'd forgotten what a vampire could do, she'd forgotten that Malvern would be able to rape her mind like that.

"Really, Laura," Malvern said from the ceiling, as she scuttled around up there, coming closer. She was no more than twenty feet away now. "Really. Thy little blunderbuss can't harm me now. I've drunk so much blood I'm invulnerable, immune to every weapon you have."

Caxton forced herself to take careful aim. With a shotgun you could never count on real accuracy. But sometimes you didn't need to.

She fired again, even as Malvern began to laugh once more.

She didn't laugh for long.

The shot in the round blasted upward across Malvern's left leg, high up on the thigh in a tight grouping. The special shot tore through muscles and bone, cracking Malvern's femur, shredding her flesh.

The vampire screamed and fell from the ceiling to land in a heap on the floor.

"Immune, huh?" Caxton asked.

[2008]

The screams of the mortals all around her barely reached Justinia's ears. "More," she said, and the half-deads performed her will, dragging more of the captives to her. She slashed and tore and sank her fangs in them, their blood coating her body, clotting in great clumps on her skin. "More!"

She was the last, the only vampire left. She intended to make a good showing of things in the morning. "More," she growled. With every drop of blood that slid down her throat she grew stronger. Her skin grew harder, her bones more durable. She grew faster, and stronger. The blood pulsed through her, it suffused her with energy. It was almost too much to bear. She grew full for the first time in centuries, felt sated in a way she never had before. "More." She grew bloated like a tick with the blood, felt like she would burst. "More!"

For so long she had starved herself. Rationed the blood she took to minimize the evidence she left behind. There were so many humans looking for her, looking to destroy her. Only by keeping a low profile had she survived. But not now. Now, she would have as much as she could stand. She would have more than that.

Everything was in place. All her enemies would gather, as she had planned. They would resist her as best they could. She would possess a small army of half-deads, and the power of her own body, her own mind.

If she died in the Hollow, if Caxton destroyed her, it would be the end of her kind. Justinia felt no pangs about that. Fitting it was, she thought, that she, the most brilliant, most devious of vampires to ever live, should be the last. But if she lived, if she killed them all—

There would be no stopping her then.

"More!"

59.

Malvern climbed to her feet, not without difficulty. Her leg was a ruin, a mess of fibrous white tissue barely clinging to a scored and cracked bone. She stared down at it with her one red eye, and a hissing noise escaped her lips. She tried to take a step toward Caxton, and the leg buckled. She fell to the floor again, howling, and her arms flailed wildly as she tried to push herself upright again.

Caxton hoped it fucking *hurt*.

She'd bought herself a precious fraction of a second. She used it to reload—a series of motions she'd practiced over and over again until she could do them with inhuman speed. She cracked open the shotgun and ejected the spent casing. She took another shell from the stock and shoved it home, then swung the barrel up to complete the process. Malvern looked up and staggered toward her, moving no faster than an Olympic athlete could run.

Caxton pointed the weapon and pulled the trigger. The accuracy of the shotgun was terrible, worse than any of the times she'd practiced with it over the years. Still, she didn't miss.

The shot tore through Malvern's left shoulder. None of it hit her heart, but damage was done. The tissue split and fell away, the bones shattered. Malvern's arm fell off and landed on the floor of the cave with a wet plop.

Already the flesh of her leg was healing itself, knitting itself back together. Caxton couldn't see the femur anymore—the skin had already closed over the wound.

"What have ye done?" Malvern rasped.

Caxton broke open the shotgun and pried out the spent shell.

"Sharpest thing in the world," she said. "The only thing in the world that could even scratch you right now, I imagine."

"No!" Malvern said.

Caxton reached for the last of her shells. This one had to count. "What is it?" Clara asked.

"Vampire teeth," Caxton replied. She kept her eyes on Malvern. "The teeth of a vampire named Congreve, to be exact, loaded into a perfectly normal shotgun round. It was Jameson Arkeley's idea originally. He knew you could hurt each other. He thought maybe your teeth would retain some of their power, even after you were dead."

She finished loading her last shell. Then she took a step toward Malvern. Nothing was finished yet. Not unless she got a clean shot at Malvern's heart. That was her only vulnerable spot. The only way to kill her. She took another step.

Malvern moved then, as fast as she'd ever seen. Caxton was certain she was dead. She'd been counting on the vampire's surprise, the shock of actually being wounded, to slow Malvern down.

She'd figured wrong.

It could have been over right then and there. Malvern could have fallen on her before she could get the last shot off. She could have torn Caxton to pieces where she stood. But Justinia Malvern had never been one for the direct assault.

Instead she liked to do nasty things. Sneaky things.

So she went for Clara.

It happened so fast Caxton could barely keep up. Malvern was a white streak across the floor of the cave and then she was standing still, holding Clara in front of her with her remaining arm, holding Clara like a human shield.

Clara, the person Caxton had loved more than anyone else in the world. Clara, her lover. Clara, her girlfriend.

Caxton steeled herself. She'd spent two years trying to forget all that.

"Perhaps," Malvern said, "we should discuss this."

Caxton gripped the shotgun in both hands. They were no more than five feet away from her. Point-blank range, even for the lousy shotgun.

"Ye can kill me, oh, yes, we both see that now. Ye've been clever, Laura. So damnably clever. Ye've outwitted me."

"Flattery won't get you anywhere," Caxton said.

"Ye have one shot remaining. Why don't ye take it? Slay me, girl. Do what ye will. It's what Jameson would have wanted. But make sure ye don't hit this one, hmm? Make sure ye don't kill thy lover."

There was no time to think. If she gave Malvern a second to come up with a better plan, it would be all the time the vampire needed. Caxton brought the shotgun up and pointed it right at Malvern's heart.

Which happened to be behind Clara's chest.

Clara's human flesh wouldn't slow the teeth down at all. They would pass through Clara and kill Malvern. All she had to do was pull the trigger.

Everybody was expendable. She'd promised herself that. When the plan had included sacrificing her own life, she hadn't blinked at the thought.

"Laura," Clara said.

"Don't," Caxton told her. "Don't make this hard, don't say—"

"Do it."

Caxton stared at the other woman. She couldn't believe what she'd heard.

"It's worth it," Clara told her. "If you don't take the shot right now, she'll kill us both! Just do it."

"Child," Malvern howled, "do ye even know what ye say? Do ye?"

Caxton brought the shotgun up again. Adjusted her aim. She just had to pull the trigger. She just had to shoot.

"No," Malvern said. "No! Ye can't! Ye can't do it!"

Caxton steadied her hands. She wiggled her trigger finger to limber it up.

Then she lowered the shotgun. "You're right. I can't."

Malvern started to laugh. She didn't get very far, though.

Holding on to Clara with only one arm meant she couldn't control what Clara did with her hands. Without any warning at all, Clara grabbed the carbine hanging around her neck and fired off her entire clip. Not into Malvern's body, of course—that would have been a waste of ammunition. Instead she pointed the barrel straight up and fired into the ceiling.

The quartz crystals up there were fragile at the best of times. They couldn't take that kind of abuse. Chunks of rock crystal fell like rain. Stalactites fell like spears, dropping right on Clara's head. Clara's head, and Malvern's.

The vampire panicked and let go of her. Malvern sprinted away from the falling rocks, even as Clara was buried under a pile of blue crystals. Malvern started to laugh again as she danced free. "Did ye think I'd be crushed by a little rock, dearie?" she demanded. "Did ye think—"

Malvern stopped talking abruptly. She must have felt Caxton's presence directly behind her.

Caxton placed the barrel of the shotgun up against Malvern's back, just to the left of her spine. And fired.

[2008]

"No," Justinia howled. "No!"

She felt each individual fang tunnel through her body. She felt them gouging out deep tracks as they plunged through her flesh, felt them tearing at her, ripping her apart. When they reached her heart she started to scream.

"No! No! No! No! It isn't fair! Ye've rigged the deck! Ye cheated!"

That was how the game was played, though. She had made every trick she could of the trumps in her hand, and she had laid them down. Laura had just had better cards.

"'Tis not possible! It's a cheat!" Justinia screamed as she fell to the

ground, her fist beating on the floor, her feet kicking at the unyielding rock. She could see nothing with her remaining eye. Everything had gone black. She could feel Laura behind her, though. She could feel Laura moving back there.

Every gambler must know that a bad hand is coming. Every card-player dreads it, but sometimes the cards are worthless. Sometimes luck frowns.

Justinia couldn't accept it, even as the last of her life drained away. Even as she lay dying.

"No," she whimpered. "No. No. No."

"Shut up, you old hag," Caxton said, and then stamped on Justinia's head until everything went away, until it was over. All over.

60.

Clara had never hurt so much in her life.

She'd broken bones before. She'd been stabbed, and shocked, and hurt plenty of other ways. But she'd never had a mountain fall on her back before. Most of her was buried under the blue crystals, which weren't heavy on their own but added up to quite a weight. She did not want to move. She didn't want to even breathe deeply.

She was absolutely certain she had broken ribs, and probably a broken leg and a broken arm, too. The rocks had come down hard.

But—and here was the kicker—she was still alive.

Caxton hadn't shot her. Laura had refused to kill her, even if it meant killing the vampire. She had been forced, in the most horrible way possible, to choose between Clara and Malvern. And she'd made the choice.

And Malvern was still dead.

"Laura," she said. "Laura, honey. Please. I need help."

The other woman didn't respond. She just stood there, barely visible in the low light. Standing, holding her shotgun, not moving at all. Like she couldn't believe what she'd done. Like she didn't know what to do next.

"Come on, Laura. I'm all banged up," Clara said.

Nothing.

In the end she had to free herself. It wasn't easy. She used her probably-not-broken arm to move the rocks away, one handful at a time. It took forever. When she was finally free, though, she found one nice little surprise. Her leg wasn't broken. It was just really, really badly sprained. If it meant life or death, she could probably even walk on it.

Not that she wanted to try. She crawled over toward Laura and grabbed her ankle. The fearless vampire hunter barely flinched.

"Laura, snap out of it!" Clara said.

Laura turned to look around as if she wasn't sure who was talking to her. Eventually she looked down. She threw the shotgun behind her and then reached down to help Clara up to her feet. Clara hopped around a bit, leaning on Laura, until she got the hang of not falling down and crippling herself. It took a lot of pain, and a lot of trial and error.

"She's still dead," Laura said.

It was the first thing she'd said since Malvern died.

"What?" Clara asked.

"I keep expecting her to come back to life. To jump up and attack us. That seems like something she might do."

Clara looked down at Malvern's corpse. Corpse was definitely the word. Laura's boots had done a number on Malvern's head, but the real damage was in her chest. The vampire teeth had carved a hole right through the body. There were a few black shreds of Malvern's heart left, but they weren't moving. That was how you killed a vampire. They couldn't survive without their hearts. Anything else, maybe, but they needed their hearts.

"I promise you," Clara said, "she's not coming back."

Then she held her breath, just in case she was wrong. But the corpse just lay there, completely inert.

Laura didn't say anything in response.

"Come on. We have to get out of here," Clara said. Even knowing it was a lot easier said than done.

Clara grabbed the flashlight. Then she hopped—with Laura's help—back toward the entrance to the cave. It turned out that Urie Polder's spell had no effect when you tried to leave the cave. For the first time Clara saw how narrow the creek really was, and how wide the tunnel that she'd thought she would never get through. When they reached the outermost chamber, though, she saw that the wall of rocks was still there, still blocking the way. Dust still hung in the air from the explosion. It felt like that had been hours ago, but in fact only a few dozen minutes had passed.

"Jesus, what are we going to do?" Clara asked.

Laura had no answer. Of course, Laura had never intended to leave the caves. She had wanted to make sure Malvern couldn't leave, either. The cave was sealed off.

Clara wondered how long the air inside would last. Probably best not to think about that too much.

She tried pulling at the rocks that blocked the entrance, but most of them were far too big for her to lift. She figured maybe she would rest a minute and then try again, as hopeless as it might be. What else was she going to do?

So she sat down on a big rock and closed her eyes and tried to rest.

Laura interrupted this attempt by talking. "I guess you hate me now," she said.

"I'd have good reason," Clara told her, opening her eyes.

Laura nodded.

"You've been a total asshole for what, two years now? It would take a lot to make me trust you again. You understand that, right?"

"Yes."

Clara nodded. The adrenaline was starting to wear off and the pain in her arm especially was beginning to announce itself. She really wished she had some aspirin. Or a rock drill, for that matter. "I don't know if we can ever be like we were before. Not that we even ever had a chance to be what—what I wanted us to be. I just don't know what I feel for you now. I'm not being unreasonable, am I?"

"No."

Clara gritted her teeth. Breathing was starting to hurt. She was probably going to die here, in pain, and all she could think to do was give Laura a hard time.

Screw it.

"You could have shot me back there. You probably should have."

Laura looked at her with empty eyes.

"There's still something human in you. The vampires didn't take it all," Clara pointed out. "You should have shot me, but you didn't. You hesitated. We both might have been killed because of that hesitation."

"I'm . . . sorry," Laura said.

"No! That's not the point," Clara insisted. "The point is, when you had to choose, when you had to make the sacrifice—you made the human choice. You aren't dead inside. Not entirely."

She got up—carefully—and hobbled over to where Laura stood, just staring at the rock wall in front of her. "Come here," she said when Laura didn't seem to take the hint. "Jesus, come here and kiss me."

Laura's eyes went wide. But she bent down and kissed Clara, a gentle peck on the lips.

"That was very chaste of you," Clara said. Then she grabbed Laura around the neck and stuck her tongue in Laura's mouth.

Laura pulled back a little. "You don't . . . have to do that, just to cheer me up."

"Maybe I need cheering up," Clara replied. "And anyway, I told you once. I think vampire hunters are sexy."

"I'm not." Laura shook her head. "I'm not a vampire hunter anymore."

"Cool. So what are you going to do next?"

Laura had no answer for that. Clara hobbled back to her rock and sat back down. "Is it getting hot in here, or am I just about to pass out and die from my injuries?" she asked.

It was definitely getting hotter. Eventually the rocks in front of them started to glow with heat. They moved farther back down the tunnel, having no idea what was happening. After a while they had to climb up on fallen rocks because molten stone started pouring from the wall that sealed the cave mouth.

Then something gave way, the rocks sagged, and fresh air blew in through a hole in the rock. The pale face of Patience Polder looked in at them.

Laura looked confused. "How?" she asked.

"An old spell my father taught me," Patience explained.

"But . . . why? I told you to leave us in here. I told you I was going to die in here, with her," Laura insisted.

"You told me many things, Miss Caxton. But you always seem to forget I can see the future. I knew exactly how this would end. Now, step this way, please. And be careful—the rocks here are still hot enough to burn you."

[EPILOGUE: 2012]

In the Polder house, Patience stood on a stool to wind the ancient grandfather clock in the front entrance hall.

"Do you know what happens if it stops?" Laura asked.

"I do," Patience said. Her face darkened for a moment. "But it won't stop, not in our lifetimes. I'll always be quite careful to wind it every day, until I am old and quite frail. And then I will have children to do it for me."

Laura shuddered a little. Even now, after so many years, Patience Polder still kind of freaked her out.

The girl always dressed in black now. She had traded her white pinafores and modest bonnets for the black shapeless gowns her mother Vesta had always worn. It didn't seem right, her wearing black, at least not this day. But Laura didn't question Patience's decisions.

Laura was wearing baggy pants, herself, to cover the electronic monitoring anklet on her leg. It would be another six months, even with good behavior, before it could be removed. It was a hassle, but it definitely beat going back to prison. She also wore a man's white dress shirt, a cheerful tie, and a black frock coat. She had a sprig of baby's breath pinned to her lapel.

So maybe she shouldn't be the one to criticize other people's fashion choices, she thought. The outfit had seemed appropriate to her for her role in the day's events, even though most of the Hollow's inhabitants would have preferred her to wear a dress. Laura Caxton didn't wear a lot of dresses.

Maybe she would wear one to her own wedding.

She took Patience down the long path to the Hollow while a jug band played "Here Comes the Bride." She took Patience's arm for the last stretch. Nineteen years old now and a good bit taller than she used to be, Patience didn't have to stand on tiptoe to hold on. The two of them marched with a stately gait into the clearing, and Laura saw how well the witchbillies had rebuilt. There was no sign anymore of the fires or the battle that had taken place there, except for a scar in the trees on the opposite ridge where the helicopter had crashed. Eventually even that would fade.

The witchbillies had all turned out for the wedding, dressed in their humble clothing. There were fewer of them than there used to be, but still enough to make a decent crowd. They stood and cheered as Patience came among them. The girl did not acknowledge the racket.

At the altar, Simon Arkeley stood waiting. He still had an ace bandage around one wrist. When Malvern threw him against a tree on that fateful night, he should have died. He broke most of the bones in his body, punctured a lung, and completely crushed his gallbladder. Patience had nursed him back to health, staying with him night and day in the hospital and then bringing him back to the house on the ridge to convalesce once his health insurance ran out. At first he had rejected her presence, losing his cool every time he saw her, having flashbacks every time he thought about what had happened.

She had started to heal his soul, as well as his body. In time he'd grown quite dependent on her. Not the best way to start a relationship, maybe.

When he saw her coming toward him at the altar, though, he wept. Big gooey tears. It was one of the sweetest things Laura Caxton had ever seen, and she felt a tear of her own break free from her eye and roll down her cheek.

The rings the happy couple exchanged were old, dull gold. Laura had seen them before, on the fingers of Vesta Polder. The tuxedo Simon wore didn't fit him—it was huge across his shoulders and too short in the sleeves. It had belonged to Jameson Arkeley, though Laura still couldn't believe Jameson had ever worn it.

The ceremony was short and formal. One of the witchbillies officiated. When the vows had been accepted, he said, "In the name of the earth, the sun, and the stars, I pronounce you man and wife."

They did not kiss. That wouldn't have been humble. Yet when they walked back up the aisle together and headed for the house, everyone jeered and made crude jokes about exactly what the two of them would get up to once they were behind locked doors.

That was just the way the witchbillies were, Laura supposed.

When her part of the ceremony was over, Laura walked over to the rows of chairs and found Clara waiting for her. Clara had put on a gorgeous vintage sundress, the color of cool spring grass. Her eyes were red with crying and she was dabbing at her makeup with a tissue.

"I still don't get this no-reception thing," Clara said, jumping up from her chair. "You mean we don't get any cake?"

"Nope. They don't really go in for special occasions. There's a big communal dinner next week if you want to come back, but it's not for celebrating the wedding. It's just what they do once a month, on the day of the full moon."

"Um, no offense, but I don't think I want to come back here that soon," Clara said. She glanced over at the far ridge, at the place where the cave had been. It was sealed off for good now, with Malvern's body still inside. Nobody—not even the cops— had wanted to touch the thing, so they'd just left it to rot.

"Believe me, I understand," Laura said.

"No dancing, though!" Clara said, to break the mood. "How can you have a wedding without dancing!"

"Oh, they never dance. That would be intemperate or something," Laura explained. "Except, of course, when they get naked and dance in the woods. But that's different. That's religious."

"Uh-huh." Clara shrugged and turned to go. "Alright. It's a long ride back to Harrisburg, and it'll be dark soon."

Laura nodded. Then she stopped and grabbed Clara's arm. There was something she had to say.

The other woman turned and looked at her with expectant eyes.

"I love you," Laura said.

"You should," Clara replied.

Laura smiled. This time, she thought, Clara was just joking. There had been a time when she would have been serious. But time had a funny effect on people. It definitely had had an effect on her. "There's a place in Mechanicsburg," she said, "where they have an eighties dance night every Friday."

"Tonight's Friday," Clara pointed out.

Laura nodded. "They've got good margaritas, too."

"Oh, boy," Clara said. "I think you've got a date."

Laughing, they headed back to the car. Not, unfortunately, the old Miata—that had been totaled years ago. These days they drove a Prius. Clara drove, steering the car north, toward their lives. The sun set while they were driving, but there was no reason to be afraid of the dark.

ACKNOWLEDGMENTS

This is going to get a little soppy. You have been warned.

When I started work on *13 Bullets,* it was going to be a four-thousand-word short story. I had just read some forgettable book about vampires falling in love with human women because they were . . . I don't know. Special or something. I threw the book across the room and said, "Dracula would kick this guy's ass. And then eat his girlfriend for dessert." I sat down to write a quick scene of a hard-core vampire fight, featuring the nastiest, most brutal vampire I could think of. Laura Caxton and Justinia Malvern came later—at the beginning it was just Arkeley sitting in a car, wishing he was ready for what was to come. Knowing he wasn't. I wasn't ready, either. *Monster Island* hadn't even come out at that point. I was a professional author, but I had yet to see a published book; and I could not predict what the future would hold.

Five books later, here we are. It's been one hell of a ride.

I wish I had room to thank every single person who helped me out along the way. That would require an additional volume. So if you don't see your name here, please don't think I forgot. Let's start at the beginning with Alex Lencicki, who is no Johnny Halfways. The man single-handedly got me to a place where I could do this. Then Byrd Leavell came along and made sure this wasn't just a trilogy. Jason Pinter loved the first book. He *believed* in it, on pure faith. Carrie Thornton took over and taught me more about writing with her red pen than all the workshops I've ever taken. Jay Sones sold the hell out of the books for years, while remaining one of the nicest guys I've ever met. Russell Galen (about whom little need be said—far better writers than I owe him big-time) helped me pay the rent and buy new laptops as I wore out the old ones. And Julian Pavia brought us home. Every single one of them a class act.

Then there's the small army of copy editors, publishers, marketing folks, publicity people, sales reps (some of the most important and most criminally neglected people in the business), bookstore owners (chain and indie—Del Howison is a hero out of a mythic age), bookstore grunts (those staff recommendations made my day, every single time), cover artists, advertising designers, bloggers, book critics, reviewers (Curt Purcell, of *The Groovy Age of Horror,* I'm looking at you), Amazon reviewers, eBook packagers, audiobook voice artists, all the people who put books together, who print them, who sell them, all the people who just simply love books, love them so much they put up with the frustrations, the discouragements, the prophecies of doom, the big failures and the little triumphs. Every single person who ever worked on behalf of creating the book in your hands (or on your Kindle, or wherever you're reading this) deserves my utter and heartfelt thanks.

And then there's you. This book is dedicated to you, the person who read it. The person who read all five of them, and let me know you enjoyed them, or told me I got the guns wrong, or asked when the next one was coming out. The person who read them and recommended them to your friends, or read them with your family, or who just, you know, enjoyed them. I wrote them to entertain you. Maybe to scare you a little, too. How'd that work out? You, my friend, have made it possible for me to do the thing I love. You have kept me going through a divorce, health problems, economic downturns, family crises, and existential dread. Because I knew you were out there waiting for the next one, and that was all the spur I needed to keep going. To write again.

Thank you. I cannot say it enough. Thank you.

Sincerely,
David Wellington
New York, 2011

CURSED

Revenge in the face of bloodlust is seldom sweet . . .

There's one sound a woman doesn't want to hear when she's lost and alone in the Arctic wilderness: a howl. For Cheyenne Clark, there's a bad moon on the rise. When a strange wolf's teeth slash her ankle to the bone, her old life ends, and she becomes the very monster that has haunted her nightmares for years. Worse, the only one who can understand what Chey has become is the man – and wolf – who's doomed her to this fate. He also wants her dead.

Yet, as the line between human and beast blurs, so too does the distinction between hunter and hunted . . . for Chey is more than just the victim she appears to be. But once she's within killing range, she may find that – even for a werewolf – it's not always easy to go for the jugular.

978-0-7499-5238-9

RAVAGED

Be careful what you search for. You just might find it . . .

When a strange wolf's teeth slashed Cheyenne Clark's ankle to the bone, her old life ended, and she became the very monster that haunted her nightmares for years. Worse, the only one who can understand what Chey has become is Powell, the man – or wolf – who's doomed her to this fate.

They vow to find the release to the curse, yet as the line between human and beast blurs, so too does the distinction between hunter and hunted. Because someone is on the trail of Powell and Chey, determined to get revenge – someone as deadly and as fierce as they are . . .

978-0-7499-5243-3

And in case you missed it, check out the first novel in the Laura Caxton Vampire series …

13 BULLETS

All the official reports say they are dead – extinct since the late '80s, when a fed named Jameson Arkeley nailed the last vampire in a fight that nearly killed him. But the evidence proves otherwise. When a state trooper named Caxton calls the FBI looking for help in the middle of the night, it is Arkeley who gets the assignment – who else? He's been expecting such a call. Sure, it's been years since any signs of an attack, but Arkeley knows what most people don't: there is one left. In an abandoned asylum she is rotting, plotting and biding her time in a way that only the undead can.

But the worst thing is the feeling that the vampires want more than just Caxton's blood. They want her for a reason, one she can't guess; a reason her sphinxlike partner knows but won't say; a reason she has to find out or die trying. Now there are only 13 bullets between Caxton and Arkeley and the vampires. There are only 13 bullets between us, the living, and them, the damned.

978-0-7499-5426-0

Do you love fiction with a supernatural twist?

Want the chance to hear news about your favourite authors (and the chance to win free books)?

Keri Arthur
S. G. Browne
P.C. Cast
Christine Feehan
Jacquelyn Frank
Larissa Ione
Darynda Jones
Sherrilyn Kenyon
Jackie Kessler
Jayne Ann Krentz and Jayne Castle
Martin Millar
Kat Richardson
J.R. Ward
David Wellington
Laura Wright

Then visit the Piatkus website and blog
www.piatkus.co.uk | www.piatkusbooks.net

And follow us on Facebook and Twitter
www.facebook.com/piatkusfiction | www.twitter.com/piatkusbooks

piatkus